HOBO ASHES

A Novel

Including the short stories
Conversations with Clete and *Carrying Kerrie*

STEVE SPORLEDER

Hobo Ashes
© 2013 by Stephen L. Sporleder

ISBN: 978-1-61170-137-1
Library of Congress Control Number: 2013947916

This is a book of fiction. Most of the characters, names, incidents, organizations, and dialogue in this novel are either products of the author's imagination or are used fictitiously.

All rights reserved.
Without limiting the rights under copyright reserved above, no part of this publication may be reproduced, stored in or introduced into a retrieval system, or transmitted, in any form, or by any means (electronic, mechanical, photocopying, recording, or otherwise) without the prior permission of the copyright owner.

The scanning, uploading, and distributing of this book via the internet or via any other means without the permission of the copyright owner is illegal and punishable by law. Please do not participate in or encourage electronic piracy of copyrighted materials. Your support of the author's rights is appreciated.

Cover design and illustration by: Letty Samonte

Printed in the USA and UK on acid-free paper.

Robertson Publishing™
www.RobertsonPublishing.com

Additional copies of this book or of Steve Sporleder's other works are available through:
    www.rp-author.com/Sporleder
    amazon.com
    barnesandnoble.com

Dedicated to my parents, Louis and Virginia Sporleder

and

In memory of James Clayton Fanning.
You caught the west bound way too soon, J.C.

Acknowledgements

Hobo Ashes came about with great cooperation from many wonderful people in my life. At the top of the list is my dearest friend and confidant, Mary Wolf. Without her in my life I'd be nothing. She is my rock and I am a very lucky man. Her support and encouragement provide the wind that carries me.

To my best girlfriend, Susie Kankel, who gets to see my work first and last. Her spelling, punctuation, grammar and sense of timing are unsurpassed. She inspires me to be a better writer.

I will be forever grateful to my friend and editor, Parthenia M. Hicks, a beautiful poet and author, who encourages me to keep taking steps forward in my writing. Her enthusiasm and creativity helped heighten the drama of *Hobo Ashes*, and other works.

To have the talented and beautiful Letty Samonte once again design the cover for one of my books is a true gift. People will pick up my book because its cover tells a story and invites readers to begin the journey. Her ingenuity and sense of detail are greatly admired and appreciated.

Thanks to Janet Samo, who read the manuscript early on and wanted to know more about hobos. Her request led me to more research and to carve more historical and detailed substance into my characters and their environment.

Thanks also to Peggy Conaway, Lyn Dougherty, and Jade Bradbury for their insightful critique of the manuscript early on. And for their heartfelt and supporting testimonials.

I will always be grateful to Jonathan and Alicia Robertson of Robertson Publishing for their formatting skills and patience. They make it look pretty.

I will always be indebted to Marnya Campbell, who told me long ago, "You can write." Her words will stay with me forever.

Special thanks to my family: To my parents, Louis and Virginia Sporleder, who provided foundation and a sense of home. Their stories of Los Gatos when they were growing up are an ever-flowing resource fountain. To my brothers, Doug Sporleder and Bert Sporleder, my best friends. They are what big brothers are supposed to be. Talk about having my back!

To my children, Lou and Elisabeth Sporleder and Jessica and Michael Erkiletian, you are my light and I thank you so much for the wonderful gifts of my grandchildren, Addie and Jakob Sporleder and Ethan and Sion Erkiletian. Blessings and love to you all.

Last but not least, I want to pay tribute to the most profound character in my stories: the town of Los Gatos, the Gem City of the Foothills. What a rich environment, rife with history, tales and incidents that provide a plush fabric for storytelling.

HOBO ASHES

A Novel

Thinning the herd, that's what a veteran of the jungle called it. A hobo getting murdered is what he meant. That was a raw deal, no matter how ya looked at it. Nobody deserved that, not even a bum. Even though I was livin free, could go where I wanted, do what I wanted, or so I thought, it grated on me, ya know. Just like the loss of my wife and son. Christ, I'd hear a child yell, "Daddy!" and I'd turn, wishing like hell he was calling me.

All along the shoreline of my life there was debris from the shipwrecks I caused. Hell, you'd a thought I would've learned to jump into a rescue boat or at the least put on a life jacket, but no, I went down each and every time. I kept doing the same things expecting different results. But there always seemed to be another campfire in another jungle to pick me up.

—Grady Prescott, former cop, hobo

I got all my belongings in a bindle slung over my shoulder. I got a gray fedora I wore when I was a businessman, before I hit the road. It's got a few holes and some nicks about it, but that's okey-dokey; it's kinda like me, ya know. There's nothin behind me and nothin in sight. I'm as free as the breeze doing as I please, mac.

—Overheard in a hobo camp

1

This is a seamy section of town, a pitiful place most people call "over there;" a region derelicts, whores and various other criminal types inhabited, only a few miles from where the forest meets the Great Plains. I watched the hobo from an alley between a vacant hardware store and a boarded up bakery. He lumbered along the darkened street, his slouch hat was pulled low on his brow and the black and red checked lumberjack coat was tied around his waist by the sleeves. My heart was beating like a tom-tom and my hands were flailing like I was trying to air-dry them. He heard my rapid footsteps behind him and turned. The thrust was powerful and the pain in his gut had to be severe. He looked down at the hunting knife sticking out of his belly and the blood oozing through the fabric of his blue work shirt. "Oh my," he gasped as he fell. His wine breath, his last, gave me a rush when I inhaled. He was deader than a doornail before he hit the ground and didn't hear the "whoosh" when the match landed on his lighter-fluid soaked clothing. I darted down another alley, crossed a boulevard and disappeared—another successful elimination.

I'm getting rid of these bastards, but the one I really want is still out there. I'll find him sooner or later. I just know it.

2

"You've been nominated for Senior Citizen of the Year," a woman said over the phone. "Please drop by the Town Manager's office so we can make it official and fill you in on the ceremonies." They must have the wrong Grady Prescott, I thought. Why would they want an old fogey like me?

When I asked, "Why me?" the woman just said brightly that the selection committee had all agreed. So I still don't know why anybody would want to honor me, a doddering old fool whose pride won't allow him to use his cane. Maybe because I've lived so long. Or maybe one of my relatives nominated me, but nobody is fessing up to it.

The Town of Los Gatos was celebrating its 100th anniversary of incorporation and events were planned all through the autumn of 1987. I was supposed to give a twenty-minute speech about my life in Los Gatos, but far too many things had happened since I'd first arrived to capsulize into a short talk, so I was just gonna hit the highlights. Some things are best left unsaid, you know.

It was a cloudy day and rain was in the forecast, but I insisted we walk the creek trail to Oak Meadow Park, and my family yielded. It had been years since all of us were together. My wife and her nephew, my sons and their wives and children, teenagers now, were present. Even my ex-wife and her husband and their son came. I was proud of my kinfolk. I looked at my ex and she gave me a nod and held her hand over her heart. There were good reasons she was my ex, but her gesture caused an emotional surge in a morning that promised more emotional surges. I just didn't know how intense they would be. I wasn't prepared.

The trail was well maintained, level, and manicured to accommodate walkers and bicyclists. Decades away from the footpath it once was, to be sure. The creek meandered along, creating a pastoral scene. The Billy Jones Wildcat Railroad locomotive blew its toot and kids in the miniature train cars waved while passing by. It reminded me of the Southern Pacific locomotive that traveled the tracks above the park when it was a quarry before the line to Los Gatos was discontinued. Every so often I can hear the faint whistle of a freight train that still comes out of the cement plant above Cupertino as it rolls through the Vasona Junction headed for San Jose.

Uniformed Boy Scouts were handing out programs and seating elderly folks in folding chairs in the first rows in front of the stage. The Los Gatos High School Orchestra played familiar tunes and everyone seemed to be having fun. The master of ceremonies was at the podium that stood beneath a sycamore tree, asking people to find a seat.

My wife looked at me and asked, "Are you nervous, dear?" I kissed her on the cheek and told her I was fine. I stepped onto the dais, and the mayor, in a maroon blazer and gray slacks, with white loafers, shook my hand and said, "Congratulations, Mr. Senior Citizen of the Year," and motioned for me to sit next to him, alongside town council members, the town manager, and other civic dignitaries. Gazing down at the senior citizens in the front, I wondered again why I was the one being honored.

I looked around at the setting and tried to picture where things had once been. The creek had been diverted many years ago and all the earthmovers and quarry buildings were long gone. I thought I had the area where we had cooked spotted. My wife's nephew, Byron, was giving the landscape a hard gaze, too. I was proud of the man he'd become, a Korean War veteran and a retired Navy officer. He gave me a crooked grin, like the cat that ate the canary.

Sometimes I think back fondly on those days, how free everything seemed. But I was holed up in a fake sanctuary then. What I have now is what I always wanted, but I reflected on those who had been in my orbit in the earlier years and about the broken bones and the noggin thumps I'd received so long ago not too far from here. Nothing ached any longer, but I still remembered the injuries.

The memories from those days are mixed. There was a time I'd lost everything I had, and a group of strangers let me into their lives. It was the lowest point in my life, and they helped pick me up. It was subtle, but a pick-me-up none-the-less. I learned many life lessons back then, and met some of the most significant people you can imagine. I can almost smell the stew and cigarette smoke and body odors, and can practically hear the sing-alongs and harmonicas filtering through the trees. Then there were the benders. Man, oh man, I'm glad I don't have to do that anymore. The faces of the cast of characters seem blurry at times, and other times I remember every facial crease, scar, and mole, every vocal peculiarity and wisdom. The Billy Jones whistle dumped me into the present. That was then, this is now, and this is better.

The Los Gatos Poet Laureate was finishing up a spirited ode to The Gem City, Los Gatos' nickname, and then it was my turn. I was introduced and received a louder applause than expected. I thanked the luminaries and the nominating committee for honoring me, then started my speech, "When I arrived in Los Gatos it was just a sleepy little town…" Then I heard a loud and obnoxious raspberry emanate from somebody on the right. I glanced in that direction, then continued, "As I was saying…"

"Why don't you tell us about when you were a bum, you piece of shit!"

The crowd quickly separated itself from the heckler and he took off up the creek trail at a trot, with Byron in pursuit. The heckler had a head start and vanished into the bushes. My nephew came back just as I was finishing my speech. Even with the interruptions, I received a standing ovation. I was upset with the outburst from the man and wondered if anybody, other than my intimates, knew what he was talking about. Almost all of my contemporaries from those days are dead or suffer from dementia. But, there is still one who is alert and oriented—the heckler.

I'm Grady Prescott and I was a cop before I flushed myself down the john. I never wanted to be "free." I just made bad choices. Hard to believe I'd end up sitting around a campfire with the same kinda types I used to roust on vagrancy beefs. Nonetheless, here I sat.

It was around 1944 and many of us had ended up on the skids for various reasons, not all of them avoidable. The crash of 1929 was the most talked about state of affairs. But that had happened over a decade and a half ago, and we'd been through a war. Then there were those who had been on the skids for so long that they could never climb out from under. Some Bo's talked about their homes and their families. You could tell the bull-shitters from the real deal. When the real deal guy talked about hearth and home, he had a longing in his voice and a mist about the eyes. The BS artists talked with a crow and a bluster that was as transparent as wet tissue. But in sobering moments, Bo's would tell you they loved the freedom, "No ties, and mac, that's how I like it," a veteran hobo told me early on.

Hobos have been around since the Civil War, hitching rides toward better circumstances and economy. Hopping trains is a dangerous undertaking, and ain't for elders, young'uns or sissies. Gals hopped freights from time to time, too. Gotta admire their grit, I mean entering into a hobo jungle or camp where it's mostly a stag affair. The fact was, in order to get from one job and town to another job and town, it was better to hop the freights. Those with dough rode the gray dog.

"Why in hell's sake would I pay for a ride on a bus when there's one for free on a freight train?"

"No cops on the gray dog, mac," was usually the answer. The cops on trains were called bulls and a whack to the head with a pick handle was how they got you off the train.

Lots of Bo's worked the fields and orchards. Some say the name hobo comes from hoe boy or farm hand. Others say it's a greeting; "Ho, boy!" Still there is always the definition—one I don't think is true—of hom beau, for homeward bound. Don't know any Bo's that were homeward bound; most were gravitatin' away from home.

See, my greed got the best of me. My nightmares and heavy drinking had escalated. Violent dreams, where people are fighting. I even hit Janey, my wife, from time to time while dreaming. Booze numbed me and I discovered that I didn't dream if I passed out, so I was drunk most nights. Times were tough for everybody, but I was getting by, so I didn't think about others; just me and my wife and boy, and then they became incidental. I was a selfish bastard. I was like the goons taking cash and goods from storeowners to "protect" them. Guys were losing their jobs, the banks had taken their homes, and wives and kids went home to mama. "Ain't nothing left here for me, I'll try Frisco or maybe Spokane," guys said.

Me, I was living high on the hog back then; sacks of groceries, trinkets, and nick-knacks were plentiful, while others were starving. They were saps. I coulda stopped the nutty merry-go-round, but self-indulgence had its glue-hooks in me. The girls at Dago Rose's whore-house fed my hunger for power and control. Who's the real sap? Why, I was so full of myself in those days that I didn't even bother to clean up before I went home. Whiskey, sex and sweat wafted from my uniform tunic. I ignored my son when I entered the house. Every day, before my corruption, he'd rush into my arms and squeal, "Daddy, you're home!" Then it became just a look up as I passed him on the living room floor playing with a toy or reading the comics. That didn't stop me. See, conceit was running my life. Janey finally got fed up. My thought was, Jesus H Keerist, look what ya got! Quit yer belly aching, fer crying out loud. She was such a cute little thing, but then my arrogance took its toll on her and she stopped taking care of herself. I clobbered her from time to time, knocked any self-esteem she had down the street like loose marbles. I'm not proud of it. Who woulda blamed her if she'da shanked me? I was a run-around guy and a drunk and a wife beater. Then I came home one night and she and the boy were gone. I had a load on and the despair of the situation didn't hit me until the next morning. The end result was that I'd been abandoned, again. The first time wasn't on me, but this was mine, all mine. Lately all that had happened to me was either my own doing, or I allowed it to happen. "How could she do this to me?" I remember wailing as I walked through the empty house when I realized she was gone, like it was all her fault. I crawled deeper into the bottle then and stayed for a good long time. I showed up for roll call drunk once too often, and the precinct captain, a loud mouth about as tall as a fire hydrant, ordered me into his office and told me he was suspending me until I dried out. "Ya been seen boozed up sporting the buttons," which meant drinking while on duty and in uniform.

"Screw you," I screamed. But I didn't say, "screw" if ya get my drift. Everyone in the station house heard it, even a deputy chief. I won't go into detail about how hard I hit him. Suffice it to say I lost my job, my pension, and my friends. I surrendered my badge and sidearm, which, looking back on the whole shebang, was the wisest thing I had done in a long time. If I'd kept my revolver I woulda plugged a few on the way out, or maybe myself. I did keep the nightstick my grandfather gave me when he retired from the department. It was made of highly polished maple, the color of honey, with a white ceramic knob on the end by the leather strap. It's one of my dearest possessions. His police career ended about the same time mine started.

That was the only time I was glad my grandparents were dead—when I got bounced from the police force. I tried to enlist in the military, but they rejected me. I was over thirty-five, ya see. Just a drunk and not even fit for the Army now. It wasn't too long before the house went into foreclosure and the bills went unpaid. I was a goddamned disgrace and I didn't want any of my friends or former co-workers to see what a stumblebum I'd become. But did I stop drinking? Hell, no. A guy gave me six hundred bucks for all the furniture, appliances and my car, and I went on the lam. I thought about keeping the car, but the thought of buying gasoline instead of a bottle, seemed like a simple choice—another bad decision. I kept one hundred dollars and put the rest in a savings account. Thirty-six years old and homeless. The nation was in mourning for FDR. He put guys to work, Franklin did. But did I try and find one of those jobs? No, I didn't. I didn't even look into it; I just skedaddled. I told ya I made bad decisions. If I'da dried out I'd still be a cop and have everything I lost.

My wife and boy went south to King City. I heard she got a job as a cocktail waitress at a joint called the Corner Club. I couldn't see her waitressing in a lounge, what with her shy ways, but that was part of the debris in my wake. Anyhow, I left San Jose, California, and headed north for San Francisco. I thought about hopping a train. But that idea only lasted a second. First of all, I'd never been on a train before in my life. At times I'd investigated crimes in the train yard and stood next to boxcars, but never studied how to climb onto one.

It was wet and miserable when I arrived in the city. The gray dog pulled into the bus depot with a grind of brake shoes and the diesel fumes swirling around. I visited the restroom and stood at the sink looking at my reflection in the mirror. I'd been sober for ten days, only because I managed to save my money for an uncertain future instead of buying a bottle. The face staring back at me I hardly recognized.

My once sharp jawbone was jowly, and veins lined my cheeks. Crow's feet bracketed my eyes, which had dark circles. Overnight, it seemed, my brown hair became streaked with gray. There was a note scribbled in pencil next to the mirror. It read, "You're looking at the problem." Man, that honked me off.

Most jungles were near rail yards and bus depots, but in Frisco they were remote. Railroad bulls and bus station managers weren't so friendly around these parts. I was taking in my surroundings, when a heavy hand landed on my shoulder, which scared me stiff.

A big man with a black scraggly beard said, "Ain't no camp here, best move on. Cops show up here regularly and put Bo's in the clink as soon as they touch ground."

He showed me a marking on a wooden pole that had three diagonal lines, which meant this place wasn't safe for Bo's. He gave me directions to the nearest camp. Along the fringes of Golden Gate Park in the shadows of a football stadium and not visible from the streets. There were two pots with fires under them. Smoke hung in the overcast air and at first stung the eyes. Every once in a while a breeze would pass through, scouring the atmosphere. But the tobacco smoke was constant. One of the pots was for cooking, and the other, remote from the "living section" was for boiling clothes to exterminate lice. I shuddered. An unofficial greeter, a broad shouldered mug, gave me the lay of the land. "First off, mac, ya don't just go barging in on a camp. Ya stand on the fringes and wait for someone to call ya in." I apologized to the guy and he waved it off.

"The shitter is beyond the juniper bushes, clean up the best ya can. We don't want the sanitation cops on us, ya see. There's a spade for burying." I shuddered, again.

My clothing was pretty neat compared to some of the others I met along the way, and they could tell I was new to the life. The men were friendly for the most part and I listened to the so-called camp rules. Pretty simple these rules: "Be nice to others and they'll be nice to you. When you meet Mr. and Mrs. John Q. Citizen, be respectful, or you'll get the bum's rush. And, we ain't bums, ya see?" the greeter explained. Bums were lazy and not willing to work; they begged. Tramps worked when they had to, and Bo's worked to get a stake so they could move on. "Too bad the folks in town lump us all together. They'll call a Bo a bum or tramp. Now, tramp ain't as much of an insult as calling us bums," I was told. When I was a cop, there was no distinction.

I had a heavy navy blue woolen overcoat, which I found out was a luxury, and I could use it for a bedroll until a better bedroll became available. Some guys used newspapers for bedrolls. These were called California Blankets. I found out pretty fast that I had too much stuff to carry, so along the way I traded my shirts and slacks for cigs and canned food. I only kept a change of clothes and my socks and underwear.

I laid my bindle down and cozied up to the fire and nodded to others warming their hands. "What's yer story, mac?" a grizzled old man asked in a clipped mid-western cadence, his breath visible with each syllable.

"Just trying to go along to get along," I replied.

"Yeah, we're all wanting that," he said softly. The tan coat and gray trousers he wore were shabby and frayed, but clean. His gray hair, while uncombed, appeared to be washed. His bushy mustache was nicotine stained under his nostrils. A slouch hat was propped on one knee as he sat. The man's face was creased and leathery. A week's worth of beard covered his chin and cheeks.

Most of the Bo's were clean, due to the fact that they took a PA bath every other day or so. PA stands for pits and ass. There were those, though, that had a stench that could be detected from a block away.

He told me his name was Bob Billups, or Double B. "What did ya do before hoboing? Ya look like ya might a run a store or something."

"How'd ya guess," I said in an amazed tone. "I ran a hardware store in San Jose," I lied.

"Looking at the veins in yer nose, I'd say ya tip the bottle a bit. What's yer name, anyway?"

I put my hand out and said, "Grady Prescott, pleased to meet ya." I don't know why I gave him my real name; after all, honesty wasn't a strong suit of mine of late. I just lied about my previous occupation. That was survival, I thought. Telling this crowd I'd been a cop might cause a ruckus. I just got here and didn't want trouble. This guy, Double B, gave me an identity.

"What about it? Ya got a bottle?" Double B asked. I shook my head no, and his face shrugged. "Might be nice on a night like this," he said as he blew warmth into his hands. A drip from a branch landed down my collar, causing a shiver to progress through me and leading me to agree with him; a small nip might be nice.

"What are the prospects like here?" I asked Double B.

"Hah, ya want prospects? Ya should a stayed home, mac."

After a few moments of silence, Double B said, "Frisco's a friendly place, for the most part. The top cop got tired of us giving the city a bad name, so he put us to work cleaning the alleys behind saloons and cafes. Show the decent citizens we earn our keep, for that we'd get a voucher for a meal at the mission. Ya wanna avoid south of Market Street, though."

"Why's that?" I asked.

"Bums, whores, and all around bad guys. Hell, they'll kill ya and think nothing of it." He told me there were lots of dark alleys that could be troublesome. "It's funny—a Bo will stop shaving and taking a PA and his hands won't quit shivering wondering where his next drink is, and that's called going south of Market. But in Frisco the place for the down trodden is in an area actually called south of Market Street."

"Are they the ones thinning the herd, Double B?" I asked with wonder.

"Nah, it's somebody not hoboing, I'm sure," he said with a yawn. "It's no jungle buzzard." When I asked, he told me a jungle buzzard was a hobo that preyed on other hobos. "There was a guy called Sidetrack that killed over thirty Bo's a few years back. He was a jungle buzzard. I heard he turned himself in."

I looked up the word hobo in the dictionary once. Webster's New World, I believe it was. I was doing an incident report, and wanted to make sure I had the spelling right. It said the word, hobo was a noun and the first definition was a migratory worker. The second definition called them vagrants or tramps. It referred to bums as drunken derelicts.

"In the jungles I habituate, the hobos have an ethical code—be polite, don't bring undue attention, share, and don't get caught stealing," Double B admonished. He didn't say don't steal, he said don't get *caught*. Was I gonna become a thief?

As darkness fell some guys left and others arrived after being out all day. Anyone new to the ensemble, like me, would create a slight stir. The friendlier ones asked what I was about, and if I ran into so-and-so along the way. Others might as well wear a sign that said, leave me the hell alone. The rain was getting heavier and I started to wonder if I could find a dry spot to sleep. Double B saw me looking around and said, "You can bunk in my hovel tonight, but ya gotta set yourself up tomorrow, Grady." Double B's hovel was nothing more than a tent fashioned out of cardboard boxes. A strong gust of wind would surely cause the cardboard to take flight. But I'd worry about that when it happened, and it might not. The wet boxes smelled, but the ground underneath was dry. Double B had a one-pound empty coffee can with the top and bottom cut off. It was sitting on some flat rocks in front of his hovel and had a fire going under it. Vent holes cut into the sides provided combustion air and the flame could be used to cook something or provide warmth. I guess I should say the look of warmth.

Somebody was playing a sad rendition of "Big Rock Candy Mountain" on a harmonica and men talked in whispers as they dipped their cups into the thin stew simmering over the open fire. I heard one say, "They gaffed another one of the boys up along the Sacramento River. A guy told me about it earlier today." After a few tongue clicks he continued, "They's not only sticking 'em in the gut, they's torching em too." A tremor ran through me. Over the past several years the San Jose Police Department and other departments in Santa Clara County had had several stabbings and burning of hobos. The cop in me started to run through what I remembered from those unsolved cases. Be careful, Prescott, you start talking like a cop, you may get it next. That was the last I remembered as I fell off to sleep, right into a bad dream.

Since childhood I'd gotten nightmares that infused me with terror, and the violence intensified as I got older. It always started the same. I'm hiding in a dark closet; it's stuffy and smells like mothballs. I open the door a slit and see my mother fly across the room and land head first into the wall next to the radio cabinet. My father is standing over her, his fists moving like a boxer, and he's flexing his biceps. He is grimy from his plumbing job and he smells like beer. My mother's head is bleeding and she isn't moving. I feel her pain; my head aches something awful. I see my grandfather rush into the room and spin my father around. I shut the closet door and plug my ears to muffle the grunts and grumbles and toppling furniture. That's usually when

I wake up, and this time was no different. I crawled out of Double B's hovel and made it to the bushes where I vomited. I heard somebody say, "That Bo just flashed the hash."

The early May morning sun slashed down through the cypress and eucalyptus trees, at first causing a sense of warmth, but then the breeze started. This was spring in Frisco. I remembered the quote from Mark Twain, "The coldest winter I ever saw was the summer I spent in San Francisco." Men stood around the fire shuffling their feet like they were stomping bugs. Most were smoking and sipping coffee. Double B was on his haunches putting more wood in a fire ring that had a scorched coffee pot in it, a cigarette dangling from his lips. Every man had a cup of some sort, ceramic, tin or paper. Me, I had no cup. "Throw yer feet, pal," Double B said to me. I gave him an odd look. He moved his index and middle finger in a walking motion. "Check the trash pile yonder," he indicated with his chin toward the outskirts of the encampment. "I saw a Dixie cup there."

The coffee was strong and hot and full of grounds. I didn't dare ask if there was any sugar or cream. "Yer gonna need to get a mess kit, Grady," Double B announced. "This is no catered event, ya see." I thought about my camp kit in the basement at my house in San Jose. It's full of pots and pans, utensils, a coffee pot, and tin plates and cups. The last time I used the camp kit was with my boy, Calvin. We'd spent a few days at Big Basin State Park, back when we were father and son. A quiver of sadness took hold.

"Ya got a look about ya I didn't see yesterday, Grady. If ya got second thoughts about hoboing, act on 'em. This life ain't for everyone," Double B said as we walked toward the football stadium.

"Just thinking about my boy is all." I asked him if he ever had second thoughts.

"Every Goddamned day," he whispered. "Never act on 'em though. I guess I like being free."

3

"Where we headed?" I asked as we crossed a busy street.

"Getting some supplies," Double B replied matter-of-factly. "Every guy in camp is a procurement officer of sorts. I'm gonna show ya what needs doing and getting, so you can do it and get it." He told me the basics were food, any kind of food. Paper was also a commodity. "Newspapers, grocery sacks, and the like. For toilet paper, ya know." We ducked down an alley behind a café. He showed me a marking on a signpost. It was two shovels, which meant there was work in the area.

"They got an outdoor dishwashing station. Some guys back at camp work there from time to time, to get a stake so they can move on." Double B peeked around the corner and whistled to a man scraping food from plates. The man looked around, then motioned us over with a head jerk.

"Hey, Choppy, this is Grady, he needs a kit." Choppy nodded to me and said, "Knife, fork and spoon is all I got now."

He saw me looking at a tin measuring cup, and squinted. He picked up the cup and tossed it to me. "Now get outta here before I get the axe." My new possessions rattled in my coat pocket. All I had to my name was my new mess kit and a change of clothes and two sawbucks, my nightstick, and a toiletry kit. In the toiletry kit there was a bar of Ivory soap, a Gillett safety razor, and a toothbrush and can of Colgate tooth powder.

Under Double B's guidance, I was learning the lingo of the jungles, more of the ethics code and how to read signs other Bo's left.

"We try and stay clean, so a stray bar of soap is a nice thing to pick up. Boil up yer duds as often as ya can," he told me. "Respect handouts and don't wear out yer welcome. Another Bo will come along and need something, too."

"Do most guys work, or do they panhandle?" I asked. He told me he didn't like the word "panhandle."

"Bums panhandle. To fit in with the town is what a Bo should try and do. Help anybody you can whenever you can. Do the jobs no one else wants to do. I try and work as often as I can; gotta always have a road stake for emergencies." He told me that a guy who stays with the same job for more than a year was called a barnacle. When I asked what his occupation was before hoboing, all he said was, "Insurance."

Behind an apartment building Double B showed me a sign on a doorjamb, a crude sketch of a cat. "That means a kind lady lives there. Go knock on the door and ask if she has any work."

She had nothing for me to do, but she gave me a can of condensed milk and a can of chicken noodle soup, which I carried to where Double B was standing. I felt like a hunting dog bringing a duck to his owner.

"The boys will like that," he said. I held the cans closer to me. He grinned and shook his head. "One thing ya gotta learn is to share. Yer new to this jungle; adding something to the stew will put ya in a good light. Share, son, share."

Later in the afternoon, I dragged a roll of chicken wire into camp. When Double B asked me what I was gonna do, I told him I was gonna make a tent. "Don't make it too permanent, or the cops will think it's something that's not so temporary," he warned me.

"When I get cardboard over it, it'll be just like the others," I told him while shaping the wire into a tent. By supper, my hovel was all set up right next to Double B's. The cardboard was new and bright, not faded and weather-stained like most. The stew was warm and multi-flavored. There were some pieces of meat the Bo's called gump in it. But if you weren't one of the first to dip your cup, you got mostly broth and some limp carrots or celery.

Double B and me carried trash to the large green garbage barrels near the stadium after supper, and when I got back, there was somebody rummaging through my stuff in my hovel. "Whatcha think yer doing?" I asked the bird.

He looked at me with darting eyes and a constant sniffle and said,

"Just looking for my... er, my..." he stammered. His nose and mouth twitched constantly and he made an annoying sniff noise.

"I don't have anything of yours, so scram, bub," I hissed.

Double B said, "Where've ya been, Jitters? It's been a long spell."

Jitters ducked out of my hovel and told Double B that he'd been riding the rails in Washington. He never took his eyes off me when he spoke, like he was sizing me up. I wondered if he knew me. I stepped around him and scanned my interior to see if anything was missing. "I didn't take nothing. What's the billy club for, mac?"

"To clobber guys like you with. Stay out of here. You read me?" He gave a gesture with his hands up, patting the air that said, "Take it easy. I got it." Jitters moved over to the stew pot and reacquainted himself with the boys. He kept looking at me, which was putting me off. "What's that jerk's story?" I asked Double B.

"He's harmless, and is a good scrounger when he's not elevated." I looked at him with a head tilt.

"Ya know, sleeping under the Tokay blanket." I shook my head. Impatiently, Double B said, "Ya know? He's an alkie." My cop instincts were kicking in. I had the nagging feeling there was gonna be trouble. I turned and Double B was staring at me. "What?" I asked.

"Why do you have a billy club, Grady?" Do I reveal to him I had been a cop? Tell him my grandfather was a cop? Why not? "My grandfather was a cop; it was his."

One morning, a week or so later, I could hear a jackhammer a few blocks away from the jungle. I headed for the clamor and saw a beefy man with huge arms in bib overalls and a white tee shirt digging up the sidewalk. When he stopped, I asked him if he needed any help. He squinted, wiped his forehead and said, "Why not? Once I get the sidewalk dug up, I'll need some pick and shovel work from the meter to the house," he said, pointing the line out. "Gotta replace the main. If ya want, ya can start hauling these chunks to the trailer, there in the driveway." I started to pick up pieces when he asked me, "How much ya want?" I just shrugged and carried the piece to the trailer. "Fifteen okay?" I nodded in agreement.

I thought about my father a lot that day; he was a plumber before he ended up in prison for beating my mother to death. I wondered if he was still alive. I also thought about my grandparents and the life they provided for me. I never lacked anything, except my mother and father. I know I wasn't the only boy without parents, but I still felt different.

By the time we finished, my back was aching, but it felt good. "Come back tomorrow. I'll have some base rock to strew out, ya up for it?"

I stopped at a mom and pop store and bought two pints of Four Roses bourbon to ease my sore back. Double B's eyes popped when he saw the pint. My plan was to share one with him and to down the other by myself. But as the swig party progressed, I pulled the second bottle, and it was gone in no time.

In the middle of the night, I was awakened by people running, and loud and excited talking. I stuck my head out of my hovel and asked what the matter was. A guy scurrying by pointed to a pile on fire. My thought was, why are they starting a fire there?

"I think it's Jitters," the guy said. My head was throbbing and not quite understanding.

"What're ya talking about?" I asked.

"Jitters was sleeping there, and now he's on fire, that's what I'm talking about, mac."

4

Well, what do ya know? I pulled it off. They think that Bo is me. I let the air out of the guy and before it gets bloody, I swap coats. His was better than mine anyway. They think Jitters, that's me, is a goner. I'm gone alright. I stood in the crowd that was buzzing around the burning body. "Poor Jitters, he was a good scout," somebody sighed. Almost had me in tears, I'm tellin' ya. I staged my limp and walked through the junipers and across the street and into the Frisco night. Hasta la vista, Jitters.

Changing getups was second nature to me. Getting the stuffing knocked outta ya on a daily basis as a kid makes ya tough. After the first beat down, at the hands of my step-brothers, Simon and Reed, I determined that they'd never see tears from me. No-sir-ee. I held it all in and bided my time. They had no idea how often I planned their deaths, the number of ways to do it and the disguises I would wear. I love animals, but I hated their collie dog. I'd kick that son of a bitch every time it got close to me. Then one morning I put rat poison in its kibbles. Maybe the dog didn't deserve it, but its owners sure as hell did.

5

"This isn't good, Grady. The cops will be here and we'll probably have to move on," Double B exclaimed, startling me. "Grab yer shit and let's split."

"Won't that look kinda suspicious?" I asked. "I mean everybody knows me and Jitters argued the other day. Now he is dead and I take off? I think I'll stick around."

"You sound like a cop."

"I told ya my grandfather was a cop; I ain't." *Not anymore, anyhow.* "Some copper instincts rub off on ya." My thinking was that there are always a few guys awake all through the night. Did somebody see something? How could a ruckus like this start and nobody see anything? *Knock it off, Prescott. Yer acting like a cop.*

A Bo in a rust, yellow, and green plaid jacket, the guy who told me about Jitters on fire, said in a raspy rhythm, "I seen him getting the fruit on last night."

Double B braced the guy in the plaid jacket square on and hissed, "Jitters is not a queer."

Plaid guy said, "He was the life of the party up along the Spokane River. Maybe not here, but up there his dance card was filled up, I ain't lyin." To me, when a mug finishes his statement with "I ain't lying," or "that's the truth," I get suspicious. It's the cop in me. Double B had warned me that plaid jacket man was a bully of the first water. He'd cut guys down, make fun of any disability somebody had. I didn't like this guy and hoped he'd stay out of my way. But I felt we'd have issues.

Double B warned me about him. "He's a hacker. He'll hack on a guy just to be hacking. It's always at somebody with a weakness or smaller than him. I've known him a long while."

I figured out fast that he moved in and out of the camp like a draft. You'd be talking with a group of guys and suddenly the mug in the plaid jacket was there giving some contrary statement on a previously voiced opinion.

The homicide detectives gathered the information that the hobos were willing to share. I must say it wasn't a very complete investigation into what was surely a murder. "The mayor will raise a stink about this," Double B said. "Probably send in Public Works and Parks and Recreation to tear us down. I'm gonna shove off."

I told him I was gonna work one more day for the plumber and would move on that evening. "Which way you headed, Double B?"

He scratched his head and replied, "Probably north. Hop a train, maybe." He told me about a site along the delta in Sacramento that had a nice spot for camping and the locals usually didn't bother Bo's.

After my day's work, I skirted the edges of the park. I saw the black smoke rising into the blue sky. All the hovels and any debris left were on fire. *No chance of finding any clues now.* A red fire engine sat idling as firemen and city workers tossed material onto the bon fire. What had been my home for three weeks was going up in flames. "That's what it's like when yer a citizen of the world," Double B told me once. He was my mentor, Double B was, and now I wondered if I would ever see him again. I purchased two pints of booze and headed for the rails.

During my first weeks of hoboing in Frisco, I heard various views on hopping trains. I'd never done that in my life, and now I'd have to see if I learned my lessons about hopping freights. "I don't do that shit anymore; too dangerous at my age," Double B said. Now, he always got on the train before it departed, being careful to avoid the authority. "Usually a train will stop before it enters the yard you want to get off at. That way you usually avoid the bulls." He told me that a slow moving train was the only one ya wanna jump on, for obvious reasons. "If yer between yards wait at a sharp turn. They gotta slow way down. Then find an open boxcar and toss yer bindle in and grab the side and hang on. The momentum will carry ya along, then swing into the space." Another Bo told me to carry a rock large enough to block the rail of a boxcar door.

"Doors can't be opened from the inside if they slam shut, ya see."

"And fer Christ's sake keep yer feet off the rails," a grizzled codger admonished. "Had a guy I was on the road with," he continued, "Ran for an open car and slipped and his foot landed on the rail." He shook his head and got a far off look on his face. "I saw his boot with the foot still in it flip off a wheel. I looked down the track and he was scrambling to get away from the train. That's the last I saw him. It was like he didn't know his foot was cut off."

I crossed several sets of tracks, headed for a northbound train. All the while I kept thinking, *why didn't I take a bus?* I had no idea whatsoever which of these trains was headed to Sacramento. From under a car, I saw the black boots of a man walking on the other side. I thought this might be a bull, so I tossed my bindle into an open car and climbed in. "Hey, shitbird, I seen ya climb on my train. No free rides to Sacramento today," a pasty-faced railroad cop yelled into the car. He had dark eyebrows that slashed above his eyes with no space in between them. When he spoke, his double chin jiggled. He was carrying a wooden axe handle he kept tapping the door rail with, but the gun on his hip concerned me more. "Get outta here, and if I see you again, I'll thump yer skull."

I got out and crept across the tracks. When the bull was out of sight, I heard a faint hoot from another car and the sleeve of an olive-colored coat waved me over. I ran to the car and a blond man, younger than me, put out his hand and helped me up. "Thanks, mac," I said. He gave a shrug that meant, "You'd do it for me."

The blond man assured me that this train was gonna stop in Sacramento. "Where ya headed?" he wanted to know, and I told him. He just nodded.

"What about you?" I asked.

"Tacoma, maybe. Heard about field work there," he replied with a sniff that became a sneeze. I wished him luck, and took in my surroundings.

6

So far, so good. This mug don't suspect nothin. I'm glad to be done with the Jitters getup. I mean all that fidgeting can take over. Hell, I found myself ticking and twitching when I wasn't acting as Jitters. It just happened with this guy; I covered my sniff with a sneeze. The sniff became part of me. I perfected it. I just gotta be careful. I watched this mug, trying to figure out what he was doing. He's not from the road, or he's new to it. I can tell. Always cozy with Double Bob, or whatever his name is. They don't have any idea how close death is. His billy club must be in his bindle.

7

I didn't expect the car interiors to be so dirty, but once the train picked up speed, debris swirled around like a sand storm. Nobody told me how cold it would be either. It was about sixty-five degrees out, but going over sixty miles an hour for most of the ride, well, the cold went clear to the bone. I curled up with my head toward the front of the train.

"I wouldn't sleep that way, pal. Always put yer feet to the engine." I spun around and gave the guy a questioning look. "If the train stops suddenly, you'll fly forward; better to get a broken leg than a broken neck," he said matter-of-factly.

No bulls were to be seen, so I hurried away from the tracks. I turned and the young guy from the boxcar was right beside me. "Go down that ditch about three hundred yards and you'll pick up some signs," he said pointing to a reed-lined graveled path.

"Where you going?" I asked.

"I was going to Washington State, now I ain't sure."

"Why not stay here?" I asked.

"Sac ain't been kindly to me. No, I think I'll shove off. Be careful. And move on before the rains start." I gave him a funny look, and he said, "Too much rain and the levees can fail and guys drown, so head for high ground when the rain starts." I asked him what his name was when he turned and walked away. All he did was salute.

Double B was sitting Indian style talking with a Bo in a dove-gray overcoat. When he saw me standing above the camp on the gravel path, he waved me in. The camp was bordered on one side by the path and on the other side by a trapezoidal levee. Several Bo's were fishing with homemade fishing poles atop the levee. Except for the age of the men, the scene reminded me of Tom Sawyer. The Bo talking with Double B gave me the head-to-toe scan and continued his conversation. Several others sat close and hung on his every word. Double B nodded to a spot next to him and I sat.

"Anyhow, like I was sayin, my hearth and home as a kid was anything but warm and cozy. Keep in mind fellas, this was the depression in the Panhandle with dust storms." As this guy talked, I got the impression he'd been a lecturer before he hit the road. His delivery was polished and possibly canned; in other words, he told the same story to different audiences wherever he went. And that's okay; Bo's need to be entertained. There are those who are musically inclined and those, like minstrels, that can spin a yarn from fact or fiction.

"Go on, Canfield, tell us about the dust storm," somebody behind me implored.

Canfield filled his pipe bowl, lit it and puffed it to life. "Well, sir, there was days when the dust came from the ground and days when it came from the sky. And once in a while ya couldn't tell the difference—sky or ground. Now those were bad days cause ya got dizzy." He puffed his pipe a few moments. "The worst was at night. We lived in a dugout on the prairie, and every night before we went to bed we had to sweep the snakes, lizards, and tarantulas outside. Cinch bugs in the sod wall scratched all night long, and I mean every night. Son-of-a-bitch, no wonder my mama went nuts. That's why I don't like confined spaces. I spent a week in a cell in Reno, and believe you me, I thought about jumping on the west bound." Talk of suicide was pretty rare in jungles, but it was a reality.

Later on me and Double B were dipping our cups, and I asked, "Where's the town center? It seems like we are far away from everything. Where do guys find work?"

"Usually we're camped closer to the capitol, but there was a hobo killing last week and the bulls tore down the jungle. All they did was move us away from the locals. This ain't too bad—plenty of fish, out of the wind. The downside is that it's a hike to find work. Farmers are willing to hire you if they like the cut of yer jib."

At sunset Double B and me sat on the levee taking in the array of oranges and purples that sundown displayed. I was lost in my thoughts about how far I'd moved from my son, Calvin. I resolved to go south to be nearer to him. The other thought I had was that I'd moved closer to where my father was: Folsom Prison. Man, I was doing this wrong; I should be moving away from my father and closer to my son, and I did just the opposite. Jesus Christ. *It's time to start making better decisions.*

"I'm heading for Stockton in the morning," Double B announced. "Ya wanna go?"

"What's going on there?" I asked.

He looked at me and said, "Does it matter?"

"Nah, it don't. But I'm gonna go back south."

Double B looked at me and said, "South, eh?" I nodded, and he said, "There's a swell camp at a gravel quarry in Los Gatos. Maybe we'll give that a shot."

It was a balmy night, so I didn't need a hovel. I just covered myself with my overcoat and slept under the stars. I'm not certain what time it was when I awoke to the sweet, but acrid aroma of burning flesh. I sat up and on the levee was a burning body. I woke Double B and said, "I ain't waiting for daybreak. I'm leaving now. This place is no good."

"Why? What's going on?" Double B asked. He scrunched his nose and looked at the flame atop the levee. "Oh. Wait for me."

The farther south Double B and me got on the freight, the better I felt. Even getting chased off the train by bulls in Davis didn't change my disposition. We caught another train that stopped just outside the terminal yard in San Jose.

I was getting my bearings, when Double B said, "This way to the creek trail, pal."

I figured I was only a short distance from where my house sat before I bombarded my life. "I think I want to go see my house."

Double B turned around and walked toward me. He saw my look and said, "And you want to do it alone." I nodded and he shrugged and said, "I understand. I'll see ya up the road a piece." He took a few steps, then turned around. "The trail follows the train tracks. It goes off a bit, but ya can always find the way by following the tracks." He saluted and walked away.

I climbed up an embankment of pink and white oleander and walked down to the street where I used to live. It was around ten o'clock on a damp, misty night, and the pearl glow from the street lamp gave me an eerie feeling. When I saw the plywood over the windows and doors of my house I felt a sense of foreboding. I opened the gate on the side and walked into the back yard. My son's bike was lying in a patch of weeds that grew through the spokes. The tire swing hanging from the magnolia tree swayed gently. "Push me higher, Daddy, higher," I could hear my son saying. I fell to my knees and sobbed. It was one of those cries that seemed to clean you out.

I fell asleep and had the nightmare, but this time there was a new installment. The closet door is whisked open and I fear that my father is going to make me fly, too. I peek from under a woolen Polar King blanket and see the kindly face of my grandfather. His knuckles are nicked and bleeding. "It's all over Grady, come on out." He hurries me to the kitchen door where my grandmother is standing wringing her hands. I look back into the living room and see my father sitting on the sofa, his face lumpy from a fight, and my mother is still on the floor. *Is she dead?* Grandma takes me next door where my grandparents live. I hear a siren while I'm sitting at her kitchen table. I woke up from the dream when the siren turned into the brake screech of a train in the Southern Pacific yard a few blocks from where I sat on my dry lawn. I had a bout of dry heaves.

Before I departed the yard, I picked the weeds from the spokes and put Calvin's bike under the overhang of the garage next to the kindling pile. I watered the geraniums in a flowerbed next to the back porch stairs, which was useless because they looked like straw. I sat in the swing, my legs dangling, and looked up at the gnarled branches and sighed, "Shit."

I could smell the coffee and cigarettes before I actually saw the camp at the quarry in Los Gatos. On a piece of wooden fencing next to a stream was a mark—a square with the top missing—which meant this was a safe place to camp. I called in and a couple of Bo's waved me over. I didn't see Double B and asked if he was around. "Ain't seen hide nor hair of him for some time," a ruddy-faced man, shorter than me and wearing wire-rimmed glasses, answered.

"He was in Sac two days ago. Said he was headed south to a quarry," I offered.

"I hear Jitters took the west-bound," another said to no one in particular. "Dying that way is rough."

My new neighbors were giving me the lay of the land and prospects for earning. "The quarry guys look the other way when we use their privy, just don't leave a mess. They're good to us," a man with a gray beard said as he lit his pipe. This was definitely a step up from Frisco, and a might warmer too.

A short bald man with a squeaky voice told me, "There're several churches in town and they always have work for us. Course, ya gotta listen to them talk on God and whatnot before ya get any angel food or a spiff."

I was figuring out that each jungle had a unique lingo; in this case it is *spiff*, which meant a handout, and getting a meal after listening to the clergy was called *angel food*. "There's a man that has a hauling company up by the train depot; he puts Bo's to work. He's a gruff bastard, but he pays fair," a fellow, shorter than me with a huge mole on his cheek, added in a tough tone.

"How do you know, Maurice? Y'all just got here the other day" a mug said as he rolled a smoke. I looked at this Maurice, and he stared right through me. He looked kinda familiar, but I wasn't sure. Maybe we crossed paths in Frisco or Sac. Couldn't be any place else, including when I was a copper. A shiver shot through me.

Around noon, I was setting myself up with a hovel. Most Bo's were out working, and those that remained were most likely hung over and sleeping it off. Out of the corner of my eye I watched a man in a brown suit wearing a beige snap-brim hat with a purple hatband approach. He looked vaguely familiar. I dove into my new digs and pretended to be sawing logs. The man kicked the sole of my oxford and said, "Don't try and duck me. I saw ya standing just a few seconds ago. C'mon out from there."

I hadn't seen Jack Calloway in years. He was rattling doors on patrol, the last I heard. Now he's in a suit, a detective. We'd gone through policing classes at night school together. His black hair had streaks of silver around the sideburns. He squinted in recognition, and then an expression crossed his brow. "What did you call me?" he screamed. "Put yer hands behind yer back," he ordered as he roughly spun me around. The distinct clink of the cuffs engaging woke some Bo's up, the loud talking didn't faze them, but the metallic click put them on high alert. "Take care of my stuff," I yelled over my shoulder to nobody in particular as Calloway jostled me away from the camp. My thought was, *what is the ass up to?*

"Jesus, Grady, I heard ya got bounced from the force," Calloway said when we got to his sedan and out of earshot. "Wait a sec, are you working undercover? Is that it? The hobo murders?" he asked in amazement. I didn't expect that, so I said nothing. "C'mon, you can trust me," he said. I just tilted my head like a dog hearing a strange noise. He told me that Los Gatos had been the scene of one hobo murder. "One just last night, an old codger named Billups."

I felt my heart sink, but I had to keep it to myself. "I hadn't heard about that one, Jack. I just blew in this morning," I told Calloway as I tried to cover my grief. "The Bo's in that camp haven't heard about it. What have ya got?" I whispered and pointed back to the camp with my shoulders because I was still cuffed. He fished in his front pocket for his key ring and removed the cuffs. My cop instinct was taking over, or maybe it was survival. That and not wanting to be disgraced. But when I cut to the chase, I knew I wanted to solve Double B's murder. He was my friend and mentor. I couldn't believe he was gone.

"I knew there had to be more to Grady Prescott getting the axe, I just knew it," Calloway grinned and shook his head. There it was for the second time, somebody giving me an identity. First, as a storekeeper, and now an undercover dick.

I asked Jack where the murder took place. He told me it was along the railroad tracks between the back of a lumberyard and a creamery. "I can show ya, if ya want," he offered. "We'll just do a drive by, like yer a witness or something. It might look kinda funny if you don't ride in the back. Goddamn, Grady Prescott, undercover."

"Listen, Jack...I'm, I'm..." I stopped to gather what I was gonna say. I intended to tell him that I *was* on the skids and *did* get the axe, but an inkling of hope hit me. Calvin, my son just might be able to brag about his father one day. This could be my last shot at doing something good. Doing the next right thing, ya know.

"What is it, Grady?"

"There is only one person in San Jose that knows about me. I can't give you his name. Nobody was supposed to find out, so when I saw ya walking into the camp I tried to hide."

"Yer story is safe with me, Grady. I know how these things go. I won't blow yer cover. You feed me info, and I'll do the same."

From the backseat of Calloway's sedan I stared at the last place Bob Billups, AKA Double B had been alive. I'd known him for only one month and I was in mourning. He was a decent man who didn't deserve to die like that, goddamn it. "Where is his body, Jack?"

"At the moment he's at Melvin's Mortuary. Not much left of him, though. They'll cart him over to the county morgue later, I suppose." I told Jack to take a close look at the knife. "Check with other departments around and see if there are any similarities." I felt I was talking out of my ass, because I felt sure this had already been done. But when Jack said, "Man, that's a good idea," I wondered what *had* been done. I doubted if the agencies looking into, or *supposedly* looking into the hobo murders, gave the cases much effort. "Jack, I'd like to look through his bindle. Can you arrange it?" I also asked when the last murder, before Double B's occurred. "Late summer, early fall. I'll look it up."

When I re-entered the jungle, guys came up to me and asked if the cops had walloped me with a rubber hose. I told them that it was all a misunderstanding. "The copper thought I called him a name. I told him he hurt my heel when he kicked my foot. He thought I said, Yer a shit heel."

When the mug named Maurice asked, "What *did* ya call him?" I just grinned.

"These cops here can't catch a cold; they're real clucks," the guy in the plaid coat from Frisco chimed in. *When did he arrive?* I wondered.

I kept the info about Double B to myself, just to see how it played out. Bo's straggled in at the end of the day. Most presented an item of food—pilfered vegetables, cans of broth and gump of some kind. This camp had a designated chef, of sorts. He concocted stews from whatever there was available, and it was pretty decent, too. He had a pan going with some potatoes and onions frying. It was a delicious aroma.

I was washing my cup out when I heard a long, low train whistle up above the camp. Somebody said, "She's just a little late tonight." I instinctively looked at my wrist that didn't have a watch on it. I saw several Bo's do the same thing, and it transported me back to my house and family when we could always tell the time of day by the train whistle, but my reverie was quickly interrupted by a horrible squawking coming from a small rise behind some heavy equipment just below the railroad tracks.

"What in hell is that?" I asked.

"Cock fights," a Bo said in disgust. "Those stupid bastards waste their doe-ray-me on chicken fights, I don't get it. Bring those birds down here; we'll put 'em in the stew. Hey, Cookie, ya know how to make dumplings?"

I remembered from my cop days that cockfighting was a real blood sport. Two birds would go at it in a ring called a cockpit. They'd fight until one was dead or critically injured. Some of the bird handlers strapped small knife blades on the bird's legs with a leather strap. Usually the betting was hot and heavy, and the crowds less than savory. Judging from the human yells coming from above the camp, this bout was a doozy.

Davy Holcomb—the guy in the plaid jacket finally had a name—plopped down next to me and whispered, "I hear tell in town that Double B caught the west-bound. I thought ya might like to know."

I stared at him for several seconds then asked, "Where did ya hear that?"

"There's another camp up the creek from the train depot, that's where he was staying. Mostly gypsies up there, though. I think old Double B was messing with some of the women." It was difficult to tell if he, Holcomb, meant Double B was annoying them or buying their time for companionship. I didn't think it was either. This guy was no-count, fer sure. I didn't trust him, but thought if I'm gonna be an undercover operator I best start *acting* like it for real. As repugnant as it was, I cozied up with Davy Holcomb.

"Hey Davy, ya say they got women up there?" I asked with a jerk of my thumb up stream.

"Ya bet, I'll take ya there tomorrow," he replied, as he rolled a smoke and lit it with a brushed chrome Zippo lighter.

"Can't tomorrow. I'm helping that hauler move furniture. Maybe on Saturday, though," I said with a grin that was as bogus as a three-dollar bill. What I was really doing tomorrow was meeting Jack Calloway; he was gonna let me go through Double B's bindle.

I met Calloway in front of the two-cell jailhouse behind city hall. He opened the huge wooden door and let me go in ahead of him. His thinking was that seeing a Bo entering the jail with a detective would be less suspicious than meeting someplace else. The room smelled like Lysol and had a clammy atmosphere that gave me the creeps. Double B's belongings were sparse to say the least. The guy lived for over sixty-odd years and his worldly possessions were wrapped in a blanket. That saddened me considerably. A dinner knife, fork, spoon, a tin cup, and toiletry items were bundled tightly in a dishtowel and tied with twine. There was also a six-inch hunting knife in a leather scabbard. Folded in a Shell Oil road map of the San Francisco Bay Area was an index card with the name, Maude Billups, and an address in Iowa. I wondered if Maude was his wife, daughter, sister or mother. A photograph showed a picture of a young Bob Billups looking quite successful in a double-breasted suit holding a fedora, smiling at the camera. His foot rested on the running board of a four-door automobile. A lady in a flowered dress stood next to him, looking into his eyes. Could that be Maude? There were several citations for vagrancy folded neatly. I knew most Bo's would move on from a place if they were cited. I asked Calloway, "Did Billups have anything on his rap sheet?"

"Just a couple of petty larceny beefs. Nothing recent. No wants or warrants, and nothing local," he said with a shrug. When I asked if the person, Maude, had been notified, Jack shoved his hat back on his head and said, "We contacted the Clayton County Sheriff in Iowa and they told us the dame didn't want anything to do with him. I thought that was pretty severe." I agreed with him. I picked up the map and opened it. Marked faintly in pencil were x marks of what I thought were hobo jungles. "Say, Jack, do you mind if I keep this map?" He told me that all the stuff that belonged to Double B was going to be destroyed. "There's nothing of evidentiary value, so yeah, take what ya want, Grady." I took the map, the hunting knife and the photograph. I held the knife and asked, "Did you find out anything from the other agencies about similarities to the knives?"

"Oh yeah, thanks for reminding me, all the knives were eight inches or longer and were manufactured by the Schrade Knife Company. All appeared to be new and inexpensive, but that's all. Oh, and there weren't any good fingerprints. The guy must have worn gloves."

"How many killings were there, Jack?"

"We put it out on the teletype to all departments in California, and fourteen positives came back."

I wondered if any of the cases had been solved. "Anybody arrested, Jack?"

"Nope. Nary a one. All open and unsolved. Also, the last murder was eight months ago, in September of last year." I asked if Jack would let me look at the crime scene photos. I wondered why the District Attorney wasn't involved. "Is the DA doing any investigation, Jack?" He told me they weren't putting much effort into these cases.

8

What are these two shit-birds up to? I thought the cop was tossing the Bo in the hoosegow, but I can hear them talking real friendly like. I can't understand the words. Even though this straw hat I'm wearing makes me look like a gardener from the city, I don't dare get closer.

The jail door opened and I stood with my back to them and pretended to be inspecting a leaf. They didn't even notice me, and I like that. Sometimes, though, I want to be noticed. Like when ma married my step-father. They did it at a Justice of the Peace. I was supposed to stay in my "new" home with my step brothers. They ridiculed me, and one of them beat me while the other urged him on. I ran off the place and into town. I found the Justice of the Peace's office, which was in his house and rushed through the door. My ma smiled and my new daddy scowled. But they definitely noticed me. Ma told me to go back home and she'd be there in the morning and make flapjacks. Her and her husband were gonna spend the night in the fancy hotel in town. I sat near the Civil War cannon in the square and tried to figure out a way to get the cannon out to my new home and send a ball into the center of the house killing the old man and my new brothers. I woke early and headed back to the farm before ma got there.

9

To avoid scrutiny, I darted down a small hill next to the police station, which was located in the basement of a church, and crossed a field where a baseball game was being played. Behind the left field fence was a trail. I made my way through some Scottish broom bushes and down an embankment along the creek. There was a small wooden bridge that spanned the creek. On the other side was a rodeo ground where a trainer was trotting a palomino. Up the hill from the horse corral was the rail tracks that would lead me to the depot and the gypsy camp near it.

I heard accordion music, cheerful talking, and children laughing, but when I entered the camp, all the cheerfulness dissipated and the music stopped. Parked adjacent to the camp was a truck with a high canvas tarp over the flat bed beside various other automobiles. A dark faced man in a multi-colored vest and straw hat said in a tone disguised as friendly, "Can I help you?" He smiled and a gold-capped tooth glistened in the sunlight. His eyes, however, betrayed his fake smile. I said to him, but loud enough for all to hear, "I'm a neighbor from downstream. Came by to say howdy is all." Murmurs and a wheeze from the accordion started up. A raven-haired woman in mismatched calico and striped clothing with eyes like obsidian offered me a hard biscuit. To decline her offer would have been an insult. It was her way of calling me in, which I should have waited on before intruding. She sashayed away from me with the jangle of her bracelets tinkling the air and her wide hips moving suggestively. I got the feeling that if I turned my back, I'd get shanked. I saw movement from the back of the truck and Davy Holcomb and a young girl with a darkish complexion climbed out. Her age was anyone's guess. If she were underage, I'd blow the whistle on this hump. One thing that isn't tolerated by Bo's is preying on children. That's the quickest way to get run out of town or end up in a ditch.

10

"Hey, Grady. I thought you were hauling today," Holcomb said in a jovial manner.

"Small load. I thought I might find ya here," I replied. I looked around the camp at the brightly dressed inhabitants. Some were making baskets, and others were carving wooden figurines, and some of the women put up card tables to read palms. These were called mitt camps. What was of particular interest to me was the man sharpening tools with a whetstone. Hoes, loppers, scissors, and knives were on a crimson blanket at his feet.

"Did ya meet the Rom Baro?" Holcomb asked me.

I shrugged my shoulders and asked, "What's that?"

He told me the head of a clan was called Rom Baro. I assumed he meant the man who met me when I entered their camp. I was surprised when he led me to the grinder sitting on the crimson blanket. He had on a colorful knit cap and a violet silk shirt with billowing sleeves and a pair of rust colored corduroy trousers.

"Sir, I'd like you to meet a friend of mine, Grady. Grady, this is Rye," Davy said.

Rye put down his stone and extended his gritty hand with filthy black under his nails. His palm was rough and his grip strong.

"Pleased to meet you, sir," I said. He just nodded. I got a closer look at the knives and noted several hunting knives that looked like they just might be ten inches or longer. "How much do you charge for knife sharpening?"

"Two bits a blade," he snarled in a European accent. "Best price you'll find, I ain't lying." I pulled out my Case pocketknife and handed it to him. He took it from me, looked at the bone handle and nodded. "It'll take ten minutes," he said as he opened the blade.

"I'd like to wait for it, if that's okay." He gave a "suit yourself" shrug and rubbed the blade of my knife across his stone.

The girl who had been in the back of the truck with Holcomb started to do a dance as the accordion and a mandolin picked up the tempo. Her bare feet were raising puffs of dust as she did a can-can of sorts around the people there. Holcomb was eyeing her with flared nostrils.

"Is that yer gal, Davy?"

He swung his head in my direction and grinned. "That's Rye's daughter, Malina. She's everybody's gal, mac."

"How old is she?"

"Old enough."

Rye caught my eye and motioned me over. He pulled up a sleeve and exposed a thick forest of black hair covering his wrist. He opened my knife and scraped it across the hair; a white spot of skin developed and the wrist hair fluttered to the blanket. I paid him with a quarter and thanked him for his hospitality. Before I left the camp, I said to him, "Your daughter is beautiful. Does she go to school?"

He looked at me with narrow eyes and whispered, "She gets education every day."

"How old is she?"

He, too replied, "Old enough."

When I walked out of the gypsy camp, I thought to myself, *Well, Rye ain't lying; my knife is razor sharp.*

I heard a "yoo-hoo" of sorts behind me and saw Malina hurrying my way. I stopped and she said, "Do you like me?" I told her I did, and asked her how old she was. When *she* told me she was old enough, I told her to go home. To my back she said, "Maybe you'd like my mother." I waved my hand in the air, dismissing her and her offers. I did feel that I would have to visit the gypsy camp again if I was going to investigate these murders. Those hunting knives were just too much of a coincidence to ignore. Hell, I was acting like a cop. But by the time I entered the quarry camp I was a hobo once again.

I decided to stay up late. A question that kept jabbing me in the ass was, *where does Holcomb sleep?* I usually went to bed at dark and woke up with the morning light. I never saw him around or in a hovel. In the morning he wasn't around either. Just before supper this day, he came sauntering in with a sack of hard biscuits to share. He started in on a smallish man with a severe limp. He called the poor guy "gimp" and "lame-oh."

Finally the cook said, "Why don't ya leave that Bo alone. He's done nothing to you. You don't always gotta be a bully, Davy."

He came over to me and sat. "Well, what did ya think about the gypsies, Grady?"

"That Rye did a bang up job on my pocket knife."

"Let me see," he said with an outstretched hand. I gave it to him, and he opened it and ran his thumb over the blade. He whistled, and said, "Real sharp, but that ain't much of a knife, mac."

"What have you got?" He pulled a sheathed knife from his jacket pocket and handed it to me. I took it out and noted the brand, a Winchester. I thought for sure I was gonna see a Schrade.

"Nice edge, too," I said. "Rye hone that up for ya?" He told me he took care of his own weapons. He pulled out a sack of Bull Durham and some papers and rolled himself a smoke. He offered me his fixings, which I declined. He used a stick match to light up, and I pulled a bottle out and offered him a snort, which he gladly accepted. We got a bit tight, but him more than me. When the bottle was empty, I faked a yawn and crawled into my hovel. I heard Davy riding somebody, and then his voice stopped. I peeked out of my hovel and saw him head for town. He looked back at the camp then disappeared into a stand of sycamores. I scrambled from my hovel too quickly, and was light-headed. After several steps, my noggin was right, and I went looking for Holcomb.

I caught sight of him as he walked in front of a cannery on Santa Cruz Avenue. He never looked back and I felt sure my surveillance would go undetected. Automobile traffic was light, and there were no pedestrians, except for me and Holcomb. He stopped in front of the bus depot and chatted with the cab driver stationed there. He ducked into a bar called the New Yorker. I stood at the entrance and heard a gruff female voice say, "I told ya not to come in here anymore." The door opened quickly, and I barely made it into the doorway of a barbershop between the depot and the bar before he saw me. I hugged the doorway to be as flat as possible in case he went back in the direction of the camp. He continued up Santa Cruz and passed the Gatos Theatre. He entered a joint called the Top Cat Tavern. The automatic closer was slow to shut the door, and I heard a man slur, "Where ya been? Wanna a chance to get yer money back?"

I was baffled; why would Holcomb get the boot from one bar and receive a friendly greeting at another? It just didn't add up. I crossed the street and stood in the shadows of a nickel and dime store watching the door of the Top Cat. An hour later the door opened and Holcomb and Rye walked out and headed toward the train station. I couldn't hear what was said, but Rye seemed mad. He kept jabbing his finger in Davy's mug and Davy kept deflecting the jabs. I followed them all the way to the gypsy camp. "So that's where he's staying, huh."

I entered the Top Cat Tavern and for a moment the din in the smoky barroom stopped, and guys looked at me, then the chatter started again. "Can I help ya, sport?" the bartender asked as he dropped boiled eggs into a jar. He had gangly arms and a pocked face. I told him I didn't see who I was looking for and left. At the New Yorker they weren't quite as friendly. The New Yorker catered to a more upscale cliental than the Top Cat. The lady behind the bar asked, "Yeah?" She had a bottle job of red hair in a bun and a dark mole on her upper lip, and out-weighed every man in the joint. I asked her if she had any jobs that needed doing. "Unless you can make a buck outta two bits, I got nothing," she said, with a not so cordial chuckle. I thanked her and left. *A Bo would have to wear his Sunday best to get respect in the New Yorker. Hell, my Sunday best is no different than any other day of the week's best.* Not that I could afford cocktailing in barrooms, mind you.

I was starting to think more like a cop than a hobo, and brother, I was conflicted. I hoped I could find a balance. The stress was starting to get to me, and I needed a drink. Presto, I was a hobo again. When I got back to the camp around midnight, a couple of guys were passing around a split of Thunderbird. A tune I didn't recognize played on a harmonica down by the creek. Some Bo's were standing and some were sitting in groups smoking. This was a culture I missed while sleeping. It was calmer and cozier, I guess. Guys seemed more comfortable in the dark.

"Where ya been so late?" the cook inquired.

"Looking for nourishment," I replied.

"If it's female nourishment, I can't help. But if yer thirsty, help yerself," he said handing me the bottle. Later, I crawled into my hovel with a sour stomach. *Jesus Christ, Thunderbird.*

I was breaking down cardboard boxes for Gene, a short dark-haired man who owned Gene's Country Store. He wore a white dress shirt and charcoal slacks under a khaki shop apron. His cordovan shoes were highly polished. "Bundle 'em up, too, Prescott," he said as he tossed me a ball of twine. He always called people by their last name. "Ya want cash or a bottle today?"

"Four Roses would be good," I told him.

"Aw' right, but ya gotta sweep up back here and dust mop the floor inside."

Jack Calloway walked in the front door while I was using a dustpan to sweep up sawdust from the floor behind the butcher counter.

"Hi, Calloway. What can I help ya with?" Jack told Gene he wanted to talk to me. "He's been here for two hours, he didn't do it," Gene joked with a chuckle. Jack nodded to the back of the store and I followed him. In a whisper he said, "I got the photos in the car; when do ya want to see em?"

I shrugged and said, "Now, I guess."

Gene stood in the doorway and asked, "Calloway, are you gonna be here for a sec? I gotta run across the street to the post office." That gave us an opportunity to be alone. Calloway went to his car, leaving me by myself in the store with all the booze. For a split second I thought about stuffing my pockets. But sanity showed up when I realized I would never work here again. I liked Los Gatos, and if I pilfered from a decent guy like Gene, I'd be shown the town limits and probably squirrel any future work for other Bo's. When Calloway returned I asked him if he could spot me a loan. "Being undercover, I can't get to my bank account and I need some things. I'll pay ya back." He nodded as he handed me the file folder.

The photos were gruesome to say the least. All the victims were on their backs with their arms and legs slightly up. From police classes, I knew this was called the pugilistic pose. When a body is burned, the heat causes the sinew to tighten up, making the victim look like a boxer ready to start jabbing. The clothes were charred. Their faces were similar with exposed teeth in a horrible death grimace. I tried to concentrate on the weapons used and not try and figure which one was Double B. "Hmm," I hummed.

"What do ya see, Grady?"

"All the coats were unbuttoned or not on. Look," I said handing the photos one by one to Calloway. "That would make sense," I continued. "In warm weather, jackets are not always worn. A Bo will always have his jacket with him, though." I took the pictures back. "Ya see, in the cold months a Bo wears lots of layers. Heavy woolen jacket, a couple of heavy shirts and long johns." Calloway gave me a shoulder hunch. "It would take a mighty stab to get through all the clothing."

Calloway nodded and said, "A real sharp knife and long, too."

There didn't seem to be any link to times or dates. Often crimes such as murder and assault follow a lunar pattern. "Can you check the newspapers for the death dates of these and tell me if there was a full moon or not. Actually, you won't need to check Billups. I know it was a full moon that night." The bell over the door rang, and Gene came back.

"By the way Jack, do you have any info for me?" He winced, and replied, "Sorry, Grady. The Chief has given this a low, low priority."

"What has a higher priority than murder?" I asked, with my arms out stretched. "Oh, I get it; if it were some honorable local gentry it would move to priority status. But, since it's just a vagabond, no need to put too much effort into it," I said with some heat. *Would you listen to me? It wasn't too long ago I would've agreed with the top cop. Now I'm on a soapbox yammerin' about the discrimination toward hobos.*

"Look, Jack. I know you didn't make the call, the brass did. It's just I get the feeling I'm working alone on this."

"You are, Grady. I'll give you the credit when there's a collar, don't worry."

"Jesus, Jack, the last thing I want is credit." He shook my hand, and folded in his palm was a sawbuck. I grinned and thanked him. "One last question, Jack, before the hobo murders dropped to the bottom, did anybody look into a gypsy connection?"

He nodded and replied, "I'll get you that file."

I walked to the counter, and Gene gave me my pint of Four Roses, which I slipped into my coat pocket. I slapped the ten-dollar bill on the counter and said, "Give me a split of Thunderbird and a fifth of Four Roses, please."

Gene grabbed the bill and held it up to the light to make sure it wasn't counterfeit. He did this as a joke and with a grin on his face. With the rest of the money, I bought a pound of stew meat, a soup bone and several cans of broth and vegetables, a bag of bow tie noodles and a handful of cigars. As Gene was putting my goods in a paper sack, he asked me, "You informing to the cops, Prescott?"

I just stared him in the eyes, and he sort of stepped back. "Not that anybody knows about," I replied.

"Sure, sure, I got it, Prescott."

I checked the community bulletin board that hung inside next to the front door of Gene's. People posted items for sale, help wanted, and lost or missing people and pets. I was taking note about a missing terrier, whose owner was offering a reward, and the last location the dog was seen. On the sidewalk, a few doors away, I heard Jack Calloway talking to the police dispatcher on the blue call box attached to a wooden telephone pole. He caught my eye and held up an index finger in a hold-on-a-sec gesture. I heard him say, "Oh, I see the smoke now. I'm on my way." He pointed behind me and said, "The gypsy camp is on fire, Grady." Most pedestrians were headed in the direction of the fire. I declined Callaway's offer of a ride. I thought it might be too conspicuous and he agreed. I left my groceries with Gene, and joined the parade headed to the fire.

I approached the gypsy camp from behind the train station. The smoke seemed to be less there. A couple of kids from town were hiding in the bushes watching the blaze. When they heard me, they spun around; their eyes were as big as saucers. I noted their clothing and general facial and hair description. I was acting like a cop again. I walked toward them and they took off in the direction of North Santa Cruz Avenue. They ran up Broadway and ditched behind the hotel. I followed them and noticed that an alley ran behind the hotel from Broadway to East Main Street. They were gone.

When I got back to the scene of the fire, citizens were standing side by side watching the fire department put out the fire. I felt the firemen were just going through the motions. All the tents were burning, but the hoses squirted water around the cars and kept the vehicles from going up in flame. Through the smoke and heat vapors, the colorful clothing of the gypsies could be seen. I decided to walk to the other side of the camp and stand with the gypsies. Rye looked at me with stone cold eyes. His jaw and cheekbones were crunching as much as his knife grinding ever did. "Is there anything I can do for you, sir?"

"Find out who did this. I'll pay when they are in custody." His accent seemed to get thicker as emotions took over. His eyes misted and his daughter sidled up to him and put her arm around his waist.

"It'll be okay, papa," she murmured. All the while she was looking at me suggestively; so young and always on the make.

I noticed someone slight of stature standing by the stew pot with a child when I walked back into the jungle. My heart started to beat faster because the person was about the same size as my wife and the child could be Calvin. I hurried to them, but the closer I got, I could see the man and boy were not my family. I gave Cookie the groceries after removing the whiskey and a couple of cigars and dashed to my hovel. Cookie yelled to me, "Thanks for the bottle and stogies, Grady." I tried to catch my breath and hide my tears as I sat Indian style on my bedroll. Later I saw the boy tossing a rubber ball up in the air. I got near him and said, "Toss it here."

He threw it over and I tossed it back. This went on several times, and then the father joined in and we had a three-way round of catch. We came together in a circle and the boy said, "That was fun." He had sandy blond hair, pale blue eyes, and a smattering of freckles across his nose and cheeks. Their clothes were shabby and the soil of the road clung to them like flies on flypaper. "Where ya headed," I asked.

The man told me they were going to Santa Cruz. "They got some sort of carnival going there during the summers. I hear they got work for guys." He must've meant the Boardwalk.

"It must be rough traveling with your son from place to place."

"This punk ain't my son. He was locked in a boxcar after the door slid shut." Punk is what Bo's called a young person in the jungles, without the negative implication most are used to. "That was in Fresno, across from the Santa Fe Hotel." The boy's name was Byron Wanell and the man's was Larry Dolan. When I asked the boy, he told me his father ran off and his ma got mean and beat him for no reason. A jolt went through me like a rifle shot. *Christ all mighty, is that what could happen to my boy?* I didn't think so. But I didn't really know how deeply I might have wounded my wife. Maybe she looks at Calvin and sees me. Man oh man. I had started to distance myself from my feelings and then this ragamuffin shows up. I never really did want to shut the door on my past. But I kept trying. "Look, ya ain't got time to set yerself up with a hovel before dark, so ya can share mine. Oh, it'll be cramped, but I'd like the company, ya know? Lets get some grub, and then ya can boil up yer duds."

We lay in our bedrolls, Byron in the middle. "Boy, would ya mind if I put my arm over you?" He told me that it would be okay.

The man said, "No monkey business."

"It ain't like that. Ya see, I just miss my boy is all." Byron grabbed my hand and held it to his chest. My sniffles and gasp I'm sure were noticed. This kid, wise for his age, sensed my longing and reacted with this simple gesture that meant the entire world to me. In the morning they were gone. On the floor of my hovel was Byron's rubber ball. "He forgot his ball," I said aloud and looked up the trail to see if they were still around. Then the thought came to me, *He left this just in case Calvin and I do reunite.* He seemed to be such an intelligent kid, that Byron. Being on the road, you pick up not only street smarts, but also a sense of compassion. I prayed that I would catch up with Byron and Larry at some point.

I met Calloway again in the storeroom of Gene's, which seemed to work okay for our info exchanges, and Gene was square with it. "I looked in the file about the gypsies," Jack told me. "Not much in it. Just the names of the families and vehicle plates." Jack grinned and added, "About the only real municipal complaint is they swim and bathe in the town pool at night."

"I saw a couple of kids looking through the bushes as the fire was going. They seemed pretty scared, Jack." When I told him they were white kids wearing bib overalls and white tee shirts and work boots, he replied sarcastically, "Well, that pretty much narrows it down to every kid in town, I'll get right on it."

"Rye told me he was offering a reward for the arrest of the person or persons responsible for the fire. I think I'd like to look into it, Jack. Do you have a problem with that?"

"Yer gonna keep looking into the murders, aren't you?" I assured him that the murders were my priority assignment. *Would you listen to me?* At times I felt I was really a cop, trying to solve the slaying of my mentor, Double B, and, at times I felt as if I were playing pretend like I did as a kid. Back in cop mode, I asked Jack, "Do you know what was going on just before the fire started?"

"The fire chief told me that he interviewed some of the gypsies and was told that there was a matinee going on." I gave him a puzzled look. "Some days around lunch time, men gather around the area where the fire started and some of the gypsy ladies put on a dance show. The men toss cash into a basket. The more fanny the gals show, the more money is thrown." My immediate reaction was Rye's wife and daughter. I had a theory that the young boys I saw were there getting a free show when the fire started. Maybe they were having a smoke and a discarded cigarette started the dry grass and bushes on fire. I was going to try and see if I could locate those kids. That was as good a place to start as any. I wondered how much Rye was gonna pay. "By the way," Calloway continued, "Rye told me the money basket went missing during the confusion when the fire started."

I went across Santa Cruz Avenue and up Broadway and walked the alley behind the hotel, following the route the boys took when they ran away from the fire. I spent some time around the back kitchen door of the hotel. I wasn't sure what I was gonna find, nothing most likely. But I felt sure the kids ran this way. That was two days ago, though. With a squeak, the screen door opened and a short, wide Mexican woman came out. She said something in Spanish I didn't understand. I just raised my hands and moved on. "Hey, you want *comida*?" she said to my back. I turned and looked at her. She motioned me over and moved her hand to her mouth in an eating fashion.

I sat at a small white wooden table next to a huge refrigerator and the senorita set a plate of beef brisket and boiled potatoes in front of me. It had been a long time since I had a kitchen-cooked meal. Not that I'd been starving, but eating out of a tin cup can get tiring. The lady, Yolanda was her name, refilled my coffee cup and put a slice of apple pie in front of me.

Suddenly, the swinging door from the dining room opened and a boy in a starched white busboy's jacket entered. He wasn't wearing bib overalls, but sure as heck he was one of the boys I'd spotted at the fire. We eyed one another for what seemed like a long time. I nodded and then concentrated on the pie. He picked up a tray and walked around me a few times, then said to no one in particular, "Does my old man know yer feeding this lay-about?"

Silence fell over the room. I put my fork down, stacked my dishes and carried them to the sink. The kid had a smug look on his face.

I whispered as I passed him, "Did you enjoy the hoochie-coochie show the other day, boy?" Saucer eyes again. "I hope you and your buddy weren't the ones that started that fire."

"We didn't start nothing," he snarled.

"Ya sure about that? Discarded cigarettes and matches were thrown about in the area you were standing," I lied.

"What's it to you? You ain't no cop." I told him that was a fact, but I heard the cops talking about the cigs and matchsticks.

"Ya best go to the cops and tell em' yer story, or I will." I could smell this kid's fear and see it in his eyes. "Arson ain't something ya want on a rap sheet," I continued, and the more I pushed the more bluster flaked off of him. I was a hobo, but my cop talk was working.

"Look, we was there, ya saw us. But we didn't start the fire. We was just trying to get close enough to get a peek at the gals." He told me that they didn't see who started the fire. "Man it went up with a whoosh, though. Dry grass and brush I guess," he told me as I was washing my dishes. He leaned his backside to the counter and said, "Are we good?" I nodded and he took his tray out to the dining room. I felt certain this kid was telling the truth, and I'd need to look for other clues. I took the alleys behind the stores on the west side of Santa Cruz Avenue. I entered the back door of Gene's.

"Got anything for me to do, Gene?" He told me he was caught up and added, "When you talk to Calloway again, would ya mention that I called the cops the morning after that guy along the tracks was killed, and they never showed. I found something in my front doorway that could be important."

"Why didn't ya say anything to him? He's been here lots of times."

He looked at me intently and said, "Because I didn't know where you fit in the equation. Nothing personal, Prescott."

"None taken. It's just that the guy that got killed was my friend, and I'd like to catch the son of a bitch that did it." Gene went into his office and came out holding a tin can of Ronsonal Lighter Fluid. The yellow container was smudged with what appeared to be blood smears all over it. I was thinking about Gene's fingerprints wiping out anyone else's, when I took it from him, holding the top with my right index finger and the bottom with my left. Gene was looking at me strangely. I eased the can onto the counter and replied, "I seen coppers do that with evidence when we had a burglary at the hardware store where I used to work, before…ya know, I hit the road." I told Gene to put the can in a sack and give it to Calloway the next time he saw him. I assured Gene that I would call Jack and that the lighter fluid was important. "Let's keep this on the QT, okay, Gene?"

I was in a part of town I wasn't familiar with. I was carrying a lost brown and white terrier. I'd spotted him behind an appliance store sitting in the sun. When I called the dog's name, Frisky, he ran into my arms. This street, Glen Ridge, was wide and sat a few blocks above town. The houses were old and big with manicured lawns and well-kept garden beds. Cars slowed when they saw me. I'm certain that Bo's weren't regular pedestrians in this neighborhood. It wasn't too many minutes later that a cop car stopped at the curb where I was walking. When I told him about the lost dog and the reward, the cop gave me a ride to a house on Walnut Avenue. Sensing he was close to home, the dog started to squirm and took a leak on the back seat of the cop's car, which I kept to myself. The lady in the yard had on a flower print blue housecoat and a sunbonnet. Her cheeks were red, and when she spotted her dog they colored even more. "Frisky," she screamed, as she put the basket of freshly cut flowers on the grass. The dog was out the door almost before the cop opened it. Frisky was doing a shimmy at the lady's feet. She was crying and thanking the cop, as if I weren't even there. The cop pointed to me and the lady, tears dripping, held out her hand and said, "I don't know how to thank you."

"There was a mention of a reward, madam."

"Yes, yes, of course. But do you need anything? I have a loaf of fresh baked bread that's still warm. Maybe some butter?" I told her that anything she wanted to give me would be fine.

The cop shoved his cap back and said, "Well, I guess things are okay here, I'll get back to patrol." His words were an assessment to see if the lady was comfortable. She was snuggling the dog in her arms and Frisky was licking her face. The cop looked me up and down and uttered, "All right, then," and took off.

I walked away with two fins and a sack of canned goods, a loaf of bread and three sticks of butter. Not a bad reward, not bad at all. On the walk home—*was I really thinking of the camp as my home?*—I analyzed my prospects. The work I did for Gene kept me in booze. I did, however, take cash from time to time. I was undercover investigating the hobo killings, which was no pay, and looking for lost dogs, which had rewards and other benefits. I was starting to have a pretty good stake saved up and could pay Calloway back the sawbuck he loaned me.

I grabbed my stake out of my hovel and walked to Crider's Department store where I bought a new pair of off-the-rack tan trousers, a white dress shirt and a pair of brown brogans. I took a room at the Lyndon Hotel; I wanted to sleep in a bed and take a long soak in a tub. The desk clerk gave me the once over and must've determined I was legit. It felt good, ya know, not getting the evil eye or being singled out. I called Jack Calloway to meet me in the lounge at the Lyndon at six. I was gonna buy him dinner.

Steam covered the mirror and rivulets of water dripped down and disappeared into the wooden frame. I lay in the tub with a washcloth covering my face. The sweet smell of Yardley's Lavender soap permeated the bathroom. I drained the water, and filled the tub again to bathe longer. The months of sleeping on the ground had taken its toll on my body. *Enjoy this, because tomorrow you'll be back in your hovel.*

I slid onto a barstool and asked for a Four Roses on the rocks. The bartender flipped a napkin in front of me and placed my drink on it. I gave him four bits and told him to keep the change. I could get used to this. Man, I walked in the front door like a real square guy. *Just don't get snockered, Prescott, or you'll end up back in your hovel or the hoosegow.* Calloway showed up a little past six. There was a brunette woman standing behind him dressed in a navy blue business suit that fit her form real fine. Black high heels accentuated her shapely legs. I stood when they approached. Jack introduced her as Hazel Kane. She appeared to be about thirty years old. Her smile was fleeting as she extended a veined hand sans jewelry.

"Can we move to another seat?" Jack asked. We sat at a tiny round cocktail table.

"Jack tells me you can find people, Mr. Prescott."

I shot Jack a look that he met stoically. With squinted eyes, I asked, "Who's missing?"

"My nephew, Byron. Here's a picture of him." My stomach flopped like it had a live trout in it. I hoped my expression would not reveal that I recognized the Byron in the photo as the Byron who passed through Los Gatos a few days ago. "How do you know he's around here?" I asked.

"I saw a boy that might've been him standing outside my gift shop in downtown Saratoga. When I opened the door, he turned and walked away. I called his name, but he kept going."

"Where are the boy's parents?" I asked.

"My brother-in-law lit out almost immediately after he came home from overseas after the war. And my sister is sort of fragile, you see," Hazel Kane replied as she touched a finger to her head. "She's in a…a…a place to help her calm down."

"If young Byron is located, where will he go? Not to a fragile mother, I trust."

Hazel Kane assured me that Byron would live with her in Saratoga, which is only four miles from Los Gatos. Jack Calloway said, "I told Miss Kane that you required the usual, Grady, a twenty dollar retainer and ten dollars a day, plus any additional expenses."

"I don't know, Jack. I'm kinda booked right now." *Listen to me negotiate. What a hot shot I thought I was.* I caught a glimpse of Calloway grinning. I was given another identity, again.

"Oh, please, Mr. Prescott. I'd be most grateful if you could give some time to this," Hazel said as she pulled a twenty from her wallet. Her face softened, and she managed a sincere smile. At that moment the layers of hoboing were wearing off. In the back of my mind I knew I needed to solve the hobo murders, but the thought of seeing Larry and Byron inspired me; and I was gonna make some dough doing it.

I held Byron's rubber ball in my hand the entire twenty-mile bus ride to Santa Cruz, California. I squeezed the ball so much I thought there would be no bounce left in it. I exited the bus and walked to the Beach/Boardwalk. Seagulls squawked as they flew along the shoreline. The salt air was a nice change from the cooking and tobacco smells of the camp. A slight breeze cooled the summer day, but didn't stop children from running from the waves while parents sat bundled in robes and sweatshirts on blankets. I walked through the arcade which had all the usual sounds—bells, horns, sirens and clangs. The smell of cinnamon from the candy apples, along with fresh popcorn, attacked me. The floor, gritty from sand, crunched under my feet.

I stood inside the door of the management office for the Boardwalk. A tall lady with a cigarette dangling from her lip asked if she could help me. She had on a pair of men's chinos and an un-tucked, light blue uniform shirt. When I told her I was looking for Larry Dolan, she asked, "Are you a cop?" I snorted a laugh and replied, "Not hardly, just an old friend." She referred to a clipboard and said, "Right now he's running the kiddie boat ride at the far end," she said, pointing away from the arcade end. I walked along and heard the click-clack of the Giant Dipper roller coaster as the trail of cars climbed the steep hill toward the extensive plummet, screams and laughter emanating from riders. The calliope music from the carousel took me back to another time when Calvin would sit astride a painted pony and I'd stand next to him to make sure he wouldn't fall off. Every time we came to where his mother stood, he gave out a hearty "Halloo!" I watched a father and son for several turns and walked away saying, "Goddamnit."

I watched Dolan for a few minutes. He was a decent guy, and seemed to enjoy watching the children having fun. I felt good that he was the one to take Byron Wanell under his wing. There are so many on the road that would exploit a punk. *Thank you, Lord.*

Larry Dolan spotted me and gave me a "what in the hell are you doing here?" look. I held my hands out to my side and grinned. He pointed to his wrist, which meant wait a few minutes, even though he didn't wear a wristwatch.

"Good to see ya, Grady. Good to see ya," Larry said as he gave my hand several healthy pumps. He told me that he and Byron landed here and got jobs and a room right away. "The guy that hired me told me we could stay in the nurses' station at night. We just have to call the police if any monkey business happens after hours."

"Where is Byron?" I asked. He told me he was a pinsetter for the bowling alley across from the Boardwalk. "He's having a rough go. Kids in town resent him. He's had a few scraps," Larry said as he threw a couple of jabs in the air. "The Boardwalk Company wouldn't hire him because he wasn't old enough. And he's having trouble fitting in." I thought it rather funny that a kid could fit in at a hobo camp, but not in a town with people his own age.

When I told Larry about Hazel Kane, he looked at the ground for several minutes, and shook his head a few times. His eyes were misted over and he whispered, "I'm sure gonna miss him. But this is the best for him. Don't you think, Grady?"

"Why don't we let him make that choice, Larry? If he don't wanna go to be with his aunt, I'm sure as hell not gonna make him. That boy has been making his own decisions for a long time."

The clamor of pins tossing around on hardwood greeted me as I entered the bowling alley. Greasy cooking smells from a poor hood vent system over the griddle infiltrated the entire structure. I heard the whistle and looked above the pins along the lanes, and then I saw a hand waving at me. When the group he was setting pins for finished their game, Byron came over and shook my hand. I gave him his rubber ball and he grinned. We had colas in the coffee shop. He had the remnants of a shiner over his left eye and scabs across the knuckles of both hands. I picked up his right hand and looked closely. "Hit 'em in the gut, Byron; less chance of getting an infection." He grinned and shook his head. "It's not such a friendly place here, Grady."

"Did you ever think of going home, Byron?"

"No way! There I can't fight back. Here at least I win a few."

When I told him his aunt Hazel was looking for him, Byron just stared at me. "She asked me to try and find you. She wants you to come and live with her in Saratoga. It's a good chance."

"You met my aunt? Why did she come to you? I mean, a Bo."

"Hey, kiddo, I wasn't always a Bo. I had a life before hoboing. I even went to college for a bit. Plus I know a cop in Los Gatos, and he didn't have time to find you. So, he hooked me up with your Aunt Hazel."

"And here we are. You've found me. Now what?"

"That's up to you, Byron. I'll get you a bus ticket to Saratoga if you want, or you can stay here behind the pins. It's your call, son." We strolled to a chili parlor down the street from the Boardwalk near the train trestle that crossed the San Lorenzo River toward the south.

11

What's he doing with that boy? Is that his kid? That guy is something else, always cozy with that cop. Is he onto me? Maybe I should let the air outta him. He didn't know I sat right behind him on the bus ride. I'm good at this, he's not onto me.

Being on the bus gave me such a swell of excitement and reminded me of the Friday afternoon I snuck onto the rally bus headed to a high school football game in the next town over. I was in sixth grade, but dressed like a teenager and sat behind my brothers as they made complete asses of themselves with girls. I was getting better with makeup and clothing. Heck, I think I could work in the clothing field. I matched patterns and fabrics that give a hint of wealth to my ensembles. The old man called me a sissy because of what I enjoyed. He can go pound sand.

12

I waited in front of the Fun House while Larry finished his shift at the wooden slide where he handed out burlap sacks so the patrons could go down the slide without getting floor burns. Byron said he needed to be alone and think about getting off the road and living with his aunt. It seemed like an easy solution to me, but then I wasn't sixteen.

People passed us at a rapid pace while we sauntered the Boardwalk.

"Where's everybody going, Larry?"

"To the Fire Slide, c'mon." The Fire Slide, a dangerous stunt, was very popular. A man stood on top of the casino wearing layers of heavy clothes. They doused him in gasoline and tossed a book of lighted matches on him. When he flamed up, he dove into a saltwater pool forty feet below. Given the hobo murders, I wasn't amused.

We were almost back to Larry and Byron's crib and I heard Larry say, "What the…?" Then suddenly I felt a crack on my head. I went down, but was still aware, and I scissored my legs around the ankles of my attacker, toppling him. He scrambled to his feet and took off with Larry chasing him.

"You okay, Grady?" Larry asked, panting when he came back to me. I was sitting up touching my skull to see if I was bleeding. No blood, but a good size goose egg was growing. "What was that all about?"

In the nurses' station Larry was applying an ice bag to my head. Byron walked in and said, "What happened?"

"Grady got sapped by some guy. I chased him but couldn't catch up," Larry said. When Byron asked who did it, I shook my head, which caused me to wince in pain.

I woke with the ice bag sloshing sloppily next to my face. My headache was thunderous, worse than any hangover I ever had, and that's saying something, because brother, I've had my share.

The three of us had waffles in the coffee shop of the Casa del Rey Hotel. It was hard to believe, but six months prior, this hotel had been a Naval hospital.

Byron was just swishing his waffle through syrup. "What's up, boy?" Larry asked. "You ain't said two words since ya got home last night."

Byron added cream and sugar to his coffee took a slurp and said, "I gotta make a decision, and it's hard, ya see. Someone is not gonna like it." He set his spoon on the saucer, cleared his throat and said, "Larry, ya been like a father to me, but I need to get with kin, and trust my ma will get well." He took a huge breath of air into his lungs.

"Don't think for one second that I care if ya stay or go. I've had pards leave before, it ain't no big deal," Larry said matter-of-factly. "It ain't like I won't know where yer gonna be. So go, and I'll catch ya down the road." Larry got up and walked away from the table.

Byron started to go after him, and I stopped him, "He needs to be alone. Leave him be."

We got on the gray dog and Byron exclaimed, "I should've gone to him." I told him that when Larry said, 'I'll catch ya down the road,' it was his way of saying good-bye. Bo's are that way."

Byron and I got off the bus in Los Gatos. I took him to Crider's and outfitted him with a new set of clothes, and then took him to my room at the Lyndon for a good scrubbing before I checked out of the room. It was gonna be back to my hovel for a while. A few steps off the hotel porch and I knew I'd be back. Maybe not in a hotel, but a place that had a bed and a flusher.

On the bus ride to Saratoga, I asked Byron what his plan was. "Don't know for sure. See my aunt and find out if she really wants me to stay with her. She's my mother's sister and I wouldn't put it past her to fake me into thinking she was doing me a good turn, when she might be in cahoots with my ma."

"Listen Byron, ya know where I'll be. Look me up if the bees land in the butter. If I ain't at the quarry camp, try Gene's or the Lyndon," I told him. "Ya can always go to Jack Calloway. But will ya promise me you'll try, son?"

We stood under the marquee of a show house looking across Big Basin Way at the storefront of Hazel Kane's gift shop. Byron was shuffling his feet and couldn't stand still. "Ya nervous, kiddo?" I asked.

All he said was, "Yeah." He let out a sigh through pursed lips and told me, "Being on the road has been a good deal for me. Nobody tellin' me what to do and don't do. I'm used to it, ya see. What if it don't pan out?"

I reminded him where he could reach me. We crossed the street and approached the shop. Byron let out a deep sigh and opened the door. A bell tinkled when he entered. His aunt let out a screech and I saw her embrace Byron and I feared for his ribs. I pocketed the envelope Hazel gave me and motioned Byron over. I put my hand on his shoulder and pointed my finger at him in a fatherly manner and said, "Remember what I told ya, and keep yer nose clean. You're gonna have more street moxie than any ten kids in this town. Use yer knowledge wisely. Go along to get along."

I waited in front of a Dodge Dealership for the bus back to Los Gatos. I opened the envelope and saw three saw bucks. *She spiffed me ten, which would cover our bus fares and meals, well I'll be.* Truth be told, I would have done this job gratis. I was feeling pretty good about my lot. I got on the bus and looked out the window at The Derby Burger across the street and saw a man looking at the bus. He turned quickly away when he spotted me. He was vaguely familiar, from where? I didn't have a clue. Funny how it works on the road; ya see lots of Bo's, and they take on a certain look, almost like they blend together. The turnover rate in a jungle is baffling. No farewell party, no welcome back celebration. Just, "Where ya been? Who'd ya see? What's going on there? Any sight of so and so?"

I had a fitful night's sleep, not because I missed the softness of the hotel bed or the flush toilet, but because of the conversations going on around me. They seemed to be louder than usual. I'd doze off and waken in the middle of a conversation. "Dago Rose's on Bird Avenue…" Another was "the Boardwalk," and yet another, "Calloway."

Were these mugs talking about me? I needed to figure a way to get outta the camp.

"Where is everybody, Cookie?"

"Whadya mean? They's all out already. It's past eight a.m., Grady. Some mush left, ya want it?" he asked as he handed me the coffee pot. The sun glistened off his pink scalp. Cookie squinted and said, "Ya been gone longer than usual. Ya got a gal or something?"

I stared at him for a few seconds and told him I'd stayed at the Lyndon for a couple of days. "Get a bath, sleep on a bed, got some new duds."

"Ya gonna go home, Grady?"

"I ain't got a home anymore. No, I think I'll stick around here for a spell."

"What's here for ya?" he asked.

I looked over my shoulder to see if anyone was around and whispered, "I'm trying to figure out who the guy is killing the hobos, Cookie."

"Hell, everybody knows that. It ain't a secret. The way you cozy up with that copper. We all know you and Double B were tight."

"What are they saying about me?"

"Some think the cops ain't doin' shit and are glad somebody's doin' something," he replied as he tossed a pan of dishwater into the bushes. "Then there are those that think you think yer better than the rest of us."

"What's yer read, Cookie? What do you think?"

"I think yer a temporary hobo. Yer situation is changing. Oh, ya came here broken and on the skids, but yer grinding to get back to hearth and home. I say more power to ya. Don't dally too long, though. The next thing ya know a year's gone and then another and presto; ain't no going back."

I was silent for a minute or two and said, "Maybe yer right, Cookie."

He raised his hands in a who-knows fashion, then said, "Look at Holcomb. He lives in a boarding house, beats the crap outta me why he hangs around here. He does bring in some good grub, though. I just wish he'd quit ragging on the weaker guys. He's like a school yard bully."

"You mean to tell me Davy Holcomb don't stay with the gypsies?"

I asked skeptically. "Where does he get his dough to stay in a room?"

Cookie told me he wasn't sure. "Ain't none of my business, either." He also told me that Davy didn't want anybody to know he wasn't from the road. "He's been in more than a dozen camps over the past few months. I guess he finds a flop in the towns near the jungles." I asked Cookie if he could tell me the closest jungles to the quarry.

"Well, sir, going north there are camps in Redwood City and South Frisco, and of course Frisco itself. Those are the bigger ones. Some small burgs might have some," he said in a professorial manner. "In San Jose, Bo's hang out in Saint James Park during daylight; at night they camp along the Guadalupe and other locations." I knew these spots all too well from my cop days.

"Going down 101 there's Morgan Hill and Gilroy. Lots of field work there. I had a pretty good time in a little road house called the Coyote Inn," he said with a wistful grin. "I spent a week there one night," he chuckled. "Course I was much younger then." He stared off into space, lost in his thoughts. "Out toward the San Joaquin, there are lots of towns, but Stockton has the most prospects, though, being a port town and all along the Sacramento River. I gotta hit the can. Keep an eye on the fire, will ya?"

Before he came back Cookie stopped at his hovel and picked up his toiletry kit. He strode to the creek and motioned with his head for me to follow him. "The problem with Stockton is they got real rough characters there. River people seem to have a way of handling matters—over the side or shanghaied."

"You sure seem to know a bit about California, Cookie," I stated.

He told me he got off a merchant ship in San Diego and never went back. "Too many people tellin' me what to do and what to say and how to say it." He washed his hands and face and teeth and used his coat sleeve to dry off. "Now, heading further south on 101 to Salinas is where there are lots of camps. Work, though, can be dicey; too many migrants jockeying for the jobs." He started to slice onions and other food stuff to begin a lunch Mulligan. "Greenfield, King City and Soledad got some thriving camps. The one in King City is along the Salinas River and seems pretty peaceful. I spent some time there one fall. Real mild."

I helped him with cutting carrots and said, "So ya kinda took the

Mission Trail, eh, Cookie?"

"Well, gosh darn, I never thought of it that way, but yeah, I did. I'm a regular Father Serra."

I thought long and hard on Cookie's comment about me being a temporary Bo. He was right; I was yearning for hearth and home, but the prospects were slim and few. I knew the longer I stayed in the camp, the farther away domesticity became. I needed to talk to somebody about this. If I asked five Bo's, I'd get five different answers, so that wasn't an option. I thought about Hazel Kane, but nixed that idea. She didn't need to know about me. The logical person was Jack Calloway.

I met Jack at Gene's, but before I said anything, he looked me straight in the eye and said, "A guy I know, a San Jose detective, swears up and down that you got the boot. What gives, Grady?"

I hung my head and shook it several times before I answered. I knew this day would come sooner or later. "It's true, Jack," I said. "I'm so sorry that I duped you."

"Why'd ya get the axe?"

"I socked a captain on the jaw. I was shit-faced most of the time, ya see." Calloway stood with his feet spread and his hands on his hips. "Eventually I lost everything—my family, job and house. I skedaddled to Frisco. Then I show up here and we run into one another, and you gave me an alibi. I didn't plan on trying to solve the murders, but when you told me about Billups—well, things changed. He was my best friend in the hobo life and some son-of-a-bitch knocks him off."

"Why didn't ya level with me from the start?" Calloway demanded.

"It seemed like a nicely wrapped package, too convenient to pass up. I'm still gonna try and solve the murders, Jack, as long as you don't have a problem with it."

He told me he needed to think about it for a day or two. "I'll see you at Gene's on Saturday." Before we parted, I asked if he was gonna tell anybody about me. He shook his head and walked away.

Betraying a friend is a horrible thing to do. Jack Calloway aside, all my hobo brethren were deceived by me also. I needed to start damage control and the best thing to do is come up with a plan. So I got drunk. How's that for a damage control plan?

My life was never gonna be the same again, I just knew it. If Jack kept my secret about being a copper I might be able to get along in a non-hobo life. On the other hand, if he puts the kibosh to my murder investigation plan, I'm headed for another town and another hobo jungle.

I was sitting on several cases of Acme Beer in Gene's storeroom when Jack Calloway walked in dressed in casual clothes: dungarees, a blue plaid sport shirt and sandals. He carried a white envelope. "Are those my walking papers, Jack?"

"Kind of," he replied with little emotion. "Let's take a walk, Grady." We stood at the corner of Saratoga Avenue and Santa Cruz Avenue. Lou, the guy who owned the Shell station was talking with old man Nolan, owner of North Gate Drugs and Norman O'Conner, an insurance broker, neighboring businesses on either side of Lou's. All three acknowledged us and continued their conversation.

"What's in the envelope, Jack?"

He handed it to me and said, "Open it." It had no name on it, but the return address was Town of Los Gatos Police Department. I looked at Jack and he nodded. My hands were shaking as I slid my finger along the flap. Inside were a gun permit and a Private Investigator's license with my name on it. I looked at Jack and he said, "I applied for them on your behalf. I stuck my neck way out for you, Grady. I hope you realize that," he whispered. "But then I find out that yer bogus. Shit man, I don't know what to do now."

To think that Jack had that much confidence in me and my ability as an investigator stunned me. However, I felt his faith waning. "Look Jack, the only thing I wasn't up front about was getting kicked off the force. I know that is huge, but all the rest is legit, I swear."

"Oh, I believe you're determined to find out who snuffed yer buddy. I wonder if ya really care about the other stiffs, though. You found that lady's nephew and that lost dog. Those weren't real tough. A private dick needs cases, and I can feed stuff your way, but I gotta know how you plan to set yer operation up. Ya can't work out of a cardboard tent, fer crying out loud."

"What are you saying, Jack? That yer gonna let me have this?" I asked as I held the envelope up.

He told me that I could have them, but if there was one misstep, he'd snatch them from me lickety-split. He asked, "How ya gonna get out of the camp, and where ya gonna go?"

"I found out that most Bo's know that I'm looking into Double B's killing. Until yesterday I thought I was fooling them," I said motioning in the direction of the jungle at the quarry. "So probably the best thing to do is be upfront with 'em and to let them know I'm not an infiltrator."

Jack added, "Maybe tell 'em you really did hit the skids, but found out ya had a knack for finding out things. Mention Byron and Frisky, ya know?"

"I need a stake. I got my stash, but that ain't enough. Maybe a room for a week or so but after that, I dunno," I said aloud.

"I wish I could help out, Grady, but my apartment is pretty cramped. Didn't ya say that there was a bank account you had?"

"Dang, I completely forgot about it. I need to get to San Jose." Jack drove me to the Bank of America building in downtown. I took $475.00 from my savings and felt that would be enough to get a room until I started to find more work. Things were looking up, except for the fact that I needed to come clean with my hobo brothers.

Most of the Bo's in the camp couldn't care less about what I was gonna do. For that matter, they didn't care what anybody did. I thought when I told them I was a disgraced cop they'd push me to the curb. Nobody said a thing. I couldn't believe it. Then, "Some of us figured ya were," Cookie said.

I shook my head and wondered aloud, "Why would ya think I was a cop?"

"There was something perplexing about you. Ya got elevated on a regular basis, but then you'd hang around all palsy-walsy with that detective. Some of us guessed that you were a bull," Cookie explained, and then added, "Are ya leavin town, Grady?"

"No, Cookie, I'm just leaving the camp. I'd like to know if I'd be welcome from time to time."

"Sure. Why not?" Cookie replied. Others there also chimed in with approvals. "Well, I just hope ya find the bastard that's doing the killings," Cookie added. "And if we hear anything, we'll funnel it to ya." There were more murmurs and "yeahs" and "you betchas." I was starting over with a clean slate.

"I need to find a place to live and maybe set up an office," I mentioned to Gene when I stopped to tell him my plans. He told me, "I know a guy that owns a building across the bridge. Maybe I could talk to him." Gene made a phone call and thirty minutes later I met with a man, Donald Wilcox, at the building on the corner of Main Street and College Avenue. He had on a tan suit and a straw hat. A bar, Reggie's, occupied most of the ground floor. A barbershop and dry cleaners took up the rest. Wilcox led me up a narrow set of stairs with black rubber on the risers. The wooden handrail was smooth and worn from years of use. At the top of the stairs was a long corridor with black and white linoleum on the floor. Frosted glass doors with transoms over them led to doctors, dentists, and insurance offices. Before it had become an office building, it was a flophouse hotel. At the far end of the hall was an open door. I could see tarps and ladders and the smell of fresh paint lingered. "This was a real estate office until last week," Wilcox explained. "Gene tells me you need a place to live and work. I don't usually like to combine the two, you know, living and working. Seems like you'd be getting two for one."

"I think it would be temporary, Mr. Wilcox. Maybe I could help out with janitorial services or night guard," I offered with hope. He rubbed his chin and looked me up and down. "Tell me again what it is you do."

"Up until a year ago I was a cop. I had a rough patch and I'm no longer a cop. Last week I was living in a hobo jungle." One thing I learned from Calloway was to be truthful, so I was up front with Wilcox. "There've been several hobo murders and I'm trying to solve them."

"Why don't you let the police do that?" he wondered.

I told him it was not a real priority for them. "Besides, that's not all I'll be doing. Missing persons, lost animals, run around spouses, and bill collecting, the whole gamut." Of course, I had nothing on the horizon, but those are all things a private dick does.

The painter was folding his tarps and removing tape from trim. "Is the paint dry, Frank?" Mr. Wilcox asked the painter. "All but the efficiency kitchen," Frank answered as he fished a rag from the front pocket of his white coveralls. "Another few minutes."

I looked around the room with a new coat of off-white on the walls and ceiling. The wood trim was a shade darker. One wall had two large windows that looked out onto College Avenue and the beige stucco sidewall of the Baptist Church. In a corner near the back door was a full bathroom. A small closet was situated between the bath and a back door with outside stairs that led down to a dirt patch that served as a parking lot. An old wooden building with peeling and faded paint stood adjacent to the parking lot. Barely visible on the front was a sign: Los Gatos Soda Works.

"Well, what do you think, Grady?" Wilcox asked. I said the place looked fine, but wondered if I could live here.

"We can figure something out. You said you could do janitor duty. That won't be too much," he announced as he pointed back down the hallway to the front stairs. "Most of the tenants clean their own offices or have a company come in and do it. The common areas—hall, stairs, and public restroom are my bailiwick," he said as he ran a finger on the top of the wainscoting. He looked at his dusty fingertip and shook his head. "Once a week I ask the bartender to have one of his customers clean up for a few bucks and a couple of drinks. That doesn't always work out." I assured him I could do a job that he would be happy with. "You gotta clean the cigarette butts out of the sand urns, too," he told me as he opened a hall closet where cleaning supplies were stored. "Besides Gene, do you have anybody to vouch for you?" I told him about Jack Calloway. He seemed impressed. "If I was to go down to the police station and ask Calloway about you, what would he say?"

"He'd tell you I was a stand-up joe. Matter of fact, I'll go with you." Mr. Wilcox told me that seeing Calloway wouldn't be necessary.

Frank, the painter was taking a final load of his equipment to his panel truck and told Mr. Wilcox that the paint on the efficiency unit was dry. With the tarps and ladder removed I took a real good look at the space. It was a large well-lit room with a desk with a telephone and file cabinet.

"I'll have somebody take those out, Grady." I told him I could sure use them if that was okay. He shrugged as if to say, "If you want."

I opened a set of accordion doors that revealed a sink and the smallest refrigerator I'd ever seen. A two-burner stove with an oven and a small counter with a cabinet above and below made up the rest of the kitchen. I was starting to think this place would be out of my price range. "How much is the rent, anyway?"

Wilcox was quiet for a couple of moments, and then said, "Thirty a month, but you have to do the janitorial stuff and provide security at night." I looked at him and nodded my head. "We get bums sleeping in the hallway. Scares the ladies when they show up for work in the morning." He looked at me and whispered, "Sorry about the bum comment." I educated him on the difference between a bum and a Bo.

He pulled a rental agreement from his coat pocket and sat at the desk and filled it out, and then I signed. On the bottom he wrote my duties as they affected my occupancy; once a week wax the hall floor and dust surfaces. Daily I was to clean and re-stock the restrooms and empty the sand urns of cigarette butts and lock the front door at 10:00 p.m. I gave him sixty smackers to seal the deal, and when Mr. Wilcox gave me the keys to my own space I was walking tall. I wondered what I was gonna sleep on, and then reality set in. The last year I'd been sleeping on dirt. I needed to be grateful I had a roof and a kitchen and a flusher. *Where am I gonna sleep?* Jesus.

Downstairs in Reggie's, the guy behind the bar let me borrow a chair for a few days until I could find a real desk chair. I moved the desk over toward the window, which gave me a nice view of Main Street, the bridge and the side of the Foothill Apartments. I walked to the phone company, which was across the street from Crider's and set up an appointment to have a new phone number and get my name in the phone book. I knew I needed a business license, but felt I could wait on that expense.

At Clanton's Used Furniture I found an oak wooden desk chair for five smackers and a sofa for fifteen. Mr. Clanton and I were jockeying the couch down the hall toward my place. I was walking backward when I heard Jack Calloway say, "Gimme yer key, Grady. I'll open the door." Clanton left and Calloway and I put the couch next to the bathroom. We sat and took in the new digs. "Well, what do ya think, Jack? Pretty nifty, eh?"

"I think it's real swell, Grady. Donald Wilcox stopped by the department and asked me about you. I'm glad ya told him yer whole story." He kept looking at the desk by the window and said, "You could divide this into two spaces, Grady. Put up some sort of screening and that would be the office," he said pointing at the window, "And this could be your domicile," he said moving his hand in a circle. "Nobody wants to see yer cot when they come in to do business."

"Ya got time to have a beer downstairs, Jack?" He looked at his watch and announced, "I'm off duty, so heck yes." On the sidewalk Jack told me," I got something in the car for ya. I'll meet ya inside." He brought in a laundry shirt box. Inside the box was a good amount of binder paper, pens and pencils and paper clips. "If yer gonna do this right, you'll need to do reports. Under the paper are some Manila folders." Jack waved me off, when I told him I'd repay every cent. Pointing to the box he announced, "That's your new business gift from me to you. You *can* buy me another beer," he said as he drained his glass of draught.

"What are ya gonna call yer outfit, anyway?"

"In the phone directory, it'll be Grady Prescott Investigations. I been thinking about getting some cards made up. And in the left corner will be the initials, GPI, for Grady Prescott Investigations. My name will be in the middle, Private Investigator under it and the address and phone number under that. How's that sound, Jack?" He looked at me and squinted and then whispered, "Part of me is jealous, pal."

"How so?"

"You know, working for yourself and all. Kind of appeals to me."

"Don't do anything dumb, Jack. Get yer pension."

"Yeah, I know. What are ya gonna do for your first day on the job?"

I told him my plans for seeing the insurance companies in town to let them know I was an investigator. "Then see the bankers and find out if they need bill collections done. Throw my hat in the ring, so to speak."

At the used car lot of the Ford dealership I was thinking about getting some transportation. I had to turn down a job from an insurance company because the agent wanted me to tail a truck driver, who they suspected was bilking the company he worked for, because of a "bad back." He was getting his insurance money and working for another company doing the exact same job. It would have been a snap. But I couldn't afford to take a taxi or ask a bus driver to "follow that car."

A salesman, clad in a white shirt with a bright red bow-tie approached me and said, "I've been watching you, and you got a good eye. That little 40 coupe has yer name written all over it." He reminded me of a carnival barker.

"Is that so?" I replied. I hadn't even settled on any car yet.

"Yer darn tootin' it's so." We bantered back and forth for several minutes. Man, he wanted me to take it for a spin, but I declined. I needed a car, but would have to wait, so I walked away. "Don't wait too long, mac. That ride is a peach and some guy is gonna see what a good deal it is and scoop up the coupe. Hey, that rhymes."

My funds were running low and rent was due in two weeks. I needed a payday real soon. I decided that I would see Rye and look into the gypsy camp arson case.

When I passed the depot I heard no music, which I thought odd, but when I saw no cars, I knew why there was no music. They had moved on. The arson payday was as gone as Rye and his clan. I needed to catch a break. Had I known what was going to happen next, I would have had second thoughts.

I was checking the bulletin board inside Gene's Country Store for notices about lost animals. Three new ones had been tacked up. I copied the info and realized that the lost dogs were from the same general vicinity near an area of Victorian homes called Fairview Plaza. I trudged up to Fairview from a path at the end of West Main Street. A huge rooming house called Abbey Inn stood on the left. The place was painted white with dark green trim. I heard a screen door slam and saw Davy Holcomb dash down the stairs and head for a stand of oaks next to a creek. I scratched the idea of knocking on doors to inquire about lost dogs and followed Holcomb. I hid behind a huge Hawthorne bush and saw Maurice sitting on the ground looking at the creek. He handed a bottle to Holcomb as Davy sat down. "How long do I gotta keep cleaning up after those mutts?"

"Just a couple more days. Don't get yer water hot." Davy replied.

"This ain't what I wanna be doing, and you know it, Davy."

"Just be patient."

"The last dame gave us a reward that didn't even cover the cans of dog food," Maurice whined. "Maybe we should hold em for ransom, ya see. Tell 'em they ever wanna see Fido again leave fifty smackers in an envelope."

"No, this works better than most scams. It can last longer than doing a D and D."

Doing a D and D is a deaf and dumb gig. A guy knocks on the front door of a house and when somebody answers, he hands them a note that says, "I'm deaf and dumb. Can you help me out with the price of a bus ticket so I can visit my son in the hospital? He has polio." The resident feels sorry for the guy, so they give him a couple of bucks. The problem with a D and D is that it's real temporary. One clown even went back into the neighborhood where he pulled his deaf scam, knocked on the same door and asked the same lady if she had any work. Makes me think this cat was elevated at the time. The lady says to him, "You were here last week with a note that said you were deaf and dumb. Get off my porch before I call the police."

The guy was quick; I'll give him that. He told the housewife, "It's a miracle. Praise the Lord." Nonetheless, she slammed the door in his face.

So Davy and Maurice were stealing dogs, and when a notice goes up offering a reward, they return the dog and pocket the cash. I felt these two were up to no good; however, I thought it would be more serious. I was thinking they had a part in the hobo murders. Think about it; one guy pretends to be a Bo, but lives in a rooming house and the other joker is a toady to the fake Bo. "Why don't they get legit work?" I whispered to myself.

Holcomb looked in my direction when he heard kids laughing and talking while walking up the path. I backed away into an open garage. When Davy turned back, I scurried down Bayview Avenue to Bean Avenue.

Jack Calloway was walking down the stairs from my office just as I opened the door to go up. "Oh, there you are. I just left a note on your door," Calloway told me. I could smell booze on his breath, and it was just after two in the afternoon. It wasn't the first time I got a whiff of alcohol from him.

"What's up, Jack?" He told me that his department received a wire from the Salinas Police Chief about a hobo murder. "Seems like the same MO as the others, Grady. Only difference is they didn't torch him." I didn't say anything and Jack asked, "Are ya gonna go down there?"

I mentioned about transportation and he said, "Shit, Grady ya can use my car." I looked at him oddly and he said, "Not my cop sedan; my Ford. It's just sitting in the garage."

The dark blue 1939 Ford Tudor had good tires and ran like a top. The interior was beige mohair and the three-speed gearshift on the floor had a pearl-white knob. I agreed to take down the mileage each time I used it and after every hundred miles, I'd pay Jack $5.00. I was responsible for maintenance and I had to get insurance. "You still have an operator's license, don't you? If not, get yer ass to the motor vehicle department and get one."

I had the license, but I stopped at Norman O'Conner's office to get a policy because the next day I was heading to Salinas. That afternoon I stopped at Gene's and helped him sweep and tear down boxes. I needed a few extra bucks to get me through the next day or two. I had $75.00 to my name, so another fin from Gene would help. After all, I was on a no-pay jaunt; a vow is a vow, though. And I vowed to solve these hobo murders.

Reggie's has two windows on the corner of the building. One faces Main Street and the other faces College Avenue. As I walked by, Jack Calloway rapped on the Main Street glass and waved me to come in. A bottle of Lucky Lager was on the bar in front of him. *This guy is going down a bad road.* "C'mon Grady have one with me," he slurred. I sipped my Four Roses and Jack had another beer. I don't know how many he had before I got there, but I guess a few. I looked at him and saw myself, and a shiver hit me from head to toe. I knew what drinking on the job could do and wrestled with whether or not I should say something. I knew when I was hitting it hard I wouldn't listen to anybody's advice. I'll mention the dangers and if he pays attention great, if not? Well, at least I tried, right? Lately *my* drinking had diminished a bit, and the dreams had increased. You'd think having a saloon at the bottom of the stairs would be convenient, but the fact was I didn't have cash to support the habit. I knew that I was just a tinkle of an ice cube in a glass away from sleeping on dirt again.

"Ah, hell, Grady, it's just my Irish blood. We like a nip now and then, don't worry," Calloway scoffed and gave a dismissive hand gesture.

"I know what drinking on the job can lead to. Don't become a disgrace. There's no future in it, pal. Believe me."

The sun was just coming up as I was headed down Highway 1, and the rolling hills with clumps of scrub brush and oak trees looked brown and tender dry. The air was sticky already until I got a few miles from Salinas where a sea breeze refreshed me and the landscape got greener. The fertile aroma of freshly tilled soil was pleasant and my spirits lifted, until I saw a sign for King City. I gripped the steering wheel tighter until my knuckles were white. I looked at the file folder Jack loaned me with notes about the hobo killings and said, "Ya got a job to do Prescott, stay focused."

The desk officer at the Salinas PD led me through a squad room with desks where police officers were writing reports, their typewriters clicking constantly while they talked on phones and interviewed witnesses. He knocked on the door and a deep voice said, "Come on in." Dante Verducchi got up and walked toward me and stuck out his hand. His face was dark and he had a huge nose. Not because of family genes, but because it looked like it had been broken a few times. Scars over his eyebrows shouted: boxer. His hair was black and shiny and he seemed to be one of those guys that needed to shave a couple of times a day. "Calloway told me you were a cop and now you do PI stuff. How's that working out?"

"I just got started, so not so good. Insurance work mostly at the moment," I replied.

"Get yerself hooked up with a criminal attorney, and you'll be busy all the time," Dante announced. That was a damn fine idea. "I'm not real certain our murder is like yours. Tell me about them," he said in a business-like manner. I told him that all of the hobo murders were committed in warmer months by stabbing the Bo in the gut with a ten inch or longer Schrade hunting knife. He kept shaking his head.

"Then they douse em with lighter fluid and toss a match on 'em. Pretty ugly, ya know?"

Verducchi's face was grim with a downturned smile. He tossed a paper clip he'd been twirling onto his desk blotter and said, "Our guy was attacked from the rear. His throat was slit," he said as he made a move with his index finger across his Adam's apple. "No weapon left and no fire." After a moment he whispered, "The only similarity is this guy was a bum."

"Our victims were hobos, Dante."

"Is that so? What's the diff?" So I educated Dante Verducchi on the diff. He asked, "How can ya tell them apart?"

"Did your victim have a job?"

"Yeah. He worked at the Boardwalk in Santa Cruz." My heart was pounding and a cluster of bile jumped up into my gullet. *It can't be Larry Dolan. Please don't let it be Larry Dolan.* "What was his name?" I asked in almost a whine.

"Hmm, let me look. Ah, here it is. Lawrence Peter Dolan."

Two of the most decent Bo's—hell, forget about being a Bo—two of the most decent men I've ever met were killed. Murdered. I must have looked pale, because Verducchi asked me if I was okay. I told him I did a runaway investigation, and I met Dolan while doing it. Verducchi let me copy his notes and I told him I was going to visit the crime scene and ask a few questions.

"You have a PI license on ya, right?" I showed him my ID and he stood and told me good luck.

I sat in the Ford parked behind the police station and wept. I wept for Double B, Larry Dolan, and Byron Wanell *and* for me. Who knew this would be such an emotional roller coaster? In the hobo camps life was easier. At that moment I understood what a Bo meant when he said, "I like being free, mac, nothing behind me and nothing ahead."

13

This son of a bitch is all over the place. He's gotta be the fuzz. How could he have heard about this slash job if he wasn't? What in Christ's name is this Bo doing in Salinas? I shoulda hit him harder in Santa Cruz. I'm changing up my routine to throw em off. But still this guy keeps showing up.

Working the dog scam with Holcomb gives me some coin, but the dough I get, fifty smackers, every so often from Davy is what I crave. Ass-bite brothers send him a check and he shares it with me. He calls it "shut up money" and "don't ask cash" which is okay with me. Davy doesn't know the brothers give me money every so often. I've got a nice wad saved for a rainy day. Kinda funny, I had to become a hobo before I could save any money. When I was a teamster I never had dough; always broke. Now, cash gives me freedom to move from location to location. This little jaunt along the central coast is a case in point. New town, new prey. Who has it better than me?

When ma died it was just me and the old man. Brothers were off chasing diplomas, so I think he liked having me around, and I got used to him. It was better when it was just the two of us. But the fact of the matter was he knew his boys were beating on me and he did nothing about it. Sometimes I hated the old man. He did teach me how to drive a truck, though. And he was good to ma.

14

I stood in an alley behind a bar called the Garden Grill and Pub. This was where Larry got his throat slit. The chalk outline of the last place Larry drew a breath caused a chill to course through me. I walked out to the front and went in. The bartender was rolling dice with a man wearing a cowboy hat. The dice cup banged on the bar top and the cowboy gave a whoop. "What can I get ya?" the bartender asked in a friendly tone. When I told him I was a private detective looking into the murder in the alley, he seemed to stand taller and he adjusted his bib apron. "Don't know too much. That fella seemed like he was real nice."

"Did he have an argument with anyone? Did some guy have a beef with him?"

"Nah, he had a couple of drinks and went to the can and never came back. This is a real friendly place. I don't think it was any of our clientele. "What do you think," he asked the cowboy, who just shook his head and pushed his hat back. I gave each of them one of my new business cards and said, "If you find out or hear about anything, give the Salinas PD a call and give me a ring. Reverse the charges."

"Los Gatos, huh? Yer a ways from home," the cowboy said.

"Gotta go where the job takes me."

I intended to backtrack to Santa Cruz and check in with the people at the Boardwalk, but instead I walked back into the bar and asked, "How far is it to King City?" I had lots of time to think about how I was gonna break the news of Larry's murder to Byron. The closer I got to King City the more I thought about what I was gonna say if and when I ever saw Janey and Calvin again.

I sat in the Ford across the street from the Corner Club, a single story brick building. The front door was on a forty-five degree angle to the corner of the sidewalk, and I could see down both sides of the building from my vantage point. Windows lined both exterior walls and a side door was on the left. My heart was beating a drum solo and my hands shook like I was in withdrawal. Traffic was light and pedestrians were few and far between. The lunch hour was over; maybe everybody had gone back to work. I was at the front door, starting to go in and then stopping several times and finally I walked up to the structure and gripped the knob of the side entrance and stepped in. It was a lazy scene; a couple of Mexicans were playing shuffle board, the bartender was cutting lemons, and two cowboys were drinking bottles of beer at the bar. I ordered an orange juice with Calso and ice. I put a quarter on the bar, and asked where the restroom was. I took my time and checked around for my wife. I could hear pots and pans clanging in the kitchen. I opened the swinging door and saw a man in a cook's outfit and a dishwasher.

"Next door down, mac," the cook said pointing.

The bartender, a tall lanky guy with rosy cheeks and blond hair parted down the middle asked me where I was from. When I told him San Jose, he just nodded and put a flat toothpick in his mouth. A sign on the wall of the back bar said, *Kiss the bartender twice. He's Italian and Swiss.* "Is that you?" I asked pointing to the sign. "It is indeed. All of the bartenders here are Italian and Swiss." I looked at him with raised eyebrows. "We're all brothers, uncles and children of the same family."

I looked over my shoulder and motioned the barkeep over and whispered, "I'm looking for somebody that works here." His eyes narrowed and he said, "Who?"

"Janey Prescott. I heard she got a job here."

"Why are you looking for her? You a bill collector or a cop?"

"Neither. I'm her husband."

He took a step back, gave me a dirty look and hissed, "I've heard about you. And nothing I heard was good."

"I'm sure it wasn't," I replied. "That was then and this is now. Does she still work here? I don't want any trouble."

"She works here nights. During the day she works at that place across the street." I followed his pointing finger out the window to a place called the City Café. "She's working two jobs to support those boys. She worked right up to the day she delivered."

"What are you saying? She had a baby?" Air was rushing in my ears and it was difficult to catch my breath. I heard a sob come out of me that I couldn't control. I couldn't stop the tears. The cowboys gave me a strange look then turned back to their conversation about the price of feed or some other agricultural thing. "I'm sorry," I told the bartender between quick gasps of air.

"It's okay, pal. You ain't the first guy that sat on one of those stools and cried into his beer." He served the cowboys another round and came back to me. "She told us she was "with child" when she applied for the cocktailing job. We liked her right off. The customers took to her too. So when she could, she came back to work. We took up a collection for her on a regular basis to help out because… well, you know? You weren't coming across with any scratch for her."

I thought about ordering a drink, but felt if I started I wouldn't stop. That's all I would need to make a complete ass of myself waiting for Janey to come to work. Then anger took hold; I kept mulling over in my mind how unfair she was to keep that information from me. I had a right to know, God damn it. I'm that baby's father. Or was I? She might've stepped out on me. No, that's not Janey. Then I started to cry. The bartender said, "Ya better buck up, pal. She's due in any time now."

"What about Calvin? Is he okay?" I asked after blowing my nose.

"He's a good kid. Plays on the Merchant's Association softball team." He wiped the bar with a dishtowel and continued, "He gets good grades and pretty much takes care of himself and his brother when Janey is working."

Should I stay or go? Well, sir, I stayed, even though I wondered if that was wise, but I was about to find out. I saw her reflection in the mirror, face plumper than the last time I saw her, but she was glowing. She looked happy, but that vanished like powder in the wind when she laid eyes on me. She shot a glance at the bartender, and I saw him shrug. "Hello, Janey," I said softly. "When you get a chance, I'd like to talk with you."

"Not likely, Grady. *I've* got a job." The emphasis she put on that sentence was meant to berate me, and it did.

"Please, Janey. Give me a couple of minutes." I looked at the bartender and then to Janey.

The bartender nodded to the kitchen and said, "If I need ya, I'll call ya."

"Thanks, Julian. I won't be long," she said as she put her tray and towel on the bar top. She had every right in the world to chew me up and spit me out, and she did, sort of. We were sitting on a picnic bench in a patio area outside the kitchen door. "First of all, I didn't know you were pregnant. Had I known…"

"Had you known what? It wouldn't have made a difference. You were gone all the time. Oh, you may have been in the house, but you were smashed. You probably don't even remember raping me. Well, *I* sure do."

I hung my head in shame and took every bit of her tirade. "You got kicked off the police department, and let the mortgage go. That was our house and you let it go! You let us go! Whiskey was more important to you than anything in San Jose." She was flushed, her nostrils flared, and her voice was getting stronger. "When Calvin and I got here our lives improved greatly. He's doing so well," she said as she stood and crossed her arms and tapped her foot.

"Does he ask about me at all?" I inquired weakly, not really sure I wanted to hear the answer.

"As a matter of fact, he does. Why? I don't know. You crapped all over him, ya know." For her to use a word like that was out of character. She wasn't the shy one anymore. "He even brags about you."

"Do you think I can see him, Janey? Him and his brother."

"Coleman, that's the baby's name. I need to think about that. What do you do to survive? Where do you live?"

Before I could give her a recap, Julian came to the door and told her she needed to get to work, "It's getting busy, honey."

"Tomorrow is Saturday. You can see the boys then." She wrote her address on a slip of paper and handed it to me. I felt awkward in the Corner Club after that, so I left and found a liquor store and bought a bottle. I drove around until I found a place to park for the night. A motel room would've been nice, but funds were getting low. It was the longest night I ever spent, and I've spent some long nights, brother. I'd pick the bottle up and start to crack the label, then put it down again. Over and over I did that. When I woke up in the morning, my neck was stiff and my back sore. The bottle however, was unopened. That was the only thing I felt proud about. The sleep wasn't sound; I didn't dream.

There was a note tacked to the screen door of Janey's bungalow. My heart sank; she's changed her mind. Now what? The note said she forgot that Calvin had a ball game and for me to meet them there.

I drove around until I saw a school. I parked the Ford next to a cyclone fence and walked to where I thought a ball field would be. I could hear boys yelling, "Hey, batter, batter, swing!" I watched for a few minutes to see if I could spot Calvin. The players all looked the same. I wasn't feeling real good. I mean, what kind of father doesn't recognize his own son? Janey was sitting in the green wooden bleachers behind the backstop chatting with other parents. A baby stroller was on the grass next to her. I misted thinking about the events and milestones I'd squandered because of my depravity. The crack of a bat hitting a baseball turned my attention back to the field. I became aware of somebody standing next to me. Calvin! It was Calvin. His ball cap sat high on his forehead. He'd grown quite a bit and seemed tall for a ten-year-old. I knelt next to him and took his shoulders and looked him straight in the eyes. His lip and chin trembled and huge tears ran down his cheeks. We embraced each other and sobbed. He kept saying over and over, "Daddy, Daddy." Our embrace broke and he said, "Does mama know you're here? I have a baby brother, ya know?" He held my arm and when we got to the dugout he announced, "Hey fellers, this is my dad." They all turned and said "hellos" and "hi ya". God, how tough it must have been for Calvin to show up in a new town and have to explain to his new friends where his father was. As we walked away one of the boys said to another, "He's a cop."

The coach yelled to Calvin, "Hey, Cal, you're playing right field this inning, get a move on." Calvin was reluctant to let go of my hand. I told him to go ahead and I would see him after the game. He darted to the dugout, grabbed his mitt and skipped out to his position. I was blowing my nose and wiping my eyes, which was useless, because when Janey handed me the baby, the waterworks started again. I could care less as to who saw me crying—that boy in the field, that woman in the bleachers and this baby in my arms were all that mattered. Before I gave the Coleman back to Janey, he put his tiny hand on my cheek. I sensed it was his way of saying, "I've been waiting for you."

Janey introduced me to her friends, who appeared cordial. I wondered if they knew the story. But instantly that didn't matter. My mind was going a mile a minute. Can I get the house in San Jose back? I could move here. If worst came to worst, we could all live in my office. *Get a load of me; I'm planning everybody's future. Put the brakes on, Prescott.* A few minutes later a tall man in a maroon flannel shirt and jeans walked up and slid onto the seat next to Janey. "It's about time you showed up," she said to the man. Wind, whistles, and horns sounded in my head. I saw red for a second or two, but calmed down. I mean, what did I expect? She's a healthy woman with a shit-head for a husband. Of course she'd have a boyfriend. I saw her whisper to the man and nod in my direction. He looked at me, got up and walked over, grinned and extended his hand. "It's been a long time, Grady. You don't recognize me do you?" I shook my head. "I'm Tom, Janey's brother." Tom had filled out some since the war and seemed bulkier. His grin vanished and he said in a somewhat sinister tone, "What do you want? Janey has a real good life here. If you mess that up, we're gonna have problems. You read me?"

A year ago I woulda popped him one on the beak. That was then; this was now. "I don't want to cause any trouble, Tom. I'm just trying to do the next right thing." He nodded and started to turn away and I said, "Hey, Tommy, don't ever threaten me again."

He turned and looked me straight on and hissed, "That wasn't a threat, bub. It was a promise." He could have the last word. Like I said, that was then; this is now.

After the game, I sat with my family on a bench under a huge oak tree on the schoolyard eating sandwiches Janey packed. Calvin was really excited, the baby was fussy, Janey was icy, and Tommy was gone. There were so many questions we wanted to ask each other, but we just couldn't seem to begin. To say that it was awkward would be an understatement. Calvin, bless his heart, broke the ice.

"Are you still a policeman, daddy?"

"No, son, I'm not. I am a private detective now."

He said, "Oh," then asked, "That's still like the police, right?" I nodded and he gave a curt nod.

I looked at Janey and whispered, "Is there anything you want to know?"

"Yes. There were lots of things, but when facing you, I can't think of any."

Just then, one of Calvin's buddies came over and said, "There's a dead snake by the river, c'mon." He looked at his mom, then at me, then back to his mom. She nodded and told him, "Your father won't leave without saying goodbye. Make sure that snake is dead and don't touch it."

"Well, I guess you want to know what happened with the job."

"I heard you got fired. I don't know for sure why, but I can imagine. Why don't *you* tell me?"

I told her about being drunk on the job, hitting my superior officer, and getting fired. "I lost my pension, you, and the boy. Boys. The house went into foreclosure and I ran away." I told her about Frisco and Double B and the quarry camp in Los Gatos. "I got off the freight car at the train yard in San Jose. I went to our old house. It's boarded up and weeds took over." I hung my head in shame. Janey said something that I didn't understand or hear, so I just nodded.

"Did you hear what I said, Grady? Tommy picked up the mortgage. He owns it now." I didn't know what that meant. How was that important to my disclosure? One thing I noticed as I explained to Janey about my life over the last year was that her expression never changed.

"So that brings us to now, I live in an office in Los Gatos and am trying to make a living as a PI."

"You can turn it off just like that? Go from a hobo to an investigator in one fell swoop?" she said snapping her fingers.

"I wasn't like the hobos you hear about. Being free and moving from place to place, real gad-abouts. I had ties. I know you won't believe that. But I wanted to have a home with you." I looked into her eyes and saw skepticism. "Don't get me wrong. There were times when not *having* to do anything was appealing. But that's not me." She asked me about the nightmares and I told her they still occurred. "You still trying to soothe them with rot gut? You need to get one of those doctors that figure you out in your head." We were silent for several minutes listening to birds chirp. A black dog walked up and sniffed the baby's stroller and a man said, "C'mon Rex. Here boy."

"So what do you expect from this little visit, Grady?"

"I don't know. I just wanted to see that you and Calvin were okay. How come you didn't let me know about him?" I said pointing to the baby asleep in the stroller.

"Would it have made a difference?" I had to agree with her.

"You said last night that I raped you. Is that true?"

"Repeatedly. Every time you came home with a load on and your whores weren't available you took it out on me. I couldn't ever get clean enough after being with you those times.

"God, I am so sorry. I was wrong and I will never do that again," I sobbed.

"You got that right, buster. You'll never touch me in any way, shape, or form. That I swear."

From the lumpy brown brocade couch in Janey's living room, I watched her and Calvin move about. I felt like I was seeing a picture show, and the actors weren't even aware of their audience. The scene was interrupted when a knock sounded on the screen door. "C'mon in," Janey said from the kitchen. I stood up when Julian, the bartender from the Corner Club walked in. What was he doing here? Maybe checking up on her. When she gave him a peck on the cheek, I caught on; they're an item. He shook my hand and I looked him in the eye; and if there were a smirk on his mug I was gonna bust his lip. But all I saw was kindness. On some level I think this Julian felt sorry for me.

Calvin and I had a wonderful afternoon together. He was telling me about his friends and the school he went to. We even played catch. "Things are fun here. Julian takes us to the pictures.... ah," he stammered embarrassedly. I told him that I was happy about what was going on with him and his mom and baby brother, which was horse hooey, because I wanted him to tell me his mom cried out my name in her sleep and Julian was a jerk. I knew Calvin could spot a jerk; he'd lived with me. "I will always be your father, and if you need anything, I don't care what it is, call me," I told him as I gave him my business card.

Three lamb chops were thawing on the drain board in the kitchen. No dinner invite for me, I guess. "Listen Janey, I'll send you some money when I can. You know, for the boys."

"That won't be necessary, Grady, we're..."

I interrupted her and said, "I know I was a lousy husband and father," and before I could continue, Julian appeared.

"Julian, can you give us a second?" Janey asked. He backed away graciously. I wanted to dislike this guy, but couldn't quite get there.

"I can't undo the past. I mean I can't become a good husband, but don't deny me the opportunity to be a good father to those boys, please."

"If you break that boy's heart again, I hope you rot in hell," Janey hissed as she pointed a finger at me.

I walked down the walkway of Janey's house headed for the Ford, when Calvin said, "Daddy, will you come back again?" I looked at him and at his mom, as she swayed Coleman to sleep in her arms. She nodded, and I told him, "Sooner than you think, son." I could see Julian's shadow through the screen door. Driving away, I looked in the rearview mirror and saw Calvin waving to me, his tears glistening on his cheeks. I stretched my hand high out the window and waved back and honked the horn. I almost ran into a man in a slouch hat limping across the street.

My tears flowed like a fire hose. I needed to pull over and get composed. I faced the fact that my family was getting along without me. They were happy and healthy. That was an upside, for them. My upside was that I reestablished a relationship with my son, Calvin, and met my baby son, Coleman. Another plus is that I saw Janey and she didn't kill me.

Before I left King City, I remembered what Cookie said about a jungle along the Salinas River. It might be a good idea to do some investigating as long as I was here. It would be difficult to spot a camp by car, so I parked and walked along the bank. I spotted a sign, the one with the top off a square. I made my presence known and was waved in. Some Bo's were prepping for dinner and others were playing a card toss game. Judging by the number of cards on the ground next to a hat, they weren't very accurate. Still others were swimming and bathing.

I recognized some of them from Frisco and Los Gatos, Bo's who don't stay in one place long enough for a guy to get a read on or to even learn their names, just Pal, Mac or Bo. Over a week's time they could travel from San Jose to Spokane. That was the difference between me and them. I liked to land and stay, always tied to a family unit of sorts. "Hey, I seen you in Frisco. Yer a pal of Double B's," a man with curly white hair exclaimed. His face was tanned and creased like leather. "It looks like ya moved on, judging by yer clothes and shoes. Ya catch the gravy train, mac?"

I told them about finding lost pets and getting the rewards. "Then some dame wants me to find her long-lost nephew, and I found him within two days," I told those listening. "Then I got to thinkin maybe I can make a living as an investigator."

"Yeah, and how's that working out for ya?" a guy sitting on a felled sycamore tree trunk asked.

"I'm scratching a broke man's ass, if ya gotta know." We all had a chuckle.

"What brings ya here?" I told them about the recent hobo murders and that I was looking into them. "The latest was in Salinas two days ago. A guy name of Larry Dolan, any of ya hear about that?" When I started talking like a copper, they seemed to clam up. I can't say I blame them, but I planted the seed. If somebody wanted to talk, they'd seek me out. Suddenly I felt the drift coming. They migrated away from me, so I bid farewell and wished them luck.

Before I reached the car, a guy in a slouch hat limped from behind it. He put his head down and walked into the camp. I eyed him until he was out of sight. "I almost ran over that guy earlier," I said aloud as I climbed in the car.

15

I braked on a slight hill, heading North on Highway 101. The pedal seemed spongy. I pumped it several times and the system seemed to react accordingly. At a sweeping turn into a long downgrade, I braked again and the pedal went clear to the floor. Pumping them was useless and the speed increased. I zoomed past trees, fence posts and billboards. I could snuggle the guardrail to slow down, but thought about the body damage and how mad Jack would be. I tried the emergency brake and it was not slowing the car down. I looked for a road that was angled enough for me to make a safe turn onto. An agriculture road leading to an orchard was at a forty-five degree off the highway. Leaving the highway surface and onto the dirt road caused the car to pop up and down. I saw a dirt pile and headed right for it. I thought the damage would be minimal, and man, I needed to stop and I did, abruptly. I sat trying to catch my breath. Dust was swirling and my heart was thumping. I relaxed, hoping to not have a heart attack, and wiped my brow with my sleeve. I saw a farmer saunter up to the side of the car. "Howdy. Whatcha doing in my dirt pile?" When I told him about the brake pedal, he nodded and said, "Makes sense. Whatcha gonna do?"

The tow truck driver talked nonstop all the way into Greenfield. He pulled into a Signal filling station. The attendant said the mechanic was gone for the day and would be back in the morning. "Do ya think I could put it up on the hoist and take look-see under her?" I asked.

"Gotta charge a rack fee. Four bits." The three of us—me, the attendant and the tow driver—pushed the Ford onto the rack. "Smells like brake fluid," the attendant said as he sniffed his finger. "Well, look at this—yer brake lines have been cut. Somebody don't like you mister," the attendant said, as he pointed to the four brake lines.

"What about the emergency brake? It didn't work." He told me it was disconnected.

My heart started to race again and I wasn't certain how much more the old pump could take. Learning about Larry Dolan, seeing my family and realizing my wife was involved with another man, crashing the car, and now finding out someone was trying to kill me. That was hard on a guy's ticker. The Bo in the slouch hat had to have something to do with this and maybe the hobo murders. For the life of me, the only thing I remember is his hat. Every Bo wears a slouch hat, fer' crying out loud!

I had a dinner of polenta and Italian sausage at a joint called the Powder Horn. It was tasty and the people, mostly rural, were very cordial. Except that in the bar after dinner two ranch hands got into a fistfight. The bartender, an attractive bleached blond gal in her fifties, came around and shoved the combatants to the door. They were swinging and neither was connecting. "You stay outta here or I'll call the cops." She turned back and said in a huff, "Brothers. Can ya believe it? Tomorrow they'll be connecting sprinkler pipe side-by-side like nothing happened. You want another Four Roses, shug?" I did and was starting to feel that familiar glow. I was sipping more than usual, rather than my regular habit of guzzling. I needed to make sure I had enough to get the brake lines repaired and fill up on hydraulic fluid and gasoline. An hour later it was just me and the blonde and we were having a good conversation about any-and-everything. I guess she could see that look in my eye and might have felt, *This guy is gonna wanna get friendly and I'm beat, he's drunk, and I'm gonna close.* "Last call, shug." I finished and she walked me to the door. I turned to sneak a kiss, but she'd turned already and all I saw was her back. "Which way is the Signal station?" She pointed to her right without turning.

I woke up in the back seat of the car with the empty bottle of Four Roses on the floorboard. The rising sun was beating in the window and I was rumpled and cramped. I opened the door and could hear the dings of the gas pump sounding off the gallons as a car was being refueled. "Good morning, sunshine. I was wondering if you were dead," a huge man in oily coveralls said. "I coulda had ya on the road thirty minutes ago. Got a tire repair ahead of ya now. Won't be long. Coffee's in the office. Ya might find a somewhat clean cup around. Help yourself." I washed up in the restroom and took inventory of last night as I tried to neaten my hair.

An hour later I was on the road. I passed the Powder Horn and slowed to see if I could spot the bartender. Nobody around.

Santa Cruz was foggy when I pulled in front of the bowling alley across from the Boardwalk late Sunday morning. I didn't think the office would be open, but checked anyhow.

"Anytime the Boardwalk is open, this office is open," the lady I met before said. She gasped when I told her about Dolan. When I mentioned I was investigating the murder she said, "I know most of the cops around here. I saw you the other day, but didn't read ya as a cop. As a matter of fact, you *told* me you weren't a cop. Who do you work for? The Sheriff's department?" When I told her I was a private detective, she whispered, "Like Boston Blackie, eh?"

"Did Dolan fill out any paperwork that might have the name of next of kin?" I asked. She seemed reluctant to say, so I mentioned, "The murder happened in Salinas. The Santa Cruz police aren't gonna look into this. Call Sergeant Verducchi in Salinas. We're working this together."

"Aw right, just a sec. I'll get his employment card. Ya might want to get his stuff out of the nurse's station too." The only name on the card on the line for kin was Byron Wanell. Dolan's bindle didn't reveal any pertinent information and his belongings were Spartan at best. His kit and bedroll might be of use to a newcomer, so I took them with me to give out at the quarry camp. I thanked the lady and headed over the hill to Los Gatos.

After a bath and a change of clothes I headed for Saratoga. I was on a journey I didn't want to take.

Hazel Kane was locking the door of her shop when I pulled up to the curb in front of her. She told me that Byron was working at an orchard outside of town. "How's he doing?"

"He tells me he's okay. I see the bruises and nicks on his fists. I don't think he wants me to worry, but I do," she sighed. "What about you? Are you okay?"

"Maybe if you have an hour or two, I could tell you," I said with a snort.

"I do. Why don't you stay and have dinner with Byron and me?"

Byron had grown a few inches, and was my height, and his shoulders were broader. He seemed older than his sixteen years. He gave me a hardy hand pump when he saw me standing in the kitchen of his aunt's cottage. "What do ya know, what do ya hear, what do ya say?" His eyes fell when he saw my look. Hazel walked in and said, "Isn't it wonderful, Byron, that… what's wrong?" she gasped.

"I'm afraid I've got bad news, Byron."

"It's Larry, isn't it?" he whispered through tears that streaked his dusty face. "What happened?"

When I told them of his murder, Hazel was horrified, and held a hand to her lips. Byron shook his head slowly and said, "I should have gone and found him that last day, Grady. You said it was a Bo's way of saying good bye." Hazel gave him a tender hug and shushed him as he wept.

"That's how it is on the road, kiddo. Don't dwell on it. Think of the times you were together and the education you got from him."

Byron went to take a bath and every so often we could still hear him sobbing. Hazel and I sat and talked. She had a fancy bottle of wine open, and I was restrained in my intake. I brought her up to date on Janey and my boys. She reached across the Formica table and squeezed my hand. I didn't want sympathy—hell, I'm not even sure what I wanted. I felt I'd said too much. So I changed the subject. "How is your sister doing? Is she getting better?"

"Not really. I took Byron to see her and when he walked in she snapped at him. He was crestfallen." We were silent for a few minutes, each lost in thought. "Byron is going to start high school in September. He's going to go to Los Gatos. It's the closest school. He'll take the bus." I told her my office was just a few blocks from the school and he could come by anytime.

Despite the gloom about Larry Dolan, we had a nice time. Part of coping with the grieving process was to have humor interspersed with tears. Byron was telling us the story about the time he and Larry were in Sacramento and pulled a D and D on a shop owner. "The guy—the owner—says, 'Hop in my car. I'll take ya.' Well, I'm the D and D, and it's my first attempt, and I say, 'That won't work. We need the bus fare,' and Byron starts laughing. "The guy chases me out of the store and I'm scared as all get out, and I see Larry peeking from behind a lamp post all wide-eyed. It was funny, man." He then misted up, and became sullen.

"Honey, your Auntie doesn't want to hear stories about your escapades. My heart won't take it," she said drying her eyes from laughter and sadness.

Before I left, I asked Hazel if she minded if Byron and I took a walk. We stood near a creek by a park. A western swing band was playing at an open stage called Nicky's Melody Ranchland. "How you getting along, Byron?"

"It's a tough nut to crack, but it's easier than Santa Cruz, though," he said. "The kids here are all farmers. Oh, ya got some rich guys, but most are farm people. They work pretty hard, they play hard and they fight hard."

"You mixing it up pretty good, are ya?" He told me it was becoming less and less. "And that's good, ya know, Grady? I don't like to fight, but some of these guys here, that seems to be what they live for."

"Do you remember what I told you about your street smarts? Use 'em wisely."

"What about you? You out of hoboing?" I told him I was trying to make it as a PI.

"Are you gonna try and find the rat that killed Larry?"

"It is a top priority, Byron, and you can take that to the bank."

I was sitting at my desk trying to link Double B's and Larry Dolan's killing with the other ones in Los Gatos. The map I drew showing where the bodies were found wasn't making any sense to me. "I might as well be reading Chinese, fer crying out loud," I said as I tossed my pencil on the desk. It landed on the Bay Area map that had been in Double B's bindle. I unfolded it and spread it across the desk. The spots marked were all cities that had hobo camps. I added those towns to my map and a figure eight pattern developed. Jack mentioned that fourteen murders with the same MO were reported by the other police agencies. I wondered if any of them had multiple murders. Los Gatos had two, with Double B being the last one.

My thought process was interrupted when my office door opened and a huge man in an expensive brown business suit stood in the doorway. "You Prescott?" he asked gruffly.

"I'm Grady Prescott, and who might you be?" I said as I held out my hand.

"Jones, Wesley Jones, pleased to meet you." His hand was as soft as a baby's, but the grip was vise-like. He may have been an athlete at one time, but his playing days were behind him. I pointed to a side chair and he sat. "What can I do for you, Mr. Jones?"

He hemmed and hawed for a few moments, then looked me face-to-face and spewed, "It's my wife, and I think she's running around on me." I asked him why he thought that and he said that she was away from home too often.

"What does she do, I mean what is her occupation?"

"She tells everybody she's a dance instructor. But what she really does is spend my money." He pulled a picture from the inside pocket of his suit coat. His wife, Veda, an attractive raven-haired gal, had a prominent widow's peak and a smile that appeared kind. "She's an Eye-talian war bride. Yeah, I brought her here from Genoa. Hell, she could hardly speak a word of English, but I think she understood more than she let on."

I took out a notepad and got set to take notes when Jones asked, "How much do you charge anyway?"

He just nodded when I told him it was twenty for a retainer, non-refundable, and a saw buck a day plus expenses. "What expenses?"

"I may need to pay for information or grease a palm now and then. Do you want photographs? Developing costs dough." He told me he would like photographs. "If I catch her red-handed, I'm gonna send her back to mama and papa on the first ship."

I took down their address and was told that she was, at the moment, home. Jones gave me a rundown of their routine. He leaves the house by eight-thirty each morning and arrives at his manufacturing business by nine. "I think she meets with some friends at La Hacienda Inn for lunch at least three times a week. She plays canasta once a week."

"I thought you said she taught dance. When does she do that?" I wanted to know.

"Supposedly after her luncheon days." I got a description of her vehicle; a newer dark green Hudson with black fender skirts.

"Where do you think she will be tomorrow?" He told me she'd be at lunch with the gals. "It's Thursday, so she'll be at La Hacienda."

I hid behind an old camellia bush across the street from the Jones residence on Palm Avenue, snapping pictures of Veda Jones as she walked to her car. She was dressed in a brown suit with a black scarf and a black pillbox hat with a veil atop her head. She looked like a lady going to lunch with the ladies. In a log sheet I noted the date and time of the photos. I followed her to Northgate Drugs and got a shot of her carrying a small paper sack while walking to the Hudson.

I sat in front of the La Hacienda waiting for her to come out after lunch. Ninety minutes later she stood on the steps of the restaurant talking with three other women dressed similarly. They were casual in their demeanor. I watched them all walk to their cars and depart and then followed Veda to a dance studio a couple of blocks off of Santa Cruz Avenue, photographing her every move and location change. I stepped inside the studio and saw her dancing with a middle-aged man. They'd do a step or two and then stop. She'd step away and point to her feet and would do a dance move. It sure felt more like a dance lesson than a tryst to me. I sat in my car and later followed her home, and after that knocked off the surveillance for the day and returned to the office to write my report.

The next day, Friday, I tailed Veda Jones into the coffee shop of the Lyndon Hotel, where she sipped coffee and seemed to be waiting for somebody. She was dressed in cream-colored slacks, wide at the cuffs with a pair of red high-heeled shoes and a purple pull-over cashmere sweater.

Things looked normal as she walked down Main Street a little while later. But when she ducked into a cigar store with a pool hall in the rear, I was taken aback. I saw the man behind the counter acknowledge her and nod his head to the back room. Men's magazines lined a rack in front of the counter. Packages of cigarettes, pipe tobacco, and pipes and pipe filters were behind the man. Boxes of cigars were displayed in a glass counter behind the magazine rack.

"Can I get a rack of balls, pal?" I asked the cigar counter man. "In the back," he replied.

All the tables were open with pool balls racked on them. Light shades hung over the green felt tables, and cue sticks stood neatly in a wooden holder on the wall. Veda looked at me from the counter where she was talking with a gruff looking guy. "What do ya need?" the guy asked.

"Looking for my friend. I thought he'd be here."

I'm not real sure, but it looked like the gruff guy was giving Veda a racing form. "She's playing the ponies. She doesn't have a boyfriend," I said aloud as I walked back to the Lyndon.

"Jack, if a guy wanted to bet on the horses, where could he do that?" I asked Calloway as we had drinks in Reggie's. He told me the Smoke Shop up on Main. "As long as the gambling isn't broadcast all over, the Chief has no problem; same thing with rolling dice in bars. Do it the Chief's way or don't do it, and keep the unsavory types out," Jack explained.

Monday I parked across the street and took Veda's picture as she went in the Smoke Shop and again when she came out fifteen minutes later. The thought of watching her for another week rattled around in my head. I mean at ten smackers a day, that could add up. Then a better idea won out—finish this job quickly and maybe Wesley Jones would recommend me to some of his cronies.

Mr. Jones looked like he was sitting in hell's waiting room. He rocked nervously behind a mahogany desk in his office on the second floor of his manufacturing company. A huge window looked out on the machinery and machinists working below. His hands shook like an aspen tree as I handed him the large envelop with surveillance photos inside. As he took them out, I said, "Your wife doesn't have a boyfriend, Mr. Jones. She has a gambling habit."

His shoulders slumped and his face looked relieved. He sorted through the pics and said aloud, "Gambling, eh? I can handle that." He stood and shook my hand, "I don't know how I can ever thank you, Prescott." He handed me a fat envelope and my thought was, *This is the best way I know of.* Seventy-five dollars for four days of work, plus film and developing costs and a little spiff. Pretty nice and very clean. I hoped they would all be this clean, but I knew ugliness frequently invaded the investigation gig.

Bo's were sitting around the cooking fire waiting to help Cookie prepare the evening meal. "If ya help cook, ya get yer plate first. Get some protein, ya know?" a Bo explained one of my first days in the camp in Frisco. I handed Cookie a leg of lamb wrapped in butcher paper. He laid it out on a grill and started to rub seasonings all over it. "This is great, man. We all get some gump tonight. Thanks, Grady." I declined Cookie's offer to stay on for supper. I was meeting Hazel Kane for dinner.

I sat kibitzing with the Bo's for thirty minutes. They asked how my new gig was doing and if I was having any luck solving the hobo murders. "Guys in jungles seem to clam up when I start asking questions. Too much like a copper, I guess." There were murmurs and nods.

"What else keeps ya busy, Grady?" Maurice asked. I looked him in the eye and said, "Finding lost animals." He seemed to shrink back and dropped his eyes downward. I continued, "Seems several dogs from the same neighborhood go missing at the same time. The cops think people are swiping the dogs and holding them for ransom." I looked from face to face and the only Bo without a passive countenance was Maurice. "If you guys hear anything about that, let the coppers know." I paused, and then said, "I mean, what dirty bastard or bastards would steal a pet? Don't get much lower than that." Somebody replied, "Except for killing Bo's." Just then Davy Holcomb walked into camp. "Hey, Davy! When did ya get back?" Maurice asked. He seemed relieved that Holcomb had returned.

"Ya been traveling, Davy?" I wanted to know. "Just up the coast a bit is all." Then Maurice piped up, "Up the coast? I thought you said…" Before he could finish, Davy cut him off, "I changed my mind." I purposely looked at Davy's leg. When he saw me staring he said, "What?" I just shook my head and walked away.

Hazel and I tooled down Saratoga-Santa Clara Road in the Ford, passing many ranches and rows of fruit trees in groomed orchards. "The trees are so beautiful," Hazel whispered. She seemed comfortable with me, and I wondered if the time would come when I would need to tell her my entire past. That seemed too boyfriend-girlfriend like. I turned into a gravel parking lot in front of a roadhouse, Bert's Country Inn.

When Hazel called me and said that she'd like to talk to me about Byron, I had no idea that it would become a dinner date, and when she said Bert's, I was speechless. I spoke into the receiver, "Bert's? Are you sure?"

"Yes, I'm sure," she answered. "Why?" I relayed to her the times when I was on duty and we'd get a radio report from main dispatch about a brawl going on there. It was in the County Sheriff's jurisdiction. In the outlying areas of the county, one guy, a constable was on duty. He patrolled from Cambrian to Cupertino. San Jose Police and surrounding agencies would respond to help quell any melee. "Oh, it's not like that anymore, I'm sure, Grady. But we can go elsewhere if you like."

The joint was smoky but genteel. Patrons ran the gamut from ranchers to men and women dressed fancy to casual. "This is certainly a different atmosphere than the last time I was here," I said as I slid Hazel's chair out. "I told you," she answered as she looked up at me and batted her lids. I sensed a flutter in my heart I hadn't felt in a long time.

"Tell me what's going on with Byron, Hazel." She sipped her glass of red wine and told me that Byron was playing hooky. I found this amusing, but remained stoic. I mean this kid had lived in hobo jungles and on the road for that last few years and to say he's *playing hooky* sounded funny to me. "I see him hanging around Blaney Plaza in downtown Saratoga. He doesn't even try to hide his truancy."

I lost it and started to laugh. Hazel gave me a dirty look and asked, "What is so funny, mister?"

When I tried to explain that a punk couldn't become a schoolboy overnight, Hazel's lids, which had batted earlier, were now slits shooting razors at me. My once fluttering heart was as placid as a lace doily on granny's chair. I needed to go into damage control.

"Look, Hazel, I'll talk to him. Maybe spend more time with him. But don't expect miracles. He's been calling the shots, and that's hard to give up."

"That's all I want, Grady. Talk some sense into him." I didn't go into the fact that talking sense into someone, especially a teenager, who at one time was a hobo, was futile. I just nodded. We agreed that she would call me the next time Byron Wanell skipped school.

After we got in the car, Hazel scooted over next to me, turned my face to hers and kissed me tenderly on the lips. The kiss escalated into fever. The windows on the Ford were fogged up when we broke our embrace. We looked at each other with racing hearts, trying to catch our breath. Then we embraced again. I've always felt there is a time and a place for everything, and an automobile was not the place for the next stage of this evening. *Would you listen to me—I've attacked my wife, bedded numerous whores, and here I am talking about gentlemanly things.*

I walked Hazel to the door of her cottage and kissed her goodnight. She had a bluesy look and I told her, "We have lots of time, Hazel." She hugged me and whispered in my ear, "Don't wait too long."

The drive home was leisurely. The window was down and the evening air refreshing. A hint of Hazel's perfume lingered on my shoulder. I was lost in thought and didn't see the yellow caution light on the Constable's squad car parked in front of the gas station at Austin Corner's. I screeched to a stop. Harris, the Constable, came from behind the lube rack when he heard me stop. He had one hand on the knob of his nightstick and the other on his holster. I identified myself and he relaxed. "Whatcha doin out so late, Grady?" I told him I was going home. "What about you, Harris? You gotta call here?"

"Nah, just shaking doors to make sure they're locked, and ain't no bad guys around." He lit a cigarette and hiked his belt and holster up on his hips. "I hear tell you're a private dick now, Grady."

"That I am," I said as I gave him my card. "We should keep in touch, Harris. Maybe we can help each other from time to time."

"I'm glad ya stopped, Grady. I had an interesting thing happen the other night over by Ross Creek near the cemetery," he said, as he put his foot on the bumper of the Ford. "I'm driving down Los

Gatos-Almaden Road when the beam of a flashlight hits the windshield of my prowler. I pulled over and head back on foot and I seen these two jackasses wading in the creek," he shook his head and continued, "It was like they was gaffing or something. One held the flashlight and the other had a spear-like tool, and the racket was thunderous."

"What were they looking for?" I wanted to know.

He told me he watched them for several minutes and then rousted them. 'Whatcha looking for?' I says, and they jumped like they was real scared. They started to wade out of the water, and I told em, hold it right there." Harris held up his hand in a halt fashion. "I tells 'em to come out one at a time and sit on the bank. And that's when I realized the racket going on was frogs—the ones still in the creek and ones in the covered pails on the shore."

"Who were they, Harris?"

He pulled his note pad from his shirt pocket and thumbed through a few pages and said, "Ah, here we are. David Holcomb was one name and the other was Maurice Buck."

What could these two ass-bites be doing with frogs? I wondered to myself. Harris said, "I looked through the penal code and fish and game laws and the only thing I could cite them for was fishing after dark, so I let them and the frogs go." Davy and Maurice were, I realized a couple of idiots. The animal scheme, I got, but frogs baffled me.

Things became pretty slow for a while and I decided to get back to solving the hobo murders, but for the life of me I couldn't concentrate. Was it because I earned nothing monetarily while trying to solve these cases? Maybe. *Don't forget what you told Byron, Prescott. Or the vow about solving Double B's knock off.*

16

I felt the footsteps before I heard them. The frosted window in the door shuddered, and then I saw a shadow. I placed my .38 in the open top drawer of my desk in case I needed it. The door swung open and a reed-thin man stepped in. He wore a pale gray three-piece suit and a black hat and red tie. He was ashen-faced with dark circles around his eyes. It was a good thing he had a hat and tie on, because his skin tone and suit blended into drab. I stood and asked how I could help him.

"Name's Gorman and I run the Lyndon. You may know my boy, Will." I looked at him blankly. "He says ya questioned him about the fire at the Gypsy camp this recent summer. Can I sit?" he asked as he removed his hat. "Wesley Jones told me ya did some work around his plant. Said you did a bang-up job." That was a great compliment, and a referral is good business.

I pointed to the chair and said, "Your boy didn't have anything to do with that fire, Mr. Gorman." He told me he knew that and stated, "That's not why I'm here."

"What is it, then?"

"All of a sudden I've got a rodent and bug problem at my property."

"Sounds to me like you need an exterminator, Mr. Gorman."

He snapped his head up and told me, "I've taken care of the immediate problem. My point is, there has never been a pest problem in that building. Never."

He told me about some characters that had been hanging around talking to his cooks and maids and laundry workers. He called these hang-arounds, "crooked-nose Charlies." When I asked, he explained they were guys offering his employees more money if they would join the union. "So I step in and tell these vermin to stay out of my hotel. Next thing I know, there's a lady at the front desk in her nightgown and robe telling my clerk that her bed is full of bugs. Jesus Christ, can you imagine how that can ruin a hotel's reputation?" He moved his hat from hand to hand and said, "Rats have been seen in the hallways. I've never seen a rat there before now. I think these guys are bringing in pests to force me to let my employees unionize. The latest thing was that my seafood supplier sends me frog legs that are of poor quality. A specialty on our menu is frog legs. It's one of our signature dishes."

Frogs from Ross Creek flashed in my noggin. How could Holcomb and Maurice be involved with this?

"Is your sea food supplier union?" I wanted to know. He told me they were. I asked what was so bad about the union.

He answered, "I pay a fair wage and have a good medical plan; as good as the union or better."

"What do your employees say? I mean do they want the union?"

"Most are migrants. This is the first time they've worked inside. Before getting here they followed the crops and worked the fields. As long as they get a pay check every two weeks, they're happy."

"What do you want from me, Mr. Gorman?"

"I want you to stay at my place for a couple of weeks and see if you can spot an infiltrator from the union or maybe somebody working against me from the inside.

The smell of Yardley's Lavender soap and a mattress, rather than a couch flashed through my noggin.

"I got other cases I'm working."

Before I could finish, Gorman said, "That's perfect. You can be more discreet, move in and out like you got a job. Not just a guy that hangs out on the porch or lounge. We'll meet in your office to discuss anything. No, that's good."

When I told him my fees, he grimaced and said, "I'll pay your retainer. But based on the fact that you will be staying in one of my rooms and eating in the dining room or coffee shop gratis, I'll give you five a day and you pick up the expenses."

I thought this over, but before I could agree, Gorman announced, "If this gets resolved rapidly, there will be a hefty bonus." We shook, and agreed that I would move into the hotel the next day at noon.

I'd been at the Lyndon for a week and hadn't seen any union people or activity going on. I sat on the porch having coffee. The sun gleamed off the gray, enameled porch boards and the wicker rocker I sat in creaked with each rock. "You must think I'm nuts," Mr. Gorman said as he approached. "Mind if I sit?" I nodded to the side chair and he plopped down with a heavy sigh.

I asked, "Why do you think I think you're nuts?"

"Since you got here, nothing has happened," Gorman announced.

"I am good, aren't I?" Gorman cracked a smile—the first time I'd seen him smile since I met him a week ago. I asked if he wanted me to pack it in.

He shook his head and said, "Not yet." When I mentioned that I was gonna snoop around the seafood supplier's warehouse, Gorman nodded, got up and went inside.

I was parked across the street from the All Bay Seafood Company near the county fairgrounds at Tully Road and Monterey Highway. A huge marlin, the company logo, was drawn on the office front. A cyclone fence surrounded the property and delivery trucks drove in and out a gate. Several trucks were backed up to huge rollup doors at a loading dock. I observed numerous men in suits and hats standing around. Their dress appeared odd to me. It wasn't usual attire for a warehouse. I expected men in coveralls, caps and gloves. I snapped a couple of photos of the goings on and wrote in my log. My head was down and I didn't see the mug in a navy blue suit standing at my driver's side window.

"Whatcha think yer doin, bub?"

"Writing my insurance report," I lied. He eyed my camera sitting on the seat next to me.

"Why ya taking pictures?" he asked in an angrier tone. I told him something about how it's easier to submit the pictures with the written report. He seemed to buy it. But when he asked what insurance company I worked for my heart flip flopped. On the cyclone fence was a placard that said *this property protected by Acme Security Company.*

"Actually, I work for Acme Security. Say, why the twenty questions?" I snapped.

"Don't take a tone with me. I'll smack ya one," he replied.

The heft of my .38 gave some comfort. I could see several other men walking toward the street. They looked like mob muscle or bodyguards. I attempted to get out of the Ford, but blue suit guy put his hip on the door and tried to reach across me to snatch the camera. I grabbed his arm and laid the .38 on his cheek. "Back away, man, or I'll let ya have it. God damn it, I said back away." The guy stepped into the middle of the street. I peeled out, laying rubber for half a block. My heart was jumping until I got to Willow Glen.

Two hours later Jack Calloway swung open my door with the look of an angry dog. "Did you pull a gun on some guy?" he wailed.

"I'm good, and how are you, Jack?" I replied sarcastically. Calloway stood in front of my desk with his hands on his hips. "I got a call from a San Jose PD detective. He said my car, *my* car, was involved in an incident where a gun was drawn. What the hell, Grady?" Jack was breathing heavily but the anger on his mug seemed to subside.

"Sit down, Jack. Take a load off," I said.

"Well, did you pull on a guy, Grady?"

"I did, Jack. It was warranted. The guy threatened me and tried to steal my camera." Jack just sat and shook his head.

"Do you wanna hear my story or not?" I asked him.

"In a minute. You're gonna need to get your own jalopy, Grady. I can't have the cops running the license plate on the Ford and calling me every time you're involved in some escapade."

Quickly calculating my financial situation, I realized there was no way in hell I could afford a car payment. Jack continued to prattle on, but I wasn't paying attention.

"Did you hear what I said, Grady?" Jack said as he slapped the desktop.

"What?" I said looking at the desktop and his hand.

"Damn it, Grady, yer trying my patience. I said I'll sign my car over to you and you pay me off. I'll work out a contract of the terms. But we gotta get the transfer in right away. You can tell me your story on the way to the motor vehicle registration office."

After I told Jack about the incident at the seafood warehouse he said, "I would've done the same thing. Tell me more about the malarkey going on at the Lyndon." After giving him the poop on union activities and other shenanigans at the hotel, his only comment was, "Keep me posted on that."

Calloway's terms on the acquisition of the Ford were generous and basic. We agreed that $350.00 would be the purchase price and that I would pay him what I could afford each month.

"If you can muster a better deal than that, ya best jump on it, Grady." He also added that he would keep a ledger that I could look at any time I wanted. I gave him a fifty to seal the deal.

I put my temporary registration in the glove box and stopped at the Western Auto store on Santa Cruz Avenue and bought a can of Simonize paste car wax. I was gonna polish my new car, *my new car.* Did it look good? I don't know. Things were going so well for me; I decided to reward myself with a drink or two. I got drunk and never even wiped a rag on a fender.

Loud banging on my office door woke me up. For a few seconds I didn't know where I was. I'd slept in my office instead of the Lyndon. The fog was clearing; I got hammered in Reggie's with Calloway. "Hold yer horses, I'm coming," I croaked to whoever was at the door. It was Will Gorman, Mr. Gorman's son. "What's up, hot shot?" I asked, trying to mask my banging head. I'd passed out in my clothes so I must've looked a sight.

"Holy cripe, you stink," Will said as he fanned his hand in front of his face. "My old man is on the war path."

Will told me goons started a fight in the lounge and the place was busted up pretty good.

"Tell your father I'll be there shortly." I showered and put on fresh clothes, then walked up Main Street. I stopped at the Park Café, had a plate of scrambled eggs and toast with coffee and my stomach started to settle. A feeling of shame took over, which was new for me. Face it, I'm a drunk and getting drunk is what a drunk does. Very rarely did I feel ashamed or guilty after a toot. So this was new. Was I changing?

I didn't have time to process this, due to the fact that Mr. Gorman was on the porch talking with a man in overalls with a carpenter's pencil over his ear. "There you are. Where were you last night?" Gorman railed, staring me down with narrowed eyes and tight lips. I told him

I'd been working. "Well, isn't that swell. My place gets trashed and you were working," he whispered.

"Hold on just a minute, Mr. Gorman. I'm not the night watchman around here, nor am I the bouncer or bodyguard. I'm looking into labor problems and disruptive events. That's all. There would not have been a thing I could do to stop thugs from tossing your lounge. So I suggest you back off a step or two."

He dismissed me with a wave, said, "I'll deal with you later," and continued talking to the carpenter. I realized that Gorman wasn't used to being spoken to in that manner. Tough titty. That was his problem.

Calloway was in the lounge with a uniformed patrolman surveying the damage. Doors were broken off of their hinges, the mirror over the back bar was smashed to smithereens, broken booze bottles were strewn about, the smell of which almost made me heave. Furniture lay in splinters; the joint was ruined. When Jack saw me he just shook his head and gave me a look and pursed his lips and exhaled. I knew what he meant. Man, that was stupid. Let's not do it again until the next time.

"When you get the photos developed from the sea food place, can I have a look-see at them, Grady"?

"Technically they belong to Gorman, Jack."

"What belongs to me?" Gorman snarled as he approached. When I told him about the pictures I'd taken, he nodded and told Calloway that he could look at them.

Jack told Gorman, "I want to show them to patrons that were here last evening when the melee broke out. By the way, did any of your customers get hurt?"

Gorman said that he was told none of the combatants were regulars. "My bartender said these fellers walked in together, sat at the same table, argued and started busting up the place. He doesn't remember a blow being thrown. Then, he says they left together."

This was obviously a staged fight, just to inflict damage to the property. Calloway turned back to the uniformed guy, which left me and Gorman alone.

"We okay?" I asked. He nodded and started picking up debris and up-righting tables.

Over the months the expense of sending film out for developing became costly. I contacted a photographer who worked at the newspaper to help me purchase the equipment needed to have a dark room. This kid knew his stuff. He bought trays, chemicals, an enlarger, a timer and an amber safe light bulb. He calculated that it would take me four or five months to recoup my original outlay, then all I needed to buy was the chemicals, which were much less expensive than having somebody else do the developing. I fashioned a frame from pipes so I could hang a black curtain over it, which made my kitchen double in size. I had a piece of plywood placed over the counter and stove to create a workspace.

"What do these chemicals do?" I asked the photographer.

"I could tell you, but you'd forget. You got four one-gallon jugs, mark them one through four, starting with this one." He then arranged the others in order of use. There are four trays. Mark them with one to four. I'll do your first few shots, then I'll watch you do some and then yer a developer."

He showed me how to make the film into negatives, how to enlarge and dip the enlargements. The first time I did a developing job I was poking at the paper with tongs.

"Quit doing that, ya ain't cooking. Leave the picture alone. You keep messing with it you'll ruin it."

I was hanging the developed photos from All Bay Sea Food with a clothespin to a wire spanning the width of my kitchenette, when I heard somebody enter my office.

"I'll be right out. I'm developing pictures."

"Grady? It's Byron."

"Hey, buddy, how you doing?" I said from the dark room. "Give me another few minutes, okay?" The timer went off and I removed a picture from the tray and hung it.

"I didn't know ya knew how to do that stuff, Grady."

"Nothing to it, once ya learn how. What's shaking, kiddo?" I said as we shook hands.

"Aw, ya know. This and that."

Byron told me school was going okay and that the kids seemed pretty decent. "There's a couple a mugs that think they're running the show. But that's everywhere, huh."

"Are you going or playing hooky?" He waved his hand back and forth meaning he wasn't going regularly. I was about to call him on it, when he said, "I got me a girl friend."

"Does she go to school?"

"She doesn't. She travels with her family."

I asked Byron what her name was and he told me, "Malina."

Well, I darned near tossed my cookies. Rye, the gypsy's daughter! I wanted to scream, jump up and down and lock Byron up to keep him from harm, but I played it cool.

"Malina? That sounds like a European name. She from Germany?"

"No, she's Romanian." This poor kid was headed for a hard fall and all he could think about was being with her.

"Where'd ya meet her?"

"Her caravan rolled into the ranch where I work out Cupertino way. The big Slav that owns the place told her father that they could camp by the creek for a couple of days, then they'd have to leave. Well, that night the Slav and Rye—that's Malina's father—they get drunk on wine and sing songs and dance and everybody is all cozy," Byron told me. He had a far off look on his face, almost like he lost his train of thought. "That was six weeks ago," he said as he came back to the here and now.

"Ya going back on the road, Byron?"

"I'm thinking about it, Grady. What do you think?"

"Do you really want my opinion? Because I've got a definite opinion, Byron."

He nodded, and I plowed ahead. "I know that Rye and his family. They spent some time in Los Gatos this past summer. You go on the road with them, it ain't like hoboing. You'll be a grifter. Do you know what that is?"

When he didn't respond I continued, "They fleece people, Byron. In hobo jungles a Bo is protected, for the most part." Double B and Larry Dolan flashed in my memory. Officially those two weren't murdered in a jungle. I didn't have any real knowledge that Rye and his clan were grifters or not, but felt certain that being with a band of gypsies was an unsafe place for him to be.

"People in towns will shun you…"

Byron interrupted, "I know all that, Grady. I know what it's like to be an outcast. I'm from the road."

"Tell me this—is living with your aunt better than being on the road?"

He looked me straight on and softly replied, "I love my aunt, but I ain't used to being told what to do, where to go and, what to say."

"Do you think you'll have any say-so whatsoever with Rye? Hell, no! It's his way or get out. This is a very bad idea, Byron. I know you're thinking about Malina and it would be swell to be with her all the time. But she will break your heart, trust me."

"She ain't like that. I know it, Grady! We're in love."

"You aren't in love. You're in lust. Oh, you're taking trips behind the woodpile all right. But do you think yer the only one going behind the woodpile? You ain't."

Byron scratched his chin thoughtfully, then said as he walked to the door, "Well, I asked for your opinion and you gave it. I'll catch ya down the road apiece." Just like that he was gone.

My first phone call was to the sheriff. I told the dispatcher about some unsavory types in an orchard along Calabazas Creek between Saratoga and Cupertino.

"What's going on there?" the dispatcher wanted to know.

"Gypsy selling reefer around schools," I lied. When I was asked my name, I hung up. The next call was to Harris, the Constable. It took him a couple of hours to get back to me. When he did, I told him that I heard the Santa Clara County Sheriff's Department got a report of reefer being sold around schools.

"I'm on it Grady. Where did you get that scoop?" I told him I couldn't reveal sources, and he bought it. Now all I could do was wait and hope Byron missed the gypsy caravan.

I was cleaning the hallway of the office building when I heard the door from the sidewalk open. I looked down to the bottom of the stairs and a guy in a frayed sports coat plopped down on a riser and laid out flat on his belly. "Move on, pal. I'm gonna close," I yelled down the stairs.

"Yeah, yeah," the guy slurred and he waved me off.

I put my janitorial equipment away, locked my office and went down the stairs. "Ya can't sleep in here," I said as I stepped over the guy and opened the door. If he was passed out, I was going to roll him to the curb. "Let me help ya up," I said. In a flash the guy came to his feet and stood a step above me, which gave him an advantage. The crow bar landed right across the top of my head rendering me defenseless. I could feel the blood dripping down my face, onto my shirt and down my chest. The next blow landed at the base of my skull. The third, which I didn't feel at the time, got me in the ribs on my right side.

I woke up halfway out the door on the sidewalk. A light was shining in my eyes. A cop was asking me if I was okay. I guess my puking on his shoes gave him an answer. I was loaded onto a stretcher, which was excruciating. I remember wailing along with the siren as I was transported to Spotswood's Hospital on San Jose Avenue.

I sensed people moving about the room as I lay in the hospital bed. Then I heard nothing. My father made me fly, but this wasn't the nightmare. Not by a long shot.

> *There was a bright beautiful light at the end of a long spiral. The brightness didn't cause any discomfort; actually, it gladdened me and my head and rib aches were gone. I walked across a plush patch of green, the greenest grass I'd ever seen. It contrasted dramatically with a bright blue sky. A stream of clear water gurgled into a deep pond. Sitting on the bank was my mother, Double B, and Larry Dolan. I never ever remember being that happy in my life. Mother was dressed in a royal blue satin skirt and a white sweater. She looked like a young woman and her smile let me know she was okay, and she said in a voice that was the most beautiful singing I ever heard, "Grady, I am very happy."*

Double B and Larry wore khaki chinos with a crisp crease down each leg and highly polished brown oxfords. They had on starched blue work shirts with white buttons and were clean-shaven with hair neatly trimmed and combed. Their smiles also told me they, too, were fine. I tried to speak, but couldn't. I could hear though. My mother said, "Take care of the boys, dear." Dolan nodded and said, "Yeah, don't forget Byron." I looked at Double B and he told me, "We're all okay, Grady. Your mother greeted us when we arrived." I looked at my mother and she smiled and nodded her head. "We'll be here when you're ready, honey. But you must go back now."

I felt myself floating back down the spiral and suddenly my head and ribs ached again. I opened my eyes and squinted at the brightness. I didn't recognize anyone in the room, so I went back to sleep, wanting to get back to that green grass and pool of water. But my aches continued.

Calloway and Hazel stood at my bedside. His look was determined and hers anxious.

"Somebody die?" I wanted to know.

"You've been in and out for about five days, Grady. Any idea who did this to you?"

"No, Jack. I don't. But the guy played me like a fiddle. Knew what he was doing," I answered shaking my head, which caused my pain to worsen. I looked at Hazel and smiled, but that too caused discomfort.

"We've been worried about you. There were some crazy conversations going on about green grass and cool water. What was that about?" she wanted to know. I just gave them a blank look. I needed to process my dream.

"How is Byron?" I asked Hazel. She told me he was good and that he'd stop by later. I felt relief that Byron was still in the vicinity. What I didn't know was if he still hung out with Rye and his clan.

I was sitting up in my hospital bed trying not to scratch my scalp where sixteen stitches had been put in, when Byron Wanell, stern of face, walked in. "What's happening kiddo?" I asked.

"Did you drop a dime on Rye, Grady?" he wanted to know.

"What are you talking about?" Byron told me the day after he saw me in my office the coppers raided the gypsy camp. "Look, Byron, I've been here for over a week. I couldn't possibly have..."

"You could've called before ya got clobbered."

"Yeah, but I didn't," I lied. I felt justified in this ruse, especially if it kept Byron from being tangled up with a bunch of gypsies. I know his heart must've been busted because of Malina, but that was going to be one of many.

"Tell me what happened, Byron."

He told me he was in the barn at the Slav's place when a sheriff's patrol car drove down a road through his orchard. "The Slav sees this and lets out a string of swearwords like I ain't never heard. He hops in his open-cab orchard truck and takes off after the patrol car through rows of trees, and dust is flying like crazy. He cuts the patrol car off and when I got there the two, the Slav and the cop, are toe-to-toe and chin-to-chin. I could see spray from each of them landing on the face of the other. They was like two dogs getting ready to scrap. And what they said was about as understandable as dog barks and snarls."

He told me the cop said he had a warrant, and that the Slav told him where he could shove his warrant. "Next thing I know is that the cop's talking on his two-way radio asking for help, then all hell breaks loose. Sireens are off in the distance. Rye and his troupe are milling around, and the cop and Slav are wrestling in the dirt. The cop breaks free, scrambles to his feet, pulls his pistol and fires one off into the sky," Byron said holding his fist and fingers like a handgun.

Just then a nurse came in and took my temperature and gave me another pain pill. I knew from experience that I had, at the most, fifteen minutes before I'd nod off, and I let Byron know that.

"Then what happened?"

"Well, the long and short is, the Slav went to jail and is still there as far as I know, and he's a decent sort, really. He's rough around the edges is all. He don't like somebody tellin him what to do, especially on his property. If ya do your work and treat him with respect, well, sir, ya got a guy that will go ta bat for ya every time; that's the Slav. And Malina and her family were run out of town." He told me they were charged with vagrancy. "But there had to be more than that. You don't go through every bit of their belongings if it's just a vagrancy beef," he said.

"Maybe they were looking for stolen property," I offered. Byron just stared at me. He must still think I had something to do with the roust. He'd get over it.

"Where'd they end up?"

"In Los Gatos, by the train station." Shit.

"I showed the photos you took at the fish warehouse around the Lyndon, Grady. You're pretty good with developing," Calloway told me as he drove me away from the hospital. "Here's your key," he said handing it over. He told me he got non-committal responses from everyone but the bartender, who said he didn't recognize anyone in the pictures. "Do you wanna go to your office or the Lyndon?" I told him to drop me at the office.

Mail was piled up in front of my office door. You'd think one of my neighbors would've picked it up for me. I was sorting through letters and ads and newspapers when I spotted an envelope postmarked King City. I recognized Janey's handwriting. My heart was racing and my hands shook so much, I barely got the letter opened. Inside was a neatly printed note in pencil from Calvin. He wrote that he made the all-star team and wanted me to come and watch him play. The date of the game happened while I was in the hospital. "Oh no," I sobbed. "What they must think of me." I contacted long distance information and got the number of the Corner Club in King City. My hand was still shaking when I dialed.

A voice I recognized as Julian's answered. When I told him who I was he said, "Buddy, yer name is mud around here."

I told him I was sure of that. "Does Janey happen to be around?"

He put the receiver down with a wooden thump, and I heard footsteps and muffled talking and the distinctive ting of the cash register. "You've got a lot of guts to call now. I told you if you broke Calvin's heart again, I'd hope you rot in hell." I could hear her breathing. I mean it was both nostrils into the mouthpiece.

"Are you done?" I asked calmly.

"Go ahead, she sighed." I told her I just got the letter today. "I've been in the hospital for the last week, Janey. If I'd known about the game, I would've been there."

"You taking the cure, Grady?"

I felt that was uncalled for and told her so. "I got beat over the head, neck and ribs; sixteen stitches and three busted ribs. It still hurts to take a deep breath. So you jumping to a conclusion is kinda unfair."

"Grady, I'm sorry, she said. I *did* jump to conclusions. But your past..."

I interrupted her and replied, "Let's talk about my past when it isn't long distance. How did the game go?" She told me it was the type of game where no team wins, "More of an event to showcase the players' talents." I asked her if she would please explain to Calvin what happened. "I bet Calvin is disappointed in me. I'd like to make it up to him. Maybe I can come down this coming weekend."

"This weekend is no good. Julian is taking us camping up to Relieze Canyon." Now, I don't think she said that to make me feel bad, but it did. "Why don't you come the following weekend? Julian is gonna go deer hunting then with his brothers. He was gonna take Calvin, but hasn't said anything to him yet. Does that sound okay, Grady?"

I told her it sounded fantastic. "I'm gonna get a motel and stay Friday night and Saturday night. That square with you, Janey?" She told me it was. Before I hung up, I gave her my office number and the number at the Lyndon and she gave me her home number. Some reparation was made, I hoped. The next phone call I made was to an answering service so I could get calls even if I were out of the office. It was a logical step for my kind of work—more professional, you know? But more importantly, my family could leave messages.

I hobbled up Main Street. At the bridge, a half a block from my office, I wished I'd driven. But being cooped up in a hospital ward with all the smells from antiseptic to soiled linens kept me going, and allowed me to enjoy the fresh air.

"I heard they put the boots to ya, Prescott," Mr. Gorman said from his bar stool. His normally pale face had some color, could be the cocktail he was sipping. Anyhow, he was kinda cordial, for him.

I sat down next to him and he brought me up to date on any goings on. He said it had been quiet since the bar fight. I looked around and was hard-pressed to tell there'd been a brawl in the same room. When Gorman asked what my next play was, I told him it would be best if he didn't know, which was horse hooey, because I didn't have a play in mind.

17

I stepped over the railroad tracks and approached the gypsy camp. It looked like business as usual; tambourine, mandolin, and fiddles played a rhythmic tune. Ladies were dancing and men stood around clapping to the beat. Rye was grinding blades and others were carving figurines or making baskets. Rye acknowledged me and motioned me over with a head jerk. I spotted Davy Holcomb emerging from behind the baggage room in back of the depot.

"Hey, Grady, where ya been?" Holcomb asked in what I thought was a snide manner. Maybe it's just his bullying attitude that precedes him.

"Been sick, Davy. I ate some bad frog legs over in the Lyndon dining room." His face blanched and his eyes were like saucers, but he recovered quickly and he started to move with the beat of the music as he maneuvered into the crowd.

Rye motioned for me to sit with him on his blanket. His dark face and eyes were apathetic.

"Welcome back, sir. Where did you go?" I asked him.

All he said was, "Here and there." He put a drop of oil on the folding blade of a jackknife and opened and closed it until it was loose. "That boy, that Byron, you know him?" I nodded and he continued, "He's hanging around my Malina."

I waited for him to continue, but he just looked at me for a response, so I said, "He told me that he was spending time with her."

"Spending time with her?" Rye snorted. "He takes up *all* her time. Cuts in on her earning." This wasn't anything I wanted to know about, so I offered, "Why don't you run him off? I mean, if he's bothersome, give him the heave-ho."

Rye nodded his head and whispered, "I just wanted you to be okay with it." *What the hell?* He's asking me if I was okay with it?

"If she gets in a family way again, he'll be bringing his nuts home in a sack."

I acknowledged his warning and said, "Kids, eh? They can try our mettle from time to time."

All he said was, "More than you know." I sat for a few more minutes watching Rye hone blades. Holcomb was watching me and I think my sitting with Rye made him nervous. Maybe it was symbolic to sit with him on his blanket. I hoped that was the case; let that peckerwood Holcomb stew. Before the silence became awkward I asked Rye, "That Davy, he hangs around here quite a bit. What's his story?"

Rye squinted and shook his head slightly. "He's a hanger-on hoping to make a score. I can't tell you for certain what he does. He brings food, and that's why I let him stay.

"Did he follow you when you left this summer after the fire?"

"He showed up in Prunedale when we were camped by San Miguel Canyon." I let that settle for a few. I mean Prunedale is close to Salinas *and* King City.

"Rye, there was a murder along the tracks in early summer. The guy that got killed was my friend and I'm trying to find out who did it. If you hear any scuttle-but, would you let me know?"

"You a cop? I thought you were a hobo."

"I'm not a cop, I'm a private eye and I hoboed for a year or so when I hit a rough patch. I'm still trying to figure out who started the fire here, too, by the way."

"Well, yer late on that case. I know who did it," Rye said.

"You do? Who?" I wanted to know. He just smiled briefly and pointed a grimy finger to his temple as if to say, *I got all the info right here.* "My old lady saw a guy toss a lighted book of matches into the dry grass and another make off with the basket of money. Then they show up with the volunteer fire department and start fighting the fire. I told the fire chief and he canned them. But for your friend getting it," he added," I heard about it, is all—nothin' else."

I got up and stretched and my ribs hurt and I winced. Rye looked at me, picked up a boning knife, waved it and said, "Talk to the boy." I walked in front of Davy, who gave me a sinister look. I winked at him and continued walking back to my office. I needed to get to Byron and tell him the romance needed to end before he got castrated.

Friday finally arrived. I sat in the Powder Horn in Greenfield with Janey and my two boys, a family affair, and I felt normal. I didn't know I'd felt abnormal until I sat at that restaurant table feeding strained carrots to my baby son. Calvin had a lilt in his voice and Janey was cordial and I felt fantastic. The bartender nodded to me, although I don't think she remembered me.

"When I tell you, I want you to slowly look behind you," Janey said.

"What's going on?" She told me there was a man staring at me, and had been since we sat down.

"Now," she whispered. I turned and there sat the goon from the fish company, the one I pulled my gat on. *Oh boy, not now please.* Before he glanced back in my direction, I'd already turned back to Janey. When she asked if I knew the guy I said, "Could be." Suddenly somebody in a suit stood at our table. I looked at the man and it was Dante Verducchi, the detective from the Salinas PD. I looked in the direction of seafood guy as I rose to shake hands with Dante; the guy vamoosed out the door, taking one last peek at me.

I introduced Dante to Janey and my boys and invited him to join us, but he graciously declined. I felt glad; I mean I like the guy, but I wanted it to be just us, you know? All attempts to rid my mind of the goon failed, and Janey picked up on it. "When Dante stood at the table, and before you knew it was him, you had a hateful look, then relief. What is it, Grady?"

"Just a guy involved in a case years ago. Hey, Calvin how was the camping trip? Did you have a good time?"

"Boy, did we ever. I saw peacocks, a coyote, a bobcat and a pack of wild boars. We were standing above a creek and heard a bunch of rustling in the brush and all of a sudden about twenty ran through the water, huh, mom."

Janey said it was quite exciting and added, "And what else, Calvin?"

He gave Janey an odd look, and something transpired between

them and he said, "Oh yeah." He searched in his pocket and pulled out an arrowhead. "Here daddy, I found it and I want you to have it."

It caught me off-guard and as I reached for it, I mumbled, "Calvin, this is the most precious thing anybody has ever given me; thank you so much. I'll cherish this for all my life." He had a wide grin and sort of giggled. I got up, went to his chair and kissed him on the forehead.

"Daaaad," he whined. But he was pleased too. Coleman seemed to feel he missed out and fussed momentarily so I gave him a kiss on his chubby soft pink cheek. I sat back down and told Janey how grateful I was that she allowed me this opportunity.

"You have changed, Mr. Prescott, and you needed to change. These boys are yours and mine and they need you." Those were the nicest words I'd heard in quite some time and I misted up.

"Daddy, can we get ice cream?" Calvin asked.

I dropped Janey and the boys off at their house, and told them we could go fishing Saturday morning. I didn't know where we'd go, but hoped it would fall into place. I circled around the block and parked in an inconspicuous location to see if the fish goon showed up. I felt he might have followed us. Traffic was light and at midnight, I pulled out. I saw the glow of a cigarette coming from inside a gray coupe a block south of Janey's. I pulled around the corner out of sight, parked and took my .38 out of the glove box. I backtracked on foot to the coupe and hid behind an ash tree. It seemed that there was only one person in the car, but I wasn't sure. The car started and sped up the street. At Janey's house the car did a U-turn and parked in front. I ran up the street and as the guy exited the car, I pounced. We hit the ground with an audible oomph. I turned the guy over, ready to do a rat-a-tat-tat about his face when I recognized Tom, Janey's brother.

"What the hell, Tom. What're ya doing?" We stood apart trying to catch our breath.

Through pants and gasps, Tom told me, "Making sure my sister is all right."

"Look Tom, we just had a swell evening, your sister and the boys and me. This could've turned out bad," I said as I put my .38 back in my belt.

He motioned me away from the house to a spot across the street. "Janey has been telling me about some guy with a limp that always seems to show up wherever she is, so I'm keeping tabs on her. She wouldn't like it if she knew, so let us keep it on the QT, okay, Grady?" *Son of a bitch! Had I brought danger to Janey and the boys?*

"I think it's a good idea that you do that, Tom. Can't be too careful. I'm gonna be around for Saturday. Why don't you take off and I'll stay on watch."

"Are you sure, Grady? I mean, er...ah…"

"I'm as sober as a judge, Tom. I can handle this." Before Tom left, I asked him if he knew of a good place to go fishing and rent equipment. "There's a trout farm about fifteen miles south. Kids are sure to get their limits. But if yer up for adventure, I could show you a pretty nice stream. I got all the tackle, too."

Janey and Coleman sat on a blanket on the bank of the stream. It reminded me of my dream and seeing my mother. Tommy was putting fishing rods together and handing them to me so I could put reels on.

"Here, Calvin. You can put the reels on." He screwed the nut on the cork handle tightly, and I strung the leader and line through the ferrules and tied a Mepps spinning lure on. Three fishermen, Calvin, Tommy, and me, stood on the bank casting our lines warming up.

Calvin's first cast got caught in the branch of a tree hanging above the water. He looked at me embarrassed and I said, "The fish are deeper," which made him giggle.

After his line was free, I showed him a side arm cast, but my line landed on the other bank. "The fish are back this way more, daddy." We rolled on the ground laughing and tussling playfully.

Tommy told us he wanted big fish and headed up stream. I looked at Janey, who had a huge grin on her face as she prepared lunch out of a picnic basket. Nothing else mattered at that point in time. My son and I were fishing together, his mother and brother were content and all that transpired in the past was just that, the past.

I showed Calvin a deep pool at a bend where the water eddied back under a huge boulder. "See where the water goes back under that rock? Do you think you can get your lure in that spot?" He told me he thought he could. He cast back, took his finger off the line and the lure landed right on target and he cranked the reel once, which stopped the line from playing out. "Reel in slowly, Calvin. That big whopper is looking for a snack." He felt a tug and yanked, but the fish got away. "Try it again, boy. When you feel the first tug, keep reeling. When yer rod tip bends, yank and keep winding. Keep yer rod tip up."

His cast landed and several moments later his rod tip bent and he waded into the water and cranked the reel handle. The trout broke water slapping its tail at the line, trying to get free. Calvin stayed with it and landed his first fish, a rainbow trout fourteen inches long. I was busting my buttons.

"Wahoo, Calvin. That's a dandy, son." He placed the catch in his wicker creel and cast again. We spin cast most of the morning and talked. To me, catching fish was secondary; being a father and son was primary. And we were that, father and son. I answered any and all questions he asked me. After a break in our conversation, he said, "I wonder what happened to my bicycle."

"Last I saw, it was by the kindling pile next to the garage." He nodded as if to say, "Oh, yeah." I asked him if he had a bike now, and he shook his head. "Do you want a bike, Calvin?"

"I'm okay. Mama says we gotta watch our pennies. Paying the bills gets her in a tizzy, ya know? She's talking about taking in ironing." I remembered telling Janey I was gonna send her money for the boys, and I hadn't yet—another thing I never followed up on—yet.

Calvin and I sat on the bank of the stream looking at our fish—three for him and one for me. The first one he caught was the biggest by at least two inches. "I guess I wasn't holding my mouth right, and that's why you caught more than me, Calvin."

Holding your mouth right was a term I used with Calvin when something didn't go right. If he missed a ball thrown at him or answered a question wrong, things like that. When I said it this time, he curled up next to me on the sandy bank and said, "Daddy, you haven't held your mouth right for a long time."

"I know it, son, and I'm trying to change that."

He said, "Let me see," and turned my face toward him, looked at my mouth and gave a very noticeable nod and we hugged. I thought about my own father and what he'd done to blitzkrieg "our village," so to speak, and how my grandfather took over. I had done the same thing as my father, minus the killing. But nonetheless there was a "bombing" and no grandfather to pick up the slack. My family was left to the kindness of a brother, and strangers like Julian and the folks in King City. I'm so grateful that they took my family in.

Life is kinda like fishing. Getting to the fishing hole is like life's struggles. The tackle is like skills you learn to deal with those struggles. If you don't use the skills, they get lost or become rusty. And the catch is the payoff that continues the cycle.

This day surpassed any "best" day I ever had before. I felt a sense of bucolic peace overcome me as Calvin and I approached the spot where Janey, Coleman and Tommy sat. A man in a slouch hat sat on the blanket with them, wiping out any serene feeling I'd had. I held Calvin's shoulder and he stopped, not quite understanding the scene. For that matter, neither did I. Slouch hat stood and said, "Walk in easy, mac." Janey looked like my mother cowering from my father, getting ready for a beating. The man limped toward me. His knife glistened in the sun. I pushed Calvin away and went for my .38, but it was still in the glove box of the Ford.

Calvin nudged me and again I pushed him away. "Daddy, what's wrong? Wake up."

Son of a bitch, I'd fallen asleep. I sat up too quickly and became light headed. I looked at Calvin and then at Janey and Coleman. Calvin had a worried look on his face, but Janey and the baby were still on the blanket and none the wiser about my nightmare. "I must've fallen asleep, son."

"You scared me, daddy. You were kinda whining and I tried to wake you, but you pushed me away." I was glad it wasn't one of my violent dreams where I might have clobbered him. "Don't tell yer mom about the dreaming, okay."

Janey motioned us over and said, "Come and get it." We ate bologna and cheese sandwiches, potato chips, and sliced cantaloupe. Janey poured lemonade from a gallon jar. Tommy arrived a few minutes later with a string of fish.

"Let's have a fish dinner tonight," he said.

"You clean the fish, if you want me to cook," Janey stated. "Grady, would you mind if I asked Julian? He's coming home from his hunting trip this afternoon."

My heart skipped a moment, "Not in the least, Janey. Thanks for asking." To consider Julian to be an intrusion was wrong thinking. If anything, I was the intrusion. Besides, nothing could take away my best day ever. Somehow I sensed relief. Janey had moved on, my boys were well taken care of, and so I could move on also.

I used the pay phone next to the office of the motel and called the answering service and learned that Jack Calloway left me two messages earlier on Saturday. Jack told me that another hobo's body, stabbed and burned, had been found in San Jose.

"San Jose detectives are all over this and I think we should get on it and see if there are any links to the murders in Los Gatos." I told Jack that I would catch up with him Sunday in the late afternoon. "I'm visiting my boys in King City, Jack."

I left Janey's house after a breakfast of waffles and sausage on Sunday morning. I was so happy for the quality time spent and vowed to do it again. Tommy assured me he was gonna keep an eye on Janey and the boys. He told me he didn't mind if I went to the house in San Jose to get Calvin's bicycle.

I'd eaten so much food since Friday night that I was sure I'd gained ten pounds. I hadn't even thought about a drink until I drove past the Powder Horn. I let off the gas pedal momentarily. The blond bartender was sweeping the front entry. *A bloody Mary might be nice.* But I honked and continued northward.

The closer I got to Santa Clara County, the more angst I felt. What was that about? Leaving my family? I didn't think so. Not contacting Byron Wanell or his aunt Hazel? Possibly. "Damn it! I have my priorities." The more I thought, the clearer it became. I was going to help with an investigation in the San Jose PD jurisdiction where I got canned eighteen months ago. I shivered and tried to catch my breath. I could beg off from Calloway, but that would be chicken shit. Buckle down and do what you're supposed to. That's all there was to it. *How bad could it be?* I was about to find out.

As we drove over to San Jose Monday morning, Jack Calloway brought me up to speed on the recent killing. "Yesterday the county sheriff called a meeting of all agencies in the county that had hobo killings." He listed off the departments—San Jose, Los Gatos, Campbell and several unincorporated areas patrolled by the sheriff. "All agreed they have more important cases," said Calloway, "And I used your line; what takes priority over murder?"

I was curious as to why the DA wasn't calling for the meeting. He was the leading law enforcement officer in the county and he was, as far as I was concerned, conspicuously absent.

"What did they say, Jack?" He told me there were murmurs about mayor's wishes, manpower shortages, "And still others just looked down and said nothing. And then the guy from San Jose, a Captain Hardy, said he thought the meeting was a waste of time."

"That sounds like Hardy."

"Do you know him, Grady?" I told him he was the Captain I hit when I got fired.

"This is gonna be interesting," he said. "We're meeting him at the scene."

Aw, shit.

We advanced across a vacant field near the convergence of the Guadalupe River and Los Gatos Creek. The field was strewn with old tires, pieces of wood and cardboard. Discarded mattresses and box springs lay pitifully near a stand of acacia trees. A trail through the lot was bounded by the creek, the debris-filled grass areas, and the tree line. Uniformed officers were standing and pointing and others were on their haunches looking at a charred spot of landscape.

Jack and I approached and I could almost hear Hardy's sinew crackle when he saw me. He talked to those near him and they all turned in our direction. Hardy separated himself from the others and motioned Calloway toward him. I stood on the fringe of the crime scene nodding to those that acknowledged me. I'd never felt this awkward before. To hell with them. *I'm here to help this so-called squad solve a crime.* I walked completely around the burn area noting indicators that might lead to a clue. I saw nothing extraordinary except for a bent ice pick.

Calloway and Hardy continued to talk, sometimes animatedly and loud. Hardy turned on his heels and strode at me. "Stay the hell away from me, you," and pointed a finger up at me. I grinned and nodded. Jack told me Captain Hardy was against me being there.

"I told him you were a private dick assisting the LGPD on this case, and if he didn't like it to notify my chief."

"Does your chief know I'm on this?"

"Nah, but it's okay." I told Jack I wanted to show him something. He followed me to the location of the ice pick. "So? It's an ice pick."

"Look where it is situated, Jack." He looked and shrugged his shoulders.

"See the handle, Jack. Anything strange about it?" He shook his head, and suddenly he snapped his fingers. The handle ain't burned. It's sitting in the middle of a grass fire and the wooden handle is intact."

"What does the writing on it say, Jack?"

"Son of a bitch, All Bay Sea Food Company. Son of a bitch." Jack pulled a pair of tweezers from his suit coat and lifted the ice pick by the bent tip.

"You, there. What do you think you're doing?" Hardy railed. He sounded like James Cagney in a tough guy role.

"My assistant, Mr. Prescott, discovered something very interesting, Captain Hardy."

"Oh, that. Yeah we saw that earlier. It's nothing."

I asked Hardy, "If you think it's nothing, do you mind if we take it to the lab?"

I could see the others with Hardy getting prickly. One piped up, "Maybe we should take another look at it, Skipper."

"If this half-assed drunk thinks he found something, let him find out he's found nothing," Hardy growled with a jerk of his thumb in my direction.

"Captain Hardy, there isn't any cause for you to call names. This ain't a school yard," Jack hissed.

I couldn't let it go. "I was anything but a half-assed drunk, Hardy. I just wish I'd busted yer jaw. So, as long as I'm helping with this case, *you* stay away from *me,* you pint-sized underachiever. Oops, sorry. I didn't mean to call names." I whirled and walked away. I was the cool cat outside, but my insides were tossing like high tide. I ached for a long pull of Four Roses.

I wandered the tree line fifty yards remote from the crime scene trying to calm down, when the thought occurred to me—who was the latest victim? And did they find a knife? I continued with my head down and noticed an empty can of Ronsonal lighter fluid. Judging from the condition of the can, it hadn't been in the field too long. I whistled to Jack and he walked over to me. His face was stern and his blue suit coat flapped in the breeze. He stood with his hands on his hips and then grinned.

"That was interesting. You and Hardy, I mean. Whatcha got?" I asked him if Gene ever mentioned a lighter fluid can he found in front of his store.

"Yeah he gave it to me. Why?" I pointed down to the can at our feet. "Well, I'll be." Jack bent down and picked the can up with both index fingers by the top and bottom. I held a paper bag open and he dropped it in. "I gotta show this to Hardy," he announced.

"See if they found a knife, Jack," I said as I walked to the other side of the tree line. An alley ran behind houses and seemed to be a logical access to and from the field. I searched the entire length of the alley and saw nothing out of the ordinary. High solid wooden fences blocked views into backyards. A gate swung open and an old lady in a threadbare housecoat put a sack of garbage into a trash can. She didn't see me, and when I spoke she dropped the metal lid. I picked it up and said, "I'm sorry. I didn't mean to startle you." Her Mexican accent was difficult to understand, but I learned she didn't know anything about the murder or fire.

"*Vagos* go by all the time," she said as I turned to continue my walk.

The cross streets at both ends of the alley were a mix of commercial and residential structures. One place that caught my eye was a single-story brick building, a working man's bar, the El Paso Club. Music from inside bled outside. The door was open and a mixture of Hexol, tobacco and citrus battled for dominance; Hexol won. A hefty man behind the bar was reading a newspaper. His fingers looked like frankfurters.

When my shadow filled the doorway, he looked up and nodded,

"Yer my first customer today, mac. What'll ya have?" he asked as he turned the radio down.

I told him it was kinda early for me, which was bogus, because I'd been dead drunk at this time of day in the past. "I'm looking for info on the murder a few nights ago, the one in the field," I pointed out the door.

"I didn't make ya for a cop. Are you a reporter?" I told him my gig and he said, "Sam Spade, huh?"

"Yeah, just like him. Do you know anything about the other night?" He said he was off and the owner was working then. "When will he be in?"

"The owner is a she and she's in the back. Hey, Dora, somebody wants to see ya." A short redhead with black horn-rimmed glasses emerged from behind a curtain.

"What can I do for you?" she asked in a raspy, but cordial voice.

"We were busier than usual that night. This is a neighborhood joint, ya see. We don't get anybody high-hattin it. Just working stiffs," she told me when I asked about the night of the murder. She continued, "Usually by ten o'clock this place is empty. That night I poured right up to closing time."

"All regulars?"

"That's the funny part. My guys are gone by ten, like I said. But that night there were more hobos than usual. There wasn't any trouble."

"Did any of them limp?" Dora didn't recall anybody with a limp. "But, then again, I was busy."

Jack Calloway was standing in the middle of the alley. "Where'd ya go?"

"To a bar, why?" I showed him the El Paso Club and mentioned on the night of the murder the place had more Bo's than usual.

"It seems odd to me," Jack offered, "That there isn't a hobo camp close to here. Hardy told me it was many blocks away."

"Bo's go where the work is. Maybe somebody out this way is hiring. I'll see what I can find out, Jack."

Jack brought me up to snuff on the latest murder. "No knife was found at the scene; as a matter of fact the guy, a Maurice Buck, according to the medical examiner, had no wounds on him at all except for the burns. Based on the condition of the lungs, it looks like he was dead before he was torched. Do you know this Buck guy, Grady?"

I nodded, but said nothing. Where does the ice pick fit in? I wondered. Was it a coincidence? I mean, those types of things are given out freely.

18

I pulled it off again. They think Maurice Buck is dead. He ain't. I don't know who that was I torched. Adios, Maurice!

This office always smells odd. I'm used to the hobo life, but when I come here I have to dress appropriately. Don't get me wrong, I ain't a slob, but coming here feels like I'm being judged, ya know? But at least I can wear regular shoes with even heels. I can't quite put my finger on what it is I'm smelling—a mix of dust and camphor maybe. Reminds me of mother's blanket chest back home.

Here he comes, my older brother, the big shot lawyer with the stinky office. He's got a thick envelope in his hand. Who ever thought he'd be a lawyer. Not me. And the other brother is a union boss. He sees me eyeing the envelope, and puts it in his coat pocket. Gotta be in control. What am I supposed to do, beg like a dog? Fat chance.

This whole thing started because my step-dad had a trucking business, and Holcomb was our manager, of sorts. Then, whamo! We get hit with a law suit. Big deal—one of our trucks went off the road into a hobo camp and we got blamed for it!

The old man dies and we inherit the family business—three trucks and a warehouse. But those ass-bite brothers of mine couldn't wait to get out of Iowa. One brother gets in with the union guys and the other goes to law school, and me, the youngest, gets the failed business.

So much for their promise to my step-dad that they would take care of me just like I was a "real" brother. They shoved money at me and sent me on a wild-goose chase just to get me out of their lives. For good measure, they sent Holcomb, the Shadow, along to keep an eye out on me. But I convinced Holcomb we could both still collect the brothers' money, and go on our separate ways. I never needed watching in the first place. Shadow was in my way, and man, the first few days out of Iowa he almost got eliminated. Besides, he didn't have the stomach for the kind of work I was gonna do, anyway.

"Ya changed things up. Why?" lawyer brother says to me.

"That mug was already dead by the time I lit him up," I tells him.

"Hey, your kiffing is getting better." He didn't need to bring that up. I've had a nervous trait since we started the eliminations. I exhale air out my nose and it sounds like "kiff." He tosses me the envelope and I leave.

19

I dropped Calvin's bike off at the Economy Shop on North Santa Cruz Avenue. Mr. Williams told me he could make the bike like new. "I'll raise the seat and put new pedals on. I'll clean it real good. That red frame will shine like new. You'll see. I have new handle bar grips with tassels, too. Real smart looking." I was gonna take it to Calvin the next weekend.

"Yeah, I heard," Cookie said when I told him about Maurice catching the westbound. "Seems like somebody is trying to rid the world of Bo's don't it?"

"How's Holcomb holding up?"

"He's no different. Saps like that don't get attached. He'll find another flunky, wait and see." Cookie added some seasoning to the concoction and asked if I was gonna stay for supper.

"Yeah, I'll stay, thanks. You need anything?" He told me more gump would be good, "Maybe a couple a pounds of stew meat?"

"Hey, Prescott. Where ya been?" Gene asked when I entered the store. "Got a message from that boy, Byron. He's been looking for you since last Friday."

Before I returned to the quarry I stopped at my office to check messages and go over the mail. The answering service told me I had two messages from Byron and one from his aunt, Hazel Kane. I called Hazel at her shop. She was icy, and I couldn't blame her. After all, I'd been AWOL since our dinner date at Bert's Country Inn. She told me Byron took off again.

"Did he go with Rye?"

"Rye? What's that?" Hazel wanted to know. Byron kept the info about the gypsies and Malina from his aunt and now he was on the dodge. I hoped I could catch up with him by the depot.

"The dean of boys at the high school called and said Byron hadn't been to school for a week. He left each morning for school, but went someplace else." I told her I would check around.

"Let me pick you up and take you to dinner tomorrow evening and I'll bring you up to date on what I've been up to." She was thawing, which I was glad about.

Hazel and I were eating in a restaurant called Hoffler's in downtown San Jose. "You mean to tell me your wife had a baby and she didn't tell you? That's terrible." The time had come; a disclosure was necessary.

"You know I was a cop that got canned and that I went on the lam."

"Grady, I know all that. Byron filled me in. What I don't know is why you got fired."

"I'm a drunk, Hazel. I got fired for being plastered on duty. I hit my captain and lost everything. I lost my family before my bust. I cheated on my wife numerous times and I beat her. So there you have it. If ya wanna run out now, I wouldn't blame you."

"Do you still drink?"

"Yeah, but not as much."

Hazel looked at me with a crooked smile and said, "You may have been that way, but since I've known you, you've worked and you help people. I see a man climbing out of his problems and I like what I see."

I thought those were possibly the kindest words I'd heard in a long, long time.

The curtain rustled gently from a breeze drifting in the open window of my room at the Lyndon Hotel. Gypsy music played across the street. Hazel sat in the dark by the window brushing her hair. Her face had a silver hue from the full moon. Pretending to be asleep, I watched her as she softly hummed. I turned over and she asked, "Do you mind if I turn the lamp on?" The lamplight gave the room a cozy feel. Hazel looked and me and grinned.

"What time is it?" I asked.

"It's still early. Nine o'clock." She was looking at me in a way I hadn't seen in ages. What was left of my pickled noodle tried to figure it out. Then it hit me—she had a hearth and home look about her. Factions went into full scale combat—fright and refuge. If I laid there too long she'd ask me what I was thinking, and I wasn't sure of my answer.

"Let's get dressed and take a walk. It's comfortable out. C'mon," I said rising.

Hazel held my arm as we strolled by the depot. The music was loud and laughter could be heard.

"Lets go see," Hazel said. I saw Byron before he saw us. I moved her to the shadows of the depot. She looked at me, and I jutted my chin to where Byron was standing watching his girlfriend and her mother and several other females gyrate. A small boy worked through the crowd with a wicker basket full of coins and paper money.

Words that may have been, "Oh my," came from Hazel. "Is this Rye?" she asked.

"That's him sitting on that blanket with the wine bottle in his lap." She hadn't realized that Rye was a person.

Byron seemed upset. He shuffled his feet and beckoned Malina to come to him. She would throw her head back and laugh. A few times she raised her dress too high for polite company, and the only polite company was Hazel Kane. A few clucks of her tongue and Hazel disengaged from me and strode straight to Byron. This was going to be a bad scene, and I couldn't stop her. She spun him around, and he took a boxer's stance.

Realizing it was his aunt, he dropped his fists and said, "What are you doing here?"

"What am *I* doing here? A better question is what are *you* doing here, young man?" Hazel was oblivious to the fact that this confrontation might possibly have irreparable consequences. A hobo kid caught between two worlds—the road and the square life—being drawn and quartered in front of a road outfit. She might as well have pulled his pants down and spanked his bare bottom.

"You come with me right now. It's a school night." Byron shook free and ran across the tracks and down Santa Cruz Avenue. Hazel attempted to go after him, but I stopped her. The fire in her eyes caused me to take a step back. "He's all in. You shamed him."

"Are you saying it's my fault and I shouldn't act as his guardian?" she yelled. At that moment the music stopped and everybody in the camp heard her. Hazel looked around and hissed, "I'm leaving." The music started up again and the dancing resumed. Malina couldn't have cared less. She was shimmying in front of Davy Holcomb.

"It's all set, Grady. Won't be long now," Jack Calloway said over the phone. So much depended on timing in gigs like this. He was gonna take Byron Wanell into custody.

"What're ya gonna charge him with?" Jack told me the less I knew the more I could stay out of it.

A few days earlier Rye told me his entourage was heading for San Diego and he didn't want Byron tagging along. "Since that woman tore into him the other night, he is hanging around morning, noon and night. Malina is done with him. She ain't one to become too attached, ya see."

Once Rye and his troupe departed Los Gatos, I "bailed" Byron out of the clink. He looked as if he hadn't slept any part of the two and half days he'd been locked up. Flies bombarded the trays of uneaten food littering the floor of his cell. His face was ashen and dark rings around his eyes gave him an old man's sallowness.

"Are you satisfied?" he asked me when Calloway and I walked in.

"About what?"

"Bo's watch out for Bo's, that's what Larry always told me," he yelled. "But I get tossed for stealing something from a store I've never been in."

Jack took his key ring out and unlocked the cell door. "The charges have been dropped, son. Seems the grocer was mistaken. He spotted the thief and called to say the wrong boy was in jail. Sorry."

"Sorry, my ass," Byron said as he kicked a tray of food across the cement floor. I caught up with him outside and grabbed his arm. He took a swing at me, that I ducked, and I put him in a bear hug. He struggled to be free, but I didn't let up. If anybody came by at that moment they'd think we were dancing. The only sound was our feet crunching the pea gravel. Byron sagged and started to sob.

"How could you let me stay in there?" he sniffed. "Why didn't you watch out for me?" *If he only knew,* kept running through my mind.

"I'll do a better job. I promise," I whispered.

I let Byron shower at my office and gave him a change of clothes. "You want something to eat?" I asked, as he combed his hair.

"Yeah."

I got back to the office with two fried egg sandwiches on wheat toast, but Byron had split. I found him standing alongside the depot looking at the vacant space where Malina had been. Tears the size of corn kernels dotted his cheeks.

"You and Calloway dealt from the bottom of the deck, Grady. I don't think I'll get over this. I loved her, man."

We stared at each other for many seconds, then I asked, "What's next, Byron?"

"Try and find out where she went and go to her, I guess," he said wiping his nose with a sleeve. When I told him I thought that was a bad idea, he said softly, "I don't give a rat's ass what you think, Grady. You and my aunt can both go to hell."

"Don't do something permanently stupid because you are temporarily upset, Byron."

"Whatever the hell that means," Byron said as he walked away from me.

"Think about it."

"It was real unsightly, Grady," Cookie told me. "That punk stayed here for a couple of days moping around. Really wearing his heart on his sleeve, ya know. The Bo's were getting fed up with him." Byron was in a hearth-and-home frame of mind, and Malina is, well Malina—on the make to get the take.

"Anyhow, that numb-nuts, Holcomb, shows up and the punk asks if he knows where the gypsies went. Davy starts hacking on him, telling him that the girl goes with anybody that has the price, and she's worth it, too." Cookie told me Byron got up and knocked Holcomb's cup out of his hand and spilled stew down Davy's front. "Well sir, he proceeds to slap the shit outta the boy."

I saw red. The thought of Holcomb slapping Byron gave me

another thing I'd need to deal with. "Anyhow," Cookie continued, "Davy tells the boy she's probably bedding everybody in San Diego County right now."

Byron has a destination, San Diego, and a broken heart he needs to mend. Malina's father doesn't want him around and most likely will do him harm. A week later after clearing some cases, I headed after Byron.

The train ride was, at times, relaxing. The clickity-clack soothed, and then suddenly became annoying. I wanted to jump off when we went through King City.

I was downing a few in the club car to take the edge off. I swear that's all I was trying to do. When I told Hazel Kane I thought her nephew lit out for San Diego, she slumped and looked defeated. I knew I'd be on a no-pay gig, but what was I supposed to do? So here I sat traveling to San Diego.

I don't remember getting off the train in Santa Barbara and boarding another for Los Angeles, but I did. I was disoriented. Okay, I was loaded. But I could swear we were headed north. The conductor assured me we were going south. I took a nap and then hit the club car again. This time I truly just took the edge off. In the lounge of the San Diego train station I asked the bartender if there were hobo camps around. He gave me the once over. I grinned and told him I was looking for somebody.

"Try up by Balboa Park."

I drove my rental sedan up toward the foothills, passing Spanish style houses with terra cotta roofs, patio courtyards in front, and manicured lawns. The neighborhood ended and scrub brush dotted the landscape. I passed a high school and a Navy hospital and entered Balboa Park. I didn't expect to see museum types of buildings and a zoo. "There's a jungle here?" I said aloud.

A placard on a column said the California Pacific Exposition was held here in the mid-1930s. I parked the car and took in the surroundings. My hobo instinct kicked in and I looked for trails and signs. On a tree trunk I saw a sign with three horizontal lines and an arrow pointing to the ornate park buildings, meaning it wasn't a safe direction.

Another carving showed a tent-like figure and an arrow pointing up a trail to a camp. I stood at the trailhead, closed my eyes and listened. Birds chirped, bushes rustled in a slight breeze and wildlife crackled in dry leaves at ground level. No talking, no music, then suddenly a cadence of "hut-two-three" rang out behind me. A high school ROTC unit marched double time past me and onto the trail. I fell in behind the students for several hundred yards and saw indications that a camp was near. The distinctive smell of wood smoke from a cooking fire lingered under the canopy of oak and madrone trees. Filtered sunlight dappled the ground of the encampment. A Bo waved me in and I thanked him. He just shook his head when I asked him if he knew of a gypsy camp.

"He don't talk or hear," another Bo said while puffing on a corn-cob pipe. I smiled at the man and thought that he'd be the best D and D partner to have around.

20

"Gypsies hang around the ship yard, trying to lure the sailors as they get off the nickel snatcher from North Island," the man said, pointing his pipe stem toward the Pacific. When I asked, the Bo told me the nickel snatcher was the water taxi. "You a cop or something?"

"No, I'm just looking for a runaway kid. He has been known to hang around jungles. Lately, though he's partial to gypsy girls."

"Hey! Who ain't?" the pipe smoker said with a glint in his eye. "What's this punk look like? Maybe he came through."

"He's my height. Blond hair, freckles across his nose. Goes by the name Byron." I was told by those in earshot that nobody with Byron's description had been in camp.

I parked the rental car a few blocks from the water taxi terminal. Morning fog was giving way to the sun and the day was going to be warm. The canvas covered trucks and other jalopies belonging to gypsies were parked at odd angles. I heard no music or conversations. Several sailors disembarked from the water taxi, walked past the camp and into town. I wore a straw hat, blue-striped seersucker suit and dark glasses, hoping to disguise myself as a seashore tourist. From my vantage point I could see into the camp and the peripherals. Rye was grinding and others were just starting their day. Byron was not around and I began to wonder if I might be on a fool's errand. A shabbily dressed man in a brown suit got off the water taxi from Coronado. He wasn't a Bo and he wasn't square either. He was an in-between type of fellow. What intrigued me was his limp. I'd been vigilant about limping men lately. Remembering the Ford careening on a downgrade on Highway 101 caused me to shudder. I followed the limper for several blocks and observed the heels on his shoes; the right heel was worn more than the left. So what? I thought. The man removed his suit jacket and tossed it over his shoulder. Sweat stains on his blue shirt ringed his armpits. Before he walked further, he turned and looked at me, shrugged and continued. I turned up a side street and backtracked to the dock and the gypsy camp.

Two shore patrol officers were standing on the fringe of the camp. "You part of that outfit, mister?" one of them asked. I told him I wasn't and that I was looking for someone.

"Try the police substation a few blocks over. If who yer looking for is a runaway, he might be there," he told me. "I don't get it—they roust the kids, but let these rascals go scot-free," he said pointing his nightstick at Rye's clan.

"If a street kid is injured, where would he be treated?" I asked, and was told the county hospital treated the poor.

The desk officer wasn't too interested in being helpful. I gave him Byron's name and he said to me, "Never heard of him."

"What about your arrest log? Could he be listed in it?"

"Look, bub, these delinquents give bogus names all the time. Chances are he came through, but I ain't heard that name." When I asked the officer if I could walk through the cell area and see if I could spot Byron, he gave out a long sigh and said loudly, "Hey O'Malley, this guy is looking for his kid. Let him take a walk through the block." O'Malley was decent and chatted the entire way. I didn't see Byron, so asked all along the corridor if anybody knew Byron Wanell. When I said his name, a kid kind of perked up, but immediately sunk back into his jailhouse posture. "It seems you heard that name before," I said to the kid. "Do you know him?"

The kid squinted and said out of the corner of his mouth, George Raft style, "You a cop?"

"Nah, just looking for him, I want to take him home is all." He told me he didn't think the guy he knew as Byron was a runaway. "He came here chasing a skirt, is what he told me. Anyway, the last I seen him was on Coronado. That was a week, or ten days ago."

I got off the water taxi, the Barney Google IV, and walked toward a huge hotel. A sign on a post said, *City of Coronado, California—Where Summer Spends the Winter.* A cement walkway led to the del Coronado Hotel. Orange and green striped canvas umbrellas sat on the sand near the ocean. Salt air and seagulls cawing gave me a nice feeling. I didn't think Bo's would inhabit this area; it was too fancy-shmancy for them. An aristocratic older gentleman sat on a dark green bench. We made eye contact and he said, "Howsa boy?"

I answered, "Funny you should ask. I'm fine. And I'm looking for a boy. He lowered his head and looked over his dark glasses at me. "No, not that. He's a friend of mine and I need to take him home."

"What if he doesn't want to go?" the man asked. Over the next forty minutes I relayed my story and how Byron fit in. "You're now a private detective? How fun."

"What about you?" I asked the man. He told me he owned the water taxi company and lived in the foothills. When I asked where a hobo might find a friendly place or work, he told me to try the lumberyard. "As far as getting handouts, I'm not sure." He wished me luck, shook my hand, and I continued to walk around Coronado. I found the lumberyard and didn't see any Bo's. I asked a yardman if he knew where a hobo could find work, and I was told he didn't know.

I backtracked to the gypsy camp and met up with Rye. "Is that boy around, sir?" I asked him. Rye squinted and snorted, "Yeah, but he's gone." I asked him where and he said "South out of the country."

"Do you mean Mexico?" I asked. Rye nodded, then said to me, "He came here looking for Malina and she gave him the air. She even laughed in his face when he said he wanted to marry her."

"How'd he get to Mexico?"

"We took him to Tijuana. We gave him a pretty good dose of knockout pills and left him on the sidewalk in front of a cantina called the Chicago Club. I'd suspect he's in the jail in Tijuana."

"That's not good, Rye. You could've killed him," I hissed.

Rye narrowed his eyes and said, "What do I care?"

"I thought we were friends, Rye. I..." He interrupted me and softly said, "He still has his nuts. If I didn't like you, he'd be talking like a girl. Now I'm getting tired of this conversation, so leave while I still *do* like you." I got up and brushed dust from my pants, which puffed into Rye's face and eyes. I turned and could feel his stare burning into my back as I marched away.

I walked across the border into Tijuana. The stench was gagging; a mix of garbage, sewer, and greasy foods. It didn't take me long to find the Chicago Club. It sat in the middle of the block between a vacant storefront and a divorce lawyer. A small but powerful looking man was in front telling people about the beautiful senoritas dancing inside. Be-bob music could be heard, and hoots and hollers rang out every so often. Sailors in different stages of drunkenness staggered from cantina to cantina, their blue jumper uniforms disheveled and faces lumpy from fighting. Some had their white "Dixie cup" shaped service caps on and others had them stuffed in pants pockets. They were gonna have a lot of explaining to do when they got back to their base or ship.

I waited over an hour for an officer to arrive at the so-called police station that shared space with a newspaper office. The cop drove up in a pale green DeSoto with a red spotlight on the driver side windshield post. *Policia* was painted on the doors. His bulk barely fit behind the steering wheel. He had on a mismatched uniform; green trousers with a yellow stripe down the outside seams, and a blue chambray shirt with a badge pinned to the pocket. When he saw me he stopped, spread his legs, hitched up his gun belt and said, "Si, senor?" His English was understandable and my Spanish was next to nonexistent. I told him about Byron being left in the front of the Chicago Club. He smoothed his thin black mustache, and removed his aviator sunglasses and smiled. It wasn't a friendly smile, but a sinister one, and I felt this hombre was gonna try and take me to the cleaners if I wanted to get Byron out of his lockup. I knew he was going to charge me just to see if Byron was there. And if he was, there would be another fee or two on top of that.

"He was pretty sick when we put him in. Puking and shitting. Had to clean him up, senor."

"Is he still here?" I asked, and was told, "Could be."

"What do I need to do to find out if he's here?" I had fifty smackers on me and this buzzard took twenty of it just to look on a ledger to find Byron's name. "Looks like he was moved to 8th Street, which is the main jail. Go check with them there. Tell them, I, Pedro sent you," he announced officially.

"He's got some hefty fines, senor; over two hundred dinero." I knew before I was on 8th Street, Pedro was gonna call his compadre and the shakedown was set. All I had was thirty bucks and I hoped I could appeal to the jailer for compassion. Fat chance. The jailer was a bigger gob of spit than Pedro, and the price was three hundred. He did, however, let me walk through the beds of prisoners. Vomit and urine hit me like a Joe Louis punch to the gut. I gagged and retched. Byron was sleeping on a dingy mattress. I walked away and I heard him yell out, "Grady. Over here."

I waved and put my hands in front of me in a pushing type motion to let him know I'd be back soon, be patient. Back in California, I phoned Hazel and asked her to wire me five hundred dollars to the Western Union office in Imperial Beach, California. She must trust me, I thought. She never asked why I needed the money. That felt nice.

The sun was setting as I helped Byron walk into California. He was weak from malnutrition and the beatings. His face was no longer boyish. He'd passed through adolescence right into adulthood and that saddened me. He looked like he'd lost weight he couldn't afford to lose; he was withered and drained. I bought him a new set of clothes from a secondhand store and drove him to the beach so he could use the public shower. "There ain't any soap in here." I went into the ladies shower room and came back with a bottle of shampoo and a sliver of soap.

The water continued to run and I thought Byron should be done by now. He was sitting on the shower floor letting the water cascade over him and sobbing. He saw me, stood up and soaped and rinsed again. He used paper towels to dry himself off. He picked up his old clothes and tossed them into the trash drum.

We ate supper in the coffee shop of the train depot. He could only eat half of his hamburger steak and cottage cheese dinner. We got on the last train of the day, a non-stop to San Jose. Byron fell asleep in mid-sentence, and I went to the club car. It had been a real bitch of a day and I needed to medicate. I had one for each eye and sat down next to Byron and fell asleep. Around midnight I felt him stir. "You awake, kiddo?" I asked. He sniffed and sat up.

"Do you feel like talking?" Byron nodded, but was silent. I asked him what happened when he got to San Diego.

He stared off for several seconds and said, "It wasn't hard to find Malina. When Larry and I were here before, we'd seen gypsies on the dock. So that's where I went first off." He sighed deeply and hissed, "She laughed at me, man. I told her I wanted to marry her and she laughed even harder." His breathing was faster and he drummed his fingers on the armrest. "I should've listened to you, Grady."

I remembered my grandfather saying to me, "Grady, follow an old dog through the field because he can show you where the holes are." But guys like Byron and me, when I was his age, never listened. We had all the answers and no old codger was gonna tell us how or what to do.

"What are ya gonna do now? I mean when you get back. Go to school?" He shook his head and replied, "Make things right with Aunt Hazel and maybe join the Navy. I was in that jail and several sailors were tossed in and they told me how good it was."

Hazel wasn't gonna like it, but the more I thought about him in the Navy, the more logical it became. We weren't at war, even though there were rumblings about Russia invading Korea, but that was so far removed. Then again, for a guy that doesn't like being told what to do, he might have a problem. On the other hand the discipline might be what he needs. I left Hazel and Byron alone to sort out their differences. I hoped they'd come to a workable solution.

I got back to my office and saw a note taped to my door. *See me, Gorman.*

Union members slowly paced in front of the Lyndon. The signs they carried said Union-Now. People attempting to enter the hotel were berated and jostled by representatives from the Teamsters, Kitchen Workers, and Janitorial unions. Gorman stood on the veranda like a sentinel—hands on his hips and a disgusted scowl across his face.

"How long has this been going on?"

He told me they showed up this morning. "I can't get any deliveries, and my workers are afraid to come to work. Damn, I hate to give in to them," he said pointing to the pickets.

I looked at the men walking and swore I saw the guy from the fish company sneering back at me. It was him! He pointed his finger at me like a gun and mouthed the word, "Pow." To me that was a threat and I was off the porch and stood in front of the goon.

"You got something to say to me?" I asked him. I don't think he thought I'd do anything, and looked momentarily startled.

He recovered quickly and snarled, "I knew you were no insurance man. You're a patsy for that ghost standing up there." A few more strikers milled around itching for trouble.

"Mister, when you want to have a go, just you and me without your posse, let me know," I said.

"I'll do that. Hey, how is your noggin?" he snorted. I saw red and lost it. I hit him square on the nose, which started to bleed immediately.

"You son-of-a-bitch," he yelled.

Two were on me in no time. I shook one free and gut punched the other. Gorman and his son Will were off the porch and by my side. It was over before it started.

Suddenly a clear voice rang out, like a reasonable expression in a sea of confusion, "This isn't what we want. No violence. All we're trying to do is organize so the workers get a fair deal," he said firmly. The man's suit was tailored, his hair trimmed and shoes highly polished, probably a union official.

I turned on the man who spoke and shouted, "This has nothing to do with your strike. This goes way back."

The man smiled and said, "Really?"

"Pop, in order to stay in business, we gotta become a union shop," Will Gorman said to his father. We were in the lounge sipping colas. The well-dressed union guy sat, listening to our conversation.

"I mean, look around," Will continued, "It's close to noon and we got no customers." Gorman, a man who doesn't like change, scowled at what his son said.

"Nobody likes being told what to do or not do," I offered. "You told me you paid as good or better than the union and benefits were on a par too. So this could be a clear transition."

"Damn it, I want to give raises when a guy earns it, not because some goon says I gotta."

The union official listened to Gorman's concerns. He succinctly answered all of the questions and addressed all the concerns. "I'll have the pickets removed immediately," he said as he stood and shook Gorman's hand. It looked like Gorman wasn't convinced this was a good idea, but his son Will seemed relieved.

"That guy I poked in the nose, does he work for you?" I asked. He told me the guy was a teamster official. "Does he pal around with a guy that limps?" For a split second I thought I saw something in the eyes. I couldn't put my finger on it.

"I don't know who he hangs around with."

"Well, I guess my job is over, Mr. Gorman. I'm sorry I couldn't be more of a help to you."

He shrugged his shoulders and said, "Are we square on your fee?"

"Yeah, you've been paying right along." I stuck out my hand and shook with Gorman and his son, Will.

21

The 1950s started out very well for my agency. I had two associates and a receptionist working for me and we were busy with stakeouts, cheating spouses, and insurance fraud. I rented the house in San Jose from Janey's brother, Tom. Hazel and I were a couple and Byron was in the Pacific near Inchon with an amphibious landing team. I was sending checks to Janey on a monthly basis, so she could give up one of her jobs, and I felt good about that. Two years had passed since Maurice Buck got killed. The murders just stopped and so did the no-pay gigs. Calloway and I had several theories as to why. Either the murderer was in the military and had shipped out, or he was dead, or he'd found religion. Double B and Larry Dolan still weighed heavily on me, and every so often I'd dust off their files and go through them, just to see if I missed something. My drinking was under control, sort of. I'd get plastered from time to time, but lately the hangovers were getting harder to shake. With less drinking, the bad dreams came more often.

The decade after WWII put plenty of people to work. Housing tracts were springing up all over the county and ditch diggers and tradesmen got work. The water district was building a series of reservoirs for water storage and recreational use and those looking for work could find it. The population of hobo jungles dropped and a Bo's earning ability increased with the jobs offered. I'd see Davy Holcomb from time to time driving a delivery truck through town. He wore a flat-brimmed cap with a union pin on it. Cookie got a job with a boy's camp in a rural part of the county. The others just faded into the fabric of society or stayed on the road. Then one day I got a surprise phone call.

"Grady, there's a collect phone call for you from Folsom Prison," my receptionist said.

A raspy voice said, "Hey, kiddo. What's shaking?" It was my father! *What the Christ?* I did a rough calculation in my head and figured my old man was mid 80s or early 90s. "Your old man is being paroled. How about that?"

"What do you want?" I asked. He told me he wanted to see me, "Get caught up, ya know." I will admit, curiosity set in, but then the thought of him standing over my mother shadow boxing and flexing his biceps caused me to retch.

"When?" I asked.

"When what?"

"When do you get out?"

"Day after tomorrow. I was hoping you could come and pick me up." Jesus Christ. I haven't seen or heard from him in over forty years. I thought he was dead, but obviously I was wrong.

"Boyo, yer old man ain't got long to live and I'd like to see you before I croak," he wheezed wetly. Talk about a day turning to shit, this was that day.

I had a fitful night's sleep and tossed until two in the morning. I got up and took a long pull of Four Roses and then another.

As I sat with the car idling, I watched a diminutive bowlegged man, who at one time was the largest person I knew, step through the gate in the granite walls of Folsom. His brown suit and hat looked too big for his frame. His steps were faltering and he looked disoriented. The suitcase he carried seemed heavy and caused him to list to one side. I got out of the car and walked toward Sterling Prescott, my paroled felon father. I didn't know what emotion to expect, certainly not sympathy. But that's all I felt. No love, no sense of missing anything—nothing but sympathy. His shake was weak and his hand was cold as ice.

"Thanks for coming and getting me."

As we drove through Sacramento headed for San Jose, I told him my story and every so often he'd ask a question. After several miles of silence, I asked him, "What's the matter with you? Why are you dying?"

He looked at me for several seconds, then rasped, "Pancake cancer."

"Pancake cancer? What in the hell is that? Do you mean pancreatic cancer?"

He nodded and fell asleep. He snored loudly, but then that suddenly stopped. Outside Davis, California, not even half-way there, my old man caught the west bound. He was a free man for less than an hour.

"What did you do with him?" Hazel asked me. I told her I thought about dumping him in a ditch alongside of the road, and she socked my arm. "I turned around and went back to Folsom. The warden was not too keen on the idea of burying him, but the Chaplain stepped up on my behalf and a gurney from the morgue was wheeled out to my car and he was laid to rest in the cemetery there."

Hazel asked, "Was the service nice?" I told her I didn't stay, and she was aghast. "That was your father, Grady."

"That was the man that killed my mother," I said in a voice with more heat than I intended. "Look, I'm sorry I'm not acting the way you think I should, but that's how it is. You didn't know him."

At my house I laid my father's hard-boiled suitcase on the kitchen table. The clothes were neatly folded and had some order to the packing. A blue book, *Alcoholics Anonymous*, caught my eye. On the title page, there was a note from my mother's mother: *Sterling, if and when you need this, I hope you use it. Good luck.* Now, that was unexpected. Sterling kills her daughter and she sends him a book on getting off booze? There were numerous newspaper articles about the murder and his trial. One article showed a photo of me between my grandparents at my mother's funeral. Was this Sterling's trophy stash? Under the news clippings was a colored photograph of my mother, wearing her royal blue skirt and white sweater, and Sterling was wearing a charcoal gray pinstriped suit. I sat between them in beige short pants, suit coat, and a crooked bow tie. Our smiles belied what was to happen.

That night I had a dream that my mother was sitting by the stream and Double B and Larry Dolan stood behind her with their arms folded. They were watching over my mother, and even though nothing could happen to her, my friends were reassuring me she was safe. The symbolism was unmistakable: Sterling was not there.

On the lawn of the grammar school in King City, Hazel and I sat on folding chairs with Janey, Julian, and Tommy. A June afternoon sun beat down on us. Calvin was graduating from eighth grade. Coleman was sitting next to me and my world was right. When those boys called me 'daddy' or 'dad' I would burst my buttons. Janey and Julian were now married and expecting a baby. Hazel and Janey got along real well, which made me happy. I would look at Janey at times and wonder *what if.* She'd see me looking and smile as if to say, "We're where we are supposed to be, *doing what we're supposed to be doing."*

After a nice graduation party for Calvin, Hazel and I were driving with him back to San Jose. He was going to spend the week with me. It took Janey a long time to consent to have Calvin stay with me. I couldn't blame her; my skills as a father needed to be demonstrated. Soon I passed muster and Calvin was a regular visitor. Coleman would fuss, but I wasn't ready for the two of them, and Janey kept him close to her apron.

Calvin enjoyed going to my office with me. He'd sit in my chair and rearrange the items on my desk. One of the associates asked him, "Calvin, are you gonna do work like your dad?" The sound of "Grady Prescott and Sons" had a nice ring to it. Then at noon we'd walk to the Lyndon for lunch in the dining room.

Jack Calloway approached our table with a grim face. He said hello to Calvin, then turned to me and said, "Mind if I sit?" Before I could answer, he plopped down with an audible sigh. I didn't know it then, but my world was about to go topsy-turvy. Jack told me about a fire in a warehouse in San Jose that he wanted me to see with him.

"I'm with my son, Jack."

"Grady, I'm telling ya, we gotta be in on this."

Calvin didn't relish the idea of spending the afternoon with Hazel at her shop, but she promised him he could earn money by helping her stock shelves.

"Who owns the burned building, Jack?" I asked as we drove to an industrial area near downtown San Jose.

"That's the odd thing, the city owns it and the city manager's office says squatters were occupying it." I wondered why a cop from Los Gatos and a private dick were looking into this.

"Is Hardy on this, Jack?" He told me with a laugh that Hardy, the captain I'd clobbered, retired two years before.

Smoke stains could be seen around the doors and windows of a brick veneered factory building with a greenhouse roof. A gravity water tank, at the rear, loomed above the structure. Weeds sprouted along the sidewalk and inside the chain-link fence. Debris littered the entire asphalt area around the loading dock. I thought the city should be ashamed for letting property go into disrepair like that.

A tall, curly-haired fireman in uniform greeted us at the door. We showed our IDs and he let us inside. A whiff of the fire still hung in the atmosphere.

"Chief Curry said you'd be coming over. Our police was here and will be back. By the way, my name is Stannard, Don Stannard, Deputy Fire Marshal."

"Did they take any evidence?" Calloway asked, and Stannard replied, "Not that I know of."

I couldn't figure out what all the rigmarole was. There wasn't too much structural damage inside. It was mostly smoke damage. Puddles of water pooled across the concrete floor. Sunlight beamed down through skylights on the roof.

"The sprinklers put the fire out. The electricity was disconnected years ago. The gas meter was off, too."

"So, how did the fire start?" I asked, even though I knew the answer. Stannard pointed to a pile of debris in the center of a work area.

"Arson," he said. I looked at Jack and shrugged, wondering why this was so important.

"Grady, Chief Curry and my chief go back a long ways. Curry is aware of the hobo murders and called us."

My head snapped back and I turned on Calloway, "There's a body in here?"

"No, not a body," the fire officer said. "But evidence you might be interested in." Okay, I was hooked and felt a chill run up my spine, more than once, I might add.

"Follow me," Stannard said with a motion of his hand. We entered a dark recess without skylights. Stannard turned on a battery-operated lantern and handed it to me. He picked up two more and gave one to Jack. He flashed his light on a far wall, where photos were tacked up. My inner warning system went off the closer I got to the photos. The alarms and whistles in my head were blaring and air was whooshing in my ears. By the time I got to the photo display I was damn near deaf.

I couldn't believe what I was looking at. Evidence photos from the hobo murders were displayed across the wall! I lost my balance. Jack sensed this, and stood next to me. My God, this was known in the business as a "vanity display". How did this place become a *trophy room*? I stopped dead in my tracks when I saw a picture of Larry Dolan flat on his back behind the bar in Salinas. I had never seen this photo before and was sorry I was seeing it now. Why *didn't* I see this photo before? His eyes were open and blood was pooled around his torso and slashed throat. His case and the others were linked. I'd a bet the farm they weren't, and I would have been wrong. Son-of-a-bitch.

"Here we go again," Calloway said. "I'm getting too old for this shit."

"What happens now, Don?" I asked. He told us the crime scene was going to be processed to see if there might be any evidence. "Finger prints, letters with handwriting samples, cancelled checks, stuff like that." He walked back to where the fire started and said, "And I'm gonna dig through this pile and see if I can find any evidence." He told us he had to wait for the detectives to show up and give him the okay to start sifting and digging. "They sure take their sweet time. They don't need a search warrant, I mean; it's a crime scene after all," Stannard said.

I grumbled about working another clue on the hobo murders, but in reality I was happy to be on it again, even though it was a no-pay gig. Others in the office were doing pay work and that kept the bank account from overdraft.

Investigating is what I love—sifting through evidence and reports from interviews, and crime scene pictures. Looking for something somebody missed or finding something that didn't belong or fit.

I picked Calvin up at Hazel's shop. I wasn't sure what his demeanor would be. He wore a shop apron and was straightening merchandise on display shelves. He grinned when he saw me and said, "Hi ya, Dad. How'd it go?"

After a dinner at the Village Creamery on Big Basin Way in Saratoga, we dropped Hazel off and Calvin and I went home. We listened to an episode of Gunsmoke on the radio, then went to bed.

"Dad, wake up. You're scaring me. Is it another bad dream?" I sat straight up, and Calvin took a step back.

"It's okay boy, no need to be afraid," I said as soothingly as I could. My heart was pounding like a woodpecker on a phone pole. I felt tied up, but realized I was tangled in the sheets.

"Any time I have a bad dream, mom says it's best to talk about it. Do you want to talk?"

"I don't remember it," I lied. But it was *the* most disturbing nightmare I'd ever had. I was in a poker game and the stakes were high—my life was the wager. All the cards were face cards that showed the photos of the dead hobos. They were dealt rapid fire. Jitters, Double B, Larry Dolan, Maurice Buck, and other nameless Bo's. Then came the final hand—I had a pair: Janey and Calvin—and that's when I woke up.

Calvin went back to bed and I lay looking at the ceiling, willing myself to stay awake. I saw the streetlight go off and the day come to life.

I left work at noon and Calvin and I took off for Big Basin State Park to camp overnight. The drive over the summit was winding and I couldn't remember if Calvin got carsick or not.

"You okay?" I asked. He told me he was just fine. We talked about baseball and schoolwork, father and son topics. We were having a conversation and I was so glad my life had turned toward the better. To miss this opportunity would've been tragic.

We found a nice site in a campground called Huckleberry. A stream ran just below and the redwoods rimming the area were majestic.

"Look up, Calvin. Look to the sky." The tall trees swayed at their tops and let the sun flicker down on us.

"It reminds me of being in church," Calvin said. That saddened me; we used to go to church every Sunday, even if I was hung-over.

"Do you still go to church, Calvin?" He nodded. "Well, I was planning on going to Sunday service tomorrow at that outdoor chapel by the Headquarters building. You wanna go, son?"

"I didn't bring any church duds, dad."

"God wants you to show up and he doesn't care what you have on; just show up."

The tent was pitched, campstools out, and a fire going. I was cooking a hobo stew. Calvin came back into camp with an armful of firewood and said, "Gee, that smells delish, dad."

"This is what yer old man lived on for a couple of years, Mulligan stew. I hope ya like it." I felt a twinge of nostalgia, but it passed rapidly. That was then; this is now, and brother, this is much better.

A little black Scotty dog ran into our site. He stopped when he realized we weren't his owners. "C'mer pooch," Calvin said as he made kissing sounds and snapped his fingers gently. The dog meandered up, then lay across Calvin's black tennis shoes. The dog was just like a Bo; Calvin called him in and he took comfort from the camp. We'd feed him and give him a place to sleep. I was wistful again. The feeling didn't last long.

Two children, a boy and a girl stood on the fringes of our site. The girl said, "Angus, you bad dog, c'mon." Angus perked up and tore over to his owners. They thanked us and walked away. Angus was in the arms of the boy and licking his face. Calvin and I looked at one another and smiled. *Man*, I thought, *he is growing up*.

"Start peeling some spuds, kiddo," I said handing a peeler to Calvin. My stew was much thicker than the ones in a jungle; it would be better suited for a plate than a cup.

Calvin was sopping his plate with a piece of white bread and smacking his lips. "That was great, dad. Who knew ya ate so well on the road?" We sat gazing into the fire, lost in our own thoughts. Things were right in my world.

In the morning we walked to Sunday worship. There were no scheduled services, so Calvin and I sat in pews fashioned from thick redwood tree trunks in the outdoor chapel. I was thanking Christ for the life he'd given me and how grateful I was. I looked sideways at

Calvin and his eyes were closed and his lips were moving. We walked back to our site and Calvin asked me what I prayed for.

"I didn't ask for anything, son. I just gave thanks for what I have. What about you?"

"I thanked God for giving you back to me." I lost my balance and leaned into a split rail and held my hands over my eyes. "I love you so much," I said through sobs. Calvin hugged me and told me I was the best gift he'd ever gotten.

I stopped in on Dante Verducchi in Salinas after taking Calvin home to King City. Dante saw me and grinned.

"Hi ya, Grady, how goes it?" I told him about the evidence pictures displayed in the burned warehouse in San Jose.

"There was a picture of Dolan there." He looked confused. "The Garden Grill and Pub?" The throat slash?"

A look of acknowledgement flickered across Dante's face, "Oh yeah, Dolan."

"Why hadn't I seen the picture of him before?" He told me I showed up less than eighteen hours after the murder and the evidence photos hadn't been developed. "Are there any others?"

Dante left the office and returned with a file folder. He tossed it on the desk and said, "Help yourself." I saw the picture that was in the warehouse in San Jose and several others from different angles.

"How did this get to San Jose?" I asked pointing at the picture. Dante looked through notes and messages and then looked at me and said, "A Captain Hardy from the San Jose Police wanted a copy of the file." When I asked, Dante told me the date of the request, which jibed with the Maurice Buck murder. Maybe Hardy wasn't as much of a fool as I thought he was. *Oh, yes he is.* Seeing nothing new in the narrative section, I handed the file back to Verducchi.

"This is a case that has been put on the shelf. If you can shed any light on it, let me know, Grady."

I phoned Jack Calloway and told him that a copy of Dolan's file was with the SJPD and that Captain Hardy made the request. "I'd like to know who Hardy shared that file with," I said into the receiver. Jack told me he'd check into who took over the case for Hardy.

Hobo Ashes

There was a phone message from a Mrs. Muldoon taped to my phone receiver. The receptionist printed "urgent" at the top. Another person's *urgent*, I'd learned, was not necessarily mine. But I called Mrs. Muldoon, who wanted to hire me to help find her daughter. There wasn't anyone in the office to pawn this off on, so I did the preliminary footwork myself.

The Muldoon mansion sat on acreage behind an ornate black iron gate attached to river rock pillars off of Kennedy Road. Kennedy ran from San Jose Avenue up into the foothills east of downtown. Open fields dotted the road and then gave way to ranch-style houses, orchards, and a subdivision under construction, and finally into an estate-like neighborhood.

At the top of a long driveway lined with hibiscus, I pushed a button on a post and the gate opened. I parked in front of a garage with four doors. A dignified looking lady stood stiffly on the brick walkway. She wore plaid slacks, open-toed sandals and a white blouse. Though her dress was casual, she was not.

"Mr. Prescott, I'm Ardis Muldoon," she announced as I approached. "Won't you please come in?"

The foyer was wide and long. The ecru-colored tiled floor had a pale green four-leaf clover inlaid in the middle. The home smelled of vanilla and a trace of garlic. Through French doors at the end of the entry, I could see a far-reaching expanse of green lawn dotted with oak trees. To the left there was a living room with white carpeting and various shades of white furniture. A white brick fireplace dominated one entire wall. To the right was a formal dining room with the longest table I'd ever seen. Mrs. Muldoon led me into the living room and pointed to a couch and said, "Have a seat. Would you like something to drink?" I declined refreshments and sat down. I felt myself slipping off the satiny cushions. I put my foot down like pushing a brake pedal to halt my slide.

Mrs. Muldoon told me she'd heard about my success as an investigator from Wesley Jones and Mr. Gorman from the Lyndon. How about that? I asked her what she wanted me to do.

"It's my daughter, Mr. Prescott. Noelle takes off and is gone for days, sometimes weeks."

"How old is she?" When she told me she was nineteen, I said, "She's an adult. Maybe she wants to be on her own." Mrs. Muldoon's brows arched and her eyes flashed with anger.

"When she runs out of money she drags herself here and my husband writes out a check, then she's gone again."

"Do you have any idea where she goes?"

"No, not for certain. But I've heard rumors that she has been seen in downtown San Jose at a place called Rose's or Rosie's." She couldn't mean Dago Rose's could she?

Mrs. Muldoon picked up a gold knick-knack shaped like the globe with a swivel top at the equator and removed a cigarette from it. She tamped it on her thumbnail then picked up a lighter with a swordfish on it. What the Christ? That's the logo for the All Bay Seafood Company! Mrs. Muldoon inhaled her smoke deeply and exhaled through her nose. Very un-lady like, I thought.

"What does your husband do, Mrs. Muldoon?"

"He sells fish to dining establishments. All this from fish," she said with a wave of her hand. "He's never been fishing a day in his life and hates the taste. There isn't even a can of tuna or salmon in the pantry."

"I'd like to talk to your husband, also. When would be the best time to see him?" I asked.

"Oh, that will be a problem, Mr. Prescott. You see, my husband, Finis, isn't my daughter's father and doesn't take an interest in her well-being, other than giving her a check to get lost."

"Well, what about her father. Is he in the picture?" Mrs. Muldoon just shook her head without an explanation.

After the Muldoon lady signed the standard contract and paid the retainer, I asked for a photograph of her daughter. Noelle Muldoon was a cute chick with long red hair and green eyes. Her height was five feet, six inches and she weighed 120 pounds. On a sheet of paper Mrs. Muldoon listed Noelle's friends and their possible addresses. I'd planned to hand this case off to an associate, but when the All Bay Seafood connection entered the mix, I decided to work this one. However, I was going to let an associate do the legwork, which would give me time to look at the evidence from the warehouse fire.

Jack Calloway entered my office with file folders under his arm. He cleared his throat and said, "That Stannard from the fire department does a nice report. He's photographed and catalogued every bit of evidence in that pile of rubble."

"Anything to link up the previous hobo burnings?" I asked Jack. He thumbed through several photos in a folder and then put one down on my desk—a Ronsonal lighter fluid can.

"Well, I'll be." He showed me the rest of the pictures, and one of particular interest of a pair of brogans with a lift on the left heel. Was somebody faking a limp? Could that be it? If somebody was creating an identity, then they could maneuver through various crowds without too much struggle—hobos to upper-class and all people in-between. Articles of clothing, mostly suit coats, hats and wigs were photographed. Wigs? This case just got a bit tougher. Plus I had the nagging itch that the All Bay Seafood Company played in it somehow. I kept that to myself and asked Jack, "What's in the other folder?" He grinned and said, "Hardy's file on the hobo murders."

"What does that ass-bite have to say?" I snorted.

22

I'm getting my ass chewed off by my brothers. What do they expect; I'm a killer, I ain't a firebug for crying out loud. What do I know about automatic fire sprinklers? I thought the blaze would destroy all the pictures and eliminate any other evidence; the building was so dilapidated I thought it would go up like a box of matches. It was finally the end of my spree and I felt a big part of my life was leaving. What now? The brothers had put me on ice for almost two years.

Look at the two of them, will ya. Two hundred dollar suits and here I sit with an old tweed sport coat, khaki chinos, and cheap black brogans. My blue work shirt is buttoned up to the neck. I look like a migrant waiting to see an important man, for crap's sake. Man, this office stinks.

I'm gonna miss it, ya know? Killing is such a kick, and it seems to be the only thing I've ever been good at, except for makeup and wardrobes. I did other killings while on ice. I didn't kill any hobos, but I did murder others by gunshot, garroting and backstabbing. I robbed those victims, so I had some foxy pocket money that the brothers didn't know about. I always used some of it to help out at the soup kitchen at the missions. I gave some money every time I got some. Ma always taught me to think of others, especially those less fortunate who might be hungry. It was prime pickings at the mission, but I never did my hunting there. This was volunteer work.

Brother attorney said to pull the pin. "It's getting too hot.

Hobo Ashes

You've avenged enough," he told me and union brother stood in the background nodding. That's all well and good for them; they got the education and the income. Me? When I was ready for school, my dad taught me how to be a gear jammer instead. I was a damn fine truck driver, but then dad was dead and the eliminations started. I could get back behind the wheel and earn a salary. Yeah, that sounds like a good plan. I was good at it before, right? Attorney brother is telling me to lay low, maybe get out of town. Where in the hell am I gonna go, back to Iowa? That's where it all started, ya know. That BB or Double Bob, whatever his name was, is the only sucker that had anything to do with the end of our trucking company. One of our drivers goes off the road and barrels into a hobo camp killing some and maiming a few others. Big deal. It was an accident, but the insurance company makes a federal case out of it. The families of those that got run over did a blanket lawsuit and our company went kaput. Dad goes up one night and takes a bath and slits his wrists. I'll never forget his pearl-white carcass sitting in the crimson bath water and the gaping wounds, his hands dangling by small amounts of skin. I had a moment of sadness, but it went quickly. When I thought of the beatings and his lack of concern for me, well sir, I shed not a tear for the son-of-a-bitch. I got a charge out of the brother's grief, though.

It's funny, that Double Bob guy hits the skids when the market crashes and leaves his family and becomes a hobo. Attorney brother tells me to follow him. "Follow him?" I say, "How?" My brother tells me to become a hobo. It took several years to find Double B, ya know. Not only that, they hire Shadow to tail me. Thought I wouldn't figure it out. Hah!

As fate would have it, the brothers end up on the West Coast seeking better opportunities. The three brothers together again when the avenging is over; that's how I saw it. They didn't. It was them without me, really. Well, sir, I got a plan. I'll show my SOB brothers just what it feels like to be cheated and left out.

23

Hardy did write a good report. I'll give the son-of-a-bitch that. I saw the request he sent to Verducchi from Salinas PD and a note to Leo Fraser, a guy I used to be on patrol with, who must have taken over the Maurice Buck case when Hardy retired.

I called San Jose Police and asked to speak to Captain Fraser. After several transfers I finally heard a gruff voice say, "Vice, Fraser." When I told him who I was he asked, "What the hell have you been up to? And what in the hell do you want?" I wasn't sure if he was cordial or crotchety, so I played nice. I congratulated him on his promotions over the years and wished him continued success. When I told him I needed his help he said, "Meet me at Dinah's Shack on Monterey Road and you can buy me lunch."

Fraser had put on a few pounds since last I saw him. He was sitting in a maroon booth with a coffee cup and saucer in front of him. The liquid in the cup was clear as water and had a pimento-stuffed olive bobbing around. His pink neck folded over the collar of his white dress shirt. "What's up, hot shot, ya want a blast?" he asked. I declined and had iced coffee. We spent a few minutes getting caught up on families and work, and by the time we finished our salads we were down to brass tacks.

"That was the last hobo murder in our area," Fraser explained.

"Did anything happen with the lab reports on the ice pick?" I wanted to know. Fraser shook his head and said, "It was like somebody just dropped it there, like it was on purpose. No blood or charring, no prints, just the bent tip.

"Do you have any theories on why the murders stopped, Leo?"

"The hump's probably dead," he said taking a forkful of steak. "I walked through that warehouse fire and saw the gallery, pretty impressive." He held up his coffee cup and the waitress brought him another. "I was looking for any links to cases I'm working on in Vice. I didn't connect anything."

"Is Dago Rose still running a house over on Bird?" I asked.

"Nah, she's got a somewhat legit place in Willow Glen, called Rosie's." I asked what he meant by "somewhat legit" and he smiled and said, "Once a whore always a whore, eh. She's been known to run a couple of gals out of the back room."

"I'm working on a missing persons case, a Noelle Muldoon, nineteen, 120 pounds, five-feet-six inches, red hair and green eyes." I gave him a copy of her photo. "Her mother has heard she hangs around downtown at a place called Rose's or Rosie's."

"Aw, shit, the Red Rose Garden on Third Street. It's a mob hangout. If she's there, Miss Muldoon could be into a number of things—hooking, smut pictures, or dope, all of which are one-way tickets to hell." Fraser explained that this place opened about eighteen months ago as a drinking and dining establishment. "They added a small cabaret floor and the next thing we hear, they got strippers. The mayor wants to know what we're doing about it. The alcohol control folks and the city permit department are scratching their heads. Somebody's palm got greased. Every time we drop in, there's a combo playing and couples dancing. But I'll let you know if I find out anything about Miss Muldoon."

I had the impression the Red Rose Garden management was being tipped off when the cops would show up. Fraser has to see that too. When I told Leo that Noelle's stepfather owned the All Bay Seafood Company, he flashed me an odd hasty look and then he shrugged and said, "That don't mean anything to me." But still his eyes betrayed Leo Fraser. His three-martini and steak lunch wasn't enough for Leo. He wanted a chocolate sundae. I was glad Mrs. Muldoon was paying.

I gave the info I learned from Fraser to the associate working the case, a big Italian kid named Geno. "Jesus, I been working all morning and you come in with this," he said in a frustrated way.

I stopped and looked him in the eye and said, "Don't look a gift horse in the mouth. I'd prefer you said thanks and went back to work." He stared at me with flaring nostrils.

"Anything else, Geno?" I added. He asked what I thought the next move should be. "I'd go the Red Rose Garden and take in the show. Take a good look at Noelle's picture and see if she's there."

"Then what?"

"Jesus, Geno! If I gotta do yer job, I don't need you." His investigative techniques were marginal when I hired him, and now I didn't think he could work on his own. Plus the fact he was rudderless and somewhat thick-headed.

Geno Parisi came to me as a hang-around kid. His jet black hair and obsidian eyes gave him Hollywood good looks. But he was a dumb cluck. Before Geno came to work for me, his father visited my office. His denim overalls were dusty from brick residue, and his work shirt was sweat-stained and body odor swirled around him. The flat soft brimmed cap, which was once white, now gray, sat jauntily on his head of black curly hair. I've never begrudged a working man or the "pay dirt" on his clothing and body. "Can I help you?" I asked while standing up.

"Name is-a Parisi. Dominic-a Parisi," he said with a thick Italian accent while he shoved a catcher's-mitt sized fist at me. His handshake was firm and the palm jagged as coarse sand.

"What can I do for you, Mr. Parisi?" His dark complexion and Roman nose tweaked sadly, but recovered quickly.

"It is-a my son, Geno," he replied in a quivering voice. "He's headed for trouble again."

I motioned Mr. Parisi to a chair and asked him if he wanted some water.

"If it's-a no problem, please," he said while he twirled his cap in his hands. I handed him the tumbler and went and sat at my desk. The anxiety in Mr. Parisi was palatable, so I moved to the chair next to him, which made him smile slightly.

"Tell me about Geno. Why is he in trouble, again?"

"He quit-a high school, just-a dropped out. I guess he wants to be brick layer like his old man, eh? Well, he couldn't make a barnacle on a brick layer's ass. Sorry about the language, Mr. Prescott."

"Does he have a job?" Parisi sipped his water, wiped his lips with his sleeve and said, "He washed dishes at the Lyndon for a few weeks, but Mr. Gorman hadda fire him. He *gave* him the job as a favor to me. I do lots a work for the Gorman family; around the house and the hotel."

"What does Geno do?" I wanted to know.

"He runs-a all night and sleeps-a all day, that's what. And his mama lets him get away with it." He stated that his wife lets him sleep for as long as he wants. Cooks his food, cleans and irons his clothes. "She thinks she's doing what a mother is supposed to do, eh. She's-a nuts, no mother where I grew up would do that; we'd get the razor strap," he sighed. "If I get after him, and that's what he needs, the wife protects him. He should have the crap beat-a out of him."

"What do want from me, Mr. Parisi?"

"I wanna know where he goes at night. What he does. I'm afraid he's in with a bad crowd." I told him I'd check with my contacts in the Police Department, and Parisi paled and started to stammer. "No police! If he gets-a run in, he may be sent back."

"Sent back? Sent back where?"

"To Italy."

"Is that where he was born?" Parisi told me that Geno was born in San Jose.

"He's a citizen of the United States, Mr. Parisi. Nobody is going to deport him. They may send him to jail, but it will be here in America." Immigrants were told horror stories about how harsh the government was. A myth that floated among ethnic neighborhoods was if you or anyone in your family got in trouble, the authorities came in the middle of the night and tossed you on a boat back to the old country. "Why don't you have him join the armed services? They could get him on the straight and narrow." He told me the boy's mother wouldn't hear of it. "She can't let go."

It seemed difficult to categorize what this case would be; missing person? No. Surveillance and report? Possibly. I needed to check with Calloway and see if he had any records for Geno Parisi. Plus, could this man afford the fees? As if he read my mind, Parisi said, "I don't have much money, but I can do work for you. Ask Mr. Gorman, I do good work, Mr. Prescott."

I told him I didn't have use for a brick layer. He expected this, and told me, "I can do all types of work; plumbing, electric, carpentry, and painting. I am a master of them all. You maybe don't need me now, but someday you will."

When I started to fill out the standard contract form, he asked, "What about the up-front dough, eh? Will you need that?" I told him that ten dollars was required, even though at that time it was twenty-five. He pulled out a thick, well-worn brown wallet and fished two fives out and handed them to me.

"Can I get a receipt, please?"

We determined that my agency would follow Geno Parisi, try and divert him from trouble, and report to his father on his activity. This was a real loosey-goosey case, but what the heck? Maybe I could save a kid from a life of being in the criminal justice system. Before Parisi left, he gave me a photo of Geno and signed the contract.

"I don't know where to start, Mr. Parisi, any hints?"

"Try the saloon up in Holy City. Somebody said he was-a taking bets on the horses. I'd start there, Mr. Prescott."

Holy City is situated in an obscure corner of the Santa Cruz Mountains ten miles south of Los Gatos. It was founded in 1919 by Father William Riker, a cult leader. Some called him a crack pot. The religious community had no church, so services were held in Riker's home. He preached celibacy and temperance, which he didn't abide by. He also encouraged white supremacy and segregation of the races and sexes.

Riker owned some businesses, including a café, bar, gas station and repair garage. It had its own volunteer fire company and radio station. With the construction of Highway 17, Holy City was no longer on the main route through the mountains, and by the 1940s the town began to decline. In 1942 Riker was arrested for supporting Hitler, but was later acquitted. After several years, Riker lost control of the property and several buildings mysteriously burned down.

I met Jack Calloway at the police station. He was going to drive us to the Holy City Saloon. We were dressed in sport shirts and slacks. "We don't need to be goin in there looking like cops," Jack told me.

My thought was that most in there probably knew who Calloway was in the first place. We passed the Lyndon Hotel and a black haired kid was thumbing a ride. This was going to be easier than I thought.

"Pull over, Jack."

"What's going on," he wanted to know. I told him the kid thumbing it was Geno Parisi. Calloway pulled over and Geno ran up to the car. "Where ya headed?"

"Holy City," I said in a friendly tone.

"No kidding? Me too," he said as he got into the back seat. His shiny hair had an abundance of hair oil. He was dressed in a black polo-type knit shirt and tan slacks. His cordovan brogans were military polished. The kid was a looker, there was no doubt.

"I'm going to the saloon up there. That's where I work," Geno announced. I told him he didn't look old enough to work behind a bar.

"Oh, I don't tend bar or nothing, I just run errands; get ice, stock shelves, and such."

"You ever been in the Holy City Saloon, Jack?"

"Not that I recall, pal. Maybe we should have one or ten." I was glad he didn't use my given name, and was sorry I used his. However Jack was certainly more common than Grady.

"Sure come on in, I'll see ya get treated right," Geno said.

We parked in front of a vacant lot that at one time had been a hardware store. Charring could be seen on the buildings on either side of the lot. The barroom was smoky and a Dinah Washington blues song played on the juke box. The stools were occupied, so Geno led us to a table on the west side of the building. He opened the blinds and we saw a fantastic sunset.

"I'll have Rube, the bartender, come and take yer order right away, and thanks for the lift."

"Hey pretty boy, shut the God damned blinds, ya stupid dago," a fat guy at the end of the bar yelled. Geno came over and asked, "Open or closed?" Jack and I said in unison, "Open."

Geno shrugged his shoulders at fatso and continued on to the bar. The fat guy knocked his stool over when he stood and weaved his way to our table. It's like he didn't see us.

"You touch that pull, and I'll knock you into the middle of next week," Jack hissed. Fatso reached for the pull, and Jack grabbed his arm and said, "Keep yer glue hooks offa the pull." The man wrested his arm from Jack, and said, "Step outside." Jack replied, "I don't have time," and scrambled from his chair and pasted the guy in the gut and one to his beak. I stood, waiting for his friends to step in, but nobody did. The bartender said, "Anybody who takes Swifty home gets a free drink when he gets back." Nobody moved for several moments, then finally somebody said, "I'll hook his truck to my wrecker and take him home. I'll have that drink applied to my tab." Rube thanked the man for the gesture.

Rube took our order, and he had a smirk on his face. "Sorry about the beef," Jack said. "First time I'm in the place and within two minutes, I have a go. I just don't like bullies."

"Don't worry about it. Every guy in this place would like to have done what you did, but they're afraid of Swifty. He's just a tub of guts, but they give a wide berth."

I didn't notice any unlawful behavior going on. Holy City Saloon was a working man's bar and seemed friendly. We stayed until Geno was off work and offered him a ride back to Los Gatos, which he accepted. Before dropping him off in front of the Lyndon, I gave him my business card and asked him to come by my office the next day.

During the daytime Geno Parisi became our errand guy, which gave him a few bucks each week and at night he went up the hill to Holy City. His father, Dominic was happy for the work ethic Geno seemed to have, and I was happy with the bricks he put up on the front of Hazel's shop on Big Basin Way in Saratoga. It was the easiest assignment I ever had. There was one problem, though; Geno's lack of sense. He could reason things out as well as anybody, but he required a poke in the ass. Letting him decide what to do next was not going to work with him. He needed direction. When he came to me and said he wanted to become a private dick, I told him no way. Not until he at least graduated from high school. Much to his father's and my surprise he did graduate. Dominic painted my house and Geno came to work for me. He was a slow learner, and he mostly ran errands. He walked into Reggie's one afternoon and sat on a stool next to me. "Am I paying you to sit in a bar?" I slurred.

"No, you're not. I get sandwiches for you, and go to the post office and office supply store. I gotta be the boss before I get paid to sit in a bar," he hissed.

"Take the sand outta yer caw, before ya get the boot." He apologized, half-assed, and said the receptionist needed me for something. I got up and looked at Geno and said, "Ask one of the associates if you can assist them. Start making phone calls for them." And Geno became pretty good at it, but he needed constant prodding.

"Maybe you're right, Grady. I quit," he said as he started to clear his desktop. The other associates and the receptionist appeared to be busy and oblivious to our conversation, but I know they heard every word. With Geno gone, the workload got harder. My priority changed; the warehouse fire was going to have to be handled by Calloway for the most part. I needed to take care of paying gigs until I could get another associate hired and trained. Jesus, what next?

Well, what was next was that Calloway and I got sloppy-assed drunk. It started out as "Let's meet at Reggie's for one," that turned into a "Last call, boys." Calloway summoned the officer on patrol to give him a ride home, and I slept on the couch in my office upstairs.

The tinkling of broken glass didn't register at first. Hell, I wasn't even sure where I was. I saw a shadowy figure through the hole in the office door window. I saw a hand reach inside to turn the thumb latch, which by the way, I hadn't locked. The hand locked the latch, which gave me the opportunity to dart to the door. The doorknob rattled but didn't open. A hand came through again and fiddled with the lock. I grabbed the arm and swung the door open which propelled the intruder into the room with his arm stuck. I clobbered the guy several times and he slumped to the floor. It was Geno. He'd have a nice shiner and busted lip later.

"Geno, what're trying to pull?" I asked as I called the operator to get the cops here. He sat up touching his lip and looking at the blood on his fingertips.

"I asked you a question," I repeated.

He just stared at me and shook his head. "I wanted to get the copy of my PI license you have on file." That made no sense to me at all. "Why in blue blazes didn't you call? Now yer facing a B and E." My thinking was he was gonna trash the office or worse.

"I'll pay for the door, Grady, just let me go, okay." My better judgment said, *hell no*, but my headache said, *get the hell out of here and don't come back*. I canceled the cop by telling them I was mistaken. I swept the glass and went back to sleep and didn't wake up until the receptionist arrived at 9:00 am.

Later that day I drove by the Red Rose Garden. It was Moorish in design and painted pink with a huge red rose neon sign. A man in a short sleeve white shirt and brown suit pants was picking cigarette butts from the flower boxes on either side of the front door. He had blond wavy hair and a body builder's tan and physique and was obviously a bouncer. Every so often he'd wipe his hands on a towel draped over his shoulder.

I heard a truck horn beep and the butt guy stood straight and waved at the driver, Davy Holcomb, in an All Bay Seafood Company truck. Holcomb was now working for them? *He's been part of that outfit since his frog gigging caper years ago*, I thought. The man pointed to a driveway and Davy pulled behind the building. I got out of the Ford and scurried down the driveway to see what I could see or hear. Davy was backing up to the rear door of the kitchen. He spotted me and gave me a head bob. I was caught and needed to cover myself.

"Hey Davy, I seen ya drive by, how ya makin it?" I said as kindly as possible as I jumped onto the running board at the passenger side window. He put up a finger in a 'wait a sec' fashion and got out of the truck. He forgot to set the hand brake and the truck started to roll.

"Damn it!" Holcomb said as he pulled the brake handle. He seemed rattled. Did I cause him to become flustered? The man in the shirtsleeves eyed me from toe to hat and back again.

"I'll be over there, Davy," I said pointing to a bumper-nicked wooden fence. "Let's get caught up."

He tossed his clipboard in the cab of the truck and sauntered over. We didn't shake hands, no backslap either, just another head bob.

"How long ya been working the fish, Davy?" He told me a few months.

"What about you? Still looking for lost pets and kids?" I told him that he was right. He didn't deserve to know how well I was doing.

"Is the food any good in this joint?" I asked, pointing to the back of the Red Rose Garden.

"People don't come here for the food, Grady," he said with a snort. "They come to see the dancers and buddy, they got a good one featured lately."

"Oh yeah? A real cutie?"

"Yeah. Ruby Skye. Flaming red hair and a figure to die for. The girl next door, ya know. Oh, she ain't built like Blaze Starr, but she can really move and brother, she's a red head, if ya get my meaning," he said with a wink. He just shrugged his shoulders when I asked how the city let them have dancers.

Was Noelle, Ruby Skye?

"Hey, Holcomb. Ya better get a move on," the short-sleeved guy said through the screen door.

I followed Davy's truck out to the street and walked in front of the Red Rose Garden. The front door was wide open and a man in an apron and waistcoat was vacuuming the carpeting. His crew cut was so short you could see his scalp glistening with sweat. He saw me and shut the vacuum off.

"We ain't open yet," he told me. When I asked what time the floorshow started, he barked, "What floor show?" I got the hunch this was a standard response.

"The Ruby Skye show," I said.

"Never heard of her, sport." He turned his back on me and resumed vacuuming the rest of the room. I could see a set of drums, guitars, microphones, speakers and various musical instruments next to a highly polished small hardwood floor.

Driving back to my office I attempted to link recent and not-so-recent developments in various cases. I went back to Holcomb and Buck gigging for frogs in Ross Creek, and the seafood supplier, All Bay Seafood Company, selling inferior frog legs to the Lyndon. Buck is dead and Holcomb drives for All Bay Seafood. The pickets at the Lyndon, and a union official, the guy I pulled a gun on, at All Bay Seafood, walking the picket line. Mrs. Muldoon's daughter, Noelle is possibly hanging out at a mob joint that gets food from All Bay, a company Mrs. Muldoon's husband, Finis, owns.

Everything always came back to All Bay Seafood. But what about the murders? How in the hell did they fit in with this? Or did they? Maybe the hobo killings and All Bay Seafood weren't linked at all.

I was writing all my thoughts down to put in the file folder, when my receptionist walked over to my desk with the mail. "Are you limping?" I asked. She told me she twisted her ankle stepping off the curb. I watched her walk back to her desk. I tossed my pencil on the tablet and thought, *What about the guy with the limp?* There ain't a guy that limps involved in the hobo case, that we know of. But the lifts found in the rubble at the warehouse count for something, but what? And the disguises, what were *they* about?

I was doodling on my tablet—circles, squares and up and down lines and suddenly one of the doodles looked like a knife. I'd forgotten about the knives *and* the lighter fluid. I needed to do some old-fashioned gum-shoe work.

I visited several wholesale restaurant supply outfits. I told a saleslady at one place I was looking to set up a fish processing company and wondered if she could help me with boning knives. She showed me a catalog with all sorts of utensils. I didn't see any ten-inch Schrade hunting knives in her catalog.

"That's our best seller," a man in a toupee said as I looked at displays of knives in a cutlery store. "That ten-incher keeps me in business."

"How so?" I asked.

"One customer, a fish warehouse buys em by the dozens."

"I visited All Bay Seafood and they told me they bought their knives from you," I lied. The man beamed and nodded his head and gave a smug half-smile.

"Why do they use a hunting knife instead of a boning knife?"

"Don't know and don't care. There's more of a mark-up on hunting knives than any other. I ain't gonna argue with them. Why would I?"

The link between the murders and All Bay Seafood was unmistakable.

The Bo waved me in as I stood on the fringe of the quarry camp. It'd been several months since my last visit. The population was sparse, but there were a few guys who recognized me from the old days. A grill sat on rocks over a wood fire. Salmon steaks sizzled and spit up their aroma as they cooked on tin foil.

"Ya gonna take a meal with us for old times' sake, Grady?" a Bo named Butch asked.

"Not this time, Butch, but those are nice looking pieces," I said as I handed him a couple of sacks of groceries.

"Yeah, Holcomb brings stuff by every now and then. Sometimes he almost makes up for being an ass-bite, but then he hacks on someone and he's back to ass-bite status," Butch said with a snort. He asked if there was any new poop on the hobo killings.

"Haven't heard anything lately, Butch. What about around here?"

"Guys drift in from north and south and they report all quiet. Maybe the dirty so-and-so got it himself." Butch flipped the salmon and said, "Let's hope they're over. Bo's ain't like they used to be, ya know, Grady."

"How so, Butch?"

"They're younger. It's like they're runaways trying to show their independence, I guess. Always protesting about this or that."

Hazel and I sat at a table next to the dance floor. The house band played foxtrots and waltzes. It wasn't Benny Goodman, but it wasn't too bad. I knew I was taking a risk bringing Hazel to the Red Rose Garden. If something sleazy happened, I'd feign surprise and we'd leave. I was on Mrs. Muldoon's dime, so here we sat sipping wine. We danced a few and were headed for our table, when a blue light flashed and a siren blared. Somebody over the loud speaker said "Raid! Return to your seats, please!" Hazel looked at me with wide eyes. The music took on a honky-tonk type of beat and a redhead in a skimpy cop uniform slinked onto the floor—Noelle Muldoon, AKA Ruby Skye, stopped and blew a whistle several times, then circled the floor like a stalking lioness. The lights went down and she started to do a bump and grind to the music. Hazel twitched in her chair and gave me a nervous look. I'd seen enough, and scooted us out the door. As we passed the bar I heard Holcomb say, "Hey, Grady, she's the one I was telling ya about."

I explained to Hazel that I was working a missing person case and needed a shill to appear legit. The only thing Hazel was upset about was that I wasn't forthcoming from the start.

"I'm no shrinking violet, Grady. I've been around, you know. So next time fill me in so we can watch the whole show."

When I reported what I had learned about Noelle to Mrs. Muldoon, she didn't seem shocked, just sad. Nothing I said would soften the fact that her daughter was a stripper. Adding the fact that Noelle's stepfather, Finis Muldoon, probably knew this, would be rubbing salt into Ardis Muldoon's open wounds. She paid me my fee, with no spiff, which was okay. Before I left the living room, I said to her, "If I can ever do anything for you, please let me know. Would you like me to contact you if I ever hear anything else about Noelle?" She glumly shook her head and whispered, "No, thank you. She's on her own. My husband got his way. He won again."

I was just about to get in my car when the garage door I was parked in front of opened. "I'm just leaving," I said to a man in greasy coveralls. He stared at me and kept wiping his hands on a shop towel. I opened the car door and the man asked, "You Calloway or Prescott?"

"I'm Grady Prescott. Are you Mr. Muldoon?"

He told me he was. He stepped into the sunlight and his gold hair glistened and his pink face was blotchy from what appeared to be dermatology treatments. I saw Mrs. Muldoon watching us from the kitchen window. He walked back into the garage and put on a straw hat and said, "So you're the one that pulled a pistol at my place?" He put his foot on my bumper and glared.

I felt like I was the errant student being talked to by the school dean. Man, I needed to get out of that frame of mind immediately. I wasn't going to let this fat cat get the upper hand. I gave Muldoon a lopsided grin, which seemed to neutralize him. I next put my hands on my hips, which caused my sports coat to open, revealing my .38. My grin upset Muldoon more than my gun.

"That was some time ago, but yeah that guy tried to take my camera..."

"He was doing his job," he said loudly interrupting me.

"Me too," I said at full volume.

His face got pinker and his splotches became rust colored and looked raw. "Your job? A half-assed cop putting your nose where it doesn't belong. Be careful—it might get bitten off."

"You know, Mr. Muldoon, I've been threatened more times than I care to remember, especially recently. I've even ended up in the hospital. And it always has something to do with the employees at your company. I wonder why that is?" When he didn't answer right away, I forged ahead. "I don't want to think this, but here goes—there have been clues to murders that implicate All Bay Seafood Company, and you've just threatened me again. I can't let this go."

"What does that mean?" Muldoon hissed as he stood toe-to-toe with me.

"Back off before I knock you on your ass," I whispered as my nose touched his. Remembering what his wife said about how he hated fish, I hoped the tuna sandwich I had earlier would cause him to retch. We stepped back at the same time.

"Stay the hell away from me, Prescott, or I'll…"

"Or you'll what? Best not threaten me another time Mr. Muldoon. I'm starting to get the impression you don't like me." What he said next, inwardly took me right out of the fray, but my exterior remained indifferent.

He said, "Say hello to my friends in King City the next time you go there." He walked to the garage, turned, and looked at me and then pulled the rope that slowly closed the garage door.

My hands were shaking as I waited for the automatic gate to open. This ass-bite openly threatened me, more than once, which goes with the territory, but son-of-a-bitch, he's brought my ex-wife and children into it. God damn it!

Back at the office I phoned Janey's brother, Tom, and let him know what was going on and to keep a sharp eye out. I didn't want him to tell his sister, but telling Julian, her husband was okay as long as he kept it to himself. Janey would flip if she felt the boys were in danger. That was Janey, not a concern for herself, just for the kids. She's a fine woman.

24

Son-of-a-bitch, I'm getting antsy. I drift from place to place, fitting in everywhere I go. I'm that good. But, it's been quite some time, ya see. The brothers told me to lay low, so did the Shadow, who told me, "Stay out of the jungles. There isn't anything more to do there."

I'm just supposed to fade away? How am I gonna survive? My peepers are giving out, so getting an operator's license could be dicey. Maybe there's a dispatcher's job at one of the trucking outfits. Maybe my brother in the union can help. Asshole attorney brother don't seem to want to even acknowledge me, let alone help. When I told attorney brother that I would like to find a job and better circumstances, he asked me what kind of circumstances. How about being accepted into the family for starters? It wasn't my idea to start icing the hobo population; it was his, and the union brother's idea. Get the stupid one to do it. Get him to even the score for dear old dad. It came clear to me that I'd do the dirty work and their hands would stay clean. Go live like a tramp and do our bidding. Oh, we'll give you pay. You won't starve, but holidays went by and their families got together and I wasn't even invited. I was never going to be real family.

So, several days ago I show up at attorney's office and met with him and union brother. I called each and pretended to be the other and set up the meet. When I walked in and tossed a log book on the desk, attorney brother shrank away like it was infected with small pox or something. Damn, that amused me. He asks what it is and I tell him it is a log of the jobs I pulled. Both stared at me with moon eyes, and I don't mean the romantic kind of moon eyes either. I tell them to keep that one, because I have a copy. Attorney brother sweeps it off the desk top and it lands in the waste paper basket

One of them must have read it, because shadow is driving me to Fresno for a job with Navajo Trucking. A good job, I was told.

25

Wide-scale flooding took place in late winter and early spring of 1965. Streams that emptied into Los Gatos Creek backed up and did major damage to properties nearby. It was like nature was scouring our town. Sand bags were picked up at the corporation yard to help homeowners from losing any more backyards. The Quarry camp was wiped out, and I never saw another hobo spend the night there. Bo's were seen moseying through town headed for Santa Cruz or downstream toward San Jose. Some around town said, "It's the end of an era." Others said, "Good riddance." Me? I had mixed emotions; I'd needed friends and accommodations at one time and the jungles provided that. The indisputable fact was, however, that I never wanted to go back to that life. I knew there would always be Bo's, but Los Gatos was moving beyond the rural atmosphere and a new culture was developing—arts, theater, women's clubs, and other highbrow endeavors settled into the substance that made up the town. People from all over the country wanted to live in Los Gatos. Those who had been around town through the earlier years tolerated the newcomers and new ideas most of the time. And then there were those that moved in who brought a sense of entitlement with them. They bristled when an orchard truck chugged through town or a migrant worker stood in the same line at the grocery. It was okay for a Mexican to garden for them, but to buy food at the same store? Well! I loved the rural life, but also appreciated the sophistication that was now Los Gatos. *Would you listen to me? An alcoholic and at one time a hobo talking about sophistication!*

Those on the road during this time were not Bo's, not by a long shot. Their clothes were colorful, almost to the point of saying, "Hey, hey, look at me." Paisley shirts and bell-bottom pants took the place of overcoats and work clothes. The Bo of my era tried to blend in. These "kids" were trying to piss off the establishment. Some called them hippies.

"They're filthy," Gene told me one day when I visited him. "They make a mess behind my store, and I tell them to clean up and they laugh at me. No respect, Prescott, no respect." He picked up the broom leaning against the doorjamb and said, "At least you guys never left a mess. It smells like urine out back and they toss their rubbers on the ground. Son-of-a-bitch."

"Did you see the Mercury this morning?" Jack Calloway asked me as we went up the steps of St. Mary's Parish Hall. I told him I hadn't seen it. He stopped me on the porch and told me that the body of a hobo was found burned in a vineyard in Fresno.

"I'm retired, Jack," I said, "and so are you. Tell my kids about it."

He said the meeting was about to start and he'd tell me more after. We stepped in just as the Serenity Prayer was being said.

I went to my first Alcoholics Anonymous meeting six years ago. Hazel pleaded with me to get help. I went in the dry-out hospital and was okay for a few months. But over time I slipped back into the bottle. I was hanging around the office trying to stay out of Calvin and Coleman's way. Janey insisted they get college degrees before they did any work. As soon as each of them graduated, they came to work for me. I had three suites above Reggie's by 1973 and we were a big outfit. Well, as happens with drunks, I started to feel sorry for myself; I didn't have anything to do. Everything I wanted, I had. My sons were working with me and Byron was still in the Navy stationed in Hawaii and we visited him as often as we could. I had money in the bank and the bills paid, and I had Hazel, my beautiful wife. It couldn't be any better than that.

Everybody accounted for. Then I spent more and more time in Reggie's and other bars around town. I called it working the streets. "Gotta keep my ear to the ground, see what's shaking." My routine was pretty steady. I'd start at The Top Cat Tavern, then the New Yorker, which later became the Black Watch, then the Live Oak Inn, have lunch at the Lyndon, and finish my day at Reggie's. Anyhow, at the end of one of those sojourns, through a drunken stupor, I saw a look on Hazel's face that reminded me of the last look Janey gave me as her husband, and it scared the piss out of me. I felt I was going to be abandoned, again.

"I'm gonna take care of this," I said sobbing uncontrollably. That was six years ago. I was hammered at my first meeting, but more importantly, I was broken. Hit bottom. I thought they'd toss me on my ear. I must have been belligerent, because, according to reports I kept repeating any sentence or phrase that was spoken and when finished I'd say, "Amen, brother." I recalled a lady sitting next to me patting my hand and hushing while giving me coffee. Well, they didn't show me the door. They accepted me. They even took me to dinner afterwards. Some of the folks I recognized—doctors, housewives, businessmen and women, all walks of life and levels of economic circumstances. My life was saved six years ago. Jack came in several years after me and now our programs are strong. I thought I had a good life before, except for my benders, but I always went to work. My life is so much better today. That book, *The Big Book of AA*, that my grandmother gave my father after he killed my mother, is yellow with age and dog-eared to beat the band, but always within reach.

"So, what did the Mercury say this morning, Jack?"

He tells me, "A tiny article, third page of the second section, reports the long-time Santa Clara County Assistant District Attorney's estranged younger brother was found stabbed and burned in a field in Fresno."

"I didn't know Reed Mosley had a brother," I said.

"Different last names, Grady. The guy that got it was Abernathy, Chester Abernathy. He has another brother, a mucky-muck with fish cannery unions in Monterey and Santa Cruz Counties."

"What's his name?"

"Simon Mosley," Jack said matter-of-factly. That name was familiar to me, but I couldn't place from where or when. But what instantly flashed through my brain were frog legs. *What the Christ?*

"So, tell me what you're thinking, Jack."

"What I'm thinking is convince Garnett Maddox to look into this case. Oh, he'll rant about a Fresno case not having any relevance to what's going on in good old LG, or his workload is too much," he said with a grin. "Then I'll say that I'll help and he'll say for me to suit myself and I'll have access to the files, or I should say, *we'll* have the files," he finished, pointing between us. Garnett Maddox was a newly promoted detective that Calloway mentored when he was first hired.

Geno, the guy that broke into my office years ago, came back to work for me a few weeks after his crime. He admitted that he was going to break up the office that night. Anyhow, he is the most senior associate and a loyal employee. He's a mediocre investigator in the field, but a whiz in finding out about people through tenacious research. "When do you want this, Grady?" he asked when I gave him the two Mosley brothers and Abernathy names. "Yesterday, Geno. I needed it yesterday."

I sat with my sons in the Lyndon coffee shop having lunch. We do this religiously at least once a week. It's one of the great joys in my life. We don't talk shop too often; it's mostly about their families and my grandchildren. Looking back on where I was as a boy cowering in a linen closet, then growing up to be a wife beater and a drunk, I shudder. Through God's grace I broke the violence cycle and became a kindly grandfather and father. I don't have bad dreams very much anymore. Just having Hazel next to me gives me a sense of peace and serenity. Calvin favors his mother's side of the family and Coleman is a dead-ringer for my father, which sometimes gives me a shiver. But then he speaks and smiles and I'm okay.

Calvin seemed distracted, so I asked him if he was alright. "I just haven't been sleeping too well lately," he said with a sigh. He looked at Coleman and something transpired between them. "Spill it, boys. What's up?" Coleman gave Calvin a head nod that meant *go ahead.*

"A national firm wants to buy us. It's a great offer." I shook my head and stirred my coffee.

"I've had big outfits take a run at Prescott Investigations before and the offers were tantalizing, but at the end of the day I always came back to the same fact—I like working the way I work. Now I like the way *we* work. The three of us call the shots collectively, and we'd lose that with a bigger firm," I said, looking from son to son. "I get the feeling you boys have already made up your minds. Am I right?" They didn't deny it, which hurt my feelings. "Well, I'm still the president of this corporation and I don't want to sell," I said as I stood and tossed a twenty on the table. "If you want out, I'll pay you off and you can spend every afternoon at La Rinconada playing golf."

I passed the cocktail lounge and heard a blender whirring and thought about having one, but that passed quickly. I headed down the sidewalk and back to the office. "I built this company up from nothing. Nothing! Hell, I had to borrow a car to get around, for Pete's sake," I said aloud as I crossed the Main Street bridge. I stopped and watched the traffic on Highway 17 headed into the Santa Cruz Mountains. I sensed somebody next to me, but didn't turn.

"Ya look like ya wanna get drunk," Jack Calloway announced. "Don't ya, Grady?"

"I've had better days, Jack. But this isn't worth drinking over. Not even close." For the next few minutes I told Jack about the offer Calvin and Coleman received and how ungrateful I thought they were. He listened, which is what one drunk does for another, listen. No judgment, no offer of a solution unless asked. Just listening.

When I finished, Jack said, "You're right. This ain't worth drinking over." We stood and watched traffic for a few more minutes, when Jack said, "I got the files from Maddox. Let's go take a look?"

Jack was sorting the contents from a file box on the credenza behind my desk. My boys stopped and looked in at me. I got up and slowly closed the door in their faces. "That seemed harsh, Grady," Jack whispered.

"I just don't care to see them right now, Jack." The thought occurred to me that I should listen to what I told Byron years ago. *Don't do something permanently stupid for something you're temporarily upset with.*

Jack was droning on about Double B, Larry Dolan, and Maurice Buck, but I was distracted. The thought occurred to me, and I was surprised I hadn't thought of it sooner, that in San Francisco, a guy named Jitters got murdered. I had taken that at face value. But what was Jitters' real name? Those in the camp called him Jitters and that was that. He's probably buried in an unmarked pauper's grave. Who was Jitters? And was Maurice's murder as cut and dry as it seemed? It was certainly a cast of characters. Characters? Disguises, shoe lifts that caused a limp, wigs. "Jesus Christ!" I screamed causing Calloway to jump.

"What the hell are you talking about, Grady?"

"Hear me out on this, Jack," I said pacing back and forth. "What if the murderer changes disguises? Limps in one camp, wears a blond wig and glasses in another. Stays for a few days and moves on and comes back as somebody else a week or so later."

"Good theory, Grady. But who is it? And what does that have to do with the Assistant DA's kid brother getting it in Fresno?" I was silently trying to put two and two together and it just wasn't adding up.

Billups and Dolan were positively recognized through papers and identification documents they carried. Plus, I couldn't deny the fact that I personally knew them. I wasn't so sure about Jitters and Buck, though. I removed several photographs from the wall above the credenza. Calloway stepped back and asked, "Time for a story board, Grady?"

I nodded and opened a file drawer and removed Double B's map of California. It was severely creased from being folded so long and I was careful not to tear it. Jack held one end and I tacked up the other. We stood on the other side of my desk staring at the map. "Now what, Grady?"

I shrugged my shoulders and let out a sigh, "I haven't got the foggiest idea."

"Take a look at who the players are and the locations we're certain they were in for starters," Jack suggested. I listed the dead people on a legal pad: Jitters, Bob Billups, Larry Dolan, and Maurice Buck. I showed the list to Jack and he asked, "What about Chester Abernathy?" I added his name to the list. "Now," Jack said, "Let's match those names with locations we know they were in. Start with that Jitters guy." I wrote down Tacoma, Sacramento and San Francisco. "Tacoma? Where did that come from?" I told Jack that Davy Holcomb said Jitters was in Tacoma just before he arrived in Frisco. "So we gotta find out if there were any hobo killings in and around Tacoma during that time period. Do you remember the date, Grady?"

I told him I could get close. Thinking about that time caused a quake to course through me and reminded me of the hurt to Janey and Calvin. *I shouldn't have shut the door in my sons' faces.* I told Jack to hold on a second and left the office. A few moments later I returned with Calvin and Coleman.

"I wanted to let you boys know what Uncle Jack and I are working on," I announced, pointing at the dead-end files spread across the credenza and the map tacked to the wall. The boys seemed genuinely interested, but then again, I couldn't be sure.

"That looks interesting, Dad. What can we do?" Calvin asked. I didn't expect that and hemmed and hawed for a few seconds, and then said, "I don't think there is too much for you to do except maybe listen to our theories and offer advice, and I have Geno chasing down some information."

They both nodded and Coleman said, "Tell us what you've got."

I was finishing up about Jitters being in Tacoma and Frisco, when Calvin said, "Hold on," and left and came back with a framed chalk board on wheels.

"Okay, so this saga begins in Tacoma, right?" He printed "Tacoma" at the top of the board. "Now where, Frisco?" he asked. I told him to put Sacramento also. I wasn't sure if Jitters had been in Sac or not. I thought I heard that he had.

"What next, Dad?" Calvin asked.

"I worked the day for a plumber, then hopped a freight to Sacramento." My sons looked at me with shock. I just hunched my shoulders in a fashion that implied, "What're ya gonna do?" I continued, "After a couple of days in Sac, I got off in San Jose and the next day I went into the quarry camp in Los Gatos looking for Double B…"

Coleman put up his hand and said, "Lets stop a second and go back to San Francisco. Who else in this cast of characters was in San Fran?"

I ticked off on my fingers, "Me, Double B, and Holcomb. Jitters had caught the west bound already. Simultaneously my boys said, "What's the west bound?" They nodded when I explained. Coleman moved over to the map and stared.

"Do you suppose this map is a legend to the hobo killings?"

"That's Double B's map. It just shows where jungles are," I said matter-of-factly.

Calloway tripped over himself getting to one of the files. "Shit, it's amazing how much ya forget in thirty years. The booze don't help either," he said thumbing through folders. "Ah. Here it is. I put out a teletype to agencies throughout the state with the same MO as Jitters and Double B. Double B was the second one we had in Los Gatos. Fourteen agencies responded that they'd had the same stabbing and burning scene." He carried the notes from the agencies to the map and counted off the locations. "These are all cities that Double B had been in, if that's what those marks mean," Calloway whispered.

"What are you saying, Jack? That Bob Billups is the hobo murderer?"

He told me he couldn't rule it out. I stood up and said, "It can't be, men. Then did Billups kill himself?"

"Could be a copycat or revenge," Calvin offered. "Somebody knew he was the killer and gave him what for as payback."

"There is no way in hell Double B is the murderer. I knew him. No way in hell."

"How long did you know him, Grady?" Jack asked. I felt hangdog when I answered, "A month, a month and a half." I looked at the three of them and saw skepticism on their faces.

"It's getting late. I'm gonna pack it in," Calloway announced.

Calvin and Coleman got up to leave and I asked them to stay. As Jack shut the door, I said, "Look boys, I don't mean to be hard-nosed on the offer and I meant what I said; I'll pay you out. Can you please think about it some more though?" We did a three-way hug and they left.

"The Mosley brothers were born in Iowa. So was their step-brother, Chester Abernathy," Geno told me two days later, "Seems the family had a trucking company that hit the skids."

"How did you get this info so fast, Geno?" He grinned and replied, "My charm, Grady. I sweet-talked a clerk in the records office of Clayton County, Iowa and she sent all she had over the Magnavox

Telecopier. She even sent a news article about the demise of Mosley and Sons Trucking."

Clayton County, Iowa sounded familiar to me, but I couldn't figure why. I took Geno's file and retreated to my office. The map was still tacked to the wall and the chalkboard was at an angle from my desk. Neat stacks of file folders sat atop the credenza and a legal pad and ballpoint pen were on my desk blotter. I laid the Mosley file down. My instruments at the ready, and all I did was stare at the chalkboard. I picked up a piece of chalk and wrote, *Clayton Co. Iowa* and *Mosley x's 2* and *Abernathy*.

I opened the Mosley file and saw a photocopy of an article from *The Telegraph Herald*, Dubuque's daily newspaper. It was dated from December 1933. The headline said: TRUCKING PATRIARCH TAKES HIS LIFE. It read:

> "Elmer Mosley, 58, of Clayton County committed suicide last Saturday. Mr. Mosley was despondent because of a downturn in his trucking company due to a lawsuit. An insurance company, The Cedar Valley Indemnity, sued Mosley and Sons Trucking Company on behalf of numerous families of victims killed or hurt when one of the Mosley trucks misjudged a sweeping turn and went off the road into an encampment of vagrants, killing or injuring dozens in April of 1932. Mr. Robert Billups from Cedar Valley Indemnity had no comment. Mr. Mosley is survived..."

I looked at the name, Robert Billups, but it just blurred. Robert Billups. Bob Billups, holy cow! Double B from Clayton County Iowa, an insurance man. No denying the fact that the Mosleys and Billups are linked. I was beginning to descend into a malaise that had me thinking Double B could be the hobo killer.

Reed Mosley's office had a funky odor, a mix of Old Spice aftershave and mothballs that was hard to get used to. Mosley was cordial, even gracious, but that didn't last beyond our handshake, and when I told him how sorry I was about his brother, his eyes narrowed.

"What can I do for you, Mr. Prescott?"

"My investigation company is looking into dead-end files, cases that are open but unsolved…"

"I know what a dead end file is," he interrupted. "Get to the point, please, Mr. Prescott."

"The dead files just got a spark of life, Mr. Mosley." He asked what I meant and I continued. "Your brother was killed in the same way as those in the dead file, so it has now become an open case again."

"I don't understand how a murder in Fresno decades after the last killing can spur an investigation. Don't you have anything better to do with your time?" I gave him my line about nothing takes priority over murder, but he cut me off with, "Is there anything else?"

Anything else? This buzzard has given me nothing. I knew what I said next was gonna get me tossed, "Mr. Mosley, I'd like permission to look at your files on the hobo murders, going back to say, 1945."

"We don't have any files on any hobo murders."

"Why is that? This office is the ultimate police authority in the county and the District Attorney is supposed to prosecute criminals. But then, you know that."

Mosley stood, walked to the door and opened it. "There wasn't enough evidence and no suspect to convict. Have a good day."

"Not enough evidence? The same type of hunting knife was used in almost all of the killings and the same brand of lighter fluid was used to burn the victims." He shut the door on me and I stood on the other side and thought that clearly this office was hiding something.

Two bulky men in suits with stern faces appeared from behind a door next to Mosley's office. "I'm leaving, fellas. No need for force." One of the goons looked like the bouncer with the body builder's physique from the Red Rose Garden. Why the show of muscle?

On the ground floor, the elevator door opened and I ran smack dab into Davy Holcomb. He eyed me nervously. It was like when you see somebody you know, but way out of their element.

"What's up, Davy?" I asked him.

He stammered and said, "Getting a record from the clerk."

"That's in the building on the other side of the fountain," I told him pointing outside. He looked up at the directory on the wall next to the elevator and said, "Oh, yeah, my mistake." I held the door for him and watched him walk across the courtyard and enter the records office. I waited behind a column. Sure enough, a few moments later, Holcomb scurried back to the DA's office and went in. Strange, I thought. What did this ass-bite have to do with the DA?

Maybe it's time to have Geno do a little look-see into Davy Holcomb, I said aloud as I pulled out of the parking lot.

"What did you expect to learn from Mosley?" Calloway wanted to know.

"Can't be certain, Jack. Maybe looking for low hanging fruit," I whispered. "One thing I didn't expect to see was Holcomb."

Jack sighed and said, "That son of a bitch keeps showing up, doesn't he?"

I suggested we do a link analysis with Holcomb as the pivot. I erased the chalkboard and wrote Holcomb's name in the center with lines radiating out from it. The first line was SF and Jitters. From that I wrote Spokane and Jitters with a question mark. Jack told me that the Jitters and Spokane connection was a dead-end. Suddenly it was becoming clear to me, but I didn't say anything. The line for Los Gatos had Billups, a John Doe, Maurice Buck and gypsies, plus All Bay and frog legs, and the dog scam. San Jose had Red Rose Garden, Buck and All Bay and DA. Jack took the chalk from me and circled the locations of murders where Holcomb was present. It became clear to him too.

"What about the guy with disguises? Where does he fit?" Jack asked. I just shook my head.

"There is nothing to put Holcomb at the warehouse fire or anything to do with the costumes," I offered.

"Don't let that stop you from nudging Holcomb, Grady. He's involved up to his neck," Calloway said as he tossed a piece of chalk into the air several times.

"You may be right, Jack. Do we get Maddox involved or wait?" Jack rubbed his chin, leaving a dusting of chalk. I motioned with a wiping gesture and he put the chalk in the tray and used his hankie to wipe off his face.

"I say we wait, Grady. Let's see if we can find out more on Holcomb. Is Geno working today?"

Two days later Geno was in my office with me and Jack Calloway.

"This bird is kinda interesting," Geno announced. "For years he's kept rooms in towns up and down the west coast. Until recently, he's never worked."

"And now he works as a truck driver for All Bay Seafood Company," I said.

"That's right," Geno said as he straightened the papers in his file. I sensed I was taking his thunder, so I sat back and listened. He told us that Holcomb lived on Bayview at the Abbey Inn here in Los Gatos. He had no record or warrants. I was wondering how this "bird was kinda interesting." I felt he was in it up to his eyeballs, but I wasn't prepared for what I was about to hear.

"According to tax and census records he was born in Mercer County, Pennsylvania and moved as a kid with his parents to none other than Clayton County, Iowa," Geno said with dramatic flair. I damn near fell off my chair. "That's right, Grady. The Mosley's, Abernathy, Billups and Holcomb are all transplants from the same county in Iowa."

"This was going in one direction and now we've done a U-turn, a right turn and a left turn in one motion. Jesus, I love this shit. Now what?" Calloway asked sitting forward and clapping his hands once.

I asked Geno if he got this info from his source in the Clayton County records office. He told me he did.

"Send her a nice flower arrangement, Geno. She deserves it." I made a mental note to have Geno receive a bonus in his next pay envelope; he deserved it, too.

I looked at Geno's file and matched the places where Holcomb lived with the marks on Double B's map; all were in proximity to the marks, never more than a mile from his apartment to the jungles. Jack nodded his head as he looked over my shoulder.

"Holcomb is the killer, Grady. I just knew it."

"Jack, last week you had Billups as the killer."

He held his hands out to his side and said, "Holcomb is the only one we can place at every scene and he's the only one we can talk to."

The thought that kept swirling around in my head was that the Mosley brothers needed to be talked to, also. That was gonna be tricky. Maybe Garnett Maddox had some insight.

"Jack, we need to meet with Garnett, the sooner the better."

At first I thought Garnett Maddox was just tolerating me and Jack. Let the old fogeys play cops again, but I could see his interest increase.

"We don't have a lot of resources to throw at these, what shall we call them?"

"Cold case files." Jack said.

"Ok," Maddox replied. "Jack, you know your way around the records room and I'll grease it with the brass. Besides, what takes higher priority than murder?" Jack and I exchanged grins.

"You taught me that, Jack."

"You're right, Garnett, but guess who taught it to me?" he said pointing in my direction.

"If this works out, there are more cold case files. Call this a pilot program."

We laid it out for Maddox and he asked appropriate questions and added pertinent information. When I mentioned that Reed Mosley was on our list of persons of interest, Maddox blanched. "Oh, geez, I'll need to talk to my chief about that. Oh, geez. Don't talk with Mosley until you hear from me."

Maddox took on a different status at that moment. One "oh, geez," and he would have been okay; two escalated him into weenyism in my book.

26

Coleman and his wife had the family over for a barbeque. His home in Monte Sereno sat on several acres with huge lawns in the front and back. Janey and Julian made the trip from King City. I loved these events. They were something I missed from my childhood. My grandparents had barbeques, but my father always got drunk and raged. After he stormed off though, calmness settled over us. The family parties now are fun all day long, with no temper flare-ups, thank Christ.

My grandchildren played well together. Cousins are usually your first friends and these cousins were no exception. From the pool I could hear, "Marco!" then "Polo!" which made me smile. Hazel, Janey, and my daughters-in-law were preparing supper in the house. I knew my boys wanted to talk, but we didn't know how to tell Julian to go someplace else. Janey, bless her heart, asked Julian to come in and help shuck corn husks. A look of understanding came across his face as he got up and went inside. "There goes a decent man. I couldn't have picked a better man to raise you boys."

Rivulets of condensation rolled down my iced tumbler of pink lemonade and for a few seconds all we heard were the kids playing in the pool.

"Dad, we thought over what you said about taking more time to think about the offer," Calvin said. Wind was rushing through my ears and a sense of unknowing hit me. I looked to him and nodded.
"You've taught us so much about the investigation business. But more importantly, you taught us how vital family is. Coleman and I have decided that we like the way we work, too. So Prescott Investigations will remain independent."

I didn't expect tears, but they flowed like a stream.

"What's the matter with Grandpa?" I heard one of my grandkids ask.

"He's just happy," somebody from inside said. "Wrap a towel around you before coming in the house."

"You know, dad, you're right about Julian. He did raise us well, but you've given us the inspiration and courage to follow our beliefs as men," Coleman said. "It wasn't always easy to see you in the bag most days, but your sobriety is also an inspiration."

I worried about my boys not working. If they sold out they'd have too much idle time at too young an age. Hell, I'd be dead if I hadn't had a job to go to each day. I was so relieved by their decision. *My inspiration was my boys.* I'd yearned for Calvin to be proud of me again, and now I felt he was, and Coleman, too. I remember during one of my hangovers, Calvin had said to me, "Well at least you're not the mean drunk you used to be." That was the beginning of my last drunk; that afternoon I got shit-faced and when I got home, I was wobbling on my feet, waiting for Hazel to chew me out. That was the day she gave me that look. The same look Janey gave me the day she left with Calvin. I was going to lose everything again. That was then, this is now. We were still a father and son outfit and I still had Hazel. I credit Hazel with the cessation of my bad dreams. I couldn't be happier. But, I was about to find out that that happiness would be short lived.

Me and Jack were on sort of a fact-finding and surveillance operation at the Municipal Wharf in Santa Cruz. I was positioned near a ticket booth for a boat tour outfit and Jack was across the wharf standing by a chowder stand eating a shrimp cocktail. He saw me looking and raised his plastic fork and grinned. It was a chilly day for July and I thought a nice cup of Manhattan style chowder would warm me up. I jaywalked to the stand and got a cup and a pack of oyster crackers and retreated to my eyeballing spot. Seagulls ranted and raved the entire time. It was like the overcast penned them in and that pissed them off. So what did they do? They crapped on people walking along the wharf. Veterans of the wharf knew enough to stay under overhangs and awnings.

We were looking at a weatherworn wooden door between an open-air fish market and a tourist trap trinket shop. The door was the office for the Northern California Seafood Workers Union. We were hoping to get a glimpse of Simon Mosley, the head of the local. We had no idea what he looked like, but would follow anybody in a suit. An hour later a man opened the door and walked toward Jack. He wasn't in a suit, but he wore a gray herringbone sports coat, black Polo shirt and khaki pants. Jack motioned me over after the man passed. He told me a fishmonger greeted the man as Mr. M. I followed the man and Jack stayed put. I stopped at a fish cleaning station and asked a man in rubber boots if that was Mr. Mosley. He just nodded.

He stood on the fringe of a group of sightseers that were taking pictures of a pelican. I dashed into a store and bought a disposable camera. I was snapping away; one of the pelican and two of the crowd, including the man. At one point he looked right at me. Damn, he looked familiar. Then it hit me; he was the voice of reason during the one-day strike at the Lyndon, decades ago. He looked like his brother, but with a longer face.

"You don't recognize me, do you?" I asked pleasantly.

"No, I'm sorry I don't," the man said. His fingernails were manicured and his hair freshly cut.

"I was at the Lyndon Hotel in Los Gatos when the pickets showed up." He nodded and turned to walk away. "That turned out well for everybody," I said to him.

"I'm glad. That was a long time ago."

"I was sorry to hear about what happened to your brother in Fresno." His eyes squinted momentarily. "You knew Chester?" By this time Calloway was standing within earshot.

"I might have. I can't be sure. I met your *other* brother recently, though," I said. Simon Mosley just stared at me, waiting for me to say something. He eyed my camera, like he was remembering the gun I pulled when a goon tried to grab my camera. I stepped to the side and he walked away nonchalantly except that his right fist continually clenched and unclenched.

"That should get the milk curdling," Jack said. I replied that I hoped so, but that I felt edgy.

On Monday morning I was picking up the newspaper when a car pulled up to the sidewalk. The passenger window came down and a man said, "We're lost. Can you help us?" I walked to the car and unexpectedly the back door opened and a huge guy grabbed me and tossed me into the back seat next to an even bigger man. The grab was so swift I never got a look at them. The guy in the driver's seat was becoming a blur. I elbowed the guy that tossed me in the backseat in the jaw, and I gave a backhand to the goon on the other side of me. That started a whirlwind of non-stop slugs to my entire body as the car tore down my street. I curled up into a fetal position and covered my head. The pummeling stopped, I guess. I passed out.

When I woke up I was sitting in a folding chair. Silver duct tape circled my torso and legs. Briefly I thought this might be a nightmare, but that vanished when the aches started. It was very dim in the room. I could see wooden rafters and sliding doors with light creeping in. *This is like a bad B movie*, I thought to myself. I've been snatched and sit tied to a chair in an empty warehouse. I don't know how long I've been here. I had shit and pissed myself, so my guess was a long time. I remember walking to get the morning paper and being tossed into the back seat and getting thumped over and over. I heard somebody approaching from behind me, and then a cloth sack was tied over my head. A man's voice whispered in my ear through the sack, "Quit your investigations."

"Which ones?" I asked.

"Figure it out, wise-ass. We know where every member of your family lives." That's the last I heard before the knockout to the head came, putting me back in slumber land.

Seagulls squawking woke me up. I didn't think I was at the shore; what I could see of the terrain was flat and weedy. I tried to raise my head, but it hurt like a bastard to move. I could hear talking in the distance, but I stayed silent. I didn't want a beat-down again. I felt certain that another would kill me. Things were broken; ribs for sure and another fractured one could puncture a lung. My left arm was so painful, as was my right knee. In the distance a siren wailed and became more distinct as it got nearer. Then the siren stopped and running footsteps came at me. I bristled and tried to curl up. "Jesus Christ, this ain't a dead body," somebody yelled.

"He smelled dead," somebody else said. I heard the chatter of a police radio and somebody, maybe a cop, asked for an ambulance.

"What happened to you, buddy?" a firefighter asked me.

All I could manage was, "Abducted and beat up." I was aware of somebody taking my blood pressure and another person asking me to tell him if anyplace he touched hurt. I thought, *are you kidding me?*

"This must be the guy that was taken from Los Gatos," a cop announced to a gathering group of onlookers.

"Where are you from?"

I whispered, "Los Gatos," and asked, "What day is it?" I was told it was Thursday. I thought about Hazel and how scared she must be. And what about my boys? I started to cry and asked, "Is my family okay?" Nobody answered me.

I yowled and grumbled as they loaded me onto a gurney and wheeled me across uneven ground. I asked the ambulance driver where I was and she replied, "Beautiful downtown Alviso." Before the ambulance departed, the cop sat on the bench seat next to me and asked me my name and address. He told me he was notifying LGPD so they could contact my family and let them know I was alive and being transported to O'Connor Hospital.

"I'm sorry I smell so bad," I said over and over, and was told each time not to worry about it. Fluids were being dripped into me from a plastic bag hung from the ceiling of the ambulance. I looked at the needle in my arm; I wasn't even aware that the attendant had stuck me.

I could see Hazel, my sons and Jack Calloway on the porch of the emergency room ambulance entrance. They weren't allowed to come closer, so I gave them thumbs up and I heard Hazel sob.

The bottom line was four busted ribs, a broken wrist and upper arm, both on the left side, a shattered kneecap, and numerous contusions and abrasions. No head injuries except for soreness at the point of the knockout blow. The only places that didn't hurt were my fingertips and my feet. I heard my son Calvin talking angrily, "My father has been missing a week. He was brought here yesterday and we want to see him," he said as he swung the door to ICU open and let Hazel in.

"I love you honey, but please don't touch me," I begged.

She swallowed a sob and smiled knowingly. "God, I'm so glad you're alive, Grady."

A male nurse came in and said she could only stay for a few more minutes. "The doctor wants to speak with you before you leave the hospital Mrs. Prescott," he said as he left.

"I thought for sure you were dead, Grady," Jack Calloway said as he stood with Garnett Maddox by my bedside. I told him at times I'd wished I was and other times I thought I was. I gave Maddox a rundown about what I remembered; getting the paper, the car pulling up.

"It was a big Buick, maybe a Park Avenue. Four-door anyway, black or dark blue." I told them about regaining consciousness in the warehouse, the mask and being knocked out again, and finally waking up in a weed patch in Alviso. "I don't know how much time I spent in the warehouse, or how long I was in Alviso. I know it was morning when they took me, and daylight when I woke up in the warehouse and in Alviso today.

"Uh, Grady you were found yesterday," Jack announced.

"This is Friday? Jesus." Better living with painkillers, I guess.

"Can you give me anymore to go on, Grady?" Maddox asked. I told him that on the Friday before I was snatched I talked with Mosley. "God damn it, Grady. I asked you not to talk to Mosley until you heard from me."

I looked at him blankly and said, "Simon Mosley, the brother."

Maddox looked at Jack and then me, "Who is Simon Mosley?" he moaned, which by the way, made him sound whiney.

I was starting to nod off and waved my hand listlessly to Jack, a gesture that said, "Handle this for me, please." I sensed them walking to the door, and heard Jack tell Garnett that Simon was Reed's brother and a union official, then the door closed and I was out of it.

I dreamed about my grandfather; he was walking patrol on a downtown street lined with tall office buildings. He was old, but walked, almost strutted, with a younger man's gait. His uniform was crisp and clean and his black shoes were shining. He came upon a pile of fresh fish at the edge of a sidewalk. Water from the gutter was sluicing over the pile in small waves.

"Are you in there, Grady?" he asked. I removed a salmon that was on top of me and said, "Hello."

"Well, hello to you, too." It was Hazel talking, not my grandfather. I was in bed and not in a stack of fish. "Are you okay, honey?" It took me a few seconds to orient myself and become fully awake.

"The narcotics make for some incredible dreams. This one was about my grandfather finding me in a fish pile."

Hazel tilted her head and said, "Pretty powerful pain killers, huh." I could see the concern on her face and knew she was thinking about my alcoholism and drugs.

I told her that I'd talked to the doctor about my drinking habit and he assured me he would start easing up on my dosage. I stared out the window and asked, "What's it like out today?"

"Very nice. It's warm with a cooling breeze once in a while. You wanna sit outside?"

I didn't have the use of my left arm and my right knee was shattered, which confined me to a wheel chair. We sat under an umbrella in a patio adjacent to the cafeteria.

"They want to move you to a rehabilitation facility," Hazel announced.

"I want to go home," I barked.

Jack Calloway was pushing my wheel chair up the handicap ramp next to the stairs of the Lyndon. I thanked the man holding the door for us. This was my first excursion after six weeks in a rehabilitation facility. I stood out like a turd in a glass of milk and the squeaking of one of the wheels just made it worse. Will Gorman, now the manager of the Lyndon after his father retired, greeted me and told me I looked good; a lousy liar, that Will. My hair felt and looked mousey, I was as pale as sifting flour and my weight had dropped twenty pounds. If anything, I looked like I was dying.

"We've been trying to locate Holcomb, and without any luck. Your boys and I did another link analysis and came to the conclusion that Davy Holcomb is up to his neck in your attack and the hobo knockoffs," Jack said around his patty melt.

I had lots of time on my hands and did some analyzing of my

own. Holcomb was too obvious. He wasn't stupid and had to know somebody would eventually line him up with each crime scene.

27

Shadow tipped his hand before we were through Merced. I kept asking him about the job in Fresno and he kept giving me bullshit answers. He planned to ice me; I just knew it.

I asked him to pull over at a truck stop. "I need to use the can," I told him. I carried my tote in with me and put my thick leather back brace on backwards, so the high part covered my belly. I'd be ready for the thrust. I didn't know what I'd do if he changed up the routine, my routine. My brothers set this ball rolling. I just know they did. Take care of the little guy, will ya? Make sure he leaves us out of it and he keeps his mouth shut. He's become a runaway train. Now it's time to really take care of him.

The car was parked in the dark along the side of the highway about two hundred yards from the truck stop and away from the canopy lighting. Shadow was not in the car.

"Come and help me pick some peppers, will ya." I heard his voice from a few feet away.

I followed the voice and thought, "Shadow doesn't know how easy it would be for me to kill him." But I'm gonna let him "kill" me and I'll be no more and then rise up like a phoenix and become somebody else. Maybe down the road pay a visit to the brothers. That's the ticket; show up for Thanksgiving. Oh, daddy, that would be rich.

Shadow sprung up from a furrow and lunged at me. When he made the thrust, I grabbed the knife and held it in place and howled like a banshee. I fell back and played possum. He squirted lighter fluid on me and tossed the match. It was really thrilling to be on this end of the crime. He sprinted to the car and I rolled around snuffing out the flames. Shadow was a piker; he ran like a scared kid.

It didn't take me long to come across a victim. Behind the truck stop I heard the retching and saw an old man on his knees. "You okay, old timer?" I asked. "You look like you could use a snort. My camp is just a short walk." The geezer had a few days growth dotting his chin. The eyes were vacant, but when I said 'snort,' he grinned showing a huge gap between his front teeth. He followed me like a hungry dog tracking a T-bone. He was close to my build and height. When I got through with him, he'd be me. The blade tip entered his soft belly to the hilt. I changed coats with him, strewing my identification papers near the body and took his papers and doused him with the fluid, putting more on his exposed face and hands than I usually do. My own burns weren't too severe, but it did hurt to move. Switching coats with the old man I eliminated was very difficult. I walked deeper into the field rather than heading for the highway. Adios Chester Abernathy.

28

I had Geno phone the All Bay Seafood Company and ask for David Holcomb.

"Tell them you're the manager of the Purity Grocery Store and David's name was drawn for seventy-five dollars' worth of groceries." The lady on the phone told Geno that Holcomb was out on disability and she wasn't sure when he would be back to work. More investigative work would be needed to locate Holcomb—pound the pavement, visit his haunts and what not.

Calvin, Coleman, and other personnel worked pay gigs, while me and Calloway and Geno hunted for Holcomb and my attacker and possibly the solving of the hobo murders. My fieldwork was still restricted; the doctor told me to do what I felt like doing. The mind and heart were willing, but the body kept me at my desk. Geno was working the streets with Calloway, which was what Geno needed—somebody to take his time with him and show him how to be an investigator. I didn't have the patience to teach Geno long ago when I should have; too much booze running through me then.

29

"Have you ever heard of Shorepost Capital?" Calloway asked me as he plopped down in a chair in my office.

I said that I hadn't heard of them. "Who are they?"

"It's the corporation that owns All Bay Seafood Company and Red Rose Garden among other properties," he announced with a snort. "And the principals are none other than Simon Mosley and that Muldoon character.

"Do you mean to tell me that the Assistant District Attorney's brother is involved with a strip club?"

"That's exactly what I'm telling you, Grady." I just stared at Jack. I *knew* this thing was connected to the brothers. What I didn't know was how Finis Muldoon and his fish company fit in.

"Any luck in finding Holcomb, Jack?"

"The guy vanished. He's dead, sick, or gone back to Iowa," Jack replied. I asked Jack to take me for a ride. "Where to," he asked, as he stood up.

"Let's take a ride around the Muldoon mansion just to see what we can see."

"Do you want me to go up the driveway, Grady?" Jack asked as we idled along Kennedy Road. I told him to drive around the corner. The house, high on a knoll, could be seen from the next street. A service driveway to the property ran from the street to another automatic gate. I told Calloway to pull over. When he stopped the car I got out.

"Where are you going?" Jack wanted to know.

I took my cane from the back seat and said, "I need some exercise. The doctor says get more exercise and that's what I'm gonna do, Jack. Care to join me?"

Pink and white oleanders lined this driveway, and judging from the surface it didn't appear that any vehicle traffic had been on it for some time. Beyond the gate, several small structures could be seen. I rattled the gate, but it didn't open. Jack was relieving himself behind an oleander and said, "What have we here? Take a look Grady."

"Take a look at what? You better be zipped up."

"There's a smaller gate that was hidden by overgrowth."

"It's unlocked." We stared at each other, then he said, "Well, now what?"

"Take a look around."

"Let's think about this Grady. We ain't the Hardy Boys, fer cryin out loud. We're a couple of old farts. What if there's a dog in there? He'll have us for lunch. You're lame and I'm too old to..."

"You packing?" I interrupted. Jack nodded.

"Then shoot the dog if he charges." Up a slight slope I could see the French doors opposite the front entrance of the house. The back lawn was freshly mown and shaded by huge oaks that dotted the yard. The house looked empty so I edged forward, and looked back over the path I'd taken to be sure of my escape route if needed. I saw Jack behind a statue of St. Patrick. He pointed to the right and signaled that someone was coming. I hobbled behind the trunk of a tree. It was Davy Holcomb! He was wearing a navy blue polo shirt, tan Bermuda's and sandals. What the Christ? He looked like the lord of the manor. It was weird to see him dressed in sports clothing rather than the hobo or trucker garb I was used to seeing him in. A female voice from inside called out to him and he went in, giving me a chance to shuffle back to the gate. Calloway's eyes were the size of dinner plates. My breathing was ragged and my heart was pounding to beat the band.

"Holy crap, I didn't expect to see him," Jack said as we inched our way down the driveway.

I was trying to figure out why Holcomb was hiding and why Muldoon was giving him shelter. And seeing him dressed in gentrified clothing gave me pause; was he the guy in disguises in the jungles? That couldn't be. I'd seen him as Holcomb with the murdered hobos.

A sheriff's patrol car pulled behind Jack's car. The deputy announced that he'd received a report of a suspicious vehicle parked in the neighborhood. I looked at Jack's sedan and said under my breath,

"The Chevy does look suspicious." Then out loud, "I guess ya gotta have a BMW or Mercedes to park on this street."

The deputy nodded and grinned. "What are you boys doing out here?"

Simultaneously we said, "Walking."

He handed Jack his ID and asked him how long he'd been on the force.

"Thirty-five years."

The deputy whistled and said, "That's longer than I've been alive." Jack gave him a scowl and I thought, *We've seen more in our careers than this wet-behind-the-ears, snot-nosed rookie could conceive.* He told us to have a nice day and gave a two-finger salute from the brim of his Smokey Bear type hat. He reported over his radio to the dispatcher, "Two elderly gentlemen out for a walk." What a pip-squeak.

For the life of me, I couldn't solve the quandary of Holcomb. I thought he was dead or gone someplace else, and now I find him living in the lap of luxury. The Mosley and Muldoon connection was evident; not so with Holcomb. Was he living with the Muldoons? Maybe he was shacking up with Noelle Muldoon, AKA Ruby Skye. It's not like he didn't go for young chicks. I was thinking of the young gypsy girl, Malina, Rye's daughter. I came to the conclusion that more surveillance was necessary.

Just after dark I labored up the Muldoon's service driveway with a partial moon as my only means of illumination. The gate squeaked when I swung it open. I shut it and went behind some bushes. In a whisper I said, "I'm getting too old for this shit." Hell, I was too old twenty years ago. Every sound was heightened in the dark. A large bird flapped its wings and cawed as it soared into the night sky, scaring the crap out of me. I waited for my heart beat to settle before I went back to the gate. I should've returned to the car and gone home. I spit on the hinges and waited a few seconds and tried the gate one more time. The only sound was the scraping of the gate bottom on the soil. I went in the opposite direction from the day before. The sound of pool equipment gurgled. A kidney-shaped pool with brick decking lay in a secluded spot. A pool house, with interior lights on, sat across a lawn.

I hid behind the St. Patrick statue and looked at the main house. Lights glowed in almost every room except for a wing to the right of the living room and above the pool. On my first visit I thought this might be a bedroom area. The door from the kitchen opened and Mrs. Muldoon came onto the patio and turned on some stove burners. This was a complete outdoor kitchen—stove and oven, sink, refrigerator and cupboards. She opened the fridge and removed a tall pitcher with a clear liquid sloshing up the sides. She put a Martini glass on the counter and poured herself one. My mouth started to water when she speared two pimento-stuffed green olives and dropped them into the drink.

Out of the corner of my eye I saw a flash from another room; a huge television screen flickered to life. Mrs. Muldoon stuck her head in the door and said, "Do you want a refill?" A man came to the door and gave her his glass. He stood in shadows, which concealed his identity. She poured him a drink and he went back to the television set. Mrs. Muldoon set some pots on the stovetop and started chopping something. I left the safety of St. Patrick and crept over closer to the television room. From behind a potted plant with a trellis I saw Finis Muldoon ease into an overstuffed chair. There was no sign of Holcomb.

I felt movement around my bad leg, which frightened me tremendously. An orange cat nuzzled and meowed.

"Here, kitty, kitty," Mrs. Muldoon cooed, "Here Kittyboo, time to eat." She was walking right at me. I nudged the cat and she scampered away. "There you are," she said as she walked back to the house with Kittyboo following.

Whatever the Muldoon woman was cooking smelled wonderful, but I couldn't get the stuffed olives out of my head. *Knock it off, Prescott. You got a job to do. Quit thinking about boozy things.*

A doorbell sounded and Mrs. Muldoon went in the French doors and opened the front entry. I scooted back to St. Patty and saw Holcomb standing in the hall. He was trying to give Mrs. Muldoon a hug. She pushed him away, looked around the corner toward the TV room, then hurried into Holcomb's arms for a long kiss. What the Christ?

Back at the trellis, I saw Muldoon acknowledge Holcomb and wave him to a chair. Ardis Muldoon brought him a rocks glass with an amber liquid and ice. She came back outside and set three places at a wooden antique kitchen table. I thought if she goes inside, I'll make my retreat. But no, she called the men to come and eat. It was a pleasant scene—three friends sharing a meal. The only anomaly was Ardis and Davy playing footsies under the table. Wine was poured freely and the conversation got louder, but not loud enough to understand. I heard words that might have been seafood, rose garden and delivery.

Ardis got up to clear the table. When she passed behind her husband's chair she ruffled his hair and made a covert kissing gesture to Davy. What a two-timer. They all took part in clearing and when they got inside, I headed for the gate.

As I drove away, the only thing I knew for sure was that the Muldoon woman and Davy Holcomb played kissy face. "Not worth the risk, that's for sure," I said out loud. I wondered where Holcomb stayed. Possibly in the pool house. I thought about what to do next. Maybe visit Mrs. Muldoon and do a "follow up" about Noelle. Another scenario was to confront Davy. "Just go up and knock on the pool house door. Yeah, that's real smart." I decided to brainstorm with Jack Calloway.

When I told Jack about Holcomb and Ardis he replied, "Who is this guy? He pretends to be a hobo, he's at or around every murder scene, and he knows the Mosley brothers and has a romantic involvement with Finis Muldoon's wife."

"I wonder if he saw Chester Abernathy after they left Iowa," I asked. Jack stared at me with an odd look. "What is it, Jack, something on your mind?"

"What do we know about Abernathy?" he said. "He died in Fresno. Is that where he lived?" Simultaneously we said, "Geno!"

"This Abernathy character is mysterious," Geno explained two days later. "After his stepfather kills himself, Chester vanishes and surfaces in Fresno years later, dead in a field. He's got no criminal record and was a teamster." The three of us say nothing and look at one another. "His high school yearbook says he was in the drama club and Future Farmers of America and gymnastics. No other team sports or other activities. Maybe what I'll do is work backwards from Fresno," Geno announced.

"That's a great idea, Geno. Good thinking," I told him enthusiastically. Calloway winked at Geno, who left with a huge grin across his lips.

"I'm going to call the coroner's office in Fresno to find out the disposition of the remains of Chester Abernathy," I told Jack.

"Are you a relative of the decedent?" A clerk from the coroner's office asked over the phone. I explained that I was an investigator from an insurance company.

"Was Mr. Abernathy a resident of the Fresno area?" He said there was no record of his residence in the county.

"Was he positively identified?" He told me that identification was done electronically. "How does that work?"

"A photo of the deceased was wired to his closest relative, and he did the identifying. "It was a horrible picture, I can tell you that. The face was a glob of charred flesh. I asked the relative how he could be so sure, and he said the gap between the two front teeth."

"Can you tell me who the relative was?" He said his name was Reed Mosley.

"Did Mosley claim the body?"

"No. He sent a check for the cremation. And that, as they say, is that. Is there anything else?" I thanked the clerk and hung up. This whole thing stunk to high heaven, and I didn't know why. My cop instinct, I guess. *Something's wrong*, I thought.

Geno wasn't having any luck doing a reverse investigation. "He got snuffed in Fresno, that's all we know, Grady. We don't know where he lived. I gotta assume he lived in Clayton County, Iowa. But there aren't any records of him recently. The last is in 1933 when he was eighteen. He evaporated and reappeared in Fresno forty some-odd years later."

What have you been up to, Chester? You can't be gone for that much time, I said to myself. Maybe he was in jail. But he had no criminal record. Was he in the booby hatch? That's a good possibility. Maybe he went nuts when his father died. I'll ask Geno to check the asylums in Iowa. That's the best lead we've had in some time. If that doesn't pan out, I gotta confront Reed Mosley.

"Why go to Mosley?" Jack asked me after I told him my plan. "Confront Holcomb; we know there is a connection, right? That's who we should be talking to."

"That's a fantastic idea, Jack. That can do a couple of things. We can find out why he's hiding and if he knows where Abernathy has been for over forty years."

"How're we going to get to Holcomb, Grady?"

"Through Ardis Muldoon. I don't know what tactic I'm going to use, but she is the key."

30

Shadow was difficult to find, that's for sure. He'd disappeared right after he thought he'd offed me. But I knew I could find the son-of-a-bitch. Every day I dressed in a three-piece suit and hung around outside the DA's office. And then in the afternoon, I'd change into less fancy-shmancy togs in the toilet of the bus depot and ride to Santa Cruz and stand around the wharf. I walked past my union ass-bite brother and he didn't recognize me; I knew he wouldn't. I even gave a vigorous kiff while we had a banal conversation about the Big Dipper roller coaster ride on the Boardwalk, as he slurped a shrimp cocktail while I had fried clams. Man, that was a rush. Anyhow, mornings in a suit and afternoons in fishing garb. No Shadow. Then, one morning I spot the guy that owns the fish company coming out of attorney brother's office. He's with a slender guy that appeared to be the same stature as Shadow. The guy wore a Giants' baseball cap low on his brow and dark glasses. His face was tan; it looked like he'd been on vacation. My instinct said this was Shadow, and he was gonna get deflated soon. I could hardly wait; it had been such a long time. My palms itched and my pulse raced. It was kinda the same feeling I had when Shadow took me to be with the beautiful gypsy girl. She was the only person that showed me any tenderness and I still think of her. When she danced, she always winked at me, and that got me on a jag and I'd drop a sawbuck in the basket.

31

I tried to keep pace with Ardis Muldoon while she window-shopped the corridors of Valley Fair Mall. If something caught her eye, she'd enter the store. When I'm with Hazel while she shops, my tolerance is tested and I spend most of the spree sitting on benches outside stores she's in. This felt the same.

From my seat I saw Ardis through a plate glass window at the counter of a boutique. She walked out holding two large decorative sacks with handles. She headed towards me, and I got up and said, "Well, hello, Mrs. Muldoon. It's Grady Prescott, how nice to see you."

"Oh, yes, Mr. Prescott. I remember you."

It was awkward, so I said, "Well, stay well. Oh, by the way, how are things with Noelle?"

Her cheeks reddened and she stammered momentarily, but recovered and said, "She has moved to Las Vegas."

"Really, what is she doing there?" She looked me square on and replied, "She's a showgirl in the Follies Review at the Stardust."

"And how is Mr. Muldoon? I met him the last time I saw you at your house, you know."

"I saw that conversation. Finis came in the house fuming," she said with a smirk.

"I didn't mean to upset him; I'm sorry."

"Oh, you meant to upset him, Mr. Prescott. He's not used to having people get in his face. But when you bark at people long enough, eventually somebody's going to bark back; that's what happens when you become consumed with business," she said with a shrug. "Are you limping?"

I related my abduction and beat down. She told me how dreadful that had to be.

"Can I buy you a cup of coffee?" I asked. She gave a wide stare and shifted her weight from foot to foot.

"I guess that would be okay."

We sat in a booth in Stickney's sipping coffee, and I said, "You look different, Mrs. Muldoon. Younger, you look younger. What's your secret?" It'd been a long, long time since I flirted, and it felt strange, but this was work and Hazel would understand, I thought.

"Oh, knock it off. I'm just an old broad." A crude comment like that from her shocked me, but I didn't let it show.

"Mrs. Muldoon, you are anything but a broad, and no matter how old you are, you carry it well. Mr. Muldoon is a lucky fellow."

Her face shrugged and she sipped her coffee. She looked out the window and said, "Oh, my driver is here." I followed her gaze and stared into the face of Davy Holcomb. The reflected sunlight seemed to block his view into the restaurant. He was wearing a ball cap, dark glasses and had the beginnings of a mustache.

Ardis stood, and I picked up her sacks and said, "I'll carry these for you."

Holcomb's head bobbed several times as we approached. His hands shook when I gave him the sacks, so I escalated my body language; I nodded a tad and rubbed my nose, which was a grifter's sign of recognition. To top it off, I said to Ardis, "I enjoyed this. Maybe we can do it again."

She blushed and smiled momentarily. I winked at Holcomb and walked away. My heart beat like a Buddy Rich drum solo. "If that doesn't start something, I'll be amazed," I whispered under my breath. Across the parking lot I watched them get in a dark blue four-door Buick, which, by the way looked very familiar and made my body start to ache.

Driving back to the office I reflected on what had just transpired: The Muldoon woman was approachable, and she was a nice person, not like the prim and proper lady I'd met when I did a job for her. Her husband neglects her, so she takes up with the hired help. Maybe

Holcomb isn't in hiding. He's just changed jobs and doesn't drive a truck for All Bay Seafood. He's driving for Mrs. Muldoon, among other chores. Her Buick made me wonder if Holcomb was driving the same car used in my abduction. I didn't think so. I think I would have recognized him, plus he's too crafty to be involved in something that obvious.

32

Is that fish guy's wife spending time with Shadow and that hobo has-been? I watched them while I swept up debris around the mall. Now I gotta pay a cash-hungry kid to borrow his uniform and tools to maneuver around. I tell the kid that I'm a PI and I'm on the job and what or who I'm looking for. In this case, the hungry kid is a maintenance guy for Valley Fair. I wave a twenty-dollar bill in his face and tell him to take an hour off, and he gives me his broom, dustpan and uniform shirt. It's like old times; the chameleon is back. It's kind of a laugh, though; when I was drifting in and out of camps in costume it cost nothing.

The dame is leaving with Shadow! I gotta find out where the fish guy lives. I am certain that's where Shadow will be.

33

"Jack, I'm convinced Holcomb and Ardis Muldoon are doing the horizontal hokey-pokey."

"How can you be so sure?" he wanted to know. When I told him "cop instinct" he just nodded.

"Now what. Go to Maddox?" he asked.

"With what—that Holcomb and Ardis are trysting Finis? That isn't something Maddox cares about, Jack."

Jack raised his voice and exclaimed, "Garnett Maddox is giving us a chance to work on cases and we've got nothing to show."

"I know you're frustrated, Jack. I am too. But these cases are old and no one has given a shit about them, except you and me, since the late 1940s. It's now the late 70s and we are in our seventies, too." His breathing quieted and I continued, "I feel more confident now than I ever have that we will solve the hobo murders. It's just around the corner, Jack, I know it."

"Cop instinct, eh, Grady?"

I said that I thought just one part was missing. "I think it is within the fences of the Muldoon place."

I was hiding between hibiscus bushes that lined the Muldoon's main driveway, hoping to catch a glimpse of Davy Holcomb pulling out, alone. I saw Finis go to work. I saw a housekeeper walk up the drive and push in a code so the gate would open. I thought about trying to beat the gate before it closed, but looked at my cane and said to myself, *you old fool*.

I heard the scraping of the garden tool before the gardener came into view. He was hoeing weeds from the trunks of peach trees, which were missed by tractor disking. Once he had the weeds in a pile, he'd build basins around the trunks to retain water after a good hose soaking. I thought about my garden and how I missed working in it. I fell from a ladder a few years back and Hazel put the kibosh to ladder work. My boys told me to hire a full-time gardener, and I did. Now all I get to do is snip roses. I was lost in thought and almost missed the old man walking up to the gardener. In broken English the gardener asked him who he worked for, and I heard the man say, "Mr. Muldoon hired me to pull weeds and sweep the pea gravel off of the brick pathways."

"That's *my* job!" the gardener wailed.

"Well, it seems like he don't like the way you do it, so now it's my job, get it, *amigo?*"

The old man turned on his heels and headed for the house. The gardener stared at his back. He was sure-footed and wore a plaid flannel shirt, black Frisco trousers and red logger suspenders. His shoes were odd for the work he was gonna do; black oxfords. You'd think work boots would be better suited.

The afternoon sun was starting to wear me out, so I stayed in the bush line and walked down to Kennedy Road. I got in the car to head back to the office when suddenly a black and white police car zoomed up Kennedy and made a two-wheel left turn up the Muldoon's driveway. Off in the distance I heard a chorus of sirens, then another cop went by, and then a fire engine, two county sheriff's cars and finally an ambulance.

I turned down the street on the side of Muldoon's and saw the old man in red suspenders scamper away and out of sight. I raced down farther and lost track of the old coot. My first thought was to go back to the scene and tell the cops what I saw, but that idea vanished quickly. They'd want to know what I was doing in the vicinity.

At the C and J Market on San Jose Avenue I used the pay phone and called Calloway about the activity at Muldoon's.

"Yeah, I just got a call from Maddox, he's there," Jack announced.

"Is it the gardener?" I wanted to know.

There was a long pause and Jack asked, "Where are you, Grady?

Why would you ask if it was the gardener?"

Just then the man in the red suspenders walked into the market and took a bottle of Royal Crown Cola out of the cooler box. I closed the door to the phone booth except for a crack so I could hear the man's conversation. I told Jack to stop talking for a few minutes.

"What's going on?" I told him to shut up.

The old guy slapped his dime on the counter and walked to the door.

"Hey, buddy. What about the deposit?"

He grinned and said, "I'm just gonna sit on the bench out front. I'll bring it back in when I'm quenched."

"Jack, do a roll-by the C and J Market. There's an old man drinking a cola on the bench out front. I think he's got something to do with what's going on at Muldoon's."

"How do you know that, Grady? What in the hell is going on?"

"Just do it," I hissed into the phone.

True to his word, the old man returned the bottle and walked down San Jose Avenue away from town. He wasn't in a hurry, which worked for me, because my knee, the only persistent injury I had, was exploding with pain. The guy must have noted Calloway slow down when he drove past me and looked back, because he turned and I saw him mouth, "Oh shit." He made us as cops. He increased his speed and darted down a side street into a neighborhood of large up-scale houses. Jack roared down the street and stopped with a screech next to me. I said to him, "Plaid shirt, red suspenders—go! Go!"

I hobbled in the same direction and noticed that hedges or stone walls surrounded each property. This old guy could be behind any one of these walls. I heard the clang of a garbage can and headed toward the sound. An old man in a soaked-through tee shirt was tossing items into the can in front of a greenhouse. His dark hair was messed up and shiny with sweat. Startled, he looked up when he heard me.

"What do you want?" he asked in a raspy voice. When he finished his question he gave a funny sounding sniff and wiped his brow.

"I'm looking for…" I stopped when I saw his oxfords. Same as the man that approached the gardener at the Muldoon place.

He glanced at his shoes and said, "What?"

"Do they call you Maurice or Chester?" This was a long shot, but this mug's demeanor never changed.

He cocked his head and said, "Why, no. My name is Delbert."

34

God damn, son of a bitch! I should have iced that guy in Frisco. He's been a pain in the neck from day one. I thought slicing the brake lines on his car would do it, but no, he dodged that one. He's always right on my trail. I'll take care of him in due time. I need to make sure Shadow's job is complete. That Muldoon dame shows up just as I'm making my thrust into him. I didn't want to hurt her, but this is survival. I might have waited too long to see if Shadow was a goner. I heard the cop car screech to a stop, and I beat feet outta there.

Lay low for a couple of days and come out as somebody else. I hate taking the cellar door to my place. These old farmhouses, which newly rich folks clamor to buy, have unique features. This place, for instance is complete with tunnels that lead from the main house to the smoke house to the farm workers' housing and numerous out buildings. The people that live here don't know I'm living in a remote hovel on the edge of the property above the freeway. It's nothing more than a dugout, but it's home. I discovered the place quite by accident; I was walking through the fallow part of the orchard and discovered a wooden door in a mound. With some effort, I got the door open, and it was like a kid's fort. There was a crude table, a bed made of plywood and two by fours. I'd stay for a while and see what panned out. That was years ago, and I've been able to come and go as I please ever since. When there was a hobo camp at that quarry, I'd take meals and sleep there occasionally. But now this dugout is my base. I use public bathrooms for PA baths. Sometimes I bathe at Shadow's room at Abbey Inn. My extensive wardrobe is in lockers I got out of a warehouse. Over the years more lockers have been added and take up one whole wall of the dugout. When the day starts, I look over my ensembles and decide who or what I'll be that day. I even have a makeup table. My high school drama teacher taught me so much about changing appearances. She even dressed as a man one time and had me dress as a lady and we went out on the town. She gave me whiskey at a bar, and we danced. And after our evening, we went back to the school auditorium dressing room and really went to town, if ya get my drift.

Lately it's golfing attire, and I hang around my attorney brother's private golf club. At my age nobody questions me. It doesn't matter that the only time I held a golf club was when I killed cats as a kid. It was a two- iron, I believe. Fore! I know the traffic pattern in the neighborhood, so I can leave and come back unobserved, usually after dark. I can walk the tunnel to other buildings and leave from there if need be. I hate the tunnel though; wet, slimy and cold roots from vegetation growing above dangle down and always slither across my head and face when I take the tunnel, which makes my skin crawl. But I gotta take the cellar today. I put the flannel shirt over my head and carry the suspenders and white wig. The darkness in the tunnel got to me early on, so I bought boxes of votive candles and stick matches which I hide under large rocks in the tunnel along the way. I gotta stay outta sight for the time being. Shit, I can still hear sirens. They must be going up to the fish guy's place.

35

Jack parked in the driveway next to the greenhouse. He knocked on the kitchen door and a short black-haired lady in a blue print apron, possibly the cook, opened it. My knee was so sore, I stayed in the car. I heard him ask the lady if Delbert was home. In broken English she told Jack that nobody named Delbert lived there and when asked if he worked there, she also told him no. Back in the car, he said, "Who is Delbert, anyhow?" I told him I didn't know for sure.

Jack took the long way around the house, inching along slowly.

"He's watching us right now, Jack. I know it." When the orchard came into view we were surprised and Jack said, "You know, I've lived in this town all my life. I know this area was all orchards at one time, but I had no idea there was still this patch left." I asked him where this property ended. He looked around several times and said, "It butts up to the freeway." When we returned to the greenhouse, I had Jack stop again. I got out and limped to the garbage can. Inside was household garbage. I'd expected to see a flannel shirt and suspenders.

The cop at the gate wasn't going to let us go up to the house until Jack convinced him to radio Garnett Maddox. The cop motioned us up and the scene was chaotic. Emergency vehicles were parked helter-skelter and personnel were busy with the frenetic scene, racing back and forth.

Maddox met us with a grim look on his face.

"What is going on?" Jack asked.

"The Muldoon lady is going to the morgue. She was hit so hard, brain matter was oozing from her ears. Holcomb was knifed in the gut.

The gardener found them and called it in. He gave a good description of the possible attacker."

The news about Mrs. Muldoon shook me to the center of my soul; I mean, I had coffee with her two days ago. Or was it yesterday.

"Was she the target?" I asked. A war was waging in my head. Do I tell Maddox what I was doing when this incident started?

"Can't be sure, Grady. That Holcomb character is clinging to life, he might not make it."

When Jack asked if Holcomb was awake, Maddox said, "In and out. If we want to talk with him we'd better hurry."

Unfortunately, Davy Holcomb was being transported to Los Gatos Community Hospital, and the ambulance driver told us that we'd have to interview him there.

Maddox turned the crime scene investigation over to the techs and drove to the hospital to interview Holcomb and find who the attacker was. Jack and I were following so we could interview him about the hobo murders.

"You ever do a death bed interview, Jack?"

He just nodded and said, "I tried to get a confession from a guy that killed his wife when he caught her in bed with a neighbor kid and then tried to kill himself."

"Did you get the confession?"

He shook his head. "The guy told me to take a long walk off a short pier and took a last breath, ground his teeth and croaked."

Holcomb went into surgery before we could interview him. The three of us, Maddox, Calloway and me, sat sipping coffee in the hospital cafeteria.

"Did you hear what I said, Grady?" Jack asked.

"Huh? What? Sorry, what did you say?" My mind was on the front lines of the battle about revealing to Maddox what I knew.

"I wondered if you had any idea of the line of questioning we should use when Holcomb comes to." Jack and Garnett were staring at me, and Jack continued, "I know you, Grady. There's something on your mind. Spill it."

I looked from face to face and let out a sigh between pursed lips. "I was at the Muldoon place this morning doing surveillance. I wanted to see if I could confront Holcomb."

Maddox put up his hand, palm out, and asked, "Did you have anything to do with the murder?" When I told him no, he motioned me to proceed.

"I saw an old man talking to the gardener. They sort of argued. The man walked to the house."

"Describe this man," Maddox said as he looked at his wristwatch and angrily shook his head.

"No more than six feet, white hair. He was probably in his sixties or seventies. He was agile and sure-footed. He had on a plaid flannel, black pants and red suspenders." Maddox turned on his walkie-talkie and radioed the description over the police frequency.

"Your description matches the gardener's. How did you know something was going down?"

"I didn't. I sat in my car trying to cool off, when all hell starts breaking loose; cops, deputies, fire and ambulance start arriving. I pulled around the corner and saw the old man run across the road and into a field and disappear. " I waited for any questions before continuing.

"I tore over to the market and called Jack from the pay phone. And as if nothing was wrong, the man walks in and buys a soda pop, and I'm still on the phone with Jack." Maddox wanted to know the last place I saw the old man.

"On Pine Street, five or six driveways down from San Jose Avenue. I don't know the digits, but I can show you." We sat silently doing nothing. The sounds and alert tones and voices from the intercom system throughout the hospital were all we heard, except for Garnett's pencil scraping across a page of his pocket notebook. He got up and went to the bank of pay phones in the hall.

Jack said to me, "He's not showing it, but he's pissed at you."

"I know that, Jack. I think he should be pissed off at himself. A cold case that he let go of turns into a violent active case. We both have explaining to do."

"Why'd ya hold back, Grady?"

"That's a really good question. I was working the angle that Holcomb was the killer. I'm not convinced he isn't."

"I'll ask you the same question you asked me about Billups: 'Did Holcomb stab himself?'

"If Holcomb's stab wound isn't fatal, we need to take a hard look, Jack."

"What about Mrs. Muldoon? Did he clobber her? I thought they were close," he said in a devil's advocate tone.

I didn't answer his question, but made the statement, "We gotta make sure this case goes to the DA. This ain't a hobo murder, but a society lady. If the DA doesn't get on this, he's never gonna get a job practicing law anywhere. And maybe, this will be the venue to solving the hobo murders."

Jack pointed down the hall and said, "I'll betcha the guy in surgery can help us solve the hobo murders. And what do we care if the DA doesn't file. That's on him."

I felt that because we were cops, we had an obligation to make sure justice was served. But maybe I was wrong.

Eighteen hours after his surgery, Garnett, Jack and me stood at Holcomb's bedside. Fluids were dripping from tubes into his arms. Oxygen was flowing from a nosepiece. His pale face was placid until he saw us. His shoulders sagged and he took on the look of a kid caught with his hand in the cookie jar.

"Couldn't ya find younger partners," he whispered weakly to Maddox, trying to disguise his discomfort, and I don't mean because of his injuries. Once a hacker always a hacker, even with a possibly fatal stab wound.

"Nah, this is all that's available. Care to tell us who did this to you, Mr. Holcomb?"

"I never saw the guy's face. I was sweeping the pool and heard Ardis, Mrs. Muldoon, that is, scream. I turned and got it in the breadbasket. I tried to get up, but the pain was so severe, I thought my intestines were gonna spew outta me. Next thing I know Pedro, the gardener, is standing over me. He's got blood on his hands and shirtfront. Musta been from Ardis. The doctor told me she died. Her scream probably is what saved me, ya know." His breathing became labored, but settled after a few moments. "Nausea. It comes in waves."

I stepped closer to the bed and asked, "This is kinda like the hobo murders, don't you think, Davy?" Maddox shot me an angry look. I guess he didn't like being interrupted.

Holcomb contorted momentarily. If it was the soreness in his gut or a memory of past killings, I couldn't tell. My guess was the latter, based on the bags of medicine dripping into him; one of em had to be a painkiller.

His eyes narrowed and he whispered, "Those were a long time ago, Grady." He started to cough, and a nurse came in and he asked us to leave, which we did.

"God damn it, Grady. Why'd ya butt in on me?" Maddox spewed. "From now on you stay away from this investigation."

Jack chimed in, "Hold on a second, Garnett…"

"No, you hold on!" he yelled. "As a matter of fact both of you stay out of this!"

Jack's face flared up like a leprechaun's red nose on St. Patrick's Day. "All we're trying to do is help," Jack said as his voice softened a bit. Me? I was headed for the door. I wasn't gonna be talked to like that. He wants me out of this? Fine, he can do it on his own.

"What's wrong with you?" Hazel asked as I slammed the door. The noise caused the doorbell chimes to echo. She wrung her hands and paced. The worry on her face told the whole story; she was afraid I was going to drink.

Brother, I could use one, but I won't take it. Let that piss-ant Garnett get to me? Hah. I calmed myself and told Hazel, "Relax, baby. I'm not mad at you and I'm not going to drink. It's been a pisser of a day."

"I picked some nice beef steak tomatoes and onions and peppers from the garden. I thought I'd grill lamb chops. How does that sound?" Hazel asked.

Just as my wife was putting the dinner on, the phone rang. It was Coleman.

"Dad, I'm still at the office and picked up a message from that Holcomb guy. He wants to see you." I thanked Coleman and hung up. Hazel nodded and said, "I'll keep this so you can have it later."

I was hoping I wouldn't run into Maddox. I didn't spot his car in the hospital parking lot. I got a visitor pass and walked to Holcomb's room. When I walked around the screen I heard, "Can you hold on a sec? I'm changing his bandage," a nurse said curtly. I thought I could hear her say, "What next?" I stepped into the hallway and five minutes later the nurse came out and told me the coast was clear.

"Sorry about that," Holcomb wheezed. His face was still very pale and the eyes seemed sunken. I asked him what the doctor said about his prognosis. He reported, "I'm not out of the woods. The next forty-eight hours will be critical." His eyes flashed momentarily and he winced in pain. "Who'd a thought getting a new bandage would tire ya out so much?"

"What did you want to see me about, and why not Maddox?"

"I don't like Maddox, plus you know the ins and outs of being on the road." I sensed this guy didn't think I knew as much as I did.

"I don't know where to begin," he sighed.

"Start in Clayton County, Iowa, Davy." His eyes narrowed and his head seemed to hunker down deeper into his pillow as he gave me a look that asked, *You knew about Iowa?*

"That was a long time ago. I was working for a trucking outfit. We hauled for Rath Meat in those days. We drove hams and sides of bacon to warehouses to be shipped off to distribution centers. Work was slow because of the depression, so we hauled what we could."

I wanted to scream that I knew about the Mosley brothers and Chester and Billups, but I gave him his lead. "Then the old man that owned the trucking company hit the skids and lost the whole kit n' caboodle. He committed suicide; slit his wrists. We're in the middle of a depression and I'm out of a job."

"Is that when ya hit the road?"

"Pretty soon after that. The two older sons come home to clean up the old man's estate." As if anticipating my question, he said, "They were away at college. There is a stepbrother, but he's not good for anything but truck driving. Along with the will, there is a letter that asks the two older boys to take care of the younger one."

"What happened to the kid brother, I mean, where did he end up?"

His eyes shifted and he said, "I lost track of him before heading out of Iowa."

"How did you end up on the west coast?" I asked, hoping not to sound too interested in the brothers.

"We were trying to find this guy…"

"Who is *we?*" I asked.

"Huh?"

"You said 'we.' I wondered who you were with."

His cheeks flushed and he said, "I meant me, not we."

"Did you have a road stake?" Holcomb shook his head slightly.

He seemed to drift away for a few seconds and then return to the present. "I'm fading fast, Grady. I'm gonna fall asleep. Can you come back later?"

"Maddox ain't gonna like it one bit, Grady. He told you to stay away from Holcomb," Jack said into the phone.

"What am I supposed to do, tell Holcomb to quit bothering me? Call Maddox instead?"

I kept going back to what Davy said, "*We were trying to find this guy.*" Was he looking to find a job? Who did he leave Iowa with, Abernathy? But why? Maybe I'll play that hunch. Then again, Holcomb might have misspoke, maybe there wasn't anybody with him. However, my cop instinct told me he left Iowa with somebody.

"What do you really know for sure, Dad?" Calvin asked me. We were sitting in my office with Coleman and Jack going over recent developments.

"Well, son, I know Double B and Larry Dolan are dead, hobo style. And Ardis Muldoon was brained at her house. Holcomb was gutted, but is still hanging on."

"We gotta get Holcomb to spill his guts," Jack said. Our groans gave Jack a start, and then the bell went off.

"Hell, I didn't mean it like that," he moaned sheepishly. His facial contortion and embarrassment amused me, and I started to laugh uncontrollably, which was contagious and the others chimed in. It was the best laugh I'd had in a long time. I'd stop, wipe my eyes and start over again. Our faces were red and I know I was over-heated due to laughing, but needed to get back to the case at hand.

"I think you're right about Holcomb, Jack. He is the only constant we have."

"Do you still think he might be the hobo killer, Grady?"

I shook my head and said, "If his wounds were less life threatening, I'd say yes, but somebody did a job on him. Ardis screaming saved his life."

36

Would you get a load of my ass-bite brothers? They've finished their round and are changing from their golf togs and stepping into the shower room. Their suits are hanging on wooden hangers so they can don them, and go to the fish guy's wife's funeral. I placed an ice pick from The All Bay Seafood Company in the inside pocket of each brother's suit coat. I can see them in the reflection of the bathroom mirror in the men's locker room. I used the complimentary shaving materials and hair grooming products to primp. The showers here are the best I've ever been in, and the towels, oh, man, are they plush. Here they come. I wish I could stay and watch the reactions when they pull out the ice picks. My better head tells me to get going. After all, I gotta funeral to go to.

As the automatic door closed, I looked back at my brothers and wondered—which one would be first?

37

Jack and I, along with Garnett Maddox, stood under a deodar tree a few feet away from the mourners at the graveside service for Ardis Muldoon. Sprays of flowers were attached to light green tripod easels. A trio sang a laborious rendition of *Amazing Graze* followed with *Just a Closer Walk With Thee*. A late afternoon fog hung over the hills like an old lady's shawl, causing people to pull their coats tighter.

After the crowd disbursed, Maddox said, "I'm getting stonewalled by Holcomb, Grady. Would you come back to the case? I need your help." For Maddox to ask for help was a huge bitter pill for him to swallow. He didn't know that I'd met with Holcomb already. I nodded and told him I'd do my best.

Maddox and Calloway went to the after-funeral gathering at the Muldoon estate. I opted to visit Holcomb in the hospital. He was ashier than the last time I saw him, and his eye sockets seemed deeper. His head was beginning to look like a skull. Was this a sign of impending death? He asked, "Were there lots of people at the funeral?" I told him it was well attended and that the reception was at the house. He nodded and had a far off look. Was he mourning Mrs. Muldoon or contemplating his own demise?

"How are you feeling, Davy?"

He looked at me and said, "Vulnerable. I keep thinking every time that door opens, a guy is gonna come in and finish the job."

For the first time since I'd known Davy Holcomb, I felt sorry for him. To live in fear is a terrible thing.

He sighed, "Part of me wishes he'd finish the job and another says let me live so I can get right with the Lord."

This was the opening I didn't even know I was looking for. "There is always time to get right with the Lord, Davy. It's never too late. Do you want me to find the clergy?"

He shook his head and said, "He knows what I've done and will forgive me," he said pointing up. "It's the other shit I need to clear up."

My heart was beating like a scared baby bird. I was on the verge of discovery, but tried to stem my emotion. Do I ask questions or let him talk? I opted to let him talk, but he nodded off. I cleared my throat and he opened his eyes, but said nothing.

"Are you up for some questions, Davy?" He raised his hand in a gesture that seemed to say, *I suppose so.*

I decided to play my hunch. "Did Chester Abernathy attack you?"

Davy's eyes widened and bulged out so much that his head momentarily looked normal and not skull-like. Then he said, "Not likely. He died in a field in Fresno. He needed to die; he was a bad guy."

"It sounds like you knew him well."

"I knew him a long time. I can't say I knew him well, though." His eyes darted around and he sighed with submission, and said, "The Mosley brothers hired me to go with Chester to find the guy, Billups, to get revenge for their father. That's how Chester saw it. All Reed and Simon wanted was to get Chester out of their orbit," he said, and asked me to ask the nurse if he could have some juice. I reluctantly left the room. I felt when I came back he'd be asleep or maybe dead. I handed him some apple juice in a glass with a straw. He thanked me after a long sip and motioned for me to put the juice glass on his tray.

"Ya see, Chester dusted a guy, a Bo, in Des Moines and told his brothers, hoping to get an atta-boy, and all he got was an envelope with cash and a finger pointing out of town. 'Keep an eye on him', Reed says. 'We'll send you money.' Chester became like the dog that kills its first chicken; he's got the taste and the only way to stop him is to put him down, and I don't mean insulting him either."

He moved slightly, which caused him pain and a rapid intake of air. He settled into a position of comfort and continued, "I had no job, no kin, and even thought about going on the road and these guys offer me the job of keeping their stepbrother out of Iowa. It wasn't too long after Chester and I hit the road the brothers ended up in Santa Clara

County. It was after the depression and before the war. Late thirties or early forties. One is a lawyer and the other hawks fish. Chester would annoy them from time to time, just to piss them off. They'd toss him some dough and so would I, and he'd take off for a spell, only to show up again.

"How did you find Billups?" I asked.

"It took us a year or so, but we finally caught up with him in Spokane. Chester played cat and mouse with him. I wondered why he didn't just kill him and get it over. But any hunter will tell ya it's the chase, and Chester loved the chase. But, you're rushing me, Grady."

I told him I was sorry and he continued, "Abernathy carried too much stuff for a Bo. We'd get to a jungle, I'd find a room and he stayed in the camp. He felt his operation was better served by staying in the camp."

I held up my hand and said, "Sorry, Davy, but I gotta ask, what was all his stuff?"

"God damn it, Grady do you want to hear this or not? If you do, then quit interrupting me." Angrily, he told me this was a good day, because usually the narcotics seem to blur his memory. I bowed and motioned for him to continue.

"Chester was on a quest to find Billups and he wasn't going to rest until Billups was dead. He stored his stuff in the room I got and would change his appearance, and he was good at it. The only thing he excelled at in school was dramatics. He was a wizard with makeup." Davy told me about the time he was watching the gypsy ladies dance and a guy standing next to him carrying on a conversation who turned out to be Abernathy.

I was starting to get some clarity—changing appearances, limping, and possibly killing.

"Do you remember Jitters, Grady?" I told him that I did.

"You think Jitters got gored and torched?" I nodded.

"Well, sir, Jitters was Abernathy. You may ask a question at this time."

I sputtered and hemmed and hawed for several moments and said, "Who did…"

"Time's up, Grady. I don't know who the Bo was that got killed. Abernathy changed clothes with the Bo, gutted him and torched him and left the camp and the Jitters act behind. He perfected that fraud when we met Billups in Spokane. Those two would sit and drink for hours and became fast friends, Jitters-Abernathy and Double B. That was the cat and mouse game."

"Man, that makes sense, now," I said, and Davy replied, "Is that right?" The way he said it was sarcastic, and suggested a "you ain't seen nothin yet" moment.

"We end up at the camp at the quarry in Los Gatos. Then Abernathy becomes Maurice Buck."

Well, I can tell you that I pretty near fell off my chair. Holcomb is smiling because he knew I thought I had it figured out, but wasn't close to knowing the entire story.

38

This white waistcoat I'm wearing irritates my neck—too much starch in it—but still I smile and pass through the crowd of so-called mourners with a tray of glasses filled with wine. The white, a Chenin Blanc, seems to be the favorite. The pinot is not as refreshing, I guess. The group is around the pool and if you look closely you can see a faint discoloring on the bricks and grout. That makes me smile. My fake mustache and graying goatee give me an identity I haven't used in years.

It didn't take much convincing to get on with the catering crew. I gave a kid a fifty to convince the headwaiter to hire me for the day. The kid told him I was his uncle and was a good server.

I offered appetizers also; the shrimp beat out the meatballs and stuffed mushrooms two to one. I spot attorney brother and offer him a paper napkin and some shrimp. Man, I wanted to ask him if I could borrow an ice pick, but didn't. He took some, and didn't even say thank you. He moved to the number one spot on my hit parade. I carried my tray back to the kitchen and felt the vial in my pocket. The waiter tells me to work the room taking cocktail orders. I approach attorney brother and ask him if he cares for a cocktail. "Vodka on the rocks," he snaps. So far, so good. I take the vial out and hide it in my palm. The bartender hands me the cocktail and I crack the vial and pour the contents into the drink. I offer it to attorney brother and he nods. I get as close to the garden exit as I can. Two minutes later there is a commotion and people are talking excitedly.

Brother hits the ground gasping for air, grabs his chest and convulses. A doctor is kneeling over him performing CPR.

"Paramedics are on the way," somebody announces.

The doctor says, "It's no use, he's dead of a heart attack." Union brother is by his side, pleading with the doctor to do something. People are trying to get union brother away.

I start clearing glasses from the area and take them to the kitchen. I'm certain the one containing the poison is among my haul. I start rinsing and another server says that they just load the dishes and glassware into boxes and are washed at the catering company.

"I've started these, I'll finish." The other guy shrugs and walks away.

I must say, being a server has been the most fun "job" I've had lately. Mission accomplished, and I had a good time to boot.

39

A nurse came in and gave me a "you still here" look. "Time for your medication, sugar. How are you feeling this afternoon?"

Holcomb smiled briefly and said, "Can we hold off for thirty minutes or so? I'm not ready to fall asleep." She gave a "suit yourself" nod and walked out.

"Was it the same for Buck as it was for Jitters?" I wanted to know.

"It was. Chester moved from Buck to many different disguises."

"So, Davy, how do you know for sure that the guy in the field in Fresno is Chester Abernathy?" Davy said nothing and stared at the ceiling.

"Two people are dead and they were supposed to be him. What makes you think the third isn't some poor schmoe from Fresno set up to be Chester?" I asked.

"Reed Mosley identified him."

"Ah, yes. I forgot about that. Did Chester have a gap between his two front teeth?" I asked pointing to my own mouth.

"Not that I'm aware of."

I narrowed my gaze and said, "That was the positive ID; the gap in his front teeth. That's what Reed told the coroner in Fresno."

"He wore so many disguises, that I lost track of his teeth, ya know. One time, no teeth, another time buck teeth, so yeah, maybe he had a natural gap."

We were silent for a few minutes and the nurse came back. "You ready for a siesta?"

Holcomb nodded, and she put a syringe into the IV tube. "Gotta get my beauty rest," Holcomb said weakly. I asked him if I could come back tomorrow, but he was out like a light.

Jack Calloway leaned against the fender of my car. His lips were a straight line.

"What's the matter?"

"Reed Mosley had a heart attack and died at the Muldoon place. Keeled over on the bricks." I just stared at Jack.

Everything I'd thought was nothing like it seemed to be in these cases. "We better get to Maddox and set up around-the-clock protection for the Mosley families—Reed's and Simon's—and post a guard on Holcomb."

"Grady, it was a heart attack, I'm telling ya."

"Jack, I can't be certain, but I think Abernathy is alive and is the hobo killer. He could be responsible for Holcomb and Ardis. Maybe even Reed."

"Is this cop instinct again, Grady?" I relayed my conversation with Holcomb including the part about the Jitters and Buck charade put on by Abernathy.

Jack concluded, "If Abernathy pretended to be those people, then offed them, why couldn't he pull the same thing in Fresno?"

"That's exactly what I'm thinking. I was face to face with Chester at the farmhouse on Pine Street. He called himself Delbert. He's still around, Jack, and nobody is safe."

When I told Jack that I was certain Abernathy killed Bob Billups and Larry Dolan, Jack replied, "This is one bad hombre. He needs to be stopped. But shit, how do you find and eliminate a phantom? Hell, we don't even know what he really looks like. He could be that guy walking in the front door of the hospital, for crying out loud," he said, nodding to the front of the hospital.

40

Why are those two ass-bites looking at me? I'm dressed in scrubs and I belong here, or at least I look like I belong. This is too risky. I'm gonna go right out the back door and come back and visit Shadow another time. Hell, he might be dead soon and another mission accomplished. Those bastards should know they can never stop me. I've given them so many chances.

41

Before I entered Holcomb's hospital room, the nurse stopped me and said, "He's taken a downturn, so be brief, please."

He was pale and warm; he looked like my grandfather just before he died. He heard me approach and raised his brows.

"I'm glad you came, Grady," he whispered. "I got more to tell ya." I pulled a chair closer to his bedside and sat. He held out his hand and I shook it, but he didn't let go. "Simon told Chester that there was a dispatcher's job at a trucking outfit in Fresno. Reed hired me to drive him down there and kill him," he sighed as if he just had the weight of the world lifted off his shoulders. "I lured him into a pepper field and gutted him and lit him on fire."

He let go of my hand and said, "Well, there ya have it."

"Davy, you may have stabbed him and torched him, but I'm certain Chester Abernathy is still alive. He stabbed you and killed Ardis. You didn't kill anybody. You tried, but I saw him less than a mile from Muldoon's the day he knifed you."

His emotions welled up and he gasped for air. "Are you sure?"

"Yeah, and Reed Mosley died yesterday. They say from a heart attack." His eyes got wide and he started to cough. The nurse shooed me out.

Davy snored as he napped, and I hung around waiting for him to wake up. When he did it was time for a bandage change. I knew he would be tired after that, too. Quickly I asked, "Why didn't the District Attorney file any charges for Billups and Buck?"

"The DA is a patsy for Reed. He runs the show, Reed does." Davy had a coughing spell and the nurse came in and he told her to leave us alone. She harrumphed and exited. Davy labored on, "Reed knew Chester was the killer. Can you imagine if it came out the Assistant DA's little brother was a serial murderer? Man, that would upset the apple cart." Davy became very still and quiet.

Davy held out his hand again and I took it. This time it was icy cold. His breathing became erratic and bubbly. "Chester... look orchid..." Those were Davy Holcomb's last words. He thought he killed Chester, and just before he croaked he found out he hadn't. Maybe he thought he'd get redemption. The fact of the matter is, he didn't stop a killer from killing and he could have. He's just as guilty as Abernathy and they can sit at the same table in hell's dining room with my father, Sterling Prescott, for all I care.

"Orchids? What the hell does that mean?" Calloway asked as we sat in my office.

Over the next several months things fell apart for Simon Mosley and Finis Muldoon. All Bay Seafood Company was shut down due to the fact that they were involved in cyanide fishing. Divers would carry squirt bottles and squirt the poison into the coral reefs and stun the fish off the Philippines to sell to exotic fish collectors and to supply live catch fish for specialty restaurants. This practice was successful in places like Hong Kong, but in Northern California the special interest groups protested with pickets, boycotts, and lawsuits. I'm pretty sure Reed Mosley died of poisoning, possibly cyanide.

The Red Rose Garden mysteriously burned. It would be a good payoff for Finis Muldoon and Simon Mosley, but the fire investigators determined it was arson and those greedy bastards didn't get a dime from the insurance company. All of Muldoon's holdings were ruined. He was quoted in the paper as saying, "Those things can't compare to the loss of my wife." Since when did he begin to care?

Simon Mosley was embroiled in skimming funds from the union and was put in prison for six months. After his time, he moved back to Iowa and lived off his union pension.

42

Son of a bitch! Maybe I'm getting too old to keep this up. Grady is up there yapping about his piss-ant senior citizen award. I blow the raspberry and some guy starts chasing me. I had a good head start, but this son of a bitch almost got me and I didn't plan on that. Who the hell is he anyway? The idiot didn't see me duck into the creek bed; he sprinted on by and I got a good look at his face. Well, I'll be, it's the hobo kid Grady brought back from San Diego. I wonder where he's been all these years.

I tossed part of my costume and mingled with the crowd and saw this kid, a man now, sitting in the reserved section with Grady's wife. Oh, I got it, he's family. Well isn't that interesting.

My next thought was, time to start acting my age. Maybe I'll go home.

Iowa must have changed while I was out west, but in our little town everything was pretty much the same. The town square hadn't been re-landscaped, but was still very well maintained. The Civil War cannon dedicated to the Iowa Volunteers still pointed at city hall. Cars and parking stalls were more abundant. The usual trappings for gentrified folks dotted the main street—coffee houses, boutique-type stores and computer chains waiting to take in money. Bib overalls gave way to gym shorts and colorful sneakers. There were still agrarian enterprises, but hi-tech and manufacturing took over as the leading industry.

Sometimes I wonder why I left. Oh, yeah, I had a chore to do. Little did I know it would become a passion that took over my life. But in the end, it gave me a purpose, even if my ass-bite brothers never acknowledged my efforts to avenge the family.

Shadow always gave me a half a c-note every other month back in the day. I saved most of it, and had a pretty tidy sum when I came back home. Plus what I lifted off of bodies and what I burgled. He didn't know the brothers were still paying me.

Shadow told me one time that he felt sorry for me because I didn't have any friends. Is he serious? I can change disguises and maneuver in and out of parties, theaters, picnics and barbeques where everyone is my friend. No friends, hah.

I watched union brother walk out of the post office. He wore olive green Bermuda shorts, a gray Iowa sweatshirt and sandals. Sandals? Really? He held the thick legal size envelope I'd sent him three days ago from Santa Barbara. My journal. Maybe he'd finally appreciate my labors.

43

I hadn't thought about Abernathy for years. Until today, that is. I know he was the heckler in the crowd assembled to honor me as Senior Citizen of the Year. I was walking away with my family and I heard a grandfather say to his grandchild, "Honey, I remember when this was all orchards."

The child looked up and asked, "What are orchids, Gramps?"

"No, honey, *orchards,*" Gramps said.

Orchards? *Orchids?* I thought.

I drove down the dirt tractor road adjacent to the freeway and behind the orchard off of Pine Street. A mound of dirt, like a dugout sat next to the road. An old weathered door was placed in the middle of the face. I got out of the car and walked around the mound; climbed up on the top. I could see the farmhouse, and visualized where the end of the mound stopped. "Gotta be a tunnel, I said aloud."

The door was troublesome, but with more effort, it budged and finally opened. I waited for my eyes to adjust to the dark. I jumped back in terror because there was a man standing and staring at me. Damn it. It was a mirror and I was seeing my reflection. *I'm getting too old for this shit!* I lit a votive candle placed on a saucer and was stunned by what lay before me; several wardrobes lined one dirt wall and opposite was a makeup table and mirror. The clothing in the wardrobes ranged from shabby hobo attire to golfing togs. Suits and sport coats rounded out the apparel. I went several yards into the tunnel and determined it would end at Pine Street. *Man, I wished Jack was still alive.*

I think I finally got it figured out.

Several weeks later a large golden colored envelope sat in the mail pile on my desk. It was bigger than any other piece and was uneven, like something might be settled at the bottom of it. I worked my way down to it, sorting through the pile of bills, general correspondence, ads and the like, including a happy birthday postcard from Byron, still living in Hawaii.

The large envelope was postmarked from Giard, Iowa, which immediately put me on pins and needles. My hands started to tremble and my mouth was dryer than a dirt clod. I knew this had something to do with the hobo murders. I *really* missed Jack Calloway at times like this.

With a postal inspector's determination, I looked at the seal and clasp, which was covered with Scotch tape. The sides and bottom looked secure. The postage was almost six smackers. I laid the envelope in the center of my blotter and stood and looked out my window. I walked into the cubicle area where operatives were busy working on cases, computer and typewriter keyboards were clicking, phones were ringing and people were talking to one another simultaneously. I greeted my sons in their offices. All was normal at Prescott and Sons Investigations—all except for the large envelope from Iowa sitting on my blotter.

I stared at it for several minutes, picked it up and laid it down repeatedly. Finally I took my letter opener and sliced the flap. *What could it be? Nothing good,* I said to myself. *Get going, Prescott.* I laid the opener down and looked into the package. A heavy plastic wrapping surrounded a light green fabric-covered journal. I took the journal out of the plastic, noticing a large rust-colored blotch that smeared the front. Dried blood. A shiver coursed through me.

And that wasn't all. An ice pick from All Bay Sea Food and a leather sheath-bound ten-inch Schrade hunting knife were wrapped in tissue. "I'm getting too old for this shit," I said outloud for the fortieth time since seeing the envelope.

The rest of the morning I read about the hobo "eliminations." I declined lunch with my sons and read through the afternoon. I found nothing earth-shattering, except for the quantity of victims. Davy Holcomb had filled me in on some of Abernathy's deeds, but even he didn't have an inkling of the amount of people Abernathy had done in.

I closed the log, and taped to the back, was a legal sized letter envelope with my name on it.

Hello Grady,

I hope you enjoyed the reading. Every time I entered an installment in the journal I hoped one day you'd be reading it. I must say, other than Billups, eliminating my brothers was the most rewarding of my capers. You have no idea how many times I sat next to you on barstools and conversed with you. I watched you stagger home; I helped you up a few times when you tripped. When you were in the wheel chair I held the door for you. I even sat in AA meetings with you and Calloway. And you probably guessed it was me in the crowd heckling you when you got your big Senior award. I couldn't pass it up! I needed to let you know I'm still around.

Don't worry, Grady. You aren't in danger. Yeah, there was that one time in Salinas when I cut your break lines, but after that, I thought, Hell, this guy's a good guy. Got a family and all and treats his kids the way I wish I'd been treated by my old man and step-brothers. I'd rather play cat and mouse with you than do you in! If I wanted to eliminate you, I could have done so hundreds of times. As a matter of fact, I did everything I could to help you figure it out. But even a genius like you couldn't keep up with me. You could say, you became my sweet obsession, Grady! Why, we've been so close we could have been brothers! The good kind.

You know I can't stop. But I'm gonna give you a head start with a hint about my next disguise.

Goodbye, Adios, Aloha, Au Revoir, Auf Wiedersehen, Catch ya down the road.

C.A.

I sat with my eyes closed for a long time. I never knew I was so close to being killed. Even being attacked numerous times, I never thought about being murdered. And now, I get the whole story, after so many years. All the details, all the surprises, the twists and turns.... what am I going to do with this information? Man, I could use a drink. I longed for the days when Calloway and I knocked back a few trying to figure these things out.

In the mirror behind the bar I caught Coleman's reflection, peeking in the window. It had been a while since I'd sat on a barstool, but it felt pretty good. It actually felt comforting. A few minutes later Calvin entered Reggie's. *This is going to be fun*, I thought. The tall frosted glass with ice, a clear liquid and a lime wedge sat center stage. I saw Calvin eyeballing it. I picked the glass up and drained it.

"Another tonic, Grady?" the bartender asked. I shoved the glass to him and said, "Get one for my son, too." Calvin's relief was palpable. "Did you think your old man was getting pie-eyed?" Calvin just nodded.

"Don't worry. I'll let you know before I take a swig of hooch." He asked what I was doing and I told him I was thinking.

"Do you need any help, Dad?"

"Nah, I got it."

"Well, if you're sure. I'll see you later then."

Three tonic and lime drinks bloated me, so I paid the tab and walked to the Town Plaza; the post office is where the train depot used to be. Lawn and fountains cover the tracks. There is a few feet of rail left as a tribute to a by-gone era. Shit, I *am* getting too old if I remember the dog-gone by-gone era. The Lyndon Hotel had been torn down and replaced by a building full of restaurants and boutique shops.

The bench I sat on gave me a view of the depot site and the Lyndon. Tambourine music filled the air, and I glanced over to where Rye had done his knife grinding so many years ago. The music was coming from Tribewriter Jewels, a shop that sold crystals and various incense and jewelry and anything Frida Kahlo. I was thinking about Byron and how he went from being a young hobo to being retired from the Navy, with grown children. Looking at the Lyndon site made me think of grumpy Mr. Gorman, and the inferior frog legs.

But, all this nostalgia wasn't helping me figure out Abernathy. *He thinks of me as a brother*! Jesus Christ, why would he think that? Because he deemed me a worthy adversary? That son-of-a-bitch was always ahead of me. Hell, he was playing the game way before I knew I was on the other team. How can you play against someone you can't see?

He says I'm not in danger. I don't believe that for one second. He could be the old codger feeding birds on the bench across from me. He can't stop. But he *must* be stopped.

I was in the police department waiting for Garnett Maddox.

"Glad to see you, Grady," Maddox said as he shook my hand. "What can I do for you?"

He was eyeing the large envelope I was carrying. We sat across from each other at a table while I told him about receiving the journal and his eyebrows crinkled, but he said nothing.

"It's from *Iowa*," I said as if I'd solved the Black Dahlia Murder and the Lindbergh kidnapping. He shook his head.

"I think Chester Abernathy took off for *Iowa*. This book is a confession of all the murders he did."

Maddox pulled the book to him and opened the first page. He read a few paragraphs and his eyes widened and his cheeks colored slightly and he whispered, "This could solve a lot of cold case murders."

"Yeah, everything except who the killer is. All that does is give you historical facts of some names, dates and places," I replied, pointing to the journal. "The cases will never be solved completely, because we can't identify the killer, Garnett. We know it was Chester Abernathy, but who *is* Chester Abernathy? What does he look like?"

Maddox kept the book and I walked back to my office. I passed a young man in a Hawaiian shirt holding his son's hand. *Aloha!* Jesus jumped-up Christ! That's Abernathy's clue! Oh my God, *Byron*!

When I got home Hazel hissed, "What do you mean you're going to Hawaii for a few days by yourself?"

We continued conversing about my trip well into the evening. Hazel would call it a "discussion", but I'd call it a good old squabble.

Me telling her that I needed to see Byron was lame, I'll admit.

"If it's that important, call him," Hazel replied.

"You just don't understand," I whispered, pacing back and forth. To say anything about Abernathy's threat would not serve me well. As a matter of fact, Abernathy was not a name I'd ever mentioned in front of Hazel or Byron. Forget saying anything about a life and death scenario or that I'd been after this murderer since 1945. Plus, I kept hearing the spirits of Jack Calloway, Double B and Larry Dolan speaking to me; telling me to go.

The stare-down lasted a couple of minutes, but seemed like an eternity. "I *need* to see Byron, it's more important than you could ever know."

When she replied, "You're too old to go by yourself," it cut to the quick and I felt my shoulders sag. I knew it was going to sound foolish, but I said it anyway, "*So what?*"

"*So what?*" she said with her hands on her hips, "I'm going with you is what."

Later, I called Byron. He seemed almost too excited about our visit and chattered on and on. He said I must have been reading his mind because he was going to call me that night.

"Hold on a sec, Grady." He must have cupped his hand over the receiver, because in a muffled voice he asked his wife to get him a beer.

My angst ramped up when Byron said, "Your timing is perfect, Grady. Weird stuff's been going on. We'll talk when you get here."

On the flight to Hawaii I kept mulling over how to tell Byron the possible danger he was in. *Possible* changed to *urgent* and back again. Add in Byron's comment about 'weird stuff going on' and my mind was off to the races. For all I knew Abernathy was already stalking Byron. Hell, the son of a bitch could be on this plane. This would be a good time for a pull of Four Roses. But then, it was never a good time anymore; that was then, this is now.

"What did you say?" Hazel asked. I just stared blankly at her. "It sounded like you said, '*urgent danger*'."

I shook my head. I sensed Hazel staring at me. I had to fake sleep most of the way because Hazel is a smart cookie and she suspected something was fishy about this trip anyhow. I didn't want to add more fuel to the fire because she'd try and get it out of me. And believe me, brother, she could get it out of me. The less she knew the better.

Byron and his wife met us at the luggage carousel. Hawaiian music played over the loud speakers and the aroma from the beautiful leis around our necks made this feel almost like a vacation.

Byron's wife and Hazel went to get the car, while we waited for our bags.

Byron got right to it. "Grady, I swear to Christ I see Bo's from the old days every place I go. I can't put my finger on it," he said as he rocked on his heels. "Hell, just the other day I'd swear I saw Larry Dolan at the post office. It wasn't him, of course. It's just so weird."

When I didn't say anything he looked at me, and started to speak again. I put my hand up and he followed my gaze across the moving suitcases. There stood a man in a straw fedora. I thought to myself, *I got you, you bastard. If you wanna disguise yourself at this point, pal, quit wearing a hat and knock off the limp.* Goddamn, I couldn't believe I was staring right at him. I didn't know what the real Chester Abernathy looked like, but by God, I knew some of his get-ups by now. He wore a silk aloha shirt, but it could have just as easily been a blue denim work shirt; his height, posture and mannerisms were unmistakable. Maybe this was a sign the bastard was slowing down, that he was losing it a little by not bothering to come up with a new costume. Maybe Byron was gonna avoid danger after all.

What's Real and What's Not in Hobo Ashes?

A Conversation with Steve Sporleder

I'm a proud native of the great state of California, as were my parents. I was born in Los Gatos and have lived there my entire life, just as my parents did. *Hobo Ashes* brings into play many actual settings, and many composites of settings up and down the Golden State. For instance, Golden Gate Park and the football field, Kezar Stadium are real and still stand today. I don't know if there were hobo camps in the park, but I needed a setting out of Santa Clara County and this site worked. The camp along the Delta was invented by me and is fictional.

Santa Cruz and Monterey County locations were as factual as I could make them. The Beach and Boardwalk are vivid memories from my life. I can remember every zing, whistle and click-clack from there so intensely that I yearned for a sack of fresh popcorn and a candy apple. Casa del Rey was used as a military hospital during World War II and was converted back to a hotel. A parking lot occupies the spot today. The bowling alley mentioned still is operating.

The Garden Grill and Pub in Salinas was not real. The Powder Horn in Greenfield, however, was real. The Corner Club in King City was actually Nina's Cantina and has been gone many years. The building still stands. The City Café also existed. Relieze Canyon is an actual location and is my geologist friend, Bill Cotton's sanctuary. I don't know if a jungle existed along the Salinas River in King City, but it seemed like a logical stopping point for those hoboing north or south along the central coast.

San Diego, Coronado and Tijuana are real; my storyline in those areas was written after doing research about them. My Great-grandfather operated the water taxi from the Navy base to the mainland and from Coronado to the mainland. I don't know if gypsies camped on the docks or if there were hobo jungles in the foothills above San Diego. Big Basin State Park and the campsite, Huckleberry, is real.

Enough of the travelogue; I want to talk about Santa Clara County and specifically about Los Gatos locations. The quarry along the creek existed and there was a hobo jungle there. Los Gatos' Oak Meadow Park and Santa Clara County Vasona Lake and Park occupy that area. I don't know if gypsies camped near the Southern Pacific depot or not. I do remember seeing these colorful characters parked along the tracks between Sterling Lumber and Meadow Gold Creamery, near Elm Street. Melvyn's Mortuary was an actual funeral parlor on West Main Street and Tait.

The Lyndon Hotel was real and sat on what is now Lyndon Plaza on Santa Cruz Avenue and Main Street. I've used this hotel in all my stories, but called it the El Gato Hotel. I can't say why; I'm glad I finally gave this landmark its proper name. Shame on me!

The fire department was not presented in the most flattering way; they were actually an efficient department and Los Gatans should be proud of them.

Crider's Department Store, the Park Café, the Smoke Shop, Reggie's, The New Yorker, which became The Black Watch, Duncan's Pharmacy, Spotswood's Hospital and the La Hacienda Inn were authentic establishments in Los Gatos. The buildings still stand, but the occupants have changed. Abbey Inn is long gone, but Fairview Plaza is one of the oldest established neighborhoods in Los Gatos.

Bert's Country Inn, I was told, was an actual road house that existed between Saratoga and Santa Clara near Prospect Road and Saratoga Avenue. Hoffler's was an actual restaurant in downtown San Jose. Austin Corners was a spot between Saratoga and Los Gatos. Hazel Kane's shop on Big Basin way in Saratoga was made up. The theater described was once there. Melody Ranchland also existed.

The C & J Market was located on San Jose Avenue, near Caldwell Avenue, which is now Los Gatos Boulevard.

Almost all of the streets in Los Gatos mentioned are real; GlenRidge, College Avenue, Walnut and those previously mentioned.

All characters in *Hobo Ashes* are fictional except for, Gene, Lou,

Norman O'Conner and Mr. Nolan. Gene is Gene Rugani, who was a local businessman and instrumental in the growth of downtown Los Gatos. Lou is my father, Lou Sporleder, a Shell Oil dealer. Norman O'Conner was an insurance man and a good friend to my father. Mr. Nolan was the druggist that operated the Northgate Drugs next door to my father's filling station.

Any similarities to actual people, other than those already mentioned are purely coincidental and unintentional.

Steve Sporleder
2013

Conversations with Clete
and
Carrying Kerrie

Two Short Stories

Steve Sporleder

Conversations with Clete

Steve Sporleder

Chapter One

He wasn't just any soldier, not by a long stretch; he was a World War II German soldier in combat uniform. It would have been strange to see a German soldier looking in the window of a ranch-style home in this small Northern California town in the middle of the night, almost seventy years after VE Day, *even if he were visible.*

His dark green coal-scuttle helmet sat properly on his head of red hair. His slate gray tunic was neatly pressed and the insignia of a gunner adorned the collar. The trousers, also gray, were tucked into shiny black calf jackboots. He had no weapon, but he moved with the stealth of a sniper, edging from the window and making his way to the backyard, careful to "let sleeping dogs lie" just in case any were around. Like a burglar casing the place, he peered into another window. He wasn't a burglar, but he would've made a good one; *nobody could see him.*

Chapter Two

I took a big swig of cranberry juice, straight from the plastic bottle, to break up the gravel in my mouth. Each morning it's the same thing. My mouth hangs open when I sleep and I'm told that I snore. Sometimes I wake up gasping for air. That bothers me, but I sit on the side of the bed and calm my breathing down and I usually fall right back to sleep. I live alone, so I'm not hurting anybody or keeping anybody awake. But when I travel, it's different. My buddies don't want to room with me, but I'm fine with that. Meg, my steady gal of over twenty years, calls me on it regularly. She should talk! Anyhow we don't spend nights together often, and when we travel we stay in suites. She's in the big bed, and I'm on the couch, and I'm fine with that, too. She has an ample supply of earplugs, which I replenish regularly. The first time I bought them for her, the kid at the pharmacy told me that they were the type he wore at rock concerts. That convinced me they'd be just fine.

My name is Cletus Rossiter. Meg and I are just left of our mid sixties. My brown hair is going gray and I have a paunch. I don't exercise enough and probably drink too much bourbon. I retired almost ten years ago and I have a comfortable life and can do pretty much what I want. I have grown children, a boy and a girl, from a marriage that ended in divorce after twenty years, and four beautiful grandchildren. Meg has a son from her one marriage, which also ended in divorce.

Meg and I have been on vacations to Hawaii, the east coast, Chicago, and up and down California. Last year we went to Italy and France, the trip of a lifetime.

Because of language difficulties, we weren't real sure if our accommodations would be met when we made the reservations with the hotels in Italy and France. We wanted a suite at each property. But the places were fantastic and our rooms made to order. The staff couldn't have been better. The Euro to U.S. dollar, on the other hand, was like getting kicked in the shins.

I'm a travel planner. That's not my occupation. It's what I like doing prior to going someplace we've never been. I go to the bookstore and get books about our destination and visit the AAA office for maps and guides.

After gathering info for our next trip, to Cape Cod, I stopped at Meg's to set our plans in motion.

"I bought something for you," she said after we greeted each other. She is always buying gifts, usually through the mail or on the computer. Her short brown hair accentuates her angular features and her brown eyes flash when she is happy *and* when she is mad. Thankfully she doesn't get mad often.

She handed me a cardboard box about the size of a Kleenex box. It was very light and the contents rattled slightly when I shook it.

I looked at her and said, "What have you got for me now?"

"Open it and see," she said with lightness in her voice.

"I'll open it when I get home. I want to show you the books I bought."

"Please, Clete. I want you to open it now," she said with a slight whine.

I used a paring knife to cut the package open. The top of the container inside read, "*Snore no More Kit.*"

I looked at Meg, waiting for her to laugh, but she looked like she was waiting for a thank-you from me. I opened the lid and saw a mouth piece inside, just like the one a football player would use.

"What am I supposed to do with this?" I asked somewhat perplexed.

"Wear it when you sleep. It stops you from snoring," she answered back.

"Well, thanks," I said with little or no emotion. My thought was that I would put this in the drawer in my bathroom vanity next to the strips for my nose and the throat spray she's given me over the years.

"If it works we don't need to get two rooms or suites anymore," she explained.

At home I read the instructions for the mouth piece and wondered if the snoring was really *that* bad. "It must be if she bought you this," I said aloud. "But just *how* bad?"

I wandered around Radio Shack looking for a recorder to buy so I could actually hear myself snoring. I opted for a battery-operated unit that could record for eight hours. If this was really a problem, then I would use the anti-snore kit with appreciation.

The next morning, as I drank my coffee at my kitchen table, I rewound the recorder and pushed play. There was a fair amount of white noise, and I thought the recorder was defective, and then I heard my mantle clock chime eleven times. I got up from the table and looked at the mantle clock in the living room, and it said 7:20. I listened for a few minutes more and heard the rustling of sheets and a sigh as I settled in. Then a fart and grunt. "Real charming, Rossiter."

Then the snoring started, softly at first, then louder and then suddenly it stopped. It wasn't the gasping for air type of interruption, the snores just stopped. It went on like that for a few more minutes. Then I heard the toilet flush and realized it was recording my first of two nightly trips to the can. Then more snoring.

Well, it wasn't the door rattling that I've been accused of in the past. Don't get me wrong, it was definitely loud, but ear plugs should have been sufficient. I'd give it another one or two nights of recording and then make my decision if I was going to use the snore kit.

The next day, morning sun was shining in my kitchen window. I was up earlier than usual waiting for my friend, Perry, to pick me up for breakfast. I pushed play on the recorder and heard the white noise and then the mantle clock. I thought it was strange that I heard no snores or breaking of wind. And then I heard a voice say something unintelligible. At first it startled me and my heart started to beat faster, but then I realized that Perry must have arrived. I turned the recorder off and went to the door. No one was there. I stepped onto my porch and looked down the driveway. Nobody around. Out my back door I scanned the yard; no one there either.

I pushed play and heard the voice again. Then there were two voices. My heart rate was ramping up. A conversation was taking place and the language was foreign, possibly German. The more I listened, the more I was convinced that one of the two voices was mine. But how could that be? I have enough trouble with English, and here I was having a conversation in German. But with who? How in the *hell* could that be?

I was stunned and my mind raced with more questions—not just *who* but *what* and *why*? And *how* was it possible that I was speaking a foreign language? *I must be going nuts.* I held the tiny recorder in my palm and stared at. *This is used,* I said to myself and was going to take it back to the store. But, then again, there was no denying that one of the voices sounded like me.

"You're not very talkative this morning, Clete. What gives?" Perry asked. We were in the Wildcat Diner in downtown Los Gatos.

I shoved my plate of bacon and eggs away and said, "I didn't sleep too good last night. Sorry to be bad company, Perry."

"No need to apologize, pal. Your turn to buy," he said with a sly grin.

"Perry, do you still know some of the instructors at the college?" I asked, as I looked into his dark brown eyes. His face was creased with laugh lines at the eyes and corners of the mouth and his goatee was neatly trimmed.

"Yeah, a few. Why?"

"Anybody in foreign languages? German, specifically."

I walked down the narrow hallway in the faculty office area at West Valley College. The door said "Frau Baker." I knocked and she came to the door. We introduced ourselves and she showed me to a chair in her cramped quarters. She was short with strawberry-blond hair and a pleasant, freckled face. She wore a beige blouse and navy blue slacks and open-toed sandals. When I explained what I needed, she asked me, "Where did you get this recorder?"

I hemmed and hawed and finally said the work I needed translated was on a recorder I had found in the basement of a friend. To tell her the truth—that the recording was of a conversation I had last night while I was sleeping—didn't seem like it would fly. Anyhow, she accepted my explanation.

"I'll have it transcribed for you, but there is a fee," she said. "Students anticipating State Department work in a foreign country beg for this type of job, but they charge."

I told her I would pay the fee and she said she would call me when the job was done.

"It's an old dialect," Frau Baker told me over the phone. "Why don't you come in and meet the student who transcribed it? She was fascinated by the conversation, by the way," Baker said just before hanging up.

I sat in a classroom with Frau Bailey Baker and a young blond named Ruby Wayne, a tall athletic girl wearing a ball cap over her short blond hair. Her tan face was expressive with bright white teeth that, sans make-up, gave her the beach volleyball look. We chatted briefly about mundane things. I noticed Ruby was looking at me strangely, and then she took out a pencil and hastily wrote something on a pad.

"Would you please read this?" she asked as she pushed the paper toward me. It was in German; I looked at her, perplexed.

"What does this mean? These words, I mean: *was willst du*?" I asked.

"It's a question. In English it says, *What do you want?*"

She assisted me with the German pronunciation. When I finished, Ruby sat back and tapped her pencil to her cheek. Smiling, she turned the player on and fast forwarded for several seconds, stopped and pushed play. The words I'd just read came out of the recorder, and it was my voice!

"That's you speaking, Mr. Rossiter; you're speaking German," Ruby announced.

I looked from Bailey to Ruby and then to the player. I shook my head for several seconds. "How can that be?" I murmured. Then I remembered the lie I'd told Bailey about finding the tape in a basement. I admitted to my snoring, the mouthpiece, and recording myself. "Who's the other guy? This is crazy."

"This is where it gets interesting," Ruby replied with a giggle.

"The other man is a Nazi soldier and he's asking where his leather field pack is."

"You've got to be kidding!" I yelled. The two women sat back with astonished looks on their faces. "I'm sorry. I didn't mean to scare you. It's just that I have a German soldier's leather pouch on my shelf. Jesus Christ! Kruger is looking for his pouch."

"Who is Kruger?" Bailey and Ruby asked simultaneously.

"It's the name printed on the inside of the pouch. I bought it at an antique store in Fayence, France," I said. "I usually pick up some obscure piece while traveling, you know. Display it in a curio cabinet."

Ruby told me the soldier was looking for his "*soldbuch.*"

When I asked her, she told me she had gone online and discovered that a soldbuch is a pay book.

"All German military personnel are issued a pay book, which holds unit information and all issued equipment. It must be kept in the field pack."

"There wasn't anything in the pack when I bought it," I announced.

"Have you had conversations before this one?" Ruby asked picking up the player and moving it like a fan.

"No. Not that I'm aware of."

The two women looked at each other, then turned to me.

"It might be interesting to see if this happens again. Keep recording and let us know if Kruger shows up again," Bailey said.

"Why can't I see this guy?" I asked.

Ruby suggested I see a psychic who deals with paranormal activity. I walked away thinking, *If I'm talking to a dead man, am I dead too?* No, that can't be, you're walking around and talking to yourself. I passed a window and saw my reflection and somehow felt that seeing myself was an indication I was alive. This was becoming absurd. No, I'd passed absurd a while ago.

I continued to record, but had no more conversations with Kruger. I figured he'd found his field pack and was satisfied that I didn't have his soldbuch. Then I decided to try an experiment. I took Kruger's pack from the curio and put it in a cupboard above my workbench in the garage.

Chapter Three

The next morning I anxiously turned the recorder on and was disappointed to hear only loud snoring. Apparently I hadn't had any conversations during the night. A few minutes later I walked past the curio and stopped dead in my tracks; the leather pouch was sitting in the cabinet, back in its regular spot! I paced the room frantically trying to make sense of what was going on. I ran to the garage and looked at the space where I'd put the pouch. There was the initial 'K' written in the dust! I lost my balance momentarily and steadied myself with my bottom resting on my cluttered workbench. "What the Christ?" I said aloud. "I gotta get some help. That's all there is to it."

When I told Meg what had happened, she was skeptical at first, and then she whispered, "You're serious, aren't you?"

"I couldn't make up something like this, Meg. This is just too, too…"

"Haunting?" Meg answered for me.

"That's as good a term as any, I suppose."

She asked me if I was afraid. "I don't think afraid is the right word. Part of me is disconcerted; another is fascinated. What would've happened if the name on the pouch had been Hitler?"

"Now *that* would have been an interesting conversation, Clete." Meg said with a slight chuckle.

All the while I kept asking, *Why me? Why Kruger? I have other things that I've collected that belonged to other people, and they don't visit.* Then again, *maybe they do*, I thought as I remembered the "K" in the dust.

When I got home I took a picture of the K and placed a glass jar over it as if I'd caught a grasshopper. I tried to upload the picture to my computer, but it didn't show up. I got my cell phone and took the same photo, and this too didn't come out. I put the jar back over the initial.

I telephoned an old friend of mine who taught Police Science at the college. I asked him if he had a student who needed extra credit. "Hell, Clete, they all need extra credit; they just don't know it," Darwin "Hoss" Hoskins replied over the phone. When he asked me the reason, I hedged and told him that he and his students might find something interesting in my garage. "It's not a crime, Hoss. Just interesting."

He agreed to bring several students and his fingerprint materials to my house on Saturday. "We're gonna make this field trip worthwhile, Clete. We're gonna treat your entire garage as a crime scene, so get your girlie book stash tossed," Hoss chuckled.

Hoss Hoskins greeted me with a ferocious handshake and slap to the back. He's a powerful man, and although short, he's solid. His ruddy complexion and light brown hair offset his bright blue eyes. The brushy mustache, a new addition since I'd last seen him, completed the look of a retired cop. Hoss and the students, two boys and one girl, wore black windbreakers with POLICE in yellow lettering across the shoulders.

I laid out coffee and cinnamon rolls on the patio table. The students looked at the surroundings, especially the pathway to the detached garage.

"I told them they'd be doing a crime scene search for evidence," Hoss announced as he pointed his chin to the students.

"What are the facts surrounding this event?" the female student asked authoritatively. One of her male counterparts rolled his eyes.

I told them I wasn't certain there was a crime. "Maybe it's just a circumstance or coincidence. I'm not sure." I sensed the air of enthusiasm draining from them, but Hoss covered my back. "People, a citizen has notified the police with a concern. Not all dispatches result in a crime. It could be a misunderstanding, or a perceived infraction of the law. No matter what, the citizen requested help and it's our responsibility to investigate," Hoskins explained. "Why don't you tell us the reason for your call, Clete?"

I motioned with my finger for them to follow me to the roll-up door at the garage.

"Hold on just a second," one of the boys said. "Are we just gonna walk in not knowing what the circumstances are? I don't think so," he said answering his own question.

"Good, Jim," Hoss replied. "There might be some sort of contamination, or a bad guy, maybe a vicious animal. Ask more questions."

I told them that I suspected somebody had been in my garage and left something behind.

"Was anything taken?" the boy with the rolling eyes asked.

I shook my head, and waited for more questions. No contamination or animals; just a cluttered garage.

"Watch where you step!" the female student admonished.

"Gee, no kidding, Carol," roller eyes said.

I looked at Hoskins and he cracked a grin. I led the students to the cupboard and started to open the door, when Jim blocked my hand. "We can't have you contaminate the scene, sir."

I told him that I'd already opened the cabinet the day before.

"That's understandable; nevertheless we don't want to taint anything else."

"What would you do in this case, Charles?" Hoss asked roller eyes.

"I'd take out my kerchief and open it with that."

Hoskins had a frustrated look and said, "I am disappointed in all of you. You each have a pouch on your belts with disposable gloves in them, and you didn't bother to glove-up. Nobody suggested wearing booties over your shoes; you know there is a box of them in the van."

The students followed Hoskins out of the garage. They stood with hang-dog looks. Hoss picked up his coffee. Charles stepped over to the table with the coffee and cinnamon rolls.

"What do you think you're doing, Charles?" Hoss asked, impelling Charles back. He pointed to the coffee and rolls, and Hoss cut him off. "You ain't on coffee break, son. You all have an investigation to do. I suggest you apply what you've learned in class and get 'er done!"

Hoss motioned me to follow him inside. From my office window we watched the students looking at one another. "I'm waiting for one of them to step up and take charge. Jim and Charles will think they're the ones to do it, but you watch; Carol will be the lead," Hoskins said in a flat voice.

I heard their voices, but couldn't understand the words. Finally Carol separated herself from the two boys and started to direct. "Told ya," Hoss said smugly.

Charles went to the van. Jim took up a post at the garage entrance and Carol came to the back door. "Sir, we have a few questions if you don't mind."

I told her about the initial K printed in the dust inside the cabinet, and that I'd placed a jar over it to conserve it. She looked at me with a face that said, "Is that all?"

"The garage was locked. It doesn't look like anything is missing. I want to know who was in my garage; finger prints and what not."

The opaque latex gloves on their hands contrasted with the black windbreakers, and the light blue booties over their shoes muffled their footsteps. Jim was taking photos and Charles was scribing the photo info. Carol used a pencil to open the cupboard. Jim photographed the jar in place; then with the jar removed, he took a shot of the K. Hoss had them step back while he gave a talk on what had transpired so far and what was to be done next. Jim said it was time to dust for prints. That was all I wanted done, but went along with their routine. After all, I had made the request.

"We'll give you a call in a week or so, Clete. We need to run the prints, ya see."

"Hoss, does your data base cover Europe?"

He looked at me oddly and said, "We're a community college. We can't tap into Interpol info. Why?"

"No reason. I was just curious."

Then it hit me. Kruger's prints would never show up in America. What was I thinking?

"There were several prints that came out real good," Hoss told me over the phone the following week, "but no identification except for you, pal. Not all the pictures came out. We could re-shoot em."

"Thanks for all your help, Hoss. I was most interested in the fingerprints. I hope your students got something out of the field trip," I told him. "Thank them for me, please."

For the time being I'd decided to just keep recording. I didn't think anything else would come through, though. Kruger was happy that his pouch was safe and taken care of and that I didn't have his pay book. I decided not to move it again.

Chapter Four

I didn't have another conversation with Kruger or anybody else for quite some time, months actually. Then one afternoon I pushed the play button on the recorder and heard a woman sniffling and the hairs prickled on the back of my neck. *Here we go again.*

"Why are you crying?" my voice asked.

"I'm so sad." The lady's voice answered with a soft southern accent. I played the recorder back to see if I recognized her voice, or possibly the accent. This was stupid; how in the hell would I pick up somebody's accent? I pushed play again.

"Who are you?"

"I'm Zerelda, but most folk call me Zee."

"What do you want me to call you?"

"It don't matter."

"My name is Clete."

"I know." She knew my name! I wondered if she'd visited me before.

"Why are you so sad, Zee?"

"When my husband died in 1882 I got the melancholia real bad. Some days I couldn't get out of bed. I wasn't left in a good circumstance and I had to auction off some family heirlooms to pay creditors and feed my little ones, Jesse and Mary, the poor dears. I wasn't a very good mother to them, I'm afraid. But, you have something of mine, Mr. Clete. Ludwig told me you take care of his things; I just wanted to see."

"I don't know Ludwig."

"Oh, I think you know him. He's been here a few times. He's a soldier, wears a funny suit. Ain't like any army suit I ever saw, north or south."

My mind was going a mile a minute. *I* knew Zee was talking about Kruger, but the sleeping me didn't seem to have a clue. *What in Christ's name does she mean north and south?*

"What do I have of yours?"

"A beautiful jade elephant figurine that my husband gave me. It's about six inches high."

I heard a huge intake of air, and sheets rustling. Then the toilet flushed. The conversation had ended.

A jade elephant? She couldn't mean the one my mother bought at an estate sale over fifty years ago, could she? *Of course she did.* I went to the curio cabinet and removed the green elephant from a lower shelf and held it tightly, then smoothed it like I was dusting it. I placed it next to Kruger's leather pouch. I looked at the other memorabilia on the shelves and said aloud, "This could get interesting."

The more I thought about it, the more I became afraid to mention this new encounter to anyone; they'd think I was a certifiable freak. Hell, I must be, I'm talking to dead people, for crying out loud, just like the kid in the movie a few years ago. To tell somebody, *"Hey, come on over. I talk to dead people. No, I can't see them, but I got a recording. Who? None other than a Nazi soldier and a widow from the 1880s."* They'd slap a straight jacket on me in a heartbeat, and I wouldn't blame them.

The night conversations consumed me. Part of me wanted to be rid of them and another part of me couldn't wait to see who showed up next. I kept recording and listening intently each morning. I heard myself have a couple of gasping bouts, but I seemed to recover from them quickly. I tried not to let this sleep apnea thing scare me. I mean, I know it can kill people, but according to the doc, that's really rare.

The jade elephant was moved away from Kruger's pack and placed on the lower shelf where it had been originally; Zee had been here. This was getting too weird. I knew I needed help. Meg asked me if there'd been any new episodes, and when I told her about the widow, Zee, she got a look on her face that startled me.

"Zerelda? Did you say Zerelda?"

"Yeah, that's what she called herself. That and Zee."

I played the recording for her and she constantly shook her head. "This is weird, Clete."

"Tell me about it," I replied.

"Jesse James' widow was Zerelda," she whispered. "And she said her son's name was Jesse? That's just too coincidental for me. You had a conversation with Zerelda James." This was bordering on bizarre! No, that's not right; this was bizarre to the highest power.

"Just think, Clete," Meg said excitedly. "If she shows up again and you record her, maybe you can ask her questions. You know? Historical questions."

She didn't get it; I don't control the visits. I have the conversations on *their* terms, not mine. I'm in deep sleep and not capable of asking questions. I'm not consciously present. When these episodes started I thought it was unique and kind of eerie. Now I felt it was just too creepy and that I was cursed.

Strange occurrences continued to take place from time to time. Not just Kruger's initial in the dust, or his pack put back in the curio, or Zerelda's jade elephant being moved. Pictures hanging on the walls were tipped, more than once. There was a constant sense that my home had become a club house for spirits! I stayed awake all night at least two nights a week. I even recorded on the nights I was awake, but all I heard, other than household noises, was my anxiety-filled deep sighing.

"Will you please go and see someone?" Meg begged. "You look terrible, and I'm worried."

"I'm just not getting enough sleep, Doll. That's all it is."

She raised her arms and flapped them, "You have to stop recording the ghosts, Clete."

That seemed like the logical thing to do; stop recording. But I couldn't.

"What or who are you waiting to hear from?" she asked annoyed. "Your parents?"

I'd never consciously thought about my parents and whether they would visit in my sleep. Then and there I added nostalgia into the mix of emotions that I felt when I talked to Kruger and Zee. Some kind of longing for something. But, Meg was right, of course; she was always right. I needed to put the recorder back in the desk drawer.

When I phoned my doctor for an appointment the receptionist asked the reason for the visit.

"I'm having difficulty sleeping and I feel depressed," which was bogus, but I guess "depression" is some sort of signal for, "Let's get this guy in today."

I sat in the waiting room for just a couple minutes after my 3:30 pm appointment time.

"Your weight is steady and your blood pressure is normal, Clete," the doctor told me. "You've got some dark circles around the eyes. Tell me what's going on?"

I just couldn't bring myself to tell him that I talked to dead people. He'd spiff me off to a therapist and I wanted no part of that. "I want to go to a sleep disorder clinic. Can you refer me?"

"In my opinion those tests are designed for failure. If you're worried about sleep apnea, loose more weight and drink less booze." Seeing that I wasn't convinced, he asked, "What have you heard about the masks?" I told him I had two friends who used the positive air pressure masks every night and swore by them. "One guy told me he never slept better in his life and he wakes up refreshed and doesn't fade by four in the afternoon. That's what I want."

"I'll send a referral to your insurance company. In the meantime why don't you go somewhere, Clete. A change of scenery might help. Doctor's orders."

I telephoned my children and asked them to accompany me on a weekend trip to Disneyland. They were happy to go and we had a blast; no spirits, nothing peculiar. At night I slept the best I'd slept in months. I'm sure that trying to keep up with my grandchildren as they ran from ride to ride for six hours each day contributed to the restful slumber. I had a ball.

Meg met me at the luggage area at the airport. "You look better," she said as she kissed me. "Was it wonderful?"

"Better than I could hope for."

But when I entered my house, I became edgy, nervous and anxious. I passed the desk and my recorder was sitting on top of it! The same recorder I'd put in the drawer before going away for the weekend. I dropped my suitcase at my feet and opened the drawer. A slip of paper had a "Z" on it. "Jesus-jumped-up-Christ! I didn't ask for this! I yelled. "Can't you leave me the hell alone?" My mind was racing; *get rid of Kruger's pack and Zerelda's elephant; do it now! Move out of this place, it's haunted.*

I picked up my suitcase and turned down the hallway toward my bedroom and a feeling of serenity, that I was hard-pressed to explain, enveloped me. I stopped and turned back into the living room and I still felt calm. The family pictures on the hallway wall were all straight, except for the photograph of my father sitting in an easy chair; it was tipped slightly. I reached out to tilt it back, but stopped and started several times. It was like the photo might be hot to the touch. Finally I aligned it and continued to my bedroom. My feeling of calm continued until I thought about the Z. Should I keep recording? Does she have something to tell me?

I stood in the soothing serenity of my hallway and was comforted. "I can't stay here forever," I whispered. "I gotta get myself to the sleep doctor, pronto."

The sleep doctor gave me a half-assed physical; thump the chest, stick out your tongue, I'm-gonna-look-in-your-ears type of thing. It seemed bogus, but if he helped me sleep and kept me from talking to dead people, I was in.

I showed up at the clinic at eight in the evening. The nurse showed me to a room, much like a hotel room. She said, "Do whatever your regular routine is. There's cable television and I see you brought a book, that's good. When you're ready to go to sleep, push the button."

I pushed the button and her voice came over the bedside speaker, "Are you in your sleeping attire?" My sleeping attire is no attire, normally. Tonight I had gym shorts and a tee shirt. It took her twenty minutes to get all the probes and wires hooked to my head, torso, and legs. The main lead would be plugged into a computer that would track my sleep. As sure as my name is Clete, after I was hooked up, I had to use the toilet. She gave me a sleeping pill, which I started to think was all I really needed.

"If you need to use the bathroom, push the button and I'll get you unplugged." She said she was going to send some signals remotely from her desk to the computer. "I will talk to you over the speaker to get the frequency level correct."

Before I knew it, the nurse's voice came over the speaker. "Good morning, Mr. Rossiter. I'll be in to unhook you in a second. Are you ready for that?"

Two days later the sleep doctor sat behind his desk and I sat in a chair in front of him. "Look at this," he said. He showed me a chart that made no sense to me. It could have been a profit and loss statement from a Fortune 500 company. "See here, these spikes? You stopped breathing over one hundred times during the test, once for forty-five seconds. You clearly have sleep apnea." This scared me; forty-five seconds, that's a long time. *I could die.* He gave me a referral to a medical supply outfit to get a sleeping mask. "Because you sleep eighty-five percent of the time on your back, I'm…"

"Hold on, doctor. I'm a side sleeper; I don't sleep on my back."

"No, Mr. Rossiter, you sleep on your back."

"I did that night because I couldn't turn over." He stared me down with the "I'm the doctor" look. There and then I remembered what my primary doctor had said, "*Those test are designed for failure.*"

I honestly tried, but I couldn't get used to the mask, even though it was the latest design: nasal pillows. Tubing ran from an air machine to the nasal mask. It was constantly in my way. Some nights I'd wake up and the mask was dislodged and blowing air into my eye. For several months I used the machine every night, only to disconnect it around one in the morning. But the forty-five second lapse in breathing was still a concern. At a follow up session with the sleep doctor, I told him it just wasn't working. Guess what? He prescribed sleeping pills. After another month I returned the mask and told my primary doctor about my experience. He wasn't surprised.

Things seemed normal for a few weeks. My sleeping pattern became regular and there were no visits from the other side. Then one morning I turned the recorder on and heard the words, "Hey, pally. You awake?"

"Yeah. What's up?" I asked.

"Lookin for my gloves."

"Gloves? What gloves?"

"My boxing gloves. You got em? Don't lie to me, or I'll knock ya into the middle of next week."

"There are some gloves hanging on a picture of an Ingemar Johannsen and Floyd Patterson bout in my office. How do I know they belong to you?" I wanted to know.

The guy sighed and said, "Why else would I be here? Of course the gloves are mine."

We must have been in my office because the boxer exclaimed, "Those were fantastic fights between those two. They fought twice, ya know, pally. In '59 Ingemar TKO'd Floyd in the third. Ingemar knocked Floyd down seven times." He said the rematch was in '60, and Patterson knocked him out in the fifth to regain the championship. He told me his name was Petie "Kid" Pierpont. "I was a shmoe, just a club boxer always waiting for my shot. Well, pally, one night I got my shot. Or should I say I got shot."

I asked, "You got shot? Who shot you?"

"My old lady. I smacked her once too often," he whispered. "Her fights were the only ones I won."

When I told him I bought the gloves at an antique store in Reno, he told me that was where he was living when he got killed.

"That was in 1965."

I was stunned after listening to Kid Pierpont tell his story. I couldn't find any information on Wikipedia about Pierpont, and there was no mention of his name connected to a murder in the Reno newspapers from 1965. *Maybe if he comes again I'll ask him if Pierpont is his real name*, I said to myself. But as the visits go, once the ghosts see their belongings, they usually don't visit again.

I wished I could see them. I knew what Zerelda James looked like from biographies and books about her husband, but Kruger and Pierpont were mysteries.

Several nights after Pierpont's visit, I had a gasping bout. I stood in my hallway instead of sitting on the edge of the bed. There were vapors at the ceiling, but as I looked at them, they appeared to be swiftly sucked into the living room. It was like a window or door suddenly opened, drawing the image away from me, and I felt compelled to follow it. I rushed to the living room, but whatever I'd seen—vapors or a ghost—was gone. Then I realized that this was not *my* living room. It was the living room of my childhood home. I was completely at ease with a tranquility similar to the feelings of serenity I'd felt in my hallway the night I got home from Disneyland. Sitting in front of me, in an easy chair, was my father. He was talking to a lady in a long black dress with a snood on her head. Next to her on the couch was a German soldier. In front of the fireplace a boxer was throwing punches and jabs in the air. My father, Zerelda James, Kruger and Kid Pierpont; all present and accounted for. The clang of a pot from the kitchen startled me. Was it my mother? I hoped so.

The clang turned out to be a garbage can lid falling to the ground next door and apparently it snapped me out of my childhood living room. Suddenly I was gasping for air again. I tried hard to settle my breathing and get myself calm. If I was seeing my father and the other ghosts, then maybe I was dying or close to dying? *I'm not ready, I thought.* But, if death meant being in my old living room with my folks, then maybe I'd have no fear after all.

These new dreams, about my father and the living room, seemed to occur every night. The gasping for air part was starting to bother me as much as the dreams. But the most frustrating thing was that I was never acknowledged by any of the spirits in the dream. They looked at me when I entered, but they said nothing, and I was mute. And, they all talked at the same time. Four conversations at once. Kruger jawing in German wasn't a problem. The others answered him in English and it was clear they all understood each other.

I really wanted to talk with my father, but I couldn't go farther into the room, and I wasn't able to speak. It was maddening and I would wake up more anxious than ever.

Then it happened. One night I walked into the living room to see my father sitting with my mother and the others standing and smiling at me. "C'mon in, Clete," my father said.

I couldn't move. I thought if I moved I would lose this thread of the dialogue and maybe never get it back again.

"It's fine, honey," my mother said, seeing my hesitation.

"How come I can talk with you all of a sudden?" I asked.

There was a quiet pause and my parents looked at each other briefly before my father replied, "You've crossed over, son."

"Do you mean I'm *dead*?"

"Well...yes, son."

Chapter Five

I watched my children, my dear Meg, and friends grieve. "If they only knew," I thought. I had a fine funeral, just how I wanted it, more laughter than tears. Food, music and toasts to the dearly departed, *me*. My father said, "Clete, you did good. Your children and grandchildren are happy and successful."

"They're on stage now Clete," my father said.

Mother, wearing her favorite apron, was standing off to the side smiling and nodding. Kruger, Zerelda, Kid Pierpont, and my parents, watched the scenes of my old life, from what seemed like balcony boxes.

We saw the family every day, even though there was no real concept of time. I never got tired of watching. I could see all the scenes on stage simultaneously. It didn't matter if my daughter was working and her kids were at school; I could see everything happening at once. There was no judgment from us "spirits." And any indiscretions we witnessed were ignored for the most part.

"You'll know when to step in, dear," my mother told me. "Do you remember that Sunday morning at the stop light? You remember. The light turned green and your foot slipped off the gas pedal just as that car crossed in front of you after running the red light?"

"That was you, mom?"

She nodded and whispered, "You'll know when to intervene."

My son had found me in my bed the morning after I died. It had to be him; he was tougher than the others. He felt for a pulse, but my purplish skin was cold and my body was stiff. He had trouble sleeping after that. Then one night I appeared in his dream; I was pink, warm and pliable. My message to him was, *I'm okay, kid.*

I watched as they went through my stuff. Things that were important to me when I was alive were of no interest to me now. The only thing that mattered was that I was with my parents and knew that eventually I'd be joined again with those still on stage.

"May I have this clock radio?" I heard Meg ask my daughter, who said, "Sure, but it doesn't work." It was a red and cream-colored General Electric I'd received from my folks for my eleventh birthday. I wore that thing out listening to fifties rock-and-roll and the San Francisco Giants. It was part of my curio cabinet collection. By the way, Zee, Ludwig and Kid Pierpont were square with where their things ended up. "Our stuff is with yer kids, pally. We're good."

Meg had some tough moments too, and I needed to also let her know that things were okay and that I was happy. That General Electric radio seemed to be the most logical venue. Early one morning, while it was still dark, I visited Meg's stage. I turned the radio on and Jackie Wilson blared out, "*Hey, you! Come out here on the floor!*"

I watched Meg scramble from her bed. God, I wanted to hold her again. She darted into her den and the music from the radio stopped. She turned the volume dial up and down and changed the tuner knob. She picked the radio up, shook it and then saw the loose plug dangling down onto the table. I watched her as her faced slowly changed.

"Clete?"

Carrying Kerrie

A Short Story

Steve Sporleder

Chapter One

A south wind rang the chimes on my porch, and I knew rain was imminent. The fire crackled and popped in the fireplace as it consumed more fuel. A blast of air blew down the chimney and sent a wisp of wood smoke into the living room, so I opened the damper wider to allow more oxygen in. I placed my steaming coffee cup on a round cork coaster on the ancient pine chest of drawers next to my chair and went outside to get the newspapers. The magnolia trees creaked and groaned in the gusts. I picked up two newspapers from the driveway and walked back to the house. Smoke issuing from my chimney top filled me with a sense of sanctuary and comfort. Despite the cold and blustery daybreak, my world was good.

I finished another cup of coffee and my second crossword puzzle at the same time. I try to be done with this ritual by 7:45 each morning.

As I climbed into the shower, the phone rang, interfering with my tranquil morning. I let it ring. As the water cascaded over me, I wondered who would be calling me so early in the morning. If it were important, there would be a message waiting for me.

The caller ID panel on the phone read *Caller Unknown*. I pushed the play button and a weak female voice said, "*Hello, Venice. This is Kerrie. Please call me back as soon as you can.*"

"Why in Christ's name would my ex-wife be calling me?" I whined.

She didn't leave a callback number, so I decided to ignore her message. Our divorce had ended somewhat amicably decades before, although we hadn't spoken in years. Memories and events from that time are somewhat sketchy to me. I was working in the fire department at the time and was a certifiable drunk. An on-the-job injury led to my early retirement and more drinking. Kerrie ran off with a carpenter.

I got sober, moved back to my hometown, Los Gatos, California, and set up a home office in the house where I grew up. I work for Resorts International, an insurance company that writes policies for hotel properties worldwide. I guess you could say I'm my own boss. I visit the properties and do fire prevention and safety inspections. I have an expense account that seems endless, as long as it's work related. I stay in the hotel I'm inspecting, eat their food and after the inspections, I fax my report to the home office in Seattle, then I take my time and do some vacationing. My friend, Kate, travels with me from time to time, which is nice. I've been to places from Fresno, to France. However, I go to Fresno by myself.

I recently started a part-time gig doing fire cause investigations. I hire off-duty firefighters to help me investigate fires for cause and origin. I also teach Fire Scene Investigation in the Fire Science program at the community college. As I said, my world was good and comfortable, or so I thought.

"Why didn't you call her back?" my sister, Lydia, asked as we sat in the coffee shop of the ElGato Hotel where she is the manager and her life partner, Helen Gray, is the owner.

"She didn't leave a call back number," I replied quietly.

Lydia removed her eyeglasses, tilted her head and glared at me.

"What?"

"For her to call you, it must be important. Maybe something happened at your house there."

"Damn, I never thought about that."

"It's probably nothing, Sweetie. Just give her the courtesy of calling back."

I was pulling papers and address books apart searching for Kerrie's number, when the phone rang again. I knew it had to be Kerrie calling. I was breathing rapidly and I could feel my heart beating at my temples. I picked up after the third ring.

"Hello," I said flatly.

The same weak voice spoke, "Hello, Venice. It's Kerrie."

"I was about to call you back, Kerrie. I just got your message," I lied. "What's going on?"

There was silence for several seconds, and then she said, "I'm sick, Venice. I have ovarian cancer."

"Jesus, Kerrie. I'm sorry," I said. It sounded awkward, but I hoped it came through as sincere, because I was.

"It is what it is, Ven. I'm okay with dying."

She was sick *and* dying.

"I have some unfinished business that I need your help with."

"Sure. You bet. Anything you want me to do."

"Thanks. I knew I could count on you. My attorney is sending you some papers that will explain what I need. It doesn't involve any legal issues with you, but I do need some legwork done. You still do investigating don't you?"

I told her that I was still doing fire investigations, and she told me this wasn't an investigation into fires, but about finding a missing person. As we continued to talk, her voice became weaker and she had several coughing bouts.

"Kerrie, how..." I fumbled.

"A couple of months at the outside. Another day is too long, though."

"God, Kerrie. I just wish..."

"You're a good guy, Venice. Come and see me before I transition," she rasped.

"Who do you want me to find?" Before she could answer, the coughing increased, and then a female voice with a foreign accent came on the line to say that Kerrie could not finish the conversation.

I sat at my kitchen table attempting to shake off the news. My eyes brimmed with tears for Kerrie. She didn't deserve this. She was way too young. I recalled the first time I saw Kerrie. It was at a concert at a winery. She was the cutest girl there, and we ended up getting married. Just like that.

"What's wrong with you, Venice? You look like somebody just ran over your dog," Lydia said, lowering her eyeglasses. When I told her, Lydia gave me a hug and said she was sorry. She asked for Kerrie's address, so she could write her a note.

Numerous thoughts kept running rapidly through my mind. Who does she want me to find, and why? Do I want to do this? How much time will it take? The answers came quickly also. It doesn't matter who. No, I don't want to do this. But I will. It will take as long as it takes.

All I could do now was wait for the information to arrive from Kerrie's lawyer.

Chapter Two

The distinctive color of the large envelope sticking out of the top of the mail box caught my eye as I drove up my driveway. I took the bundle of mail into the house and sorted through the bills and ads. Finally I picked up the big envelope. The return address was from the law firm of Charles Donaldson in Seattle, Washington.

My hands shook as I put the letter opener to the flap. This had all gotten to me more than I expected. Inside was a manila folder and a white sheet of paper folded in thirds. My name was written in blue ink on the top fold. I recognized Kerrie's handwriting, although it was written with an unsteady hand.

Dear Venice,

*Thank you for agreeing to help me. As you know I have terminal ovarian cancer. My time is short, so I'll get to the point. I have a **daughter**, albeit estranged, but she needs to know what's happening with me. We haven't spoken in over ten years. Our lifestyles didn't mesh and she moved on. Her name is **Mandy Wilkes** and she is forty years old and the last address I have for her is in Iowa, of all places. A copy of her driver's license and social security card is enclosed. There is also her high school graduation photograph. She was studying marine biology in college, which is pretty perplexing considering she was living in Iowa. If you need any legal investigation expertise, Charlie Donaldson can help you out.*

> *I hope this isn't too much of an inconvenience for you; but you were the first person I thought of. Please come and see me.*
>
> *Fondly,*
>
> *Kerrie*

I was stunned. *Kerrie had a kid?* I was expecting to be asked to find the man she left me for or to chase down somebody who owed her money. I re-read the letter several times and each time I looked between the lines searching for a clue into this child. Was I the father? From time to time I wondered what it would be like to be a father, but always figured it wasn't meant to be, and now this. I felt sure Kerrie would have said something to me. If she was my child, Kerrie had to know I would have supported her if I had known about her. I looked at Mandy's photograph to see any resemblance to my family. One moment I saw my mother and the next there was no connection at all. Then I saw my father's chin. *Stop it!* My mind was playing tricks. For the life of me I couldn't remember the name of the contractor Kerrie took off with. It could've been Wilkes. I just didn't remember.

Mandy was an attractive high school girl but that photo was from decades before. Lots of things could've happened to change her looks—weight gain or loss, plastic surgery, a disfiguring accident or certainly hair color and style change. Drugs and alcohol could have taken their toll, also. How did I know I could find her after all these years?

I sat at my desk and made an outline of what needed to be done. The first thing on the list was to visit Kerrie. After that, the rest, hopefully, would fall into place.

Chapter Three

During the flight to Seattle, I jotted notes in my day planner about what needed to be done and what resources I'd need to accomplish this task as quickly as possible.

I had a valid social security number and an expired Washington driver's license for Mandy. I was still a sworn peace officer in the states of Washington and California, so I had access to records from police agencies across the US. I didn't relish the idea of going to Iowa, but if that's where it would take me, that's where I'd go. I'd go to Timbuktu if necessary.

I parked the rental car a few doors from Kerrie's house. The walk would steel my nerves before I saw her. *Three days ago I was in a good space; my life was uncomplicated and on autopilot, and then the call came from Kerrie.*

The weather was unseasonably warm for April and a storm that had passed over a few days before seemed to brighten up the trees and plants. The air was fresh. If I hadn't had to visit a dying woman, I might have enjoyed the day.

I turned the old fashioned key for the bell and listened for footsteps inside. After another ring, I stepped away from the door and looked in the living room window. The interior was tidy, but nobody was around. I went to the side gate and opened the latch. I saw a woman with black hair and a dark complexion sitting on a lawn chair and Kerrie on a chaise under a maple tree. She wore a white warm-up suit, fuzzy pink slippers and huge sunglasses. A multi-stripe babushka adorned her head.

"Hello," I said from the walkway. "Kerrie, it's Venice."

The woman was out of the chair in a flash. She reminded me of a protective dog getting between her owner and possible trouble. She was slight with a wide face. Her eyes were slits as she stared at me.

"Its okay," Kerrie said faintly to the lady.

Kerrie removed her glasses and gave me a warm smile and waved me over. Her eyebrows were gone, but the pencil application was done nicely. Even though she was ill, she was still the beautiful girl I'd met at a concert. She offered her cheek to me and I kissed her and squeezed her hand. Face and hand were warm to the touch.

"Vayda, this is Venice. We used to be married," she said to the dark lady.

Vayda greeted me with an outstretched hand. Her eyes wide open were dark as obsidian and kind. She asked if I'd like a drink of something, which I declined. After several awkward moments, Vayda went into the house.

"Damn, Kerrie. I'm sorry we have to meet like this. So much time has gone by; I don't know where to begin."

She grinned and put her glasses back on. "There's an old Chinese saying that seems appropriate now: *'The best time to plant a tree is twenty years ago. The second best time to plant a tree is today.'*"

She saw the confusion on my face.

"Don't look back, Venn. There's no future in it. Take the day and go with it. I don't want to dwell on what might have been, or on any mistakes I made."

My thought was that she meant *take it one day at a time*.

We sat and chatted about the next treatment she was going to have, then I interrupted her, "Kerrie, I know you don't want to dwell on the past, but I get nostalgic about Rueben and Hattie. And I want to know what your life has been like until now."

Rube and Hattie had been our neighbors on either side of us when we lived in my house in Blueport.

"Nostalgia is fine as long as the memories are good," she wheezed.

We had a nice talk about our old neighbors and the good times we had. She told me up to six months ago she was still teaching pre-school. "In fact I had three campuses and sold them all. I have a nice sum of money for Mandy, but I don't want her to come for that. I want her to come home so I can go over to the other side and have no regrets." She took in a deep breath and let it out through pursed lips.

"Would you get Vayda for me?" she said tiredly. "I need to rest and take meds. Can you come back in the morning?"

I'd planned to fly out in the morning. "Sure. What time?"

"Why don't you come for breakfast? Vayda does good pancakes and bacon."

"When did you start eating bacon?"

She gave a hint of a laugh and said, "When I found out I was terminal."

I cocked my head like a dog hearing a strange sound.

She looked at me and said, "What's it gonna do, kill me?"

Chapter Four

The smell of frying bacon permeated the yard as I walked to the door. I turned the bell key and heard footsteps.

"Good morning, Mr. Venice. Come in," Vayda said sweetly. "Would you like coffee?"

A plate of sliced oranges with powdered sugar sprinkled over them sat in the middle of the dining room table. The aroma of the citrus was comforting.

From the bedroom, Kerrie summoned Vayda, who handed me a coffee mug and went to check on Kerrie. I wandered into the living room. I recognized several pieces of furniture that had at one time been in our house. A cobalt blue vase from my childhood home sat on a side table. Several framed photographs of Mandy, and Mandy and Kerrie sat prominently on the mantle piece.

"If there is anything there you want, take it, Venn," Kerrie said as she wheeled herself into the living room. I hadn't noticed the chair yesterday.

I stepped over to her and bent and kissed her cheek. "Good morning, Kerrie. How was your night?"

"Eh. So so," she replied rocking her hand. "Maybe I overdid it yesterday."

"Miss, breakfast is served," Vayda said with a slight bow, and turned to go back into the kitchen.

"She treats me like I'm a princess."

"Where is she from? Her nationality, I mean."

Kerrie wheeled herself into position and said, "Sri Lanka."

She seemed perplexed. "Why are there only two places set, Vayda?"

"I'll eat in here, Miss. Let you have some privacy."

"Nonsense, you set up out here."

Vayda looked at me, and I smiled and pulled a chair out for her.

The meal was great. The pancakes had a nice amount of vanilla in the batter and the bacon was delicious. How bad can bacon be? The orange slices at first were tart after the sweetness of the syrup, but were counteracted by the powdered sugar.

I helped Vayda clear the table, which caused her concern. "Don't fret, Vayda. It's the least I can do after you've fed me." She giggled and started to rinse the dishes. I started to help her; she turned and faced me. With a knitted brow, she motioned her head toward the dining room and whispered, "She needs to talk with you, Mr. Venice." I looked into her eyes and she nodded and motioned with her hand.

Kerrie was sitting in the living room in a shaft of sunlight. Her eyes were closed. I walked as quietly as I could, and she said "I'm not asleep. Sit and talk with me. You must have questions about Mandy."

I asked her about the name "Wilkes" and was told that Mandy had been married briefly to a man named Russ Wilkes. "You're probably wondering if you're her father." She opened her eyes and looked at me long and hard; then a grin slowly formed. I guess my look was enough to satisfy her sense of drama. "To tell the truth, I don't know if she's your child or Pat's." That was the contractor's name, Pat Storm.

Kerrie wheeled to a position away from the sunlight. "Shortly after I took off, I discovered I was pregnant. Pat said to me that he hadn't signed up for the woman and kid thing. He stuck with me for a time, then went on the lam after the baby was born.

"Did he have anything to do with her at all?" I asked.

Kerrie shook her head slightly. "She took my last name, your last name; Webb."

I gave her a strange look, and she said, "Drunk or sober, you were more of a man than Storm ever thought of being."

"Holy crap, Kerrie. Why didn't you tell me? I mean, we were in the same county. I could've helped out. I mean..."

"Venn, we survived. We didn't need handouts."

"That's not what I meant. If she was mine, I had a right to know."

She looked at me, and bowed her head slightly. "Be that as it may, it isn't about you or me. Mandy's mother is dying and *she* needs to know. If she comes and visits, great. If not, I tried."

"What happened to Pat?"

She shook her head and replied, "He went bankrupt. Lost his contracting business and went out of state. I heard he became a merchant seaman, but I'm not real sure."

"What about Mandy's husband, Wilkes?"

Kerrie told me he was killed in an auto crash. "He was drunk. Thank Christ he was alone. He rolled over into a ditch outside of Redmond."

I asked about Mandy's work and any jobs she might have had, and all the places she'd lived over the last ten years. "I know you said the last you heard from her she was in Iowa. What about before that?"

"She worked at a café in Seattle while she was in high school. She was a waitress. When she graduated she kept the job and went to school at the University. That's when our differences started to surface." Kerrie looked tired and I asked her if she wanted to rest. She nodded and said, "Can you come back this afternoon?"

Once again my travel plans were interrupted. "What time?"

I visited the county sheriff department to ascertain if there were any warrants or wants on Mandy Webb Wilkes. Nothing showed up. She had no criminal history. I checked DMV records next and went to her last address in Seattle. The address was now a strip mall with an eclectic array of shops. Somehow I felt I was missing something, or possibly I wasn't getting all the data from Kerrie.

Vayda answered the door, and I put my index finger to my lips. She looked back over her shoulder, and then stepped onto the porch. She pulled her sweater tighter around her torso. I knew she wasn't chilled; she was nervous.

"Did you know Mandy, Vayda?"

She shook her head no. "I never heard her talk about any child until a few weeks ago." She looked into my face and winced.

"What is it?"

"She asked me to call that attorney, Donaldson? He shows up and then the energy in this house gets more forceful," she said moving her thumb back toward the interior. "It was good one way, and in another it wasn't." I looked at her and shook my head. "It gave her a purpose, but it sapped her. I've watched her deteriorate quicker since she decided she wanted to find her daughter. If you ask me, that girl is no-count. But, I've said too much."

Chapter Five

The skyscraper loomed over Pioneer Square. On the eighth floor, I entered the paneled reception area of Charles Donaldson, Attorney. My first thought was that the lawyer was just looking for a retainer to keep up his fancy office and fat-cat lifestyle. But then, I don't have too high of an opinion about lawyers. Those I know personally are okay. It's the ambulance chasers and publicity whores that give the rest a rotten reputation, I guess. The young and attractive receptionist checked her appointment book after I gave her my name.

"I don't have an appointment."

It was like her world screeched and came to an abrupt stop.

"I only want a moment of Mr. Donaldson's time. It concerns Kerrie Webb."

She left her desk and went through a large wooden door that had a *"private"* sign on it. When she returned, she said sweetly, "Mr. Donaldson will be with you momentarily."

I expected to see a guy in a three-piece suit, probably tailor-made for a thousand dollars or more, and six-hundred dollar shoes on his feet. So when Donaldson opened his office door and walked toward me, I was surprised to see him in a black cardigan sweater, gray polo shirt with charcoal slacks and black loafers, sans socks. Just before his office door shut, I noticed a set of golf clubs in a huge plaid tripod golf bag standing in front of a massive desk.

"I'm Charles Donaldson. Nice to meet you, Mr. Webb," he said with a wide grin and an extended hand. We shook and he motioned me to a conference room on the other side of the lobby.

"Taffy, hold all my calls. Do you want coffee or a soda?" he asked me. I declined. Of course, the trophy receptionist would be named Taffy.

"What can I do for you, Mr. Webb?" He asked as he pointed to a chair around a large table.

"I'm not real sure what you can do. I just want to make sure I have all the facts before setting out on this adventure." I saw him sneak a peek at his wrist watch, then pretend to be attentive. "You look like you're getting ready to leave for your tee time, so I'll be short. Is there anything I'm missing?"

"Mr. Webb, you aren't holding me up. And as far as Mandy and Kerrie are concerned, I think you know as much as I do. I know that you were married to Kerrie and that you might be Mandy's father. Her last known residence is in Iowa. You have the same info I have."

I stood up and headed for the door. "Kerrie said if I needed any expertise during my investigation that I could contact you. Is that right?"

He nodded and pursed his lips. "This started out as a will and estate deal, and has morphed into a missing person case. My fees are expensive, Mr. Webb. So when you contact me, and I hope you do, I go on the clock," he said as he followed me to the door. "Kerrie thought she could hire you, instead of using my staff; that's fine. I'm sure you're a good investigator. However, when you call me, the meter is running."

"Are you charging Kerrie for this visit?" I asked him.

"Why wouldn't I?"

I walked to the reception desk, with him behind me. "I want to pay for this visit. How much?" I asked Taffy.

She looked baffled. "The billing department handles that," Donaldson replied for her.

"I've been here for thirty minutes. Is two hundred enough?"

Donaldson bowed slightly. I dropped two c-notes on Taffy's blotter and walked out.

Bottom feeder. That's what I thought of the lawyer. I hoped Kerrie knew any time she called Donaldson, she was being charged. I walked to my car in the parking garage and heard the obnoxious beeping of somebody opening their car locks. I looked several rows over and saw Donaldson rush to the open trunk of his two-door Mercedes coupe and throw his golf bag in. He sped out of the parking lot with squealing tires as if he were late for a tee time. I grinned.

As I tooled down the boulevard, a cop was giving Donaldson a ticket. I laughed my ass off.

Chapter Six

What was the time from Mandy's eighteenth year to age thirty like for her and Kerrie? That's what kept churning in my mind. How good was it? How bad was it? What caused the split? Kerrie was going to have to dredge up the past for me before I could head out. The more info I have the more efficiently I can investigate. I also needed to tell her that she should use Donaldson for her will and estate affairs only. And if she could get out from under him she should think about it. I have a retired attorney that I go to AA with. He could do her business and probably wouldn't charge her. I'd just toss that out.

I'd been in Washington for a day and a half, and I didn't know too much more than before I left Los Gatos. The house Mandy had lived in became a strip mall and she wasn't wanted for anything anywhere. That's all I knew for certain.

I drove to her last known place of employment, a coffee-house-sandwich shop near the Space Needle. The art-deco tile on the front and the ancient glass doors made me think this joint had been around since the thirties or forties. The interior was definitely from that era, but had been retrofitted to look that way. The lone waitress stood up from a stool and grabbed a menu. I motioned with my hand that I didn't want a menu. "I'll have a diet cola is all." The grease and onion smells lingered as did a slight disinfectant aroma from the restroom.

A couple sat next to each other in a booth. They appeared to be doing a little hanky-panky. The coagulating smears of condiments on their plates led me to think they'd been there for some time. The cook and waitress were probably anxious to shut the griddle down and go home. Once in a while the girl would yelp, then giggle.

I stirred the cola with a straw and asked the waitress if she'd worked at this place long.

"Seems like all my life, Hon, why do you ask?"

I told her who I was looking for and why. "Never heard of her. Maybe Pietro knows. Hey Pietro, you ever work with a gal named Mandy Wilkes?"

"Could have. Can't remember for sure," he said as he came to the shoulder high counter where the waitresses picked up orders. "She owe ya money?"

I shook my head. "Does the owner keep employment records?" I asked.

The waitress turned to the cook and said, "Well, do ya?"

Pietro was the owner? "How long you been the owner?" I asked him.

"Since '74, that's when my father died and I took over."

I told him I had a picture of the girl I was looking for. I went to the car and brought Mandy's senior portrait in so he could have a look. When I walked in the door the booth couple was walking out. Their shirts were disheveled and they seemed to be in a hurry to get to the next level. I held the door for them and they walked away with arms around each other's waists.

Pietro wiped his hands on a dish towel and took the photo from me. He gazed at it for several seconds. I thought I saw a glimmer of something in his eyes. Then he shook his head slightly, not saying a word; then a glimmer again.

"Ya got any idea how many waitresses have worked here over the years? Hundreds, maybe thousands."

"I'm looking for just this one," I said pointing to the picture. "Are there any tax records or workers comp forms, anything would be helpful?"

He asked me how far back I was looking. I told him back to the 1990s.

"My old man was a stickler for record keeping and a hell of a lot more organized, than me, though." My heart was sinking, and Pietro could see this. "I keep records too. It's just that my files are not as organized," he replied as he walked back to the cooking area. "You're welcome to have a look, if you have a mind to."

My spirit was starting to brighten. "That would be fantastic, Pietro."

"This ain't got anything to do with anything illegal, does it?"

"A lady is dying and she wants her daughter notified. Just a missing person case, and this is the last place I know she worked."

He showed me to a storeroom office next to the restrooms. Inside were gallon cans of food and paper products. I was shocked when he booted up his computer and clicked on Records/Employees.
"Pop's stuff was all hand written. My kid is a computer geek, so he scanned the records to files. You familiar with computers?"

He may be unorganized, but his kid wasn't a geek, he was a genius. It didn't take me long to find Mandy's employment record complete with date of hire, hours worked, raises and her residence. My heart sank; it was the same place that had been turned into a strip mall. Under the heading *person to notify in case of emergency* was the name *Russ Wilkes* crossed out, then the name *Kerrie Webb*, and that too was crossed out and the name *Porter Harmon* was printed along with a phone number.

I couldn't have been more grateful to Pietro and the waitress. "I just hope you can connect them, man. Life's too short to be beefing with family. Glad I could help," he said as he shook my hand.
I called the number for Porter Harmon and got that irritating signal that comes before the voice, announcing the number is no longer in service.

A search of the local phone directory on my laptop computer didn't show a listing for Porter Harmon. I saw a library and parked my rental car and went in. The reference books were in a stack near a computer room. I picked out a phone book and scanned for Porter Harmon. The third book had his name and address. The telephone number was the same one that had been out of service. And as luck would have it, once again the address was the same as Mandy's that had been turned into a strip mall. But, at least I had a new identity to work with. I felt that progress was made. That was until I got back to Kerrie's house.

Based on the look Kerrie gave me when I mentioned the name Porter Harmon, you would have thought I'd broken wind at a formal dinner table.

"What?" I asked. We were at her kitchen table.

Composing herself, Kerrie asked, "Where in the world did you come up with that name?"

I told her about the employment records at the café Mandy once worked at and that Harmon was on the emergency contact info for Mandy.

"Who was this Harmon, Kerrie?" I asked. "Is that who Mandy took up with after Wilkes?"

"I'm sure I don't know." The clock in the hallway bonged three times.

There was an uncomfortable quiet that lasted minutes. "Did you find anything else?" Kerrie asked softly. I told her about the address Harmon and Mandy shared. Kerrie nodded slightly.

"What was Mandy like as a teenager? Was she a good student? Did she get into trouble?" I asked.

Kerrie put her hand up as if to say *slow down*. "Let's stay on course, Venn," she told me.

That's where I thought I was, *on course*. "Listen, Kerrie, the more data I have before going on this hunt, the easier it'll be. The best clue I have was her last place of employment and a name of a known acquaintance. That isn't much, but it's all I got," I announced with wide spread arms. "Do you have anything else?"

She shook her head and then took in a raspy breath of air and said, "Just that she lives in Mason City, Iowa."

I told her I was flying back to California in the early morning, and in two days I'd be on a flight to Des Moines.

"You'll keep me posted, won't you?" Kerrie asked.

I assured her that I would call her right away with any updates.

Chapter Seven

After landing in Des Moines International, I got on a Delta prop job for a short hop north. I was taken with the lush looking farmland below with its interesting patterns of yellow, green, and brown and the sun glinting off aluminum silos. A short time later the plane descended into Mason City, Iowa. For those into rock and roll trivia, Mason City Municipal Airport is where the plane carrying Buddy Holly, J.P. Richardson (The Big Bopper), Ritchie Valens and pilot Roger Peterson took off from shortly after one in the morning, the "day the music died", February 3, 1959. The Beechcraft Bonanza was found in a field near Clear Lake, Iowa later that morning. The Winter Dance Party Tour had just played its last venue, The Surf Ballroom in Clear Lake. The three stars that chartered the plane wanted to get home quickly after almost a month on the road; they never made it.

I hummed to myself *"Bye bye, Miss American Pie"* constantly as I walked to the car rental counter. Nowhere inside or outside the airport was there any mention of the crash that fateful night. No plaque, no pictures, nothing; bad business for airports to mention crashes, I guess. Before going to the car park area, I stopped at a payphone and scanned the directory. The Mandy Wilkes listed had just a phone number and there wasn't a Porter Harmon listed.

I was struck by the beautiful clear air as I drove away from the airport. The heartland, this northern Iowa, was more beautiful than I ever imagined. The traffic became lighter the farther away from the airport I got. Then it picked up again as I got closer to the downtown area.

My room at the Clarion was sufficient and appeared clean. During my insurance career I'd become somewhat of an expert on hotels and hotel rooms. Most properties my company insures are luxury locations in resort destinations; this was as good as Iowa had, and it was fine. From the information brochures in my room, I learned that Mason City was thriving with industry that included row crop farming and food production. Green technology, medical care, and home products industry rounded out the economy. Mason City was also the home of Meredith Wilson, the musician and playwright who penned the musical, *The Music Man*. And of course the infamous plane crash the day the music died.

Chapter Eight

I entered the River City Café and sat down at the counter to have breakfast. The joint was about half full. Men in overalls sat at Formica tables lingering over coffee after breakfast, their ball caps pushed back, exposing more of their creased and craggy faces. I got a cursory look and momentary silence, and then the chatter started again. All the men were big and brawny with huge hands and hairy knuckles. I got the impression this group met each morning at the same time and had on-going conversations. They seemed to be of retirement age and in no hurry to be anywhere. They'd probably worked hard all their lives on land that was passed from generation to generation.

The waitress, a splinter of a woman with red hair, pointed to the menus stacked next to the napkin dispenser and poured coffee for me. "The specials are on the white board, Shug," and then went to refill the farmers' cups. "Where ya from?" the cook asked through the shoulder high opening as he moved plates to be picked up.

When I said "California," the place got real quiet.

"What brings ya here?" one of the men at the table asked.

I told them I was looking for someone, and another asked if I was from the police.

"No. It's nothing like that. I'm looking for the daughter of a friend of mine."

I was shocked when nobody asked who I was looking for right away. Finally one said, "Who is it?"

"Her name is Mandy Wilkes. She's supposed to be with the water company."

"We know who she is," a man with a cap that said Farmers Feed America hissed.

I looked him in the eye, waiting for more.

"She ain't that bad, Fred. She's got a job to do," a younger man said. What has this kid gotten into? I wondered. "Do you know where I can find her?" I asked.

I was told to try the Engineering Department for the city.

Fred, a mountain of a man, got up from the table and stood behind me. He placed a massive hand on my shoulder and said, "I hope you take her back to California with you, mister." His tone was even and his face pleasant. The eyes however transmitted heat.

"She's from Washington State." He gave a what-ever look and walked away.

I watched him walk to the door. His coveralls were clean as was his plaid green and gold flannel shirt. The distinctive circle of a can of Copenhagen imprinted one of his rear pockets. I turned and saw the others still at the table looking at me. I was beginning to feel animosity when suddenly the waitress said, "What can I get for ya?"

I just had coffee.

A younger man took the stool next to me and said, "Don't let Fred get to ya. He's a great guy."

I told the man I was just looking to give Mandy a message. To say she possibly was my daughter was none of anybody's business. I was curious, though. "What's the beef with her?"

"It ain't her," a man at the table said. "It's what she does, who she works for and what not."

I learned that Mandy worked for the city under a grant from the state to get rid of agriculture drainage wells. Some farmers over the last 100-plus years connected their sewage systems to Ag wells, sending raw sewage into drainage ditches that leeched into the ground. The chemicals and pesticides and sewage were contaminating the drinking water.

"Shoot. Iowa was eighty percent prairie in the early 1800s," added a lanky man with wide yellow suspenders over a blue shirt. My empty stare must have let him in on the fact that I didn't know what that had to do with anything. "Tall grasses have deep roots that soak up and hold water, ya see. So the crop was hay and oats. Because of subsidies, the government encourages corn and soybean production, which don't absorb diddly squat. We grew food and the prairie went away."

"Yeah, and the heavy rains cause flooding," the younger man said.

"What does that have to do with Fred and Mandy?" I asked.

"Well, sir, we don't like change around these parts, ya know," said a man who up to that time appeared to be asleep. "Now, most of us can adapt to these changes over time, but Fred, well, he come from a stock that resists change. His pa was the same way. Even if it's good for ya, if it's different, he don't like it. He don't want no part of it."

The more I listened, the more I longed to get out of this place.

"So, old Fred, he run her offa his piece. She comes traipsing through the place with test tubes and kits and what not, taking samples and such, which by the way the law says she can do. But not on Fred's patch. She calls the cops on him and they arrest him. Picture in the paper and everything," the young man told me.

"Fred was quoted in the local newspaper after his arrest" he added. *'My granddaddy homesteaded this land, cleared it, plowed it, planted it and, at time suffered severe losses either from the elements or price drops. So somebody coming on my land telling me what I can and can't do, well sir, that ain't right.'*

A few chuckles and a couple of knee slaps later and I left. Walking away I thought that Mandy, a West Coast gal, had taken on a no-win task with Middle America farmers.

Chapter Nine

I followed a city public works truck into a maintenance parking lot behind the city office complex. Cyclone fencing surrounded the entire yard. The driver of the truck pointed me toward a light brown metal building that I passed on the way in.

Nobody was in the reception area, but I heard a radio playing somewhere in the building. "Hello?" I said down a hallway.

"Be right there," a female voice replied.

Mandy came into the reception area and said, "How can I help you?"

Her hair was light brown and cut short, but stylish. She was thin in the face with green eyes and a solid chin. She looked nothing like her high school senior portrait taken decades before. I expected an eighteen year old; before me stood a woman in her early forties. I saw her mother in posture and expressions, but not a hint of Webb. Or did I? There was a glimmer of recognition across her face.

"Mandy, I'm Venice Webb."

She seemed to lose her balance momentarily, but quickly recovered and took on a wide stance. "Yes, I recognize you from pictures that Kerrie had. What in blue blazes are you doing here?"

"I'm afraid I have some bad news."

She put her hands on the reception counter and said, "Is she dead?"

"No. But she is dying and wants to see you."

I didn't know what kind of reaction there would be. Tears, snorts, or maybe a "who cares" scenario. I didn't expect her to be stony.

"I have a ticket for you so you can go see her," I said gently.

She looked startled and stood straighter and whispered, "I'm not going to see her. She sends her ex-husband to find me and she wants me to come home; hell no."

I told her that was up to her and that I wished she'd think it over. I almost walked away then, for as beautiful as Iowa was, so far, I didn't care for the people, even though that was probably unfair. The guys in the café were okay except for Fred, and he was just standing up for what he believed in. But this little brat was pissing me off. But then again, I didn't know the whole story. That and the part where she might be my daughter kept me from walking out.

"Can I take you to dinner, Mandy?" I asked. "I want to tell you what's going on with your mother."

She hesitated for several seconds and then said, "Dinner is alright, but I'm not all that interested in her."

"Will you at least hear me out?" I asked.

She grinned and with a sudden shift in her mood, put her hand out and replied, "It's the least I can do, if you're taking me to dinner."

I shook her hand and asked where she'd like to eat.

"Just as long as it's not around here. I'm considered the ditch bitch and people would like to see me leave town on a rail."

"Yeah, I know. I met some of them at breakfast this morning."

"Let me guess. Fred Blank was one of them."

I told her his name was Fred, but I never got a last name. From my description she confirmed it was Blank.

I followed her to her house in Clear Lake, several miles west of Mason City, so she could change from work clothes.

"I need to take a shower. Help yourself to a beer. I'll be right out. Feel at home."

I wandered through her wood frame house. It was a two bedroom single story place of unknown vintage with a nice porch in front in a neighborhood of similar houses.
Mandy's furnishings were well worn and looked comfortable.

I saw no indication of anything that might belong to a male. Was Porter Harmon out of the picture?

"There's a nice wood fire steak place in town. It's decent," she said from the bedroom. I told her it sounded fine.

I was struck by the absence of anything personal; no photos, no diplomas or heirlooms. Suddenly I was saddened that this girl was alone with no legacy to cling to except for a mother who she cared nothing about. The co-dependant in me wanted to fix that. *Stay on your side of the street, Webb.*

I looked out her backdoor, through a meadow that fell off to a creek. Trees dotted her yard, which was a natural landscape and pleasing. An old weathered picnic table sat under a maple. No chairs or benches were around.

"Did you get a beer?" she asked.

I turned around and looked into her eyes. I saw them brim with tears, then her chin quivered, and my heart broke. She wasn't a stone after all.

I stepped toward her and she fell into my arms sobbing. All I could think to do was stroke her hair and whisper, "hush" to her. *This is what a father would do, I thought.*

Abruptly, she broke the embrace and said, "Well, that was unexpected," and whirled to open the refrigerator.

"Well, do you want a cold one? I sure do."

"No, honey. You go ahead. I don't drink."

She unscrewed the cap and tossed it on the tile counter top. I imagined the hearty flavor and the sting from the carbonation, and was momentarily jealous.

She offered me water and I said yes. She took a tumbler from the cupboard and held it under the tap.

She handed me the water and asked, "What's the matter with Kerrie?"

I told her about the cancer and the treatments, and about Vayda.

"How long does she have?"

"Not long," I said solemnly.

She sat at the kitchen table gazing out the window, her right hand holding her beer and her left over her mouth. She turned to me and said, "Did you really buy me a plane ticket?"

I hadn't gotten her a ticket, because I didn't know if I'd be able to find her. "No, but I will. We can fly there together," I replied with hope.

"I'm hungry. Let's eat," she said, draining her brew and standing up.

The restaurant was cozy and the aroma of rib eyes grilling made my mouth water. There was a bar lined with barstools on the right wall and a couple of cocktail tables. Straight ahead was the kitchen, which was open for all to see. On the left wall was a fireplace giving off nice heat and comfort. Tables were in front of and next to the fire place.

Mandy ordered a beer and I had orange juice with club soda. Between the salad and the main dish, I asked Mandy what had happened between her and Kerrie. She scrunched her nose and tilted her head to the left once and said, "Our lives veered away after high school. Her plans for me differed from my plans for me."

I told her that that sounded like pretty typical mother-daughter stuff.

"I guess. She wanted me to get a teaching credential and run a preschool. I wanted no part of teaching."

"She just sold three schools when she found out she was terminal," I said matter-of-factly.

"Do you mind if I have another beer?" she asked.

I gave her an intense look, but told her it was fine with me.

"Kerrie told me you were an alcoholic, and that's why she left you."

"I suppose that was part of it. I was disabled and couldn't do the job anymore. I crawled inside the bottle; felt sorry for myself, ya know."

She stared at me and said, "You guys veered too." As she said that, she sat back and looked like she wanted to shrink.

"What is it?" I asked.

I saw her look over my right shoulder to the bar. I started to turn, and she whispered, "No! Don't."

"What is it, Mandy?"

"One of Fred Blank's boys, Adam, just walked in, and it looks like he's had one too many."

Behind me I could hear the raised voices at the bar. "Ditch Bitch", "Broad and Dame" were clearly discernable.

"Just ignore him," I said.

"Welcome to my world, Venice." My thought was, *this isn't her world, not by a mile. She doesn't belong here.*

Things at the bar seemed to get quieter, so I attempted to continue the conversation about the torn relationship. "Those things certainly seem minor and easily repaired," I said. "You and your mother's relationship, I mean."

"That wasn't the only thing, Venice. There was a man."

Porter Harmon.

Mandy told me her mother was dating a younger man, and for a time it was great for her and Kerrie. "He was a nice guy. He was very helpful after my husband was killed."

"Russ Wilkes," I said flatly. "Where does Porter Harmon fit in here?" I asked.

"Wow, you really are a PI, aren't you?" She slathered butter on her baked potato and continued, "Porter is Kerrie's boyfriend and he gets tired of Kerrie, or it could be the other way around. Anyhow he starts hanging around the coffee shop and as things happen, we started dating." Mandy told me she was upfront about it with Kerrie, and that Kerrie was square with it.

"But that was bogus. She flipped her lid when she saw us together, made a real scene at the Rainier Room in Blueport. So Porter and I get a place together, and that was the last I saw of Kerrie."

"Neither one of you made an attempt to reconcile?"

"How do you reconcile with a viper?" she said with a snort.

"What happened to Harmon?"

"He was no good. He was looking for a free ride. I overheard him tell one of his friends that he was going for the money, and that he could learn to love later," she said disgustedly. "I wonder what money he was talking about."

There was a lull in our conversation as we ate, until Mandy said, "I have some questions for *you*. Do you want to know what they are?"

I nodded and she continued, "Did you ever wonder about me?"

I was flabbergasted by the question. That's what a child asks a parent when they meet years after the child has been abandoned.

"Honey, I found out about you ten days ago," I replied cautiously.

"Oh." That was all she said, and fell silent.

"What's on your mind, Mandy? Ask it."

She was peeling the label from the beer bottle, her jaw set and eyes steely. "It's just that because I had your last name, I thought you were my father," she said and hunched her shoulders.

I told her that after her mother left me I only saw her twice; once at a funeral years ago and the second time was only ten days ago. "Never once did she contact me about you. Had I known about you or that you were possibly my child, I would have been there. I hope you know that."

"You would? You would have claimed me?" she asked with brimming eyes.

"Of course, I would have. I know she's very sick, but still, I'm very pissed off at your mother for withholding that important fact from me."

"There must be some reason why she gave me your last name, Venice. I was thinking seriously about going with you to see her, but now I'm angry at her again."

"Mandy, I guess she did what she thought was the right thing at the time. Was it selfish? Probably, but that stuff has to pass. Life is too short, and for Kerrie it's down to the end game. She needs you, and you, believe it or not, need her."

"I hope you *are* my father, Venice."

That caught me off-guard and I replied with watery eyes as I placed my hand over my heart, "Mandy, that is the greatest compliment I have ever received. Thank you so very much."

We gazed at each other for several seconds and I asked her to tell me about her job.

"I got my degree in marine biology from the university and I'm full of myself. I was offered jobs up and down the coast. One in Santa Cruz, California looked nice, but I passed on it because of a better opportunity in Hawaii. As it turns out, I should've taken Santa Cruz because Hawaii went to a local," she sighed. "I thought Kerry was calling these labs and sabotaging me, but eventually I realized she wasn't that powerful."

Mandy drained her beer and continued, "I was about to accept a job in Spokane, which I didn't want, but I was desperate."

"What was so bad about a job in Spokane?" I asked. She told me she needed to get out of Kerrie's orbit.

"We sniped at each other, and I swear if I stayed, there might have been violence. Then one day I get a letter from the State of Iowa offering me this job, and here I am." She sat quietly for a few moments, almost like she'd lost her train of thought. "I hit the ground running when I got here. My boss gives me a stack of files and plot maps for drainage problems on farms. So here I am, this girl from the coast telling these farmers what they have to do and I get nothing but the air."

I asked her if she thought it was because she was female.

Just then a commotion broke out at the bar; a ruckus was brewing, and the bartender was yelling for somebody to call the cops.

The horror in Mandy's eyes caused me to spin around just as a huge young man headed our way. He was carrying a mug of beer and his zipper was down. He weaved between the tables and stopped at ours. "I got ya a brew," he slurred. Then he poured it over Mandy's head. But it was urine, not beer. Mandy screeched and retched, and I stood and pasted the guy in the jaw, knocking him into the fireplace. Tables and chairs were upended and patrons scattered.

"He pulled his schlong out and pissed in a beer mug!" The bartender yelled. The guy stood back up and took a fighter's stance and started to bob and weave, then charged me. It was a good thing he was drunk; he must have seen two of me, because he lunged and landed on the floor. The bartender and a cop got him to his feet and wrestled him to the door. I looked around for Mandy but she was gone. The waitress had taken her to the restroom.

Busboys were setting the furniture right and things started to settle down. Our meal was ruined, to say the least. I felt helpless. I wandered in the direction of the restrooms, and I could hear Mandy sobbing, and the waitress telling her it was gonna be okay.

"I wish I'd never come to this hell hole. I've had nothing but trouble here!" Mandy said through sobs and huge intakes of air. "America's Heartland, ha! This is America's asshole!"

"Honey, all roads lead out, ya know," the waitress scolded.

I went back out into the dinning room to square up the meal tag and saw the young man sitting at the bar drinking coffee. "Is tha the guy tha hit me?" He slurred.

The cop turned to me and said, "Yeah, that's him, Adam."

I was stunned; this jackass should be arrested on indecent exposure, assault, and drunk and disorderly. There he sat drinking coffee.

"Did I get any punches in, Earl?"

Earl, the cop, told him to keep quiet. "Your pop is gonna be here real soon. Just sit tight, Adam."

That's how it was gonna play out, and I wanted no part of *that* scenario. A guy pulls a shenanigan like that in a decent place like this, and they call his daddy to come and get him.

"You aren't going to arrest him?" I asked Earl with venom.

"No I ain't. He's just a little tight is all."

I turned to the bartender and said, "What kinda place ya runnin, here?"

"A real friendly place, until you got here," he said while wiping a cocktail glass. "Never had anything like that happen here, ever."

Boy, his story had certainly changed when he found out that Adam's father was coming to get his kid.

Suddenly, the front door burst open and Fred Blank lumbered in. "What in tarnation is goin on in here?" he bellowed. "Get in the truck, Adam."

"That's a real fine boy ya got there, mister. You sure are bringing him up the right way," I hissed.

Blank turned on me and said, "You. I shoulda known you'd cause trouble. You and that bitch yer lookin for."

I got toe to toe with him and could smell his foul breath. Earl stepped up and said to me, "Sir, my mind tells me to let you two have at it. But then I'll have to summon the rescue squad and all the reports about your injuries will be time consuming. So it ain't gonna happen. Fred, you get home now and sober that boy of yours up."

Fred snarled at me and spun on his heels and left.

Earl turned to me and said, "As for you. You get your date and get outta here too."

Mandy came up to my side, trembling, and said, "Take me home."

Her hair was wet from washing, as were her clothes. When we got in my rental, she started to sniffle.

"I just don't fit in here. The people in town are okay, but the rural folks hate my guts. He poured pee on me," she wailed. "How vile is that?"

I waited while she showered and changed. It seemed we were having a real good conversation before Adam Blank came to our table. I hoped we could continue it at Mandy's house.

"I don't think I'll ever be able to get clean enough," Mandy sighed as she toweled her hair.

But she looked fresh and her cheeks were rosy from her shower. She wore a baby blue terry robe, with flannel pajamas underneath.

"You asked me earlier if I thought part of my problem was not fitting in because I'm female. I believe Adam Blank is a bully, like his father, and he wouldn't have done that if I was a guy. He knew I wouldn't retaliate." She sniffled and blew her nose and gave out a long sigh.

"Are you ready to turn in?" I asked her.

She nodded yes. I asked her if I could come back in the morning and she again nodded.

"Don't you have to work?"

"The only thing I have to do tomorrow is go in and ask for a leave of absence."

Her voice was matter-of-fact, almost exactly the way I remembered her mother's.

Chapter Ten

The next afternoon I waited for Mandy in front of the Surf Ballroom. I was flying out that evening and heading for home and I wanted to see the Surf Ballroom and Museum before I left. I had no idea if Mandy was going with me or not.

The museum consisted of hundreds of pictures of rock and roll stars and numerous displays of memorabilia. My mind, however, was on the phone conversation I'd had with Kerrie earlier. Something she said was vexing me. I told her I'd found Mandy and that she seemed fine. I left out the part about her being hated by the farmers in Mason City.

"I think I've convinced her to travel home," I told Kerrie.

She said, "Okay, that's fine if she wants to. It's no big deal."

Now, God damn it, a couple of days ago she was adamant that I find her and now it's no big deal?

Before I could respond, Kerrie started to cough and Vayda picked up the phone and whispered, "Hurry, Mr. Venice."

I finished the tour and stood on the sidewalk and watched Mandy approach.

"Venice, I think I'll take you up on that ticket. Kerrie and I have some unfinished business."

Our flight from Des Moines was half full so we had a seat between us. The lights were low in the cabin and I watched Mandy sleep. My heart swelled when I thought she might be my daughter, then instantly I was angry for the years that had been wasted. I hated the thought that she knew about me and I knew nothing about her. What she must have thought about me and my character?

What if she weren't my daughter? What then? It was what it was.

It was early morning when we landed at Sea-Tac and by the time I secured a rental car the sun was up on a windy day.

Mandy's breathing became rapid and she let out huge anxiety sighs every so often. By the time I parked in front of Kerrie's house, Mandy was pale and teary eyed.

"Will it be okay, Venice? Tell me it will be okay. Maybe I shouldn't have come."

I held her shoulders and looked her in the eye and said, "This is where you are supposed to be, honey. Go make nice with your mom."

Vayda opened the door and showed us into the living room then noticed Mandy's solemn look and gave her a hug.

"Madam is just starting to wake. She won't want to see anybody until she has her bath and makeup done. Can you wait?"

I got a room at a Holiday Inn for Mandy. We took advantage of the complimentary breakfast and then she went to her room to freshen up.

The drive back to Kerrie's was filled with deep sighs once again. I reached over and gave Mandy's hand a squeeze and assured her that she was doing the right thing. She told me she hoped I was right. I felt certain I was.

Kerrie was sitting awkwardly in her wheelchair in the middle of the living room. In just a few days she'd become more fragile and the house had taken on a medicine smell.

Mandy entered with her head bowed and with cautious steps. The stare between these two, mother and daughter, seemed to last an eternity. My thought was somebody needs to take the high road. Somebody *please* take the high road, I thought.

Finally, "Hello, Mommy."

Kerrie cracked a slight smile, raised her hand and motioned her daughter closer. Mandy knelt with her head in Kerrie's lap and sobbed.

Vayda and I looked at one another through our tears, and concluded silently that we should leave them alone. As I left the room, I heard Kerrie say, "All that matters, honey, is that you're here."

A week later Kerrie fell into a coma and died. I was back in Los

Gatos when Mandy called with the news. I felt fortunate that the last time I'd seen Kerrie she was lucid and that amends had been made. She was so grateful to me for finding Mandy and kept thanking me over and over.

"You will come for the service, won't you?" Mandy asked. "Oh, and by the way, I got the results back from the lab."

I asked, "Well, what does it say?"

"I'll wait until we're together before I open it, Venice."

Chapter Eleven

My house in Blueport had been recently cleaned and accommodated me, Kate and my sister, Lydia, nicely. We arrived the day before Kerrie's service. The three of us and Mandy, along with Vayda, had dinner at the Rainier Room. After introductions were made, we settled in for conversations and toasts to Kerrie. At one point Mandy pulled a white gift box from her tote and said, "Venice, this for you, from Kerrie."

I looked perplexed and shrugged my shoulders. I looked at the faces around the table and undid the ribbon. I moved tissue paper and saw my mother's cobalt blue vase, the one I'd noticed in Kerrie's living room when I started my search for Mandy.

"Hey, I remember that!" Lydia exclaimed.

"There's a note inside the vase," Mandy said. "I wrote it, Kerrie told me what to say."

I read the short note and nodded to Mandy. She smiled and I slipped the note in my pocket. Kerrie had thanked me for bringing Mandy to her and she hoped that Mandy and I could have a relationship. There was no doubt in my mind that we would.

The service was graveside and several people from the pre-school community were present. I stood with Mandy and Vayda and we tossed a handful of dirt into the space where her urn had been lowered.

Mandy had a small reception at Kerrie's house after the services. There were just the five of us left—Mandy, Vayda, Lydia, Kate, and me. I had played out in my mind how this next segment would go: the lab result. Mandy and I would retreat to another room and open up the envelope that held the results of the DNA test.

And that's what we did. We went into the kitchen while the others stayed in the living room. The night before I'd tossed and turned, trying to figure out how I would act if I were her father and how I'd be if I weren't. Kate finally told me to leave the bed. I sat up all night, or most of it anyway. I woke with the sun shining in my face and a crick in my neck.

Mandy's hand was shaking as she slid the envelope across the tabletop to me. I picked it up, looked her in the eye and started to open the flap. "Stop!" she said loudly. "Throw it away, Venice. Don't open it."

I stared at her and shook my head slightly.

"Let's think this through," Mandy said as if she were talking to herself. "If Venice isn't my father, I don't want to know that. If he is, great. But what if he's not…"

"Honey, no matter what this says," I announced waving the envelope back and forth, "You and I are joined. I will do whatever is necessary. I'll adopt you."

"Burn the results. That's all I needed to hear, Venice. Burn it," she said.

"What? Are you sure?"

"Yes, I've never been more sure of anything in my life. Don't open it. *Burn it.*"

I couldn't help myself. I got really choked up and couldn't talk for a minute. After that, I broke into a big grin. I stood up and embraced her and she hugged me back, tight, like a little kid hugs her daddy.

"That's all *I* need to hear, Mandy," I said.

About Steve Sporleder

Steve Sporleder is a lifelong resident of Los Gatos, and the author of three books, *From Sleepy Lagoon to the Corner of the Cats*, *A Fouled Nest*, and *Gallivanting in the Gem City*, all set in the town of Los Gatos, CA. Steve, a former firefighter in Saratoga, CA, for thirty-two years, draws on his experience as a fifth-generation Los Gatos resident to infuse his writing with local flavor and history. His grandfather, father, uncles and brothers were also in the fire service and his family has served the town of Los Gatos and surrounding areas for over 100 years. His most recent novel, *From Sleepy Lagoon to the Corner of the Cats* was a Finalist in the 2012 Next Generation Indie Book Awards.

In *From Sleepy Lagoon to the Corner of the Cats*, Steve recounts the saga of four generations of *la familia Reyes* in powerful, moving terms. Through his consummate storytelling and details of setting and place, we are transported to 1917 when newlyweds Ramon and Monica Reyes flee the Mexican Revolution in search of the "American Dream." In a defining moment in the 1940s, Miguel "Mickey" Reyes, their teenage son, makes a life-altering decision late one night in the outskirts of the barrios of Los Angeles that forever shapes this family's destiny—a tragedy that propels the Reyes family away from Sleepy Lagoon and north to the quiet and lush town of Los Gatos.

Gallivanting in the Gem City – Whether it's the "Dirty Boys of Boo Gang", when a bucolic 1933 summer day turns tragic at the town swimming hole along Los Gatos Creek, catapulting three young boys toward a decision that will have consequences over three generations, or any of his other energetic stories, *Gallivanting* will leave you both longing for the gentler days of the past and eerily wary of the darkness hidden within innocence.

A Fouled Nest – Thirty years after fleeing Los Gatos, California, Venice Webb receives a call from his sister with the news that their father has died. In a startling mix of abrupt confessions, resurfacing memories, and disturbing clues, Venice is left to piece together the incidents that have forever marked his family. At once, the truth about his father's erratic behavior and neglect closes in on Venice like a freight train at full speed.

About Letty Samonte

Cover Design

Letty Samonte received her BFA with honors in Illustration in 2001 from the Art Center College of Design in Pasadena, CA.

After completing her studies there, she moved to New York City. For two years she worked full time as a faux finishing artist and muralist for Stokley Interiors based in Ridgewood, New Jersey. While living in NYC, Letty painted productions for AndHow! Theatre Company. In 2003, she had the opportunity to be part of the Williamstown Theatre Festival in Massachusetts as a scenic artist and assistant to set designer Alexander Dodge.

She relocated to San Francisco in 2004 and has been working as a scenic artist for Bay Area theaters ever since. Letty has painted for the American Conservatory Theatre, the SF Ballet, Opera, and Symphony, the Magic Theatre, Teatro ZinZanni, Marin Theatre Company, California Shakespeare Theatre, Shakespeare Santa Cruz, Joe Goode Performance Group, and for the Department of Drama at Stanford. She continues to work as a faux finishing artist, muralist, illustrator, and plein air landscape painter, as well.

Her landscape paintings have been exhibited in the national juried shows for both the American Impressionist Society and the Society of Master Impressionists. Letty is a member of IATSE, Local 800 and is a staff scenic artist for American Conservatory Theatre.

Letty Samonte
2013